Wrecking
Civilization
Before Lunch

John Ring

Chapter 1

Getting a job is not one of man's natural instincts. When Joe Caveman went out in the morning to hunt for a brontosaurus, he never thought to himself, "Hunting for things that have already been extinct for millions of years is thankless, backbreaking work, and a bit stupid, and I'm ready for something better. Something in nanotechnology maybe, or military defense subcontracting. Hell, I'd wrestle around with a stuffed pigskin in freezing weather if it'd get me some serious bling and a busty cheerleader."

No, Joe thought nothing of the kind. He just kept right on chucking spears at anything that would barbecue well, chasing Jane Caveman around the cave, and getting frozen in glaciers. And when Joe was thawed out a million years later, the first thing the discoverer would say would not have been: "I wonder what kind of work he was in."

Human beings were not meant to work. They're meant to play video games until 2a.m., sleep past lunch, watch girls go in and out of the Deb store at the mall, and then have something that once came from a cow, and beer, for dinner.

At least that's what Nathan Hamper thought.

He stared blearily at a...well, it was a blur. He blinked and a sleepy-dog crumb wedged itself between his right eye and lid, and now the blur hurt to look at. A series of rapid blinks broke up the crumb into smaller, less painful specks that did nothing to impress the blur. He decided just to close the painfully blurry eye and straighten his tie. Damn. He forgot to wear a tie. Well, at least his fly would be up, he thought, as he zipped it up...and jammed his untucked shirt in it. Crap. Now he'd have to hide his crotch during the whole interview.

Maybe he should have gotten up earlier than…he checked his watch… seven minutes ago. He hadn't brushed his hair either. The clean, pleasant-smelling shirt his mother had ironed and hung neatly on a hanger—the one he'd just jammed his pants zipper with—would nicely hide the fact that he'd also forgotten to put on any deodorant. It wasn't going to help much with the fact that his teeth weren't brushed though. The six Oreos he'd grabbed for breakfast now seemed like a bad choice.

The morning was cool and windless as he walked up a long, meandering driveway toward his destination, the blur. A moment later, Nathan stared up at an enormous house, now a bit less blurry. It looked just like Frankenstein's castle. Except it was smaller. And it had fewer bolts of lightning overhead. Well, none actually. He squinted, the sleepy-dog fragments dissolving at last. Ok, now it didn't look anything like a castle. It was very big though, with massive stone blocks that must have taken a long time to cart into this valley and glue together.

His eyes closed and reopened, trying to focus, as he approached an immense oak door. He was genuinely interested in this job…really…ok, he'd rather be sleeping but his parents said he had to get a job and this was better than stocking groceries. Hopefully. He straightened himself up to a more business-like slouch and nodded importantly. There was an aura that came from this non-castle he had felt every time he saw it, passing by on the road behind him or running through the property on his way into town. It exuded a sense of intense activity of global importance going on. Work that would change the world, inventions and devices that would allow future generations to be even more sedentary and brainless. What better thing for a teenager to be a part of? Future slackers would sing his praises, if they could be bothered to get out of bed. Unlike him.

On the other hand, having a job sounded like a lot of work.

Nathan raised a huge, brass-ringed knocker then let it crash against the door, almost making him jump. He glanced at his watch, which said it was five minutes before ten in the morning as soon as he could read the numbers. At least he wouldn't be late. He lifted up the heavy ring again before it had stopped shaking and flinched slightly as it clattered against the door once more. He could hear activity going on inside. Unless he was hearing things now.

"Who put this here?" he heard someone say, followed by quick steps across a creaking wood floor. "What in the world is that?" came from the same person a moment later. A second of silence passed before a loud crash of metal objects again failed to startle Nathan, followed by rather creative use of the S-word and the F-bomb, and more metal crashing.

Nathan rechecked the address on the job application. An interview for a job was what he was here for. And yes, this was the place. Here was where, according to the application, the "works of greatness, utilizing all aspects of science in the pursuit of knowledge and the furthering of the evolution of human endeavors" supposedly went on. The description of the lab assistant job he was here for said there would be much danger involved, lasers probably, a robot or two, maybe magnetic, gravitational, and nuclear experiments, and also some occasional heavy lifting and lab upkeep. "The wonders of the world begin in the humble laboratories of Earth's great inventors" the advertisement had said, finishing with "candidate will benefit from having some chemistry and metalworking skills, quick reflexes, and a high tolerance for unpredictable odors, unexpectedly flying objects, and occasional spontaneous detonations."

The door swung open suddenly and Nathan nearly had to resist the urge to take a step back. One of the perks in being half-asleep is being relatively disinterested when lunatics jump out at you.

The man in front of him stared with manic eyes that appeared to need a lot more sleep than they were getting and peered around Nathan as if they were looking for an escape route. The man's unkempt blondish hair, what little there was of it, spilled out over the top of his head and down in precisely that way that someone with a comb would have done all they could to prevent. Nathan couldn't tell if he was balding or the victim of one of his experiments. The lab coat the man wore was a checked shirt several sizes too large on his skinny frame. His face was pale and the glasses that sat askew on his nose were wire-rimmed with splotches of solder all over it from quick, and obviously frequent, patchwork. The man squinted as if he were unaccustomed to bright sunlight, never mind the fact that it was cloudy, and his lower jaw jutted out with the same misplaced outrage that Nathan's four-year-old brother used on everyone when he forgot to wear pants.

The man grinned immensely and Nathan went ahead and took that step back. "There's really nothing going on here," the man said through his teeth. "Ehhhrrruhm... can I help you?"

Nathan's mouth opened and closed, opened again, and emitted a single "I-".

"Aha. Yes. You're late," the man said, eyeing him more closely. "Do you intend to be," the man checked his own watch, "three days late every time you come to work, Mr. Hamper?"

"Three days? I'm not three days late," Nathan said, although it was certainly possible. He looked at his watch again, which oddly still said five minutes before ten.

"That probably won't work here," the man said, waving his hands wildly, "—magnetic field everywhere, really big, not good on fillings either—" before one hand slid out cautiously and shook Nathan's hand holding the job description. "Mark Goggin," the man said as they watched the paper float to the stone at their feet. As Nathan leaned down to grab it with his free hand, he was yanked bodily into the house.

The inside of the house looked, strangely enough, far bigger than what he would have expected from the outside. That, it turned out, was the least strange part of the place:

—The lights dimmed, it seemed, whenever he tried to look into rooms or just walk around. Just when he needed to see something, it got dark. How did it do that?

—Clouds of dust appeared and were just as quickly swept up in what could only be called micro micro-tornadoes—spinning, meandering mini-cyclones that appeared only instantly, and just as quickly disappeared. Inside the house. *Inside!*

——Nails on the walls stood out in odd places, but when he looked back, they appeared to have reseated themselves in the wall and other nails now protruded out.

Worst of all, there was a low hum that seemed to come from every direction. No wonder Goggin looked unhinged. Nathan decided he was going to need some weed to get through this. He felt around his pockets for the remnants of his last smoke.

"Excuse the mess," said Goggin. "I'm preparing for Jenna...ah...for a demonstration tomorrow."

Nathan's attention swept over to a long trough against a wall as they stepped into a large, dimly-lit room full of old, ratty furniture barely capable of carrying the weight of the dust settling and then blowing off them. The trough contained a small trickle of water at the bottom and was noticeably elevated on one end. Nathan's eyes widened as he watched the trickle flow slowly up the trough—uphill, if he could believe his eyes—cascading off the top and into a small tub that contained a pump and a tube that sent the water back to start over again at the far end of the trough.

"That's not possible," he mumbled.

"Yes, probably just our imagination," Goggin nodded. "Do you hear a hum?"

Nathan also nodded. "Ah, good," Goggin said. "Not just me then. I had this furnace installed a few months ago and ever since then this low hum—"

The wood floor suddenly began to shake, creaking in protest, as the low hum from the furnace rose in pitch, building to a scream much like any normal furnace would if it had once been a jet engine. The walls shook and the furniture rattled and skipped in random directions. Nathan grabbed a doorway frame that came loose as its nails protruded and reseated suddenly. Gradually the deafening scream subsided to give way to what now seemed to be a very pleasing low hum.

"I don't think it should be doing that," Goggin mused. "I fiddled with it a bit, you see…" His voice trailed off as his eyebrows frowned in consternation.

Nathan wondered if he might get away with smoking something during the interview as he followed Goggin into a substantial kitchen. Countertops and cabinets were on every wall, with a long, unhygienic maple table as the centerpiece of the room. The table looked as if sacrificial rites or autopsies had been conducted on it. There were unidentifiable scraps of something awful that had been decomposing for who knows how long and oozing puddles of yuck no self-respecting drunk would have thrown up. "The kitchen," said Goggin, then abruptly added "Damn."

Rolling across the floor was a round trash can on wheels that squeaked at just the right pitch for a duet with a hand dragging fingernails on a blackboard. A broom and scoop attachment in front opened to sweep up a used napkin, but bumped into a table leg instead, forcing it to reroute and leave the napkin where it was. A small cloud of dust followed it like a truck careening down a dirt road. "My cleaning bot," Goggin said doubtfully as the robot then attempted to sweep up the table leg. It gradually slowed until it was difficult to tell if it had given up or its batteries were dead.

"Now then," said Goggin, rather deflatedly, turning to Nathan. "You should probably get an idea of what you're in for. You'll be the first assistant I've had since Roger tripped over the…," his eyes widened, "…uh, tripped lightly over these very…eh…hallowed, as it were…uh…boards. Boards which constitute the core materials…although not the entirety of the materials…," he finished warily, "of the floor."

Nathan stared at Goggin. "He tripped…?"

"Well, fell down."

"Fell down."

"Or plummeted to the bottom of," said Goggin.

Nathan's jaw dropped. "Of…?"

"Yes. Nearly."

"Of what?"

"It was really his own fault."

"Of what?"

"Just a...really a very small well near the edge of the meadow down by the river..."

Nathan gaped. "A well? He fell down—"

"Nearly. Almost fell down. Great reflexes Roger has. Had."

"He's dead?!"

"No, no, no. Ha!" Goggin laughed heartily then frowned again. "Not as such."

"What is that supposed to mean?"

"Are you going to be this excitable on the job?" Goggin looked Nathan over. "I mean we're going to be dealing with a whole lot more important things than a teensy, little waterfall."

Nathan stared at him once more.

Goggin sighed. "Well it was perhaps bigger than 'teensy' or 'little' might at first seem to indicate."

Nathan mouthed a "w" for waterfall. The remainder of the word resisted making an appearance.

"But at least he didn't fall down the well," Goggin said pleasantly. "That would have been worse. Much, much worse."

"Deep water?"

"Dry as a bone. No, there are rocks at the bottom. Big rocks. Twenty feet down."

"So he just fell into the river instead?"

"Well he had to, didn't he. The flames were nearing the tops of his trousers and after that it'd be...floosh! Ha ha!" Goggin waved his hands dramatically from his belt up over his head.

Nathan resumed gaping.

Goggin fidgeted. "We should talk about this later."

"Why was he on fire?"

"No reason. Spontaneous, you might say. In fact that was our experiment. Spontaneous combustion. We'd been at it for weeks. I kept trying to get him to visualize flames and mentally set different objects on fire. All the tests thus far had been successful, except for the lack of anything actually catching fire. So Roger got a little overeager. Doused a cloth in kerosene. Got it all over the place really. He thought it would improve his chances."

Nathan was impressed. "Was he able to ignite it?"

"No."

"Oh."

"He got disgusted and chucked the cloth over his shoulder onto a heat lamp behind him."

"No!" Nathan was amazed at how eventful normally bland experiments turned out around here.

"All right, maybe it wasn't a heat lamp...maybe it was another experiment. But I had the flames on that well under control. Mostly. No way it was burning down anything other than the one table."

Nathan began to wonder whether this house had much of a future.

Goggin squinted fretfully, appeared thoughtful for a moment, reached behind a shredded gold-flecked yellow sofa that looked as if it needed a roaring fire, and lifted up a long, thick cylindrical rod with a cord that stretched from one end and curled around behind the sofa. He aimed the rod's more unpleasant end at Nathan.

Nathan's eyes boggled. Clearly he'd taken a wrong direction with this interview. Too many questions, that was his problem. Never interview the interviewer. Never, never—

"Guess what this is," said Goggin enthusiastically.

"Something besides a weapon?"

"Wrong! This is the result of my effort to build a device to clear households of pesky lint, cobwebs, pet hair, and so on, without the need for a vacuum cleaner."

"Really?" Nathan suddenly forgot his fear. This was more like it. "It does all that?"

"No." Goggin pointed the nasty end at, not surprisingly, the offensively-upholstered sofa. He squeezed a trigger, something behind the sofa began to whine shrilly, and a bolt of blinding light from the cylindrical rod screamed across the short distance, crashing into the doomed furniture.

When Nathan's vision cleared, he saw Goggin sitting on the floor where the force of the blinding light had thrown him, a stunned expression on his face. The sofa was smoking where a hole now appeared in the back. The wall behind it was well on its way to being engulfed in flames.

"Capacitors charged a bit too—Yeow! Fire!" yelped Goggin, aiming the weapon at the flames on reflex—or just in panic—as if he thought another blast might snuff it out.

Nathan ran into the kitchen, skidding this way and that, throwing open doors and cabinetry. He emerged with a fire extinguisher that made a soft hiss when he directed it at the growing blaze. Then nothing.

The two looked at one another with expressions showing conclusively that neither had a clue what to do next.

A loud scraping squeak rolled in from around a corner and the cleaning bot closed on the fire with all the haste of a fire engine whose firefighters were out trying to push it up a steep hill. Nevertheless, it arrived eventually in the vicinity of the fire, sprayed something red-colored at the wall, and the flames gradually faded and went out.

The bot reversed direction, entangled itself in a lamp cord, and disappeared into a hallway dragging a broken lamp behind it.

They stared at the aftermath, the smoking sofa and the smoking wall that dripped something red.

"Kool-Aid," Goggin said sheepishly. "I thought the bot might, you know, pour me a drink now and then."

Nathan stared wide-eyed at the curling smoke and dripping Kool-Aid, then down at the cylindrical horror resting on the floor next to Goggin.

He pointed at it. "Can I see that?"

Evening approached as Nathan's first day of work drew to a close, and the intense, earth-shattering work of building bold, new inventions hadn't actually started yet.

"Nothing's going to explode," said Mark Goggin, jumping sideways past his worried new assistant, rapidly snatching newspaper from under the dining table and wrappers lying on the kitchen floor where they'd fallen from the summit of the overflowing trash bin. The kitchen, dining room, and great room were all equally filthy, and Mark bounced from room to room, tidying here and there without much sign of improvement, chastising trash for taking the laws of diffusion to extremes, carrying things from one room to another, and later bringing them back again.

They were cleaning now. Undoubtedly, a Nobel Prize was just around the corner.

The new assistant stared unhappily after him. Nathan Hamper had been meandering in random directions, only occasionally stooping to pick up a piece of lint or a single cat hair while he watched Mark leap on trash and debris like a man searching for treasure. He stared at the lint in his hand. "Then we're getting rid of some batteries?" he asked.

"No, no, surely not," replied Mark as he picked up Styrofoam leftover containers behind a door. "Then nothing would happen. I wish we had more, but I think we cut it a little close borrowing the big one out of the Ebson's Gulfstream. They live in that, you know. Sooner or later they're going to notice." He trailed off as he tried to decide if the green on something in a wrapper was frosting or some horrible substance he'd made in the lab and left to fend for itself. If it had gotten into the house, it was doing pretty well for itself, he thought.

"But—" Nathan began, then stopped. He looked at his fistful of lint and cat hair as if a momentous decision was at hand, decided "no" about whatever it was, then apparently changed his mind and dropped the entire contents in his hand onto the floor. He mumbled a "whatever" and loped into the kitchen, where he could be heard unfolding tin foil containing brownies he had made that morning. Half were already gone.

Mark frowned after his assistant. Useless already and the boy had only been employed for…he looked at his watch. The hands were running backwards. Damn.

Those brownies smelled funny too.

He sighed and looked around. The house was in a worse mess than he had realized. It had taken him forever just to pick up the trash stuffed everywhere in the kitchen alone. At this rate, that would be the only presentable room for the demonstration of his newest and greatest invention. The representatives from General Micronet would be there at 9 a.m. the next morning. Jenna Telfair, in particular, would be one of them.

Mark's eyes glazed over and a half-smile came and went, eyebrows rising hopefully, as he slipped momentarily into the dreamy world of females and romance, that place for which science and reason seemed to work for him about as reliably as it didn't work in his lab.

He shook his head to clear it and morosely considered the overwhelming disorder of the place. It would save him a lot of time and effort if he just cleaned the one room where he would be showing off his invention—the lab—and locked the doors to all the others. If he had only stopped to think for a moment before he started cleaning, that might indeed have occurred to him. But just as he did while engrossed in the creation of his inventions, he went with the first thought in his head, which in this case was: "This kitchen would benefit from a series of contained explosions." Unfortunately, there being no explosives handy, he cleaned instead.

The stacks of equipment, books, and tools on the dining table were next. Oddly, it appeared that many of the books were ones he had just moved. How had they gotten on the table? He began lifting stack after stack, setting them on the floor down the hall, where they had been in the first place.

Nathan poked his head around the kitchen door. His eyes were oddly unfocused and it seemed to take him a second or two of staring at Mark before anything registered. "Uh, they're all charged and connected."

"Excellent." Mark dropped the trash bag he had just picked up—instantly forgetting the trash, the trashed house, and the demo looming upon the next sunrise—and bolted through the door after Nathan.

A week ago, Mark had made his first attempt to conjure up a phenomenon called ball lightning. The idea was to create enough of an electrical disturbance in the immediate vicinity to, in effect, supercharge the air, so that a luminous ball of electricity would appear. Nathan regarded the whole thing as pointless. There's a reason why no one of any eminence within the scientific community had ever bothered to find a repeatable way to generate ball lightning, he pointed out. There was no application for it. What could you possibly do with it? Scare away wolves? Light enormous cigarettes? Electrocute migrating geese?

Nathan was already getting on Mark's nerves. And it was his first day on the job. Surely there had to be some kind of special effort involved in order to be irritating that quickly.

Mark followed Nathan out the back door and stopped. The sun had set, leaving a dark, jarring red as a background to what could most closely be described as a reenactment of a UFO landing. Light beamed from every angle, pushing back the darkness in the meadow. The enormous stone house loomed behind them, the red accent of light on white limestone giving it a regal but strongly disapproving air, as if it wished it had been built at least a block further away from this dubious endeavor. Flashlights were hanging from tree branches, a car hood light hung from the basketball goal, and fluorescent lighting Nathan must have pulled loose from the lab's ceiling were held up by ropes crisscrossing the length of the meadow and affixed to the trees.

It was as if it were the middle of the day in just that small space. Crickets chirped outside the pseudo daylight, but the ones inside were confused into silence. Surrounding the brightened pocket of the meadow were ash and maple trees, a handful of evergreens and cedar saplings, and a sycamore so tall that even the blindingly vast amount of candle power at play couldn't illuminate all of it. The trees, though vivid in their fluttering October gowns of yellow and orange, quivered in the wind like the condemned before a firing squad. Mark peered sheepishly up at a hole running through one of the elders of the red maples. The hole was roughly spherical and the leaves that remained near the hole's outer edges were seared black where something had shot up through the tree. It stood as the only proof from last week's efforts that anything had happened at all. No doubt the tree would have been happier if it were otherwise.

Mark shielded his eyes as he walked. "Don't we have any more lights?" he said sarcastically.

"Oh ha ha," said Nathan.

"You realize this stadium of yours has to be turned off or we won't see anything."

"No problem. I figure it'll all go out once the ball lightning catches sight of the overhead power lines and blows every fuse in the house."

"Good thinking."

At the epicenter of all the lighting were a number of car batteries. Almost two hundred of them. It had taken a week for Mark to recharge them, and Nathan had spent the afternoon hooking them up. In the center of the batteries, sitting on a trashcan, waited an unlit Bunsen burner enclosed in an overturned fishbowl.

"Are we ready?" asked Nathan. His hand idly flicked at a large switch with tendrils of thick cables that dispersed into the crowd of batteries.

Mark waved his hand, "No, wait. Lesson time. What are we doing differently this time?"

Nathan smiled, then frowned, neither for any discernible reason. "Beats me," he said, smiling again. "Same number of batteries, same time of day from what you said happened the first time. It's just a matter of which tree gets it this time."

"Ah, but what about the weather," said Mark, pointing up.

Nathan peered up into the darkness. "It's windy. So what?"

Mark put his hands on his hips. "You call yourself an inventor?"

"No, I call myself a scientist."

There had been a brief and mostly pointless argument between them earlier in the day about whether it was better to be an inventor or a scientist. Nathan felt that scientists were interested in discovery within the bound of science while inventors were just tinker-toy doodlers, while Mark saw inventors as the true creative forces of discovery while scientists were boring note-takers who got more done when they were asleep.

"Well you're a long way from being a scientist too," said Mark. "Humidity, Nathan! More humidity. You couldn't ask for a more conductive airborne agent. Well, other than a monsoon. Or maybe a gigantic sheet of copper. And where there's high humidity, there's bound to be clouds loaded down with electrons." Mark did an impromptu stomping around that was an appallingly graceless rendition of a rain dance. "You can almost sense the barometric pressure rising." He stopped and peered up at the stars. "Something's going to happen tonight. I can feel it!" He cackled up into the night, then shot a glance at Nathan. "Where's the camcorder?"

"Right under the power lines," Nathan replied, vaguely pointing where the lines disappeared into the darkness, in the direction of the house. "I'm pretty sure we can blow that up too."

Mark nodded obliviously and quickly scanned the batteries for unconnected cables. He quit long before he had gotten very far and sped across the yard to the camcorder waiting on its tripod. There was considerable yanking and pulling and stretching before Mark had gotten it precisely where he wanted it, more or less where it had been. He set it to start recording and checked through the eyepiece one last time.

"Light the burner, Mr. Hamper," he said as he squatted down next to the camera to watch.

Nathan looked back at him in irritation. "Comfy?" he said. "So you'll just be way the hell over there while I stand here at Ground Zero then?"

Mark nodded. "Right."

Nathan sneered, yanked up the fishbowl and lit the burner with his lighter, suddenly realized what he was doing and glanced self-consciously at Mark. His parents usually scolded him for having a lighter. Mark didn't seem to notice.

"Well done," Mark called out. "Now, lights out!"

Stepping carefully over the batteries, Nathan returned to the switch and yanked at a cord reaching all the way to a fist-sized industrial plug connected to an outlet next to the back door. Sparks fizzed from the forty or so other plugs lying on the ground, and the air crackled before the meadow became dark once again. Only the small flame of the burner was visible.

"Good, good," said Mark from the safety of being twenty feet away. "Open the valve."

The valve turned just enough for Nathan to hear methane hiss slowly into the fishbowl, where it immediately ignited. He jumped as it did.

"Push the button!" Mark yelled hastily. "Push the button! Push the button!"

It was apparently an unimportant technicality to Mark that it was a *switch* Nathan was waiting to flip and not a button. Nevertheless, Nathan closed the switch as the wind whipped through the trees and made the burner's flame waver even within its glass bubble.

Just as in the previous attempt, nothing happened immediately. Mark felt the familiar electrical energy in the air, but more so. It was similar to the sensation that permeated the atmosphere beneath a severe thunderstorm. This time it felt different, he thought. And not in a good way.

Barely a minute into the experiment, they could both smell the pungent stench of rotten eggs. A sulfurous, ozony smell that would have driven back a mob of drunk, sweaty skunks.

Off to the west, a series of lightning strikes flashed. A storm was indeed only about half an hour away. Lucked out, Mark thought happily. No storm was forecast, but they were nevertheless committed to conducting the experiment that night, otherwise the batteries would lose too much charge. And right on cue was a tailor-made thunderstorm.

Nathan looked back at Mark for just a second and then froze. He saw an expression of delight and wonder on Mark's face, looking all agape at something behind Nathan. A crackle of energy discharged behind him and he spun around.

There it was. The fruition of their efforts hovered almost within arm's reach. It was the size of a basketball and hung motionless several feet in the air. It swirled with oranges and blues, seeming to revolve ever so slightly, and it sizzled and popped unpredictably. It made no move in any direction, so Nathan decided *he* would. As far as he was concerned, scientists did not put their lives on the line for their experiments. That's what defenseless woodland creatures in cages were for. On all fours like a turtle on its back, he backed slowly toward Mark, who hissed a loud "Don't move!" Nathan easily ignored it as the naïve, overly optimistic counsel of someone not very near a massive ball of electricity, and kept right on moving. He didn't fail to notice that the charged blue-orange ball was now moving too, and in his direction.

"It's going to follow you," Mark hissed again. "Don't move!"

Nathan tried stopping for half a second. If he'd only stopped earlier and allowed the ball to decelerate, it might in fact have stopped too. But it was now under the power lines, and it appeared to be more interested in them. As Nathan was also directly beneath the lines, the ball continued toward him so that Nathan resumed, and even hastened, his retreat.

Ball and boy steadily increased their pace. The ball began to hum as it moved faster and that made Nathan finally leap to his feet in complete panic, scream like a little girl, and dash straight for Mark. The ball immediately accelerated after him.

It occurred to Mark, as both assistant and experiment hurtled in his direction, that he should have mentioned to the former that the latter—ball lightning—tends to pursue moving objects. Oh well, perhaps another time.

As Nathan crashed into Mark, the electrical ball swooshed by overhead and smashed into the side of the house, phasing through and leaving a blackened stain. At the same instant, the camcorder sparked spectacularly. A wisp of smoke rose from between a seam in its housing.

From their positions on their backs, both inventor and scientist watched as lights flickered and danced all over the inside of the house. The ball appeared to move methodically for spells and then ricocheted around swiftly. In a final, sudden burst, the ball shot out through the roof and went straight up. It dispersed as it rose until nothing was left.

Nathan stared up at the stars with undiminished surprise. The whole thing had taken no more than thirty seconds. There hadn't even been time for his life to flash before his eyes.

The smell of burnt sulfur and charred plastic dissipated slowly in the breeze.

"There, didn't I tell you nothing would explode?" Mark's face was a rapturous glow and he took a big breath. "That was amazing. Okay, charge 'em all up again."

"What?" Nathan sat up from his prone position. "Why?"

"We can make them appear consistently. Now we have to figure out how to control them."

"Aw, hell."

"And Nathan? No more brownies."

Nathan let loose a cackle of his own, and fell back onto the grass to stare up at the stars twinkling apprehensively, another ball of lightning charging their way.

Chapter 2

Matthias End stood waiting outside the back shipping entrance to General Micronet's World Headquarters. A side delivery door had not yet opened. The morning air was cool, still, and expectant, though for End it felt no different than any other miserable, workday morning. Worse, he was there at that unfortunate time of the morning when he would have been late every other way in but this one, the only door without a security pad. It was his habit to enter the GMN building this way when he was so pathetically late that if he were to swipe his security card to get in anywhere else, he might as well have just put in a request to have his pay docked. In corporate-land, it takes a form even to tattle on yourself.

From under the black soft-brimmed hat that drooped over his lowered face, he checked his watch, then returned to eyeing both the door and the three other men waiting to get in. One of the men occasionally looked over at him, but as soon as End looked back, the man immediately looked off in another direction or went back to talking to the other men.

Finally, the door began to roll slowly upward and the men ambled even more slowly toward it. End walked briskly by them, his long, black Chesterfield billowing behind him, and nodded acknowledgement even when they didn't. "Good morning, gentlemen," he said, smiling broadly. "Late again, I see. Shoddy, very shoddy." He ducked under the door before it had fully opened, and disappeared around the corner.

Two lefts, a right, and another left, and End had managed to avoid most of the cubicles with people who might inform someone unpleasant about his time of arrival. He took off the heavy coat as he walked and draped it over an arm. A long hallway brought him among the cubes where Quality went on.

Slowing drastically and suddenly, End strolled leisurely past an office door, his coat only partially hidden behind him. "Good morning, Doris," he said into the office space, then accelerated hastily once he was past. He could hear steps behind him and knew the tiny, older woman had shot out the door and was following him as quickly as her undersized legs could go.

The team lead for End's group in Quality was Doris Jackson, and no finer human being existed on the planet. Even End would have admitted to that. No one worked harder or kept longer hours than Doris—certainly not Matthias End. She was fifty-eight and a twice-blessed grandmother, and all she really wanted was to have happy people all around her. Toward that end, Doris hounded the many misbehaving scalawags in her department with implacable, maternal determination until they mended their ways. Or pleaded for a transfer. In that way, her management style was unique and, mostly, effective. No one wanted to disappoint their grandmother, even someone who portrayed herself as *everyone's* grandmother. The fact that very little quality went on in Quality was important neither to Doris nor to the corporation. To Doris, numbers could always be fudged, but unhappy people needed real fudge.

Up to now, only one person in all her years at GMN had ever managed to resist her pleading and nagging, and continued with his naughty ways: Matthias End. It was not that he disliked Doris or hated grandmothers. He just didn't care to be manipulated and treated like a six-year-old. And he despised Quality to its overly documented core.

"Matthew..." huffed Doris breathlessly as she fell farther behind. "Matthew..."

End accelerated, as much to escape from the loathsome and false familiarity she always tried to instill in his first name as from the woman herself. As if by giving him a new name, he would become a new person. It wasn't long before he had left her far behind, lost amidst the chaotic throng of cubes signifying that Engineering was allegedly going on somewhere. True, it was the long way, but necessary in order to lose the pursuit. It always worked too. End could see the top of Doris's head bobbing up and down over the cubicle walls, now far away. Soon after, he pulled into his own cube, tossed his coat on the guest chair, sat down, and immediately got on the phone.

"Leave me alone, Matt," said a female voice on the other end of the line before he could speak. GMN had Caller ID, advantageous for those wanting to avoid responsibility by not answering potentially inflammatory calls, but not so much for those also wanting to avoid responsibility by pretending to be on the phone.

"Wait, wait, wait. I've got to get rid of someone," he said, glancing at the entrance to his cube. "As soon as she gets here anyway. What's going on?"

"I don't have time for this. I'm getting ready for my demo."

End laughed. "Your Tesla fusion thing, yeah right. Why don't you just marry this mad scientist, Jenna? You're sure not going to get anything else out of him."

He heard Jenna Telfair gasp, and he smirked. "Mr. Goggin has made us a decent amount of money with his work," she said. "I don't think it's too much to ask to take a look at what he's working on every once in a while."

Another female with Mrs. End potential, lost to an egocentric R&D pinhead, he thought, only half-listening.

"And besides," she went on, "what difference does it make what you think...Ohhhh, you make me so—!...goodbye!"

"No, wait—" He heard the phone click.

Doris lurched into End's cube, breathing rapidly. "Matthew, didn't... you hear me... calling you?" She leaned against the cube wall, trying to catch her breath.

End turned around and watched her wheeze with a puzzled look. "I'll have to get back with you, Doris. I'm on the phone." He held it up in case she didn't believe him.

Doris yanked the receiver from him and slammed it onto the base. End stared at her in surprise. "You're late…" she said with a raspy voice, "for the eighth day in a row."

"Doris," End said, shaking his head, "I think that senility thing is creeping up again, unless it's something more serious. I've been here for half an hour now." He took her hand and patted it. "And eight days? Are you sure it's really eight?" Her turn to be treated like a six-year-old.

She jerked her hand away. "Matthew End, that is the last straw. You've driven me to the end of my tether. I've had it up to here with you." She indicated her forehead with her hand, but had to drop it to her hip, still trying to catch her breath.

End shook his head and tsked. "Doris, my dear, are you aware that excessive use of clichés is a principal sign of at least a dozen different forms of dementia?"

For a long, silent moment, Doris Jackson stared at Matthias End, intently and ungrandmotherly, coming to a decision that he didn't recognize was happening even as he feigned sympathy. "Here," she said finally, handing him a large interoffice manila envelope. "Mr. Press would like to speak with you. I'll tell him you'll be down right away." She disappeared without another word.

$$* \quad * \quad *$$

At one time, Matthias End was known by his friends and colleagues at General Micronet as a stickler for detail. Or, as some of the ladies in the testing lab called him, "The Porcupine of Picky." Trained from the start as an arc welder, End had some time ago been reassigned—demoted in his view—to an inspector for the Quality team. He had responded with resentful aggression by going beyond "by the book" and entering an otherworldly realm where God Himself could well have gotten an unsatisfactory Quality rating for, say, putting too much water on the planet. Matthias End intended to prove to everyone—and to himself—that he could be the best at anything he did. He could be perfect.

Unfortunately, his obstinate perfectionism was met with equal indifference from his new manager, Mr. Press, who preferred sitting in Six Sigma meetings all day to having to deal with irritants like all the people who worked for him. Undeterred by management apathy and absorbed in his cause, End looked for new ways to achieve perfection. Cooperation with his peers had only resulted in unproductive chatter about cars being in the shop and children coming down with the flu. So the first step in his new initiative was to wear formal black clothing every day. A bachelor by circumstance, he had saved enough money to purchase a plentiful supply of black suits and black shirts, a black trench coat and droopy wide-brimmed hat, and even a long black scarf that dragged on the floor behind him when he walked, more grayish now from collecting dust. He drove to work every day in a black Cutlass. An imposing figure alone—he was six foot five and flattened steelworkers as a diversion—his new dark persona was instantly and easily interpreted.

Fear and intimidation became his creed. If he couldn't get results with sound reason and subtle persuasion, then he could instead ensure results with implied threats and perceived physical danger. He found that it was a satisfying emotional release to roar and rage at anything and anyone, rather than letting it bottle up inside as most people did.

For a time his fearsome persona succeeded, and he thought he was almost within reach of that impossible goal of perfection. His co-workers did as he wanted and didn't dare cross him, and his productivity increased exponentially. But his manager, Mr. Press, ignored him still.

He recognized his situation then for the doomed one it was. There was nowhere to go professionally, no way to find respect, no point in trying any more. His productivity plummeted. He became, by turns, mean-spirited, self-loathing, and cynical, and then, of all things, careless and whimsical. He remained, nevertheless, always loud and always decked full out in black. Ultimately, it was all he had and probably all that mattered to him.

The envelope Doris Jackson had given him had printed on it his name, the date, a conference room ID, and the word "Confidential" across the top and bottom in large, impersonal letters. End did not remember ever having been handed such a cryptic object or ever being sent anywhere in so mysterious a way. But he'd been asked to do plenty of strange and stupid things before for no clear reason. It seemed likely that this was just more of the same. He found the conference room far from the cubicle flotilla he normally inhabited. In fact, it was far from any employees at all.

The door said "Human Resources Conference Room," and Matthias End twisted the doorknob smartly as he swung the door open. Pushing it hard, the door shook as it clattered shut. He looked disapprovingly at the two people waiting behind a long conference table. One he recognized immediately: the manager of Quality, Mr. Press.

"Please have a seat, Mr. End," said the one he didn't recognize. End looked at both suspiciously, said, "Why, thank you so much," and didn't sit down.

"Mr. End, I am the H.R. representative for the Quality team," said the unknown man. "I'm afraid we have some bad news. Ah, can I have that?" He pointed at the envelope.

End looked down at the envelope, then handed it over. "What, more bad news?" he said sarcastically. "No, don't tell me. This year alone, the company has cut hourly wages for half the Quality department alone and laid off the other half. So rather than make up more lies, you've called me in here to at last confess that you have no clue how to set goals for this organization and no managerial guts to adjust your operating plan to something within the realm of human plausibility."

He waited expectantly. "Or are you just going to lay off more people?"

"A bit of all three actually." The H.R. man looked at a piece of paper he pulled out of the envelope.

"Well, that's just brilliant," said End, folding his arms in disgust. "Tell me, at what point will you realize that your workers are not the problem?

You lay people off and cut costs and yet you still aren't making your ridiculous numbers." He leaned down closer to the level of the two men, eyeing them intently. "The problem is not the people. Or the products. Or the cost. The problem is incompetent leadership. You set astronomical objectives in your plan and then blame the little guy when he can't meet them." Let them chew on that a while, he thought with something that felt like righteous wrath.

"Well, frankly, Mr. End, that's not my area."

End straightened. "Then I'd like to speak to the person in charge."

The man shook his head and sighed. "I'd love to let Mr. Lucy handle this sort of thing. But I'm sorry. I can't do that."

"Why don't I give it a try," said Mr. Press, grabbing the piece of paper. "This will be a pleasure."

Mr. Press looked End squarely in the eyes. "Matthias End?" he said, handing the paper to End. "You're sacked."

End took the paper without looking at it. "Sacked?" He said the word as if it referred to bagging groceries, which of course it couldn't be. "You mean fired?"

"Oh, no, but we could. We most certainly could. But the pointy-heads in Legal can't figure out how to keep away the lawsuits if we did. So instead, we're laying you off."

End's mouth opened and closed like a loose hinge while he tried to figure out what it would say. "On…On what grounds?"

"On the grounds that we want to. Now if you'll sign that waiver," Press pointed to the paper in End's hand, "we can all move on with our lives. You'll get a full severance, not that you deserve one, and—"

"But I've done everything I was asked to do. It may have been pointless and even detrimental to the good of the company, but I did it anyway." End finally looked at the paper that had come from the envelope he had brought with him. "Oh good God! I delivered my own pink slip?"

"Just being efficient," Mr. Press said with a self-satisfied smile. He leaned casually back in his chair. "Lots of people have done their jobs and been gotten rid of, End. Don't take it personally. It's just business."

End pursed his lips. "How can I *not* take it personally? Wouldn't *you* take it personally?" A rage gathered in him, a hard, acidic blackness like something stuck in an intestine and backing everything up.

"Oh no, certainly not," replied Mr. Press. "I recognize that I am just a small cog in the larger machine that is General Micronet."

End blinked rapidly, straining to compose himself. "So you're not important either," he said after a moment's silence.

Mr. Press frowned at that. "Well, no, I think I'm pretty essential. I suppose I'm more on the large side, as cogs go."

End leaned over the conference table until he was so close that Mr. Press tipped farther back in his chair, the directionless fear and tension in the room suddenly apparent even to him.

"What a load of bullshit," said End, his voice low and menacing. "You sit in meetings all day long, making up tasks that will never be done, and then you sacrifice trees to print them on and shove the stacks of paper in a corner someplace where no one will ever see them."

"Oh, I don't—" Mr. Press started uncertainly.

"What do you think would happen to this world-spanning conglomeration if you were suddenly hit by a bus?" End almost whispered.

Mr. Press was unable to come up with an immediate answer.

"Nothing!" End roared, his face suddenly contorted from anger and wasted years. "Not a thing! Oh maybe someone will come by your little cubicle there in the corner, maybe once a month, and say 'Oh, wasn't that the guy who got hit by the bus?'"

"A bus," Mr. Press mumbled to himself, looking visibly disturbed.

"And if someone were to say to Mr. Lucy, 'Hey, Mr. Lucy, how about that guy who got hit by the bus,' do you suppose he's going to have one clue who they're talking about?"

"Um," said Mr. Press, his lower lip quivering. His eyes blinked rapidly, glancing anxiously left and right at nothing in particular.

"Is that the kind of appreciation you'd expect to get, Mr. Press?" End spat. "Or did you expect there to be a corporate-wide day of mourning?

Perhaps give everyone the day off to get over your loss? Maybe ban all buses on the premises?" End threw the waiver form on the table.

Mr. Press appeared very close to tears. The HR rep had also been unable to reply, this not being the usual way that layoffs were handled. He cowered nevertheless, his head filled with too many tales of infuriated ex-employees shooting the messenger.

"No, Mr. Press," continued End, rising. "You mean nothing to this company. Well, not quite nothing. But you have obviously been judged unimportant enough to have been given the most demeaning job a person can have. A worthless person telling other people that they're worthless. How long before someone comes to tell you that you're worthless, Mr. Press? Your life spent in these hallowed halls will be forgotten the minute—the second!—you no longer work here."

The H.R. rep had noticed Mr. Press near tears and was patting him on the back, murmuring soothing words that he usually reserved for those newly reduced from the workforce. He hoped he wouldn't get fired for this.

End marched toward the door. "Well, Mr. Press, I will not stoop to the low moral standards of this company." He opened the door then stopped, glanced at the two seated men, blinked somewhat abashedly, and returned quickly to the conference table and signed the waiver. He strode just as swiftly back to the spot by the door where he had been standing. "Mark my words, gentlemen! You have not heard the last of me. I will bring this company to its knees if it takes the rest of my days! And every other company like it. I will not quit until the corporate rulers of this world bow to the might of the people, as they were meant to in the first place!"

Seconds after his words had ceased to echo through the room, End noticed his left hand had clenched in a fist and his right hand was pointing a finger righteously at the ceiling. The terrified men before him shrank into their chairs as if bracing for the ominous, black figure to drive a bus over them. He suddenly felt as foolish as he was angry.

"Uh…remember that, gentlemen." Matthias End straightened his coat and tie. "Have a pleasant day."

Chapter 3

The Missouri countryside had to be one of the most captivatingly beautiful places in the state, Jenna Telfair thought as she watched trees and hills go by from the passenger seat of her car. That was a compliment coming from someone who almost never left the city. Jenna was born in Kansas City, but had lived in most of the larger cities in the United States as a result of life as the daughter of a career beauty pageant contestant. Throughout her childhood, her mother had dragged her to pageants everywhere, and when they ran out of money, they stopped where they were to get work and save up for the next pageant. Mom had lost pageants in New York, Miami, Los Angeles, Boston, Atlanta, New Orleans, San Francisco, Minneapolis, Seattle, Dallas, and St. Louis. And they had lived in all those places, some of them more than once. Jenna had liked most of them, or at least she'd found something to like in each place.

But none of them, not even St. Louis, felt like home. She had come to appreciate the undisturbed detachment that Kansas Citians had from the harried intensity of other cities. Maybe Kansas Citians—who also regularly fought traffic, rising taxes, urban sprawl, and the same harsh competitive pace any other larger city had—would have disagreed. But she knew what everywhere else was like. And maybe somewhere far away, like in Europe or Australia, had the same serene disconnect as Kansas City, but that was just too far away from everything and everyone she knew. Her mother was now in Tampa, working in the jewelry section of a department store. Her grandparents were in a retirement home in the Keys. Far enough away, but not too far away.

For her, Kansas City was home. She had lived there longer than anywhere else, and as long as she was able to stay employed, hopefully with General Micronet until she retired, she would continue to live there. She loved everything about it. All the places to eat, all the places to be entertained. All the places *to* entertain. She loved the Starlight Theater on the East Side and Sandstone to the west. She loved the barbecue joints and the jazz clubs that were everywhere. She loved to drive over the Missouri River every morning on her way to work from her tidy split-level in Parkville. She loved to shop at the Plaza—and since dumping her boyfriend Stewart two months ago, she had shopped there a lot. She loved the size of the city. She loved the feel of it. And, except for the wheeze of burnt coffee permeating the air over the west end of downtown, she even loved the smell of it.

The countryside was another matter entirely.

She glanced with forced calm to her left. In the driver's seat of her car—*her* car—was a Mr. York. That's how he introduced himself, if you could call it an introduction: "Mr. York." Back at the office, she had said—pleasantly, she thought—"Hello," extended a hand and added, "Jenna Telfair." Mr. York had looked at her and her hand and said, "I'll drive." He had done it with such command in his voice and disdain in his eyes that she had given him her keys almost defensively. She wanted to kick herself now.

"And your name?" she had said as they got underway. She knew his name. Everyone at GMN knew his name. But introductions between two people who haven't formally met and are going to spend three hours traveling together are a matter of common courtesy, for goodness sake. At first he had not wanted to say anything, but she was determined to get the upper hand in some way, so she stared at him until he finally said "Mr. York." Rather than risk coming out on the losing side of things again, she had decided not to press him for a first name. It would probably be something awful anyway, like Adolf or Mephistopheles or Bernice. So she had kept to herself while they headed south. She was definitely driving on the way back, though. He could sit and try to look brooding and cool in the passenger seat. Assuming she let him in the car at all.

Jenna was what GMN called a Product Recruiter. Her job involved finding new products for GMN to acquire. She considered herself moderately successful at it, though it meant traveling again to all those places that wanted to reattach her to their local brand of harried intensity. Fortunately for her, Mark's home was only a few hours away, in the same state. Unfortunately for her, country life was worse for her sense of detached pseudo-serenity than non-Kansas City cities were. The lack of constant human interaction was something she just couldn't handle for very long.

Mark Goggin's home was in Brookbury, a small town south of the Truman Reservoir, one of several lakes that splashed over the map of Missouri. Jenna had never been to Brookbury because Mark had always come to the city whenever he wanted to show her his latest creation. He had described Brookbury as being as beautiful and peaceful a place as anywhere in Missouri, where mountains, national forests, and rivers elbowed one another for space throughout the central and southern portions of the state.

Peaceful sounded to Jenna like an especially appealing condition to be in at the moment, particularly with all the strange things happening at General Micronet lately. Of course, nothing was really ever normal in an environment where you were trying to find the next great product before your competitors did. If a rumor of the next miracle adhesive came out, the first available GMN rep was shoved into an airplane to investigate. No time to prepare, little time to even pack. Usually the miracle adhesive, or whatever, was not as good as it was claimed to be, or it was a hoax altogether. And then it was on to the next rumor. She had found that a reliable source of good product ideas and prototypes like Mark was a much better way to come up with new products.

Obviously, Jenna knew, the best way by far would be for GMN to have its own research and development organization. But the company had found it was cheaper to just acquire whatever new products they heard about than to actually pay people over a period of time to do the same thing. That meant that anything requiring great expense to make happen, like superconductivity or fusion or any kind of high energy or subatomic work, wasn't likely to come from corporate researchers. And because of that expense, it was even less likely to come from people like Mark, the independent 'mad scientists,' as many of the good old boys in GMN's Product Research group called them. It was discouraging to learn of massive laboratories, mostly in universities covertly funded by corporations, making so many of the advances in science and technology.

Still, things had recently been even stranger than usual. Jenna should have recognized the harbinger of bad tidings when Mr. York began frequenting the halls of her department. There were plenty of rumors about that, without a doubt. He had taken over the last assistant director's office. No one in management explained who he was or what he was doing there. He had been polite enough but otherwise aloof, even to the friendliest people. He would disappear for days and then suddenly appear in the middle of an engineering meeting. Management seemed to steer clear of him, and a recent rumor went around that Mr. York had been seen scolding a vice president of operations like he was a four-year-old.

While Mr. York's shadow now fell everywhere she looked, other events were just as extraordinary. Two major product lines were sold, and space was made on manufacturing floors in factories in a dozen countries for something that would need a colossal amount of space to build. But nothing had been put there since. German and Italian scientists prowled the halls at the corporate offices, asking lots of questions and sticking their noses into places they should not at all be. The chairman, Gibson Lucy, bought a smaller company, Fortean Composites, which made a product rivaling only one of GMN's thousands of products. He paid three times what it was worth, and then did nothing with it. All corporations acquired prior to this had been inexorably absorbed into GMN's fold. Yet this one was left almost completely untouched. Only Mr. York went there: to conduct meetings for reasons which no one, including the vice presidents and directors, knew of.

It got stranger still. Three of the most profitable sites in the company were sold, quickly and quietly. Stock analysts, the major players from the New York brokerages, were being brought in, one at a time, for personal meetings with Mr. Lucy himself. It used to be that he would hold one big meeting with all of them. This one-on-one stuff smacked of something illegal like insider trading, only without the trading.

And now here she was, best buds with one of the Horsemen of the Apocalypse. And it was the bad one, too. He just better be careful with her car.

She had heard quite a bit more about this Mr. York. The few opportunities at acquiring products that she had missed out on over the years had in many cases been mysteriously acquired later through the efforts of Mr. York. Whether he had actually negotiated and bought the rights of the various discoveries, or had copied or stolen them, she didn't know. But it wouldn't surprise her in the least if he were doing business in an underhanded way. He was completely and thoroughly creepy.

From the corner of her eye, she dared a glance in his direction. At least, he was not an ugly kind of creepy; he was really quite handsome, albeit in an elitist snobbish sort of way. And he wasn't rude or offensive, he just never talked. She knew most men didn't talk much, but this guy went beyond silence. He was positively robotic.

Since they had left town, Jenna had wondered why Mr. York would be so interested in a device built by a poorly-funded, unconventional, unscientific inventor like Mark Goggin. She didn't know exactly what the device was Mark would be showing them, but it didn't sound promising. It was more or less a series of electrically powered contraptions thrown together to create even more power. Everyone wanted to be the first to build a legitimate perpetual motion machine. Even Mark, it seemed.

They had left the two-lane highway some time ago and were nearing a county road that would take them to the winding dirt road that Mark said would guide them to his house.

Trees were everywhere now. For half the trip they had passed through mostly farmland, with the few odd clusters of trees. The second half of the trip saw a lot more hills and valleys with sizeable forestland to wind through. Jenna had never cared enough to be able to identify types of trees, but she did know what an oak looked like, and they were everywhere here. Acres of them in some places and then, occasionally, a gnarled sickly-looking one out in the middle of a pasture all by itself. Trees must be like people, she thought. They need to be with each other too.

They almost missed the dirt road, so covered was it in a dense thicket of saplings and brush. A wooden mailbox with the name 'Goggin' on its side proved they were going in the right direction. The way grew dark as they drove along. Trees, trees, and more trees obscured the sky overhead, most already turned a yellow apple or deep reddish-orange color, but a few stubbornly clinging to shades of green. The sun flashed occasionally, and then it broke through just as they did, into a grassy field, partly mown. The road had steadily inclined and now it became even steeper. When they curved around another line of trees, they spotted the house.

The driveway approached the house and then curved up to and away from the front, meeting up with itself to form a circle drive. Mr. York followed the driveway and stopped at the front steps. Both of them looked up at the architectural marvel before them. The place looked absolutely Gothic. Obviously modeled after a sixteenth century French chateau, it was replete with dormers, arched windows, and enough spires, pinnacles, and turrets on the steeply pitched roof to make Napoleon and Louis XIV both throw jealous Gallic tantrums. The steps leading up to it—in fact the entire house—were made of massive blocks of limestone that could only have been delivered on site a few at a time by truck and fitted into place by hydraulic cranes and very big men.

Where Jenna was lost amid the wilds of nature, she knew something about houses. She had fallen in love with this style when she and Mother were living in Atlanta and had gone to see the Biltmore house in North Carolina. It was majestic, simply put. How a crackpot inventor got hold of it was a wonder to her. Mark had told her he would likely be busy doing something in the lab when she arrived, so she could just come right in and seek him out. The lab extended out from the bottom floor at the back of the house. She had explained that to Mr. York, and he seemed not in the least bit shy about barging in as if he owned the place. Aggravated, she followed him in.

The inside of the house was dark and shadowy but as elaborately decorated as the exterior of the house. It reminded her again of the fabulous Biltmore house. The great room at the entranceway had paneled walls and colossally high ceilings which were carved with fine detail. The strangely flickering light made it difficult to see, but sunlight shone in and compensated. The furniture was of the correct period for the house, but the upholstery seemed a bit overly worn. If the house fell short of Biltmore stature in any way—other than being considerably smaller—it was in the lack of wall decorations. Most of the walls were either bare or had disproportionately small paintings and framed photographs. A fireplace braced the north wall, and it appeared to have been added after the house was originally built; it was made of a different shade of stone as the walls outside. Tall, neat stacks of books lined most of the other walls. Something hummed, somewhere.

"Jenna?" said a voice at the opposite end of the huge room from where she stood beside the fireplace.

She turned. Mark Goggin stood beaming and smeared head to toe in a reddish substance. Jenna smiled warmly. "Hello, Mark," she said rather more enthusiastically than she had intended. Goggin walked toward her, red grit falling like landsliding rock from his clothing to the floor, where he ground them in with equally filthy shoes.

"You did say we could walk in," she said abruptly.

"Well, of course," he replied happily. "I'm glad you could come down."

"This is such a beautiful house. Have you owned it long?"

Goggin looked around as if he had never seen it before. "A while. My family has owned it for a couple of centuries. I think it's centuries. Maybe it was decades." His eyes wandered into a long hallway that he couldn't possibly see down. "I've lived here all my life."

Jenna nodded. She saw then that it was clay he was covered in. "What happened to you?"

He looked down at his clothes. "Huh. Well…ah…I had an accident. We're getting chased by balls of lightning all the time now. Don't know if I told you about that experiment. Didn't work out. I just had one come after me out by the river while I was trying to check on a cycloidal water flow experiment." He lifted the bottom end of his shirt and inspected it. "I fell down an embankment." He tried to brush at the caked clay and succeeded only in smearing it all over his hands.

"It's a wonder you didn't fall in the water."

"Yes," he agreed, trying to brush off the clay now all over his hands. He looked up at her, grimaced weakly and tried to smooth his hair with his hands, with obvious results.

Jenna smiled at his boyish attempts to make himself presentable, not to mention the clay he was scattering everywhere. Mark had always delighted her with his discombobulated but friendly manner toward her. Of course, maybe he was that way with everyone.

"Uh…who's your friend?" Goggin asked. He found a kitchen towel and tried to stem the tide of clay enveloping his body.

"Stop that," said Jenna. She lightly slapped at his hand to make him stop, took the towel from him, and dabbed at the red mud covering his hands and face and brushed away as much of the stuff in his hair as she could reach. "Mr. York is not even remotely my friend. Didn't I tell you I was bringing someone?"

"Oh. Sure, I guess."

"You never hear anything I say to you, do you?"

He smiled. "I'm sure I hear the important stuff."

"Well, he's the someone I brought. I have no idea what he's here for, but I assume it's the same thing I'm here for. It wasn't my choice, really. There are forces at work here that are far, far beyond my control."

Goggin shrugged. "Okay." He beamed again.

It was infectious, and Jenna couldn't help but smile back. Mark was certainly in good spirits. "Shall we take a look at your latest masterpiece?" she said when the silence became too long.

"Hmm? Oh, of course." Goggin tossed the towel in the direction of any number of objects, none of which were intended for muddy towels to lie on. He moved quickly into the kitchen and vaulted through an open doorway and across the breezeway on the way to the lab. "Oh, wait a minute," he said and stopped halfway. Jenna had tried to keep up and almost ran into him. He caught her, and then they grabbed one another to keep from falling. They looked at each other for another awkward moment. "What..." Goggin mumbled, "What happened to your friend?"

Jenna found herself fascinated by the brightness of his eyes, the curves in his face, the way his mouth turned halfway up at the corners as if he wanted to smile every chance he got. "I told you," she said, almost whispering, "He's not my friend."

"I bet you guys would like to be alone right now," said a voice.

Both jumped and almost toppled over a pair of entangled lawn chairs. They looked up to see Nathan standing at the doorway, smirking knowingly and covered in leaves and more red mud. Goggin stepped modestly back from Jenna.

A shadowed figure loomed behind Nathan, and he jumped when Mr. York emerged from the darkness an instant later and spoke. "No," Mr. York said coldly. "You can fondle one another later. Goggin, if you have something to show us, get on with it."

✳ ✳ ✳

Just as the inventor himself was unconventional, disorganized, and startling, Goggin's lab was equally so. Jenna had visited hundreds of laboratories over the years, from government-run facilities encompassing several buildings, to a circular supercollider bunker, to a geeky teenager's desk. All had their idiosyncrasies, to be sure, but most if not all were immaculate to a fault. Neat and sterile. Mark's laboratory was massively chaotic and looked as if an army of scientifically-ignorant toddlers had been let loose and had moved around equipment, tools, parts, and anything else every which way, leaving them on the floor and under tables and protruding through walls and hanging from exposed rafters and strung like clothesline across the rows of tables.

Goggin stepped quickly through the tangle of objects as if he had done it every day, as he obviously did, and was comfortable enough doing it not to bother cleaning the place up any time soon. Jenna and Mr. York took considerably longer and had less success. Nathan must have taken the long way. He was nowhere to be found.

As they passed a support beam, Jenna realized that the room overall was not a rectangle shape as it had looked upon entering, but more like an L. Hidden from the way they came in, the area they were now in was much better kept up. There were still wires strung across tables and glass beakers filled with a variety of colored liquids precariously perched atop shelves. But there was a noticeable effort to maintain order. The farthest table of a close set of five was clearly the final destination of their journey.

On the table rested three distinct devices. The first on her left Jenna recognized as being a variant on a Tesla coil. The primary and secondary coils were apparent and a spark gap was plainly visible, albeit alarmingly far apart. Whatever he meant to do, Mark was going to be generating a considerable amount of voltage. The third device on her right was also fairly easy to identify. It was a Stirling heat engine, a two-piston affair by the look of it. A mesh of gears ended with a pair of wheels attached to a metal rod.

The apparatus in the middle connecting the coil and the heat engine in series was a bit harder to determine. There was a transparent tank of clear liquid suspended two feet above the surface of the table, with tubes snaking down into another tank resting on the table and disappearing into a large gray metal box. It was impossible to say with any certainty what was in it, but Mark had said he would be attempting a cold fusion reaction. So that must be the reactor. Jenna took an involuntary step back and bumped into a table behind her.

"Well," said Goggin, clearing his throat. "I think I've explained to Miss Telfair the intent of this experiment. But in a nutshell, I hope to prove that by inputting the paltry sum of five thousand volts into this collection of devices, I will be able to output enough rotary power to move a car such that it will have the equivalent efficiency of an automobile capable of completing nine hundred miles to a gallon of gasoline. For purposes of this experiment, I'm just using a scale model axle with wheels. Please don't be alarmed with the danger of excessive radiation coming from the reactor. I believe I've neutralized that with a lead vault." He indicated the box.

"The applications, I think you'll agree, are obvious," he continued. "Not only will vehicles be much more fuel efficient, but that fuel will no longer originate from fossilized petroleum. The environment will therefore benefit as well." He looked at both Jenna and Mr. York expectantly. "Any questions?"

"Am I correct," said Mr. York, his voice chilled with contempt, "in assuming that you expect to generate cold fusion?"

"That is correct. But, as I said, the radiant energy should not be excessively dangerous."

"I came down here to see sparklers, a lot of useless heat, and little spinning tires?"

Goggin shifted uncomfortably, glancing at Jenna before returning his attention to Mr. York. "I think you oversimplify the interactions that will occur, and I think you also understate the magnitude of this demonstration on social mores."

"And I think you're a self-deluded mental case." Mr. York waved his hand dismissively. "Blow it all up so I can get out of here."

Goggin stood for a moment considering Mr. York. "Of course," he said finally.

A switch was thrown providing electrical power to the devices. A harmonic chorus of energized hums grew in volume until, after a minute or so, a spark shot across the gap between the wires on the Tesla coil. There were a number of bright flashes from the spark crossing the gap, and in another five minutes, a noticeable heat was felt emitting from the lead box that Mark had spoken of.

Everyone waited to see what the heat engine would do next. Of course none of it would matter without measurements to prove that the output exceeded the input to achieve perpetual motion, a less than straightforward task, Goggin found, when matching voltages to rotary motion. But he had to make it all work first.

Several more minutes passed before Goggin happened to look over at the coil. His eyes widened in alarm. Somehow the spark gap had widened. It appeared to have expanded another inch of space. The electrical arc spit and sizzled and, just before he got there, zapped its way past the output wire and shot over to the equally sizzling fusion reaction. The jolt of the arc shook the table and further separated the spark gap. Smoke rose from somewhere.

"What's happening?" shouted Jenna just as a siren went off. That was cause for concern, Goggin thought, because that was the warning klaxon that radiation was outside the lead containment box. The heat engine at that point decided to fire up.

It was all going completely downhill. Goggin gave up as the lead box appeared to be melting, and smoke rose from several places on the table. The engine had quit after only a few seconds. He flipped the switch to shut off electrical power to the experiment.

One overhead sprinkler went off, weakly drizzling water over the experiment and its witnesses. They scooted back far enough to escape the light shower. The sprinkler fizzled out almost immediately.

"Damn," Goggin said, scratching his chin. "I made the gap too wide for the spark throwing power to the reactor." He tipped over the lead box with a broom handle, revealing a couple of containers filled with liquids, a beaker, and a test tube filled with rubber tubes that snaked out to a number of places. The glass beaker and test tube were seared black, and the plastic containers were melting. "Looks like I'm going to have to start over."

"What an unqualified disaster," laughed Mr. York, surprising Jenna. Apparently it took a virtual meltdown, not to mention indoor rainfall, to raise Mr. York's spirits to a cheery level. His lack of tact for poor Mark's hard work, on the other hand, was just awful.

"Never mind," she soothed to Mark. "Setbacks are more a part of scientific discovery than success."

"Yes, but sheer stupidity is not," replied Mr. York. "Call me back when you've gotten a high school degree." He started back toward the front of the lab.

Goggin frowned at the ruins on the table, his lips moving silently and his head jerking forward to emphasize certain points as if he were scolding the entire disappointing mess. Or scolding himself. Jenna moved next to him. "The smoke was very pretty. Like floating snow." He turned and looked at her uncomprehendingly. Then his expression cleared, and he smiled just as she did.

They walked down the same row Mr. York had left in. "I'm getting careless, Jenna. A careless man with high voltage equipment is best kept at a distance."

"Oh, please," she replied. "Until the EPA finds out about you, or you start causing mile-long fissures in the earth, you've got nothing to worry—"

She stopped where she was, staring ahead.

Goggin turned from her to look as well. In front of them was Mr. York, holding up a large pink dollhouse at varying angles, trying to peer inside the windows and doors.

"That's a Barbie Dream House," said Jenna, delight in her voice. "I had one of those when I was little."

Mr. York looked under the dollhouse, and tipped it over to look underneath.

"Hey, don't shake that!" shouted Goggin. He grabbed it back from Mr. York. "Get your own!"

Mr. York stared hard at him. "How did you make that float?" he said intently.

"Mr. York!" said Jenna, astonished.

Goggin glared back. "You know, I don't recall hearing a 'Please, may I see that?' or even a 'That looks idiotic, Goggin, what's it do?' I don't go throwing around things in your house, do I?"

Mr. York's eyes narrowed as if he sensed deception. But there were clearly few options available for getting to the bottom of this. "I apologize. The shock of seeing something hovering as it did honestly made me forget my manners. I do sincerely apologize."

"Well," Goggin shrugged and perked up almost immediately, "That's quite all right. It is a wonder, isn't it?"

"Hovering?" Jenna asked in confusion.

"It's a trick, isn't it. I don't mind admitting I was fooled." Mr. York tried to smile but couldn't pull it off. "How do you do it? Pneumatic pumps? Hidden magnets? Mirrors? Holograms?"

"You don't have to tell him anything, Mark," said Jenna.

Goggin wasn't sure what to say, or to whom. "Uh, the principle behind it is not exactly scientifically grounded."

He carefully righted the dollhouse and set it on a workbench behind them. The house remained on the workbench and did not rise.

"Well…" Goggin began and then stopped, not having thought of anything else to say.

"Why isn't it working now?" interrupted Mr. York. Impatiently, he grabbed the house again. "Do not play games with me!" he raged. The abused little house was again wrenched upside down and shaken vigorously.

"Set the little girly house down!" shouted a voice behind them. "Now!"

The assemblage turned to look at the entrance to the lab.

There stood Nathan, wielding a decidedly dangerous-looking weapon. It was long and silvery, and hefty and menacing like a flame thrower. A line of cabled wires ran from the butt to a pack strapped to his back. Judging by the way Nathan was no longer slouching as he usually did, the pack must have been heavy. Goggin recognized it immediately as the pulse laser he had shown Nathan just the other day. *What day was that again?*

Mr. York laughed loudly. "You're going to shoot me with a shiny squirt gun?"

Goggin became quite animated, wrapped up in his enthusiasm for another of his inventions. "Oh no, this is actually a high-powered pulsed laser rifle. The entire backpack is filled with capacitors. Very big ones. Each is charged to, oh, fifteen hundred volts, give or take. They discharge with considerable violence, I promise you."

"All right," said Mr. York, pointing back at the dollhouse, "let's suppose I believe this isn't some illusion. How does it work?"

"Well, it's rather complicated."

Mr. York waited expectantly.

Goggin chewed on his bottom lip. "I think it's probably too complicated to explain without some schematics and drawings and so forth."

Mr. York shook his head and waved his hands as if to say "Bring it on."

Goggin pondered the possibilities. "Well, actually, I'm afraid I can't give you a lot of details. The patent is awaiting approval at the moment, see, and I don't want to do anything to jeopardize that."

"I thought as much," said Mr. York contemptuously. "This is nothing but science fiction."

"More like fantasy, actually," replied Goggin. "Real scientists wouldn't touch this sort of thing if you put one of those pulse rifles to their heads. Isn't that right, Mr. Hamper?"

"Right," said Nathan, looking down at the weapon in his hands. "But I think I could be talked into it if that was the case."

Goggin smiled and looked back at Jenna. "I'm still trying to convince Nathan that the dollhouse really floats."

"Yes, and you never will," replied Nathan. "Unless you catch me after I've done a whole bag o' weed. I see so much light-bending, fifth-dimensional shit floating in the air, I could probably see your 'cosmic ether' then."

"If this really works, Mark, why aren't you doing anything with it?" asked Jenna.

Goggin again became noticeably uncomfortable. "Um…well, I considered the possibilities, but they don't seem altogether viable at the moment. I just don't see a true application for it. Who wants a device that just floats in the air? You know?" He tried to laugh. "Sure it's novel, but it's not really worth anything until I can set it in motion. Then we'll have something big."

He lifted Barbie's Dream House carefully and replaced it on the shelf where it originally was. It slowly rose up until it was again hovering in the air. Jenna's lips parted, and she leaned closer to look at the little house on all sides. She couldn't resist waving her hands underneath it, checking for wires or whatever made it do what it was plainly—impossibly—doing.

Goggin smiled. "But I have some ideas," he said, "and I think I'm very close. If I can make it work—you know, *move*—do you realize the effect it could have on the world?"

Mr. York stared up at the dollhouse. "Quite."

Chapter 4

Matthias End had done his best to build up a good, solid lather of rage, but it just wouldn't sustain itself. He had railed on the security guards—all five of them, he was proud to recall—who had thrown him, literally, off General Micronet grounds. He had railed at them again when they wouldn't let him near his car, which was still on General Micronet grounds. And he had railed at them a third time when he noticed his driverless car rolling at quite a brisk pace directly at him, thanks again to the same security guards. It was a durable brown sedan he had abused so badly in the past that when he sidestepped out of its way and it continued down the street before hitting a tree, a few of the more prominent dents actually popped out. He had also failed to gain any good bit of anger from hitting it with a tree limb when he caught up to it.

He was further deprived of a good jolt of angst when the car started on the first try, because he would like to have been really angry at having to walk the five miles back to his place. The traffic had also been disappointingly sedate. No one had cut him off or driven slowly in front of him. The traffic lights had all been cooperative, and everyone seemed to be using their turn signals.

It occurred to him that there was no real reason to go back home, and it being almost noon, he decided to eat an impressively large pizza for lunch and hope for stomach cramps. If he was lucky, lunch would take most of the afternoon, and he could then possibly become mired in traffic or be involved in a collision during rush hour. Stupid people out driving never failed to boil his blood.

The pizza place, after he got there and was seated, had been excruciatingly quiet and unusually free of customers, and unhappily, the waitress had been quite pleasant but not so much so as to be aggravating. End might have begun to consider some kind of insidious galactic conspiracy at that point, only it didn't make sense that the conspirators would do something like lay him off and then throw nothing but joy and happiness in his direction for the rest of the day.

The pizza arrived, and he growled on seeing that it was constructed exactly to his specifications, including the one anchovy per slice he had requested with the unexpressed hope that they would screw it up. He didn't even like anchovies. But there they all were.

End glanced outside the window as a delivery truck pulled up next door. On its side read 'HoleSale Cheeses.' Smaller letters below that read 'a division of General Micronet.'

Hmm.

His waitress approached. Impossible, he thought, as his pizza was delivered in record time. Normally, you can't get a straw when you ask for one, so how could they have possibly gotten right an order for a double king-size pizza with twelve toppings?

He found himself looking for ways to stir up trouble. Throwing anchovies at the other customers would almost certainly have made them mad, which hopefully would lead to some kind of confrontation that he could get good and hot about. If he were to proposition the waitress in as vulgar a way as he could imagine, that would surely get him slapped. Not that that would aggravate him particularly. Better still, he could start a food fight. The flying anchovies might take care of that. Of course, getting arrested would have upset him too. But he was looking for a free outlet for his frustrations, not one involving fines and jail time.

End watched as the delivery truck's driver opened up the back of the truck, pulled out three large boxes and set them on a two-wheeler. The man paused to yell obscenities at a smaller man standing next door who must be the owner of that establishment. The delivery man carted the boxes past the smaller man, cuffing him on the side of the head as he went by.

End smiled.

He finished off the slice he was eating, left too much money for the bill, and stepped toward the door, his black coat knocking drinks off another table as he swept it around behind him and put it on.

Outside, the little man was whining something about being treated unfairly. Or fairly untreated. End couldn't tell, and frankly he didn't care.

"Good afternoon!" End said jovially, putting a friendly hand on the little man's shoulder.

The little man jumped horribly and shrank back, whimpering more pitifully. The truck driver pushed his two-wheeler back out the door and went by them both.

"Hi there!" said End, smiling broadly. The driver looked at him coldly and kept on going. So End followed him. "I couldn't help noticing that you were having trouble getting along out here. I wonder if I might be of some assistance. I am quite well suited at resolving disputes."

"Get bent," said the driver with a snicker.

"Oh thank you," replied End, "that really was the answer I was looking for." With a swiftness that was all the more impressive given his size, End reached out and grabbed the driver by his left ear, and lifted it straight up. The driver had briefly cocked his arm to take a swing at End, but the pain in his ear quickly changed his mind.

"Yeaarrrrgghh!" he screamed and grabbed at End's arm.

"Let's go over here a moment, shall we?" said End. He yanked on the ear to get them started and guided the driver back to the little man, who was cringing mightily and fully expected to be torn in half by one of them, although probably not the one with his ear in the air.

End released the driver and pointed at the little man. "Apologize."

The driver took one glance at the man and launched a punch at End's chin, which was no longer there. The force of the punch spun the driver around a full circle, and there was End again.

The driver was a formidable size himself and, by the look of his face, had been in his share of brawls. But judging by the number of scars and damaged teeth and the flat nose that drooped lifelessly against his face, he had also lost most of them. To the man's credit, he did not appear intimidated by End's substantial size advantage. To his discredit, he had not recently been laid off from his job.

End himself was hoping to get hit. At this point, nothing less would stir his bloodlust. He stood his ground, his arms at his sides, motionless, a contemptuous smirk on his face. The driver circled with fists raised. As he began to move behind End, he realized that End was not moving, and he let loose a huge punch with all his weight behind it.

End turned, straightened, and leaned back, all without a moment's thought. The driver was considerably shorter and the blow clipped the top of End's shoulder. It didn't hurt exactly, just a little sting. But it would do. End feinted a jab with his left hand and then dropped the driver with one solid wallop to the ribs. Bones cracked inside the driver, his breath left him, and he crumpled to the ground. He moaned and gasped and writhed around the pavement for a while before End spoke again.

"I dislike bullies," End said. "I should probably have mentioned that at the beginning of our conversation." He leaned down to look at the driver, who was unable to even sit up. "I want to show you something. Do you think you could stand?"

The driver quickly dismissed his first inclination, which was to lash out with a heavy boot at End's shin. He knew it would only get more bones broken. So he nodded, and End helped him gently to his feet.

End walked around to the other side of the truck and waited as the driver shuffled slowly around after him. He looked alternately at the truck and its driver with a certain eager anticipation. "You'll like this," he said to the driver. "This is a trick I thought of…well, just now, I suppose. It's probably been done, but whatever." He reached over and pulled a long knife from the driver's boot. The driver did not even flinch. End then stabbed all the tires but one on the side of the truck nearest them. It took several times stabbing each tire to get them to deflate. The truck slowly began to lean in their direction. The driver seemed almost to forget about his internal injuries as he shuffled frantically to get out of the way.

End looked at the top of the truck as it leaned farther over, but he didn't move. "See, these high-centered trucks have a very bad problem with tipping. The trick is to flatten all the tires on one side, except one. Then you let the last one kind of leak slowly." He pierced the last tire and then moved to the back of the truck with the driver. "Now, the high center of weight should take care of the rest."

The truck eased gradually over as the air slowly leaked out of the last tire. It leaked too slowly though, and it became quickly apparent that the truck was eventually just going to come to rest on its rims.

End frowned.

Reaching into a pocket inside his coat, he pulled out a revolver. In one quick motion, he fired on the last partially inflated tire. Rubber exploded in all directions and left a gaping hole in the tire. Air left it instantly with a loud sigh.

The truck leaned over much more swiftly, teetered momentarily on its rims, and went over on its side, sounding like a multi-car accident. The repeated echo of things sliding and other things breaking could be heard through the truck's heavily bent metal walls.

The driver and End waited for several minutes until the dust brought up by the truck had settled. Dozens of big boxes had tumbled out the rear doors, some of them opening up to reveal what were once car stereos, televisions, DVDs, and computer equipment. Their entrails lay strewn across the pavement, mixing with one another in electronic death.

End looked it over and shook his head as he put away the revolver. "That's too bad. That stuff might not work as well now." He patted the stricken driver on the back—causing him to wheeze horribly—buttoned his coat and strolled away through a gathering crowd.

Chapter 5

"*. . . a*nd I think this is an opportunity to acquire a product that will revolutionize more industry segments than anything since the automobile, ironically the very thing this invention will eventually make obsolete. It is my recommendation that we fund research for this endeavor immediately. Given sufficient financial backing, we could well have a working prototype by the end of next year."

Jenna Telfair closed her notebook on the podium and put her hands together on top. "Any questions?"

The gathered members in the room started talking to one another first in hushes, then in agitation, growing in volume and intensity until finally the clamor of voices began to unnerve Jenna. It was difficult to tell whether they were pleased with her report or not.

Jenna adjusted her glasses, unnecessarily as it happened. She thought it made her look intelligent and professional: 'it' being, of course, both the glasses and the adjusting of the glasses. They were prescription glasses and not actually hers. Her sister had discarded them, and Jenna had snapped them up with the idea of them being a possible enhancement to her appearance. She couldn't see very well in them, naturally. In fact she only put them on when she was somewhere that she wouldn't have to walk very fast, or even at all, and so could pick out the blurred objects approaching her before she ran into them. Meetings were perfect for such a situation. She particularly liked to take them off and put one of the ear handle pieces in her mouth and squint thoughtfully at the person speaking. It made her look both intelligent and sexy. In the past, she would never have wanted to look sexy at work, but she had found it easier to compromise a little. Everyone got along better if the women occasionally smiled and teased the men, the majority of whom reciprocated by making asses of themselves. One wouldn't expect the men to feel more at ease acting like idiots, but they did relax considerably and were much more cooperative thereafter. Especially on occasions like this.

She had spoken in front of General Micronet's full board of directors only twice before. On both occasions, she had neither done well, nor had she enjoyed not doing well. But this was clearly an opportunity no one would pass up. She particularly watched Gibson Lucy, the CEO, for some kind of sign as to his inclination toward the proposal. But he appeared to be either thinking thoughtfully or just staring at the basket of bagels in front of him. His expression was almost plaintive and enamored, as if he would really like more than anything else in the world to be alone in the room with the basket and its bagels. He even licked his lips.

"Mr. York," a thin reedy suspicious man not far from Mr. Lucy shouted with surprising strength above the tumult. The room quieted. "You saw this...what was it?" He looked down the table at Jenna.

"A Barbie Dream House," she said after a split-second's hesitation. It was embarrassing to say, especially to a board of directors. "It's just something to house, if you will, the device."

"Thank you," said the reedy man. "Mr. York, what did you make of this... house?"

"Ladies and gentlemen," said Mr. York with authority in his voice. "With all due respect to the young lady, this is frankly an illusionist's trick. A good one, I will be the first to admit. But still an illusion."

"But——" Jenna started to say.

"You do not see even a glimmer of potential?" said a short squat man with nervous eyes.

"None whatsoever."

"What about the Tesla Coil Cold Fusion contraption you were sent down there to check out in the first place?" said Ms. Barlett, Jenna's boss, with venom in her words.

"It's—" Jenna again started to say.

"A total waste of time," finished Mr. York. "Not only did it not work but he practically burned the whole place down and us with it."

The board thought that was very funny, and chuckled and nodded appreciably at one another.

"Please!" said Jenna, finding her voice. "I don't think we can afford to ignore this invention."

"What the hell is going on?" Her plea must have shaken Mr. Lucy from his wooing of baked goods.

A young woman sitting to Lucy's right, probably younger than Jenna, patted his arm. "It's all right, Mr. Lucy. We were just discussing Mr. Goggin's inventions."

The room cowered, waiting for a reaction, but the fabled CEO of General Micronet had sunk back into his own muddled musings.

"Miss Telfair, I think that will be enough for now," said the suspicious man. "Thank you very much."

"But—"

"Thank you, we'll let you know. That will be all."

Jenna gathered up her notes, scanning the eyes looking back at her for some sign that they had one single clue how big Mark's invention really was. The only sign she saw was in Mr. York's eyes, but his were also glaring back at her. She walked to the doors, paused almost as if she were ready to scold all of them, thought better of it, and left.

After the door closed behind her, all eyes turned to Mr. York. He looked at them gravely. "This is it, ladies and gentlemen. This is the real thing. I saw it myself. Believe as you wish, but Goggin does indeed have a successfully realized concept for the very thing we've been re-engineering the entire corporation for, finished and running before any of our hired gun scientists have even completed their mockups. Unfortunately he doesn't seem interested in doing anything with it. He doesn't want to sell the design or partner with us."

Mr. York peered intently at the faces in the room. "Mr. Goggin and his contraption are going to be very serious problems for us unless we act now."

The group responded as most groups do when trying to reach a decision during a major crisis. They babbled like panicked second-graders.

"…Why don't we just triple our price for the damn thing? Anybody can be bought…"

"…Let's just steal it. It's not like we haven't done that before…"

"…I say we kill him. Or blow up the whole place and him with it…"

"…It doesn't do anything worthwhile. Why should we care?…"

Mr. York stepped up to the table, silencing half of the room. "One at a time, please," he said, silencing the other half.

A large balding man rose and spoke. "I would urge restraint, people. I remember forcing a company to hand over its prototype for a…what was it? A new kind of drinking glass, I think it was. Sounded idiotic at the time. But we spent millions perfecting the shape and texture and thickness. We put all sorts of people on committees to match the size and height and colors to the specifications of our target demographics, which, last I've heard, is everyone in the world. I believe we sold about a thousand of them. That was a good product compared to this impossible machine."

From the opposite side of the table an old gray-haired gentleman stood up. "I remember a few years ago when we bought a little shoe company in Kansas that most people thought was worthless too. Some of you might remember it. It's got five thousand stores nationwide now." He sat down and looked around in satisfaction.

Gibson Lucy re-entered their plane of existence and joined the discussion. "Well, I remember buying Coca-Cola."

Everyone ceased talking. With that bombshell they had no idea what to think or what to say.

"I don't think you actually did, Mr. Lucy," said Mr. York. "As I recall, you wanted to, in fact, you vowed to buy Coca-Cola, but it didn't work out in the end. The executives dropped in a poison pill clause, I believe."

"But I did buy Coca-Cola," insisted Mr. Lucy.

Mr. York shook his head. "Sir, you bought *a* Coca-Cola. Not the company."

"Kept to my word though, didn't I."

"Yes sir, you did."

"And then that Kennedy guy got in the way."

This time the room held its collective breath.

"It was him or me. All in all…worked out for the better," said Mr. Lucy as he zoned in on the bagel basket and warped out to deep space once again.

Mr. York waited to make sure that the chairman had again lost touch with reality before addressing the board once again. "I believe we all know that Mr. Lucy had nothing to do with any presidential assassinations," he said, eyeing the group. "He is out of sorts today."

Circling the table, Mr. York stood directly behind the blankly staring CEO. "Now if we may continue? Your suggestions are all well-taken, of course. As board members, you have full right to make any suggestions you desire. But, if I may, I'd like to weed out some of the less promising ideas. First, there's no point in buying Goggin's device unless you also buy the man who built it. It still needs work and the man who built it is best qualified to do that work. The same reasoning applies to stealing it. It still needs work. And General Micronet's policy is to acquire proven products, not bankroll an unknown. I also don't think we can just ignore the situation, because our competitors certainly will not. We must do something. As for killings and bombings, you are not paying me enough for that."

Mr. York folded his arms as if a decision had already been made. "The only viable solution is, I admit, a rather drastic one. It will require money and commitment to the cause in the face of immense challenges from many directions."

The directors of the board of General Micronet sat hushed, listening.

Chapter 6

Legend had it that Thomas Edison failed more than a thousand times before he succeeded in making the light bulb work. The frustration that must have gathered in him and fed upon itself over what must have been weeks and months, possibly years of failure was, in all honesty, perfectly easy for Mark to contemplate.

He'd lost count how many times he had failed to get the Tesla fusion device to work. He was afraid the next attempt would melt the rest of his experiment and irradiate the whole lab. Surely even Edison would have had as much trouble and faced easily as much risk trying to get this damnable fusion business sorted out, although Mark couldn't help thinking that Edison might have known better than to try to make it work in the first place.

The table was a tangled mess of used, unused, discarded, singed, and burnt pieces to his fusion puzzle. Those parts that he suspected had been too heavily irradiated he had shoved impulsively in a corner, and it now occurred to him that that might have been another mistake. Dozens of flasks and beakers full of chemicals he could no longer identify sat on top of a set of shelves directly above the radiating parts. He wasn't sure whether radiation rose or just dispersed in the air, but if his luck continued on its present course, it would form itself into something sentient and follow him around, irradiating him and everything in its path as it grew exponentially with each passing hour until it could melt entire cities and...

Perhaps he needed a break.

He had circled the table several times in the last...well, he didn't know what time it was, so he could only assume it was at least several hours. One of Mark's better qualities lay in his ability to focus so well on the task at hand. The downside to that was that he frequently didn't know what time of day it was, or many times, what day of the week it was. It felt like sometime late in the afternoon, approaching sunset, judging by the lack of direct sunlight coming through the windows in the lab.

Where Mark sat now, he could see across the full breadth of the lab and his eye caught the pink, boxy cuteness of the Barbie Dream House. It was amazing even to him how it hovered there, unmoving and unmoved. It had hung suspended in midair like that for the last three months. Neither the barometric pressure of heavy winds outside, nor the humidity, nor the atmospheric electricity of thunderstorms overhead, not even the numerous power failures that regularly afflicted the house and lab, could alter the dollhouse's defiance of the laws of gravity.

Assuming that was what it was doing. He couldn't really be sure. It was possible. But wasn't it impossible?

Frankly, it just made his head throb to try to think it through. The only thing that was clear in his mind right now was that the Tesla fusion invention hadn't worked and that he had to have looked like an imbecile to Jenna. An intelligent, refined woman like that was not likely to be interested in unbalanced lab rats like him in the first place, and it certainly didn't help his case that his experiment had disintegrated right in front of her.

Obviously, the thing to do was to make it work. Even if it wasn't perpetual, even if it put out less power than it used, if he could at least prevent it from starting another fire, that would be a victory. The focal point of all his troubles had to be—

Mark looked up. He sensed something was wrong in the lab. He looked around the immediate area, and then toward the far end.

A man in a huge black coat was walking—strolling actually—down an aisle of his laboratory.

Mark spluttered and stopped and started in exasperation. "Excuse me!" he called out when nothing clever came to mind. "Can I help you with anything in particular?" He approached the man who was now staring at Barbie's Dream House. "Sir, I'm afraid we're not open for business for…well… ever. This is a private residence."

The man ignored him and leaned all around the floating dollhouse in fascination.

Mark couldn't believe it. "Hello! You can't just go walking into someone's house." He looked over to the doorway. "How did you get in here anyway?"

"This is what they're after," said the man, pointing at the Dream House. "Or at least they will be." He laughed. "They sure won't care about some Tesla coil-cold fusion ridiculousness, now will they?" He laughed loudly but without malice, then stopped himself short. "I meant no offense, Mr. Goggin. Honestly. My name is Matthias End." He held out his hand.

Mark shook it without thinking, then yanked his hand loose when he realized what he was doing. "How do you know my name?" he said, trying to sound fierce and intimidating.

"Well, it's on your mail box, for one thing. But I did know your name before I arrived here. Beautiful house you have."

Mark was not to be deterred. "Thank you. You didn't answer my question."

"Didn't I? Not surprising."

"So how about an answer." Talking through gritted teeth didn't prove sufficiently menacing either.

End resumed his leisurely walk. "I'm a friend of Jenna Telfair's."

"Oh," nodded Mark, then shook his head. "That's not an answer either! How did you get in here?"

"Now that wasn't your original question. Do you still want an answer to that?"

"Yes! No! I mean…" Mark was not used to defending his home from intruders, especially ones that acted like they were there for a tour. He was about to let fly another accusation when awareness suddenly opened up before his eyes. "Jenna told you about my experiment."

End laughed again. "Yes, I'm afraid so. She actually believed it might work. She has a great deal of faith in you."

A tentative smile formed on Mark's face. "Really?"

"It didn't work though, did it?"

Mark frowned. "She told you?"

"No. It just seemed, ah, fairly predictable."

"Well, I've about got it ironed out now, so you can just tell her I'll be ready next time she wants to come see it."

They came to the table where the Tesla fusion experiment wasn't working. End looked it over from beginning to end, even leaning down closer to squint at the details. He started to chuckle, but saw Mark and stopped himself.

"Do you have any idea what the problem is?" asked Mark hopefully.

"No, I'm afraid not. I'm not much for gadgets and doodads myself. I'm just an arc welder. Until recently, anyway. But I know enough to appreciate the huge waste of time this is."

"Isn't that nice," said Mark sarcastically. "So what are you here for, Mr. End?"

"Oh, please call me Matthias." He headed back toward the front of the lab, Mark following with growing irritation. "Only people who don't like me call me Mr. End."

"Of course. What do you want, Mr. End?"

End smirked. "Touché. I know I haven't earned your trust. Yet. Certainly not by barging in like this." They stopped again in front of the dollhouse. "I'm here to warn you, Mr. Goggin."

"Well, thank you very much," said Mark, his patience a distant memory. He grabbed at End's forearm. "Glad you could drop by. Sorry you can't stay longer."

End didn't budge. "Don't you want to know what the warning is?"

"Do you think it's likely I'll believe anything you say when you've broken into my house?"

"I didn't break in. The door was open."

"The door was——? Nathan!"

As if he had been standing there all along, which he was, Nathan opened the door into the lab and stepped in, smiling. "Yes sir, Mr. Goggin sir." He saw End and said, "Hey, Matt!"

"Hello again, Nate," said End pleasantly. "Did you get that sandwich finished? Growing boys like you need to eat more. Especially if you're going to be smoking so much pot. You know, when I was a boy, I——"

"Excuse me," Mark said loudly. "Excuse me. I'm glad to see we're all friends here, but I'd like to get to the bottom of a few things. Mr. Hamper, did you leave the door open again?"

"You said I should clean out the fridge once a month."

That reply seemed wildly tangential to Mark. He rolled it around in his mind, finding only square pegs and round holes. "Okay, yes, but——"

"And you said that if the smell was so bad 'Why don't you use your head, Mr. Hamper, and open the door to disperse the contaminated atmosphere.'"

"Oh." This was becoming a hopeless situation. Mark rubbed at his temples.

"Sinus trouble?" asked End, pointing at Mark's forehead and nodding with concern. "Yes, this is the season for it."

"All right, enough."

"Definitely sinuses," agreed Nathan. "He's not usually so crabby."

Mark started to laugh. This was all too odd. "Nate old buddy, may I have a word with you?" He motioned Nathan over while End wandered back closer to the Dream House. "Haven't I told you not to bring your hallucinating friends over here? What if he thought this was some kind of doobie factory and tried to throw us out. He looks like he could do it too." He looked over at the large black figure as it peered all around the Dream House. "And I would appreciate it if you didn't go telling your friends about my experiments and the people I work with. It's a security risk and it's impolite and it's also very disconcerting having strangers come in and——"

"He's not one of my friends. We're friends now, but I didn't know him half an hour ago."

"But you talk like you're best friends."

"Oh that's just him. He's a great guy. Very friendly. Very suave. Isn't that the coolest coat he's wearing? It's so Goth, you know?"

"Yes." Mark glared irritably at Nathan, then turned back to End. "All right, Mr. End. I give. What did you want to warn me about?"

"Yes, of course." End stared a moment longer at the underside of the doll-house, then turned back to them. "Originally, I came here to warn you about your Tesla fusion device. Perhaps I should back up a tad. I was laid off recently—"

"Oh, I'm terribly sorry," Mark said without a trace of sorrow.

End didn't notice. "Not at all. Happens to everyone nowadays. All part of the new perpetually transitioning, mobile society we blue-collar workers live in. In any case. After being laid off, I found myself visiting drinking establishments much more often than usual. A couple my old welding group used to go to, in particular. I continued going to them after I was transferred to another department, and then again once I was de-employed. I find myself with a lot of idle time now, you see, and with that has come a keen interest in bringing justice to the criminal organization General Micronet. To that end, I have sought and learned a great deal from my old mates in the last week, in addition to what I have picked up from Jenna and others in the office. A covert plot of colossal dimensions is apparently in the works. General Micronet appears to be retooling its factories to build something either huge or huge in numbers. And it centers on something in this very fine laboratory of yours."

Mark laughed. "Impossible. There's nothing that impressive going on here. I guarantee you, if you'd seen the look on Jenna's face when she left, you'd have thought I was the biggest disappointment on the face of the earth. And that guy with her. York. He looked disgusted at everything he saw, including me, the whole time he was here."

End looked back up at the floating Barbie's Dream House. "Everything?" He looked back at Mark and frowned. "You mention Mr. York. For me, he is the deciding factor. He does not bother himself with minor matters where the company is concerned. When Jenna told me about him, I knew there was something big going on here. But was he really interested in your Tesla fusion device? Or was it something else?"

Mark gazed ruefully up at the dollhouse.

"I thought as much," said End. "Your danger, Mr. Goggin, lies in the very fact that he has been here and has seen this wondrous pink dollhouse of yours. Mr. York does not just make mutually equitable transactions. He conquers. He destroys. And if GMN is retooling so much of its manufacturing space now, and he is here, he will gain possession of your little girl's house at whatever cost it takes. And you know at what cost all corporations want to acquire assets."

"For free?" asked Nathan.

End smiled. "You are correct, young man. Mr. York is especially good at that."

"So what am I supposed to do?" asked Mark. "Hide it?"

"Oh that won't work," said End. "There is still you."

Mark made a face. "What does that mean?"

"You made the house float. You could make another house float," said End. "You must hide as well."

Thought and concern were evident in Mark's features. But then he made another face. "What a load of garbage," he said. "You break into my home and drop a few names of people I know and then expect me to fall for this tall tale? Listen to me. First and foremost, no one chases Mark Goggin out of his home. This place has been in my family for the last…uh, well, a pretty damn long time. A century, anyway. And second, there is nothing here worth all the fuss. I told Jenna and that York fella the same thing. Who cares whether it hovers or not when it doesn't go anywhere. It's a great gimmick for talk shows and circuses, but no one's going to be impressed about a floating anything that won't slip into gear and head somewhere."

"But if you can make it float, surely it's not that far a leap in time to making it move somewhere," insisted End.

"Yes in fact it could be a very long time, Mr. Not-Much-For-Gadgets-and-Doodads."

"Be that as it may," said End more intently, "time won't matter to GMN or Mr. York, or anyone else who finds you a threat to their business. Even if it takes you fifty years to get it working, they'll want to get rid of you now and not take the chance that you'll figure it out sooner."

Mark pondered the ceiling abstractedly. "I'll be eighty-four by then."

"Mr. Goggin!" It was End's turn to become exasperated. "You are a man of reason. Don't you see the very real danger in your situation?"

"Mr. End. Matthias, if you like. Enough. Please. I'm not going anywhere."

End opened his mouth to protest further, then closed it and smiled in acquiescence. "I can't force you to leave, Mark. I could, I suppose, but then you'd probably squirt free and come right back."

"Thank you," said Mark, smiling with some relief that he wouldn't be having to tangle with the intimidating former welder.

"Do as you will," said End. "I must, however, do the same." He sat on a nearby stool and folded his arms.

Mark's smile disappeared. "What does that mean?"

"I can't make you leave your property. That would probably get me arrested. And it's probably rude too. But I can make sure nothing happens to you."

"I don't need a bodyguard."

"Yes you do."

"What, you think you're going to just hang out here, getting in the way and eating my food?"

"It's quite all right. No need to thank me."

"I'm not thanking you!" said Mark. "You're not staying here!"

"No, of course not. I don't care to be incinerated along with the rest of your doomed laboratory doohickeys. I'll be perfectly content on the couch."

Nathan became very excited. "This is going to be so cool! This'll be like a hideout before the bad guys come and attack the place. We should get some guns. You know?"

Mark glared at Nathan as if he'd just clumsily dropped his own brain. "You know as well as I do, we don't have guns here. We'd just shoot each other."

End pulled out his revolver. He waved it around, admiring its deadly look, and then showed it to Nathan. He realized that Mark was watching him. "I'm really a fairly good shot," he said. "I've never shot anyone who didn't deserve it."

"No guns," said Mark firmly.

"Mark, I don't think you realize what's coming."

"I don't care. I don't like guns. Besides, Nathan's parents would throw a snit if they found out I let him be around guns. Get rid of it."

"And what are we supposed to do if someone comes here with guns themselves?"

"This house has ways of keeping the wrong element out."

"Oh yes, it did a fine job keeping me out."

Mark sighed and rubbed at his temples again. "Look I don't want to have to call the police and have you dragged out of here."

"And I don't want to have to call the EPA and have your lab quarantined for the next ten years due to radiation contamination."

Mark frowned. "Welcome to my home."

Chapter 7

"Miss Telfair, this is Drake Endicott," Mr. York said acidly. Drake Endicott stepped toward Jenna with his dark hair, cleft chin, broad smile—broader shoulders—white teeth, magnificent physique, and everything else.

Good God almighty, he *was* magnificent, wasn't he? she thought. Maybe not in a virile, masculine John Wayne way. More like a sly, debonair Clark Gable type.

It was always hard to think business whenever she met a man who made her knees quiver, rare though that was. But she had never let them distract her before, and she certainly wasn't going to let this one now. She held out her hand for a firm handshake and said hello. Her other hand fumbled nervously with her necklace. She was momentarily surprised that her legs refused to move her forward and so Drake Endicott had to take another step in order to clasp her outstretched hand. She smiled, a little too pleasantly she thought, after she had already done it. She must look like a dim, glassy-eyed teenager to him.

To her further surprise, he brought her hand up to his lips and gently kissed the back of it. She blinked up at him and smiled uncertainly. No one at work had ever shaken her hand quite that way. Her knees wobbled badly.

"It's a crime that so beautiful a woman is hidden away in a dull, dark building like this all day long," he said.

Outside the room they were now in—an office appropriated from a vice president by Mr. York for this meeting—the corporate offices of General Micronet bustled with an energy its employees could sense but not understand. Great things were in the making, but pawns were the last to know and the first to be sacrificed for the cause. Jenna hoped she wasn't being prepared for sacrifice.

"Oh," Jenna breathed and then jerked as if awakened. "Um, thank you very much, Mr. Endicott."

"I mean that," he said with an immense, ivory smile.

She nodded in agreement but could think of nothing to say but "Of course." Turning to Mr. York, she was startled by the unpleasantness of his expression. He looked even more irritated than he had at Mark's lab. The contempt was focused mostly on Drake Endicott, but she could see that he was in no small part scornful at what he must have considered her weak level of resistance to Endicott's charms. She tried to sneer back at him in equal disgust but it felt to her more like she was about to sneeze.

"Mr. Endicott is here——" Mr. York started to say.

"Hey, Yorkie! Man! We're on first names here, aren't we?" Drake Endicott turned to Jenna, sweeping her hand again up into his. "Call me 'Drake'."

Jenna was lost as to what to do next. She met Mr. York's loathing stare.

"Mr. Endicott," resumed Mr. York, "is here as a representative for a coalition of firms that are interested in your Mr. Goggin's efforts. They are very much fascinated in what we saw the day of our visit. I have already described events as I saw it. He would like to hear your recollections——"

"You see, Jenna— oh! May I call you Jenna?" Drake Endicott waited for her reply as if that was all that mattered in the world. Jenna could only nod. "Jenna, I know it's hard to recall sometimes what has happened, especially when it's been, what, a week since you were down there? Ha ha! I can't remember what day it is sometimes! Thursday, Monday, Sunday, who knows?"

"That *is* appalling," replied Mr. York blandly.

Drake Endicott raised his eyebrows, glanced over at Mr. York, and guffawed in appreciation. "You got me there, Yorko! What a kidder. I had no idea he was such a cutup. Now, sweetheart, my people are really, really, really interested in this floating house gizmo. I know we've sunk a pile of the green stuff on that testy chilly fusion whatsis, but I just don't think it's gonna pan out. Do you?"

Jenna blinked.

"I didn't think so. Now, from a purely corporate perspective, we're looking to leverage this guy for all he's worth. Cut him a check and then cut him off, that's the gist of it. No disrespect of course. Just don't want loose ends. Are you with me so far, Jenna sweetheart?"

Jenna nodded quickly, but with a worried expression on her face.

"I'm not," said Mr. York.

"Ha, ha! Cut it out!" chortled Drake Endicott. "Okay, Jenna. Take me back in time to that little house on the prairie. Feed me the sights and sounds as they come to you."

Jenna wasn't sure she wasn't on some kind of game show, but she explained what she had been told to expect when she arrived at Mark's house.

"Good, good," said Drake Endicott. "You're doin' fine."

She related how impressive the lab seemed. A tad disorganized, but a lot going on.

"I'm with you, I'm with you," murmured Drake Endicott. "Go on."

The Tesla fusion device had looked promising, she had recalled, but the experiment had not worked. Poor Mr. Goggin was terribly disappointed.

"Oh I'm sure," Drake Endicott soothed. "Tragic. Just tragic."

Mr. York had been rude through the whole visit and had grabbed the floating dollhouse when he saw it.

"Ha! Well, the Yorkster is paid to get after it. What else?"

"That's about it. We asked Mark some questions about the dollhouse, but he doesn't seem to think it's a very promising idea."

"Not surprising at all, Jenna dear. I've been around innovators all my life—heck, been one too—and none of them are good judges of investment possibilities. *None* of them. They just want to make their silly whosits and then toss them in the corner and start on something else. A fully functional intergalactic warp drive is probably sitting right now in some middle-aged loser's basement gathering dust even as we speak! Ha ha ha!"

He beamed at Jenna for just long enough to make it awkward—for her, not him—and to give her time to conclude that he was something that had probably been spawned in the bowels of marketing or the entrails of sales. For her, the luster had quickly worn off, leaving only a superficial gray sludgy residue.

Mr. York, like Drake Endicott, was also immune to awkwardness, but he was not immune to impatience. It was, in fact, a natural occurrence in much of his analysis regarding communication between individuals. People were stupid, he often concluded; stupid, generally unproductive, and prone to long silences for no good reason. In all likelihood, he would have found the hypothetical fool with the warp drive by now if he hadn't had to wade through the sea of aimless, pointless, stupid people surrounding him. And now to have to baby-sit a conniving schmoozer like Endicott was an insult. He had better get a bonus in his paycheck out of this whole deal or heads would roll.

He sneered in disgust. *Heads would roll*, he thought. He was beginning to sound just like the flatulent ass. It was too much. "Thank you, Miss Telfair. I'll be in touch."

"Yes, Jenna, thank you so much," added Drake Endicott. "You're a credit to your profession and gender. We'll be in touch." He winked with sufficient suggestiveness to make Jenna back out of the room even faster. She was gone without so much as a "You're nuts."

"Did you see that? She was giving me the eye, my friend," said Drake Endicott. "She wants me. Bad. Pretty obvious, don't you think?"

"I couldn't possibly care less, and I am not your friend."

"Oh I know, babe. Just a figure of speech."

"It is not a figure of speech. A figure of speech is a rhetorical expression or a metaphor; an idiom; a cliché, even. I'll certainly not deny that you spew out plenty of that. But calling yourself my friend is implying some form of intimacy, which is so revolting a thought that I am tempted to put my fist through your face."

"Hey, hey. Yorkshire, man. Let's not split hairs here, guy. We've got to work together on this. Don't get me wrong. You're the man as far as I'm concerned. You're in the know, you're happenin'. And you've been at this a lot longer than I have. But guys that have been at something a long time tend to circle the wagons. Know what I mean? Go soft, hang back, play zone coverage. But I'm not there. I've got to shake things up. Fire all my guns. Hey, call it youthful exuberance. That's not to say I'm a rookie though. I've been around the pistol range a few times myself. And I can spot the obvious as well as the next schmo."

"And what is obvious, Mr. Endicott?"

"Now now, there, Yorktown. I don't want to cloud your vision. You're the bomb, my man. You're on the pulse of the problem. You see it and you know what to do, i.e. you've got a plan. I'm just eyeballing it from my perspective. You say 'whoa' and I'm quiet as a church mouse."

Mr. York so wanted to end the unrelenting babble, but he had enough trouble bringing himself to say a word like 'whoa' that it was too late.

"All right," said Drake Endicott, teeth flashing. "I knew you'd come around, big guy. The gist is this: the Goggin goon has got to go. Pure and simple. Am I right or am I right? Or am I right?"

Mr. York eyed him with suspicion and some alarm. He'd heard of Endicott and his favored tactics in a pinch. Still it might be profitable to play dumb. "Go where?"

"Adios. So long. Farewell. Shuffling off this mortal coil. Scragging the ninth life. Telling tales to the big CEO in the sky."

Mr. York pursed his lips but said nothing.

"Hey, your Yorkfulness, you've got your way and I've got mine. Frankly I don't know what your way is, but my way is a bullet through the kitchen window into the left temple. Not that I'm above the judicious use of carpet-bombing. It does have its place."

"And what if we want him alive? The potential of his invention is quite staggering."

"Not worth the risk. He could turn on us. Better to cop the house and frag him now and let our own science guys work out the kinks."

Mr. York watched Drake Endicott for some sense that he was being misled. But the man had no subtleties that he could discern. "I'll consider it. In the meantime, you will take no action. Understand?"

"Yorks, Yorks, you're runnin' the show. I'm on the sidelines until you let me into the game. I'm a team member, guy. Always have, always will."

Mr. York was already out the door and gone.

"Until you fuck it up," said Drake Endicott, beaming once again.

Chapter 8

This can't be what it's like to have a family.

Mark Goggin had been raised in a home where his father worked horrendously hard, nine days a week it often seemed to him, and his mother worked harder still to keep the house and the family in one piece. He only had a brother and a sister, but with cousins and kids from neighboring farms stampeding in and out, home had always seemed like a packed stadium. With a town as small as Brookbury, where everyone knew everyone else, there was probably no other way. But it was always so noisy, so busy, so frantic, going from one chaotic maelstrom of activity to the next. It never felt like he had a real family. He never remembered a real conversation with either of his parents, something with substance and meaning. Oh, there were rare droplets of encouragement and smiles and pats on the back. He knew they loved him. But it was disappointing not to be able to seek their advice on things like school, or growing up, or girls.

He sighed wistfully, then looked up to see Matthias End and Nathan Hamper pointing fingers and bickering about something, rules for a debate or some such thing.

It would never even have occurred to him to ask his parents the answer to the current item up for debate among his companions: 'If a dragon happened to be approaching the earth—having presumably been on an exhilarating jaunt around the moon and so forth—would it survive re-entry?'

Housework had always been a torturous affair for Mark and Nathan. Both blamed the other for the abysmal state of home affairs and expected the other to pull more of his weight. Both could also recall having just recently cleaned the place, or part of it, and didn't see much reason to go at it again so soon.

It was left to Matthias End to find a way to smooth frail nerves, a startling position for him, as he was more in the habit of making a mess of people's nerves. He suggested that Nathan think of a question for debate. Any question would do. The stranger the better. They could then argue it out and not even notice they were cleaning up.

End nodded approval of the topic, then attacked immediately. "The dragon would have collapsed from lack of oxygen as soon as it reached the upper atmosphere, long before it could ever have escaped the Earth's pull into space." He said it matter-of-factly as he gathered up scattered socks and t-shirts.

"That's not the point," said Nathan, holding a cloth he meant to dust with. "The question has to do with its surviving re-entry. You're not supposed to look at the other things."

It all seemed fairly obvious to Mark. "An impossible supposition. Flying dragons do not exist. Therefore one could not have gotten into space in the first place. Unless you are suggesting that someone launched one out of a cannon or sent it up on the next shuttle. Then the questions become numerous and rampant: how did you catch it? How did you keep it from setting fire to the shuttle? Did you build a spacesuit for it? Wouldn't animal rights people sue you? How could you justify spending taxpayer money to send a dragon up into space? I could go on and on, but it would diminish the importance of my first point." He swept repeatedly at something dead, stuck between two pieces of maple flooring.

Nathan frowned. "Which was?"

Mark looked up from his chores. "That there is no such thing as a flying dragon."

Nathan quickly became exasperated. "You're completely missing the point. Don't say 'What if'. *Assume* that there exists a dragon, like in the Arthurian legends, with wings and scales and fiery breath, and what if it somehow found itself in space, ready to re-enter the atmosphere."

Mark shook his head. "What do they teach you in school anyway?" he said. "You do go to school, don't you?"

"A very difficult question," admitted End.

"Is anyone listening to me?" Nathan whined. He had yet to dust anything.

Mark would not be denied. "All right, it would have burst from the vacuum of space. Exploding dragon everywhere."

"Listen to me!" said Nathan, his interest was now more on being understood than in actually finding out anything about interstellar dragons. "You're supposed to consider whether its scales would protect it from re-entry. That's the whole point. I swear, you are such an unimaginative prick."

Mark's mouth opened and closed in consternation. "I am positive you did not just call me a name. You know, we can just stop those silly little laser triangulations you like so much. After all, we pricks are much too busy dealing with mouthy high school know-it-alls."

Nathan slouched and scowled at Mark from underneath his eyebrows.

"Good," said Mark, "now where were we?" He had gathered up a pile of dirt and debris, and looked around for somewhere to put it.

"Flying dragons in space," said End.

"No, we were past that and on to something else."

"There was nothing else."

Finding nowhere convenient to dispose of his swept-up dirt, Mark opened the front door to toss it back out where it came from. He stopped suddenly.

"Great Edison's toast!" he shouted. "There's a dead chicken at the door!"

Nathan came running, and End was not far behind.

"Oh no, it's Don!" cried Nathan.

A healthy-sized chicken—though probably not doing so well now— was pierced through its midsection with a large knife, whose sharp end was lodged a good inch into the solid wood door. Judging by the feathers at their feet, Don had been dead for some time.

"Technically, it's *on* the door," offered End.

Mark turned to him, his voice a nervous tremor. "Technically, it's *on* the *knife*! Are you wanting to argue about something *else*?"

"Who'd want to kill Don?" said Nathan, on the verge of tears.

"Okay, okay, let's not panic," said Mark, holding his hands in the air as if he was ready to. "It could just be an accident."

"An accident?"

"Sure. Someone could have been passing by and wanted to practice throwing their very large knife. They threw it at our front door, and the chicken just happened to be flying through the air—coming down from the roof maybe—and, you know, the knife...you know, stabbed the... chicken."

"What a great idea," said Nathan sarcastically between angry sobs. "That must be how you come up with your fabulous experiments. Sort of a mix of the stupid and the impossible."

Mark continued to stare at the dead chicken as if it was helping him with his thinking. "Yeah, yeah, I'm not convinced of that either." The chicken didn't appear to be all that helpful.

"Well, I'd say this was a warning," said End, calmly dislodging the knife from the door. The chicken slid lifelessly off the knife and flopped to the floor.

"Ewww!" said Nathan.

"A warning?" Mark said. "What, someone doesn't like chickens? Or just *our* chickens?"

"No, no, no," End said, shaking his head. "Remember what I said about the Dream House?"

"Chickens are dying over a damn dollhouse?"

"Apparently so."

"We've got to put a stop to this. Nathan, bring all the chickens inside."

"They're not our chickens. We only had...Don."

"It doesn't matter. Someone's got to protect them."

Nathan ran out into the yard while Mark frantically began closing and locking all the windows. "My God, the corporocrats will stop at nothing," he mumbled under his breath.

"Now, now just a minute. There's no reason to get out of sorts here," said End. "We've just got to leave for a bit."

"We shall not abandon the ship!" grunted Mark as he fought with a stubborn window.

Nathan returned with a chicken in each arm, kicking another one into the doorway. He released the two in his arms and leaped back out the door. In the next five minutes, he rescued a dozen more. "This is all I can find," he said and shooed them into the clean kitchen.

"Why don't we just calm down a minute?" said End. "After all, a warning is just supposed to make you think, not panic."

"Nathan, seal up the lab," Mark called from somewhere upstairs. Nathan disappeared again.

"It's just a chicken," End shouted at the ceiling.

Mark reappeared seconds later from around a corner, leaping at the front door to close and bolt it shut. He stopped long enough to answer. "First it's the chickens, then it's the women and children, then it's us. You've got to draw the line somewhere." He ran through another doorway.

End stared after him. "What women?"

Nathan ran back into the house. "Okay, it's all closed up. What do I do now?"

"Just relax," said End. "We just need to calm down and think about the situation. Everyone's just getting a little too—"

"Generator's going," Mark said as he came back in. He came to a sudden stop.

"That's better," said End. "Now why don't we think about this—"

"Should we fire up the pulse laser again?" asked Mark.

Nathan barely nodded once before he was gone again. Mark made hastily for yet another door, when End grabbed him by the back of his shirt and pulled him backward.

"Stop!" he roared.

Mark tried to pull away, his arms waving wildly. "What's the matter with you? Let go of me!"

"Quiet! Listen to me. There's no need to panic. We're in no danger."

Mark stopped for a second to hear the words, then tried swinging at End's arm. But the angle was all wrong, and he looked rather like a pre-schooler getting the worst of it from a bully. Getting picked on by bullies was a sore spot for Mark, and it momentarily took his thoughts away from dead chickens and the apparent start of intergalactic war in his front yard. He folded his arms and tried to look angry and intimidating while hanging by his shirt collar.

End spun him around and dropped him, checked around the room for Nathan, started to speak, pursed his lips grimly and said very quietly "I killed the chicken, all right?"

Mark's anger gave way to shock. "You?"

"Yes!" End hissed and looked around again.

"You killed Don? Why?"

"I just wanted us to…sort of…leave for a while."

"And you thought killing a chicken would do that? Don was like a pet to Nathan."

"It's just a chicken!"

"Tell that to Nathan, chicken killer."

"No, no, we can't tell him. He'd hate me." He straightened his coat in sudden agitation. "There aren't too many people that think I'm a…an okay person."

"Oh yes, I'm sure that would be just too bad. You're okay with me hating you though, aren't you?"

"Well, I'm not sure you cared much for me to start with."

"You're not far wrong, that's for sure. I'm beginning to think your whole story is a lie."

End's eyes widened. "No, no, no, it's all true. I swear. I wouldn't have killed the chicken if I was lying about the danger you're in. Really."

Nathan leaped back into the room, the energy rifle draped over an arm while he struggled to get the backpack on over a shoulder. There were loops for the legs to fit through, and he had only got one leg in, so that he looked like he was wrestling with the backpack and losing.

He saw that the two men had stopped to talk. "What's the matter," he asked, stopping just as the pack was about to throw him on his face.

"Ah! Uh...All done?" Mark said awkwardly. He wasn't sure what to say.

"Almost. Just need to let it warm up."

"Good, good. Plenty of time for that." Mark glared at End.

Nathan was doubled over and appeared to be in a little discomfort. "Would someone help me with...this leg won't go through and now I can't...what's the matter with this thing!"

End came over and unraveled the straps from Nathan's snared shoulder and leg. The backpack slid to the ground in a clanging heap. "So what's happening?" said Nathan as he set the rifle down on the heap. "Are we all secure?"

"Well, Nathan..." Mark started to say.

"False alarm," End said hastily.

Nathan looked first at one, then the other. "A false alarm? What do you mean? It wasn't false! Don's dead. Someone put a knife through him. On purpose! We saw it."

Mark made a face at End that spoke of surrender.

"We think it was poachers," End said quickly. "It was a hunting knife, after all. They must have thrown it at the chicken...uh, Don...and when it hit the door, they got scared away."

"Poachers?" Mark sputtered. "That's the best you could—"

"Yes, it is shocking, isn't it, Mark?" End glanced meaningfully at Mark, then looked at Nathan.

Nathan looked at both of them, then stared at the pile of feathers that used to be Don. "I guess I'll go bury Don, then. Do you think they're gone?"

Mark frowned. "Who?"

"The poachers."

Mark raised his eyebrows and shrugged. "As a matter of fact, they're a lot closer than one would...ooooph!" End jabbed at Mark's kidney. "Oh, they're long gone, I'm sure." Mark rubbed at his lower back and glared at End.

Nathan nodded and went to get a shovel.

"I'm going straight to hell," mumbled End dejectedly.

"I'll be glad to give you a push," said Mark.

Chapter 9

It had been weeks since Mark had seen Jenna Telfair. And his first thought on recollection of that last meeting made his insides twist painfully. It seemed at times that the disastrous demonstration lived in him as a permanent, unwelcome guest. His saving grace was in remembering how perfect her face was, how much she smiled at him before the demo, how bad she felt, and how hard she tried to comfort him afterward. It almost made him want to blow something else up, just so she would be near him again, searching his eyes to make sure that his inventive spirit hadn't been obliterated along with his experiment. Of course it hadn't, but he had let just a flicker of anguish show through, and she was immediately at his side. It was manipulative, sure, but it had become clear to him over the years that if the right woman was to be won, a man had to go after her like Pickett's Charge. Hopefully things would work out better than they did for Pickett.

Mark and Jenna were meeting at a roadside grill just off the county highway. It was the closest thing to a restaurant in a five-mile radius around his home, and he felt certain she would not want to eat at his place. After all, if he incinerated his work, something he really cared about, what horrors would he inflict on food?

There was no denying that dating women was not one of Mark's strong points. Of course, this was not a date. Of course not. They were just needing to discuss what he was working on now, and they needed a place to be in order to have that discussion. No, nothing like a date at all. But he so wanted it to be. If he did well, if he impressed her, maybe he could later recall it fondly as 'The Pre-Date'. The optimist in him, the one that kept him going in his lab through disaster after disaster, thought a nonviolent lunch well within his abilities. The pessimist in him expected their table to spontaneously de-molecularize into a pulpy puddle before they had even opened their menus.

He accelerated the pickup involuntarily down the road as his imagination unveiled molten linoleum and screaming, flaming waitresses for his bemusement. Now all he needed was for a majestic twelve-point buck to trot across the road so he could run it over and demolish his pickup at the same time. With any luck he would be thrown from the truck into the path of an oncoming cement mixer. Then if only a massive meteor shower would enter the atmosphere directly overhead...

It's not a date. It's not a date. He said it over and over in his head and made himself slow the vehicle down. His faculties gradually pulled themselves together, blanketed with the unhappy thought that it was in fact not actually a date.

It appeared that his only possible mental approaches in which to enter the grill were either sweating out an impending date, or depressed by the notion of what might never be. He didn't like either one. If only he were able to just switch off his thoughts, swagger in, dazzle her with his charm and wit, sweep her into his arms, and...

The pickup pulled into the gravel parking lot of Bilbo's Shire. The proprietor was a big fan of J.R.R. Tolkien, but only the name of the place resembled any of his work. Inside, it was dark, smelled like spilt beer, and had more two-by-fours wedged between floor and ceiling—presumably to hold it up—than there were chairs to sit in. It seemed obviously to be a losing effort, and Mark expected the roof to collapse at any moment. That was not really a problem, because any one of the massive truck drivers who ate there could have held up the ceiling while everyone else finished their meals and exited safely. The truckers worried him more than the structural integrity of the Shire. If any made advances on Jenna, Mark would be hard pressed to fend them off. All of the available weaponry were busy holding up the building.

Mark scanned the parking lot for Jenna's royal blue Audi. Amid the pickups, motorcycles, unhitched semi-trucks, and unrecognizable and probably abandoned wrecks, she would have stood out. But she wasn't there yet. He wasn't sure whether to go in or not, and so, just as he did with his work, he went with the first thought that came to mind. He sat in his car and waited.

* * *

The trip down was faster than Jenna had expected it to be. She no longer had any trouble convincing herself to take the long drive. Her thoughts were already in Brookbury, wondering how Mark would be feeling, wondering whether that extraordinary if discombobulated brain of his was still down about the Tesla Fusion demonstration.

About fifteen miles back, she thought maybe she had missed a turnoff onto one of the county roads. Or maybe she was supposed to turn off a county road. Perhaps what she should really have done was go to Mark's house instead and let him drive to the restaurant. She was terrible with directions.

It was extraordinary—Mark's brain, that is. There was no longer any doubt of that. As word spread at General Micronet about the floating dollhouse that defied the venerated laws of reality, pressure on her to acquire it had grown. Every facet of the conglomerate— from chemists to plastics specialists to aerospace engineers to astrophysicists to robotics technicians—they all wanted to know how Mark Goggin had made Barbie's house float. They were all convinced that, whatever it was, it had some grounding in their particular area of expertise. Every meeting Jenna attended, there was some vice president demanding to know if she had learned the secrets of the dollhouse. What was worse was that she was starting to get emails and phone calls from people outside corporate headquarters. The last call had been from an impatient brusque woman from the Brussels office who had harangued her over the phone about her inability to wrench the secrets from 'that Brookbury kalkoen.'

Out of perverse curiosity, she looked up 'kalkoen'. It was Flemish for 'turkey.'

The Audi was gradually becoming more chalk-colored than blue as she careened through another gravel side road. She suspected she had already been down it once.

Jenna had had no idea what to say to the woman from Brussels. She was in complete shock, first, that yet another person—on the other side of the planet, no less—knew about Mark. He had sworn over and over to her that she was the only one he had talked to about the floating house. And he was so uncomfortable talking to *her* about it that she believed him. Even if she wasn't involved, she doubted he'd have talked to anyone. So it was someone on the GMN board who had leaked it.

Secondly, the call had surprised her that it was all the way from Europe. It had not even been a month since she had reported on the little house, and she had expected the board to have guarded the knowledge of the great prize with their very lives. But, again, apparently not. Third, how could the woman have known he lived in Brookbury? It was like Mark Goggin had suddenly become a major celebrity inside the company itself. It was only a matter of time before the general public knew about him.

All right, she thought as she passed through a cloud of dust, she had definitely already been down this road. Another dusty affair with trees on all sides.

Someone *wanted* all of it to happen. Someone *wanted* word to spread. But why? It would just send more prospective suitors Mark's way, and his price for a deal would go up. Unless of course, that 'someone' wanted everyone's attention in order to make Mark look bad. Then the dream house would be easy pickings for GMN. Mark would have to take whatever was offered.

Who would do such a thing? A clever idea, it was, but a little overly elaborate.

Jenna wondered where Mr. York was keeping himself these days.

Ah, this is more like it, she thought, turning down a road that would not have allowed room for another car to drive the other way. She hadn't seen this road before. It was something along the lines of progress toward reaching her destination.

Mark was not rich and GMN was, so she would have thought he'd have taken a reasonable offer eagerly, just to cover the cost of the many scorched or just completely missing parts of his home before winter hit. The place was of mansion-like proportions, but it was also obvious that its owner was not financially equal to the task of its proper upkeep.

She drove by a used car lot for the third time when she noticed that the name of the place didn't have the word 'used' or 'car' in it. 'Bilbo's Shire', it said. Her destination. She must have seen all the mud-caked, rusty, ruined vehicles surrounding a building that she could only see the top of, and she had just assumed it was a used car lot. It was entirely possible that her subconscious had recognized it, and that was why she had been by three times. She was quite respectful of her subconscious, or maybe it was better called intuition. Whichever it was, it had saved her many times.

It was her intuition that had made her interested in Mark. Or maybe it was attraction. No, that was unprofessional, it had to be intuition. She had recognized that he had an inventive streak that would take him far. And she wanted to be at his side when that streak ignited. Professionally speaking, that is.

Three times she drove around the parking lot, if it could be called that. The absence of lines in the gravel to denote spaces had encouraged everyone to park at all angles and variations on the imagined size of the space their respective vehicles needed. She could probably have fitted into two or three different spots, but they almost guaranteed a door ding. So she parked next to the trees at the farthest point from the front door, next to a large gold car with no window glass—or wheels. It was six feet from her car, but she still wasn't sure the door couldn't reach hers. Still, it was the only place she could find, so she locked and armed the security alarm and stumbled in her heels over the uneven white stones.

She rarely ate at places outside the city, and she hadn't been sure what to wear. It seemed inappropriate for a business lunch to wear something like jeans, although she expected that to be the haute couture of choice among women locally. It also seemed unsafe to be dressed in a business outfit, for fear of getting mugged by hillbillies or attacked by biker gangs. That was probably wise because she could pick out a few trucks in this parking lot that the Beverly Hillbillies themselves might have thumbed their noses at in disgust, and there were as many huge squat-looking motorcycles as there were the four-wheeled variety. So, she wore a nondescript sweater and slacks, and pumps. As she twisted an ankle with every other gravel-strewn step navigating through the parking lot, only the shoes had been a definite mistake so far. But there was plenty of time left for the rest to go wrong as well. She hadn't even gotten inside yet.

She knew this lunch was nothing other than a meeting between two professionals, but she had to admit that she felt something different about Mark. Call it motherly concern, or sisterly protectiveness, or girlish attraction— no, no, not that—but she wanted very much for Mark to be happy. When he wasn't dwelling on his foul-ups in the lab, he was so naively exuberant and boyish. There wasn't anyone she enjoyed being around more when he was that way. Not that it meant anything other than that she had a good solid professional relationship with her client, Mr. Mark Goggin.

'Goggin' would not have been her first choice for a married name, she thought, and then wondered briefly why she had thought that.

She reached out to open the door to the Shire.

"Jenna!" said a voice behind her, and she half-turned at the same time as the door opened and hit her squarely in the face. She heard a cracking sound and saw the door shake. A voice snickered, "She hit her head," as several men walked through the doorway and past her. Stepping backward involuntarily, she almost fell, but someone caught her and helped her through the door. She sat heavily on a bench just inside and glimpsed the swimming face of Mark Goggin, apparently smiling uncertainly at her. Her left cheek alternated between numbness and sharp pain, and she prodded at it to check for…she didn't really know. Something ruptured or broken, she supposed.

"Are you all right?" Mark said and dabbed at her cheek as well.

Jenna winced and jerked back involuntarily. "Oh, sure. I just didn't see the door open." She rubbed vigorously one last time at her cheek, as if trying to revive it or impart a little energy. Then she held out her hand to be helped up.

Mark grasped her hand and helped her rise, and without noticing, continued to hold her hand as she reassured him again that she was fine.

Mark compared the abused cheek to the unscathed one and pronounced it as being 'puffy.'

"You *are* a genius," she said with a pained smirk.

His face brightened, his relief evident that she was not upset. They stood a moment, waiting to be seated. "So how are you?" he said finally. "Besides the swollen cheek, I mean. Did you have any trouble finding the place?"

"I had a terrible time," she said. "Did you know there are no signs in this part of the world? How do they expect to get any tourists to come around if they don't put up a few street signs once in a while? I didn't even see any mile markers." Passersby had to dodge as Jenna's arm shot out repeatedly to indicate the many directions where signs were missing. She didn't seem to notice their hands clasped together either.

Mark led Jenna after the hostess, around a dozen two-by-fours, to a table in the center of the room. "There are signs," he insisted. Neither seemed to notice releasing hands as they pulled out their chairs, and sat down. "You just have to know they're there before you see them or you'll miss them. Trees grow around them and the weeds along the roads get tall. And some get covered in dust from the roads. Or shot up for target practice."

They waited for someone to take their order, and Jenna finally noticed the décor. It was early Heavy Renovation. There was wood sticking up everywhere. She looked at the ceiling to see if it was about to cave in.

Orders placed, they talked about Jenna's drive down, the sudden chill in the weather, the sturdiness of a typical two-by-four, and, of course, Mark's continual failure to fire up the Tesla fusion device.

"I honestly don't know what's the matter with the thing," said Mark. "I've tried every combination I can think of. I'm almost to the point of doubting the very fundamental concept of the whole idea."

"You mean like cold fusion being a contradiction in terms?" Jenna had been watching a two-by-four vibrate after being buffeted by a fast-moving waitress, or she might have thought a little more carefully about what she said. She watched him to see if he'd take offense.

"Exactly," he said.

She was surprised at his reaction, especially given his dogged pursuit of success in the matter. She leaned forward, flashing her warmest smile. "You haven't taken another look at that Dream House, have you?"

His expression soured. "I have not, and I'm not going to either."

"Why not?" Jenna asked with sudden animation. Their unbalanced table quivered as she leaned on it. "It could be huge. It could be the greatest invention of the twenty-first century."

Mark blinked several times and appeared to look everywhere at once. "Well, it's got some severe...I just, I don't care for the way it..." He gave her a determined expression. "A good scientist never abandons an experiment on the first setback."

"Mark, you've had a thousand setbacks on this fusion thing. Don't you think maybe it's a hopeless cause? At the very least you could just set it aside and do something else. If you come back to it later, you'll be refreshed and energized with a new perspective."

"Oh, that's what that idiot End keeps saying. When he's not telling me I should run and hide in the woods from corporate bogeymen, anyway."

Jenna straightened. "End? Matthias End?"

"Yeah. He's big on the Dream House thing. Seems like everybody is."

"What is Matthias End doing at your house?"

"Well he sort of invited himself. He says you know each other."

"How does he know you?"

"He doesn't. Or rather he didn't. He showed up one day and announced himself as my bodyguard. Pretty useless, if you ask me. I've no doubt he can shoot straight; the question is really whether he can tell the good guys from the bad guys. He is a much better cook than Nathan or me. We devour everything he fixes. Good thing there's not much to eat, or we'd be getting fat."

Mark explained End's rationale for being there, the threat GMN and any number of other companies posed to Mark, and End's prowess as a body-guard. "He's awful though. He's the last one there if we hear strange noises, and I'm waiting anytime now for that gun of his to go off and bring the entire sheriff's office down on us. One afternoon we had a car drive up the path from the main road and stop within a hundred yards of the house. Was he anywhere to be found? No! He was lost in the woods somewhere. Search-ing for creeping corporate spies, apparently. And he fell into the creek, for Pete's sake. Does that sound to you like a capable bodyguard? I'd feel safer with the creeping spies."

"He has a gun?" Jenna had spilt her water on hearing that. She put nap-kins on the small pool on the table and soaked much of it up, but when she pressed on the napkins, water escaped and dribbled across the table in all directions. She saw Mark watching her, tickled to the point of laughter, and she threw a sopping wet napkin at him. It hit a two-by-four behind him that she had been particularly concerned about. It didn't budge, but as she half rose in horror, expecting the ceiling to cave in, her chair skidded back into an enormously tall biker seated behind her. Startled, he appeared to have stabbed the inside of his throat with a fork, because he rose up and unleashed a roar of pain. Jenna reacted quickly, and thinking he was choking, slapped him hard on the back, which made him roar louder.

"Quit hitting me, lady!" he raged, fending off her well-meaning whacks. Jenna stopped in surprise. The huge man turned back to his girlfriend, or wife, or whatever, gripping his throat with concern and letting his tongue loll out of his mouth like a stunned cow that had just stabbed its throat with a fork.

Jenna returned to her seat and held her hands to her head in complete embarrassment until she thought maybe only half the restaurant was staring at her. She looked up to see Mark looking at her with concern. When he saw that she was only embarrassed, he grinned again with that wonderful warmth of his. "I think you almost killed him," he observed.

She pressed her lips together, nostrils flaring, but saw it was useless to get upset. And she didn't really want to. She sighed and glanced involuntarily at the two-by-four behind Mark one more time.

Lunch arrived, lying on cheap cellophane in little baskets. Jenna hadn't expected much and dug right into her greasy blob. At least it smelled like a cheeseburger.

"He killed a chicken and stuck it on the front door," said Mark, chewing. "Your friend, Mr. End, I mean."

The blob sat idly in her mouth while she imagined End killing whole pastures full of farm livestock. She nodded as if it was entirely in character and went back to eating. "He's not my friend. But it doesn't surprise me a bit. Did he say why, or did he think it would be funny or something?"

"He thought it would scare me into leaving the house."

"Because he thinks you're in danger"

"Yes."

"He's an idiot."

"I know. But he sounds very sincere. And he makes great pizzas. We souped up an old stove a while back so it would go up past eight hundred degrees. His pizzas taste like the real thing, let me tell you."

"Just watch him. He got laid off from General Micronet a couple of weeks ago. He may be a little crazy."

"Oh, I have been."

Jenna bit into a pocket of solid grilled onions and had to force it down with half her glass of water. She stopped to catch her breath and saw that Mark had been watching her eat. She smiled and looked expectantly back at him. He blinked self-consciously, gave her a weak smile, and went back to eating. Then it was her turn to watch him eat.

The food had disappeared before either had said much of anything else.

"Would you do something for me?" said Jenna, wiping the grease off her fingers.

"Of course."

"Give the Dream House some serious thought. See if it has some potential for improvements. It could be very important, Mark."

"Right," he said, staring into her eyes.

"You didn't hear a thing I said, did you?"

"What?"

Chapter 10

Mark's face felt warm and intense from forehead to cheeks and his chest swelled like an over-pressurized air compressor as he drove behind a couple of pickups in the direction of home. Not even the billowing clouds of exhaust and dust from the gravel road that obscured existence on all sides could smother his elation. And the fact that two more pickups were tailgating him barely came to his attention.

Jenna Telfair *liked* him. There could be no doubt about it. She smiled at him every time she saw him. And it wasn't the polite, though clearly irritated expressions of so many other women he had encountered. They all seemed to wish he were going the other way. Jenna's eyes twinkled when she looked at him, her cheeks dimpled in a barely discernible way, her head tilted in the most adorable angle—she seemed even to lean toward him ever so slightly, although he might in fact be the one who was leaning.

At Bilbo's Shire, they had finished eating and talked a little longer about nothing of importance. At least Mark didn't remember any of it. He hoped none of it was important. She hadn't knocked anyone down or broken anything, and she seemed relieved to have gotten out of the place without a single two-by-four snapping in half. She had terrible difficulty walking back to her car, and it had been his greatest pleasure to put his arm around her and help her. He thought it was strange that she didn't just take her shoes off and decrease the risk of sprained ankles, but he was not one to complain. She had held his arm and had even clung to him two or three times as she was about to come crashing to the ground. He had not wanted to let go when they got to her car, and apparently he had held her too long because her complexion turned to a shade of pink and she pressed a hand gently against him. He got the hint and let go. Mustn't push things too much. She had a job to do, after all.

And so did he. Before he had returned to his truck, he had already decided to shelve the Tesla fusion meltdown menace and return his attention to the Barbie Dream albatross hovering in his laboratory. He knew sooner or later he would have to deal with it. He had just hoped it would be later. Much, much later. Like after they had married and had a few kids, maybe even grandkids. Better still, after he was long dead. But he could no longer bear to have Jenna look even remotely disappointed in him. It was obviously of tremendous importance to her. Her career might even be hanging in the balance, right up there in the rafters with the stupid Dream House.

The trucks in front of him had slowed enough that he could see them even through the poor visibility. They didn't appear to be hauling anything so Mark couldn't figure out what the problem was, but in his present mood he was inclined to assume for the best. There was probably a combine crawling along ahead of them, just out of his sight. The road was narrow enough to prevent them from easily passing it. That was all right, he had plenty of time.

Jenna had seemed a little worried about End, although she had acknowledged knowing him. That eased Mark's mind a bit. The fact that she seemed so upset about him being armed was a bit more disturbing. That bothered Mark, too. But End could have done them in that first day if he'd wanted to. No, Mark was of a mind to believe him, however much End continued to overreact about the situation. The Dream House was a marvel, sure, all modesty aside, but not worth having an army of company-paid soldiers descend into the heart of Missouri.

Even combines don't go this slowly, Mark thought, and he moved into the oncoming lane to pass, or at least to get a better view. The truck in front of him apparently had the same idea and moved left to pass, blocking him from doing so, which was strange because the driver hadn't seemed at all interested in going around up to then. Mark slipped back into his own lane. The truck did as well. They had slowed now to the point where he could see both trucks clearly and, though they were winding considerably through hills and trees, there was no sign of a combine or ducks out for a stroll or wandering drunken cows or anything of the kind.

It all looked awfully suspicious. The two trucks behind him were still there, and they also seemed satisfied to sit behind him, no matter how slowly they went. It was almost as if they were all positioning themselves to seal him off, or at least force him off the road.

Mark began to feel just a bit nervous. Was this what End had been warning him about? If not, then it was the worst traffic he had ever seen in Brookbury. He looked through the rear view mirror at the driver behind him. The man wore sunglasses and had an arm hanging out the window. He wore a green ball cap. Even from such a bouncing angle and on-again-off-again view, Mark could tell that the cap was new, completely uncreased, and ungreased.

No one had clean hats around here. Not even the women.

It suddenly became absolutely vital to get away from there. He looked for another chance to pass, and the truck in front again blocked him. This time, it didn't return to the right lane when Mark did. Instead it continued on, and the truck at the front of the small convoy slowed drastically so that both vehicles were side by side. Both drivers talked through their windows as if they knew each other, but it still seemed frightening, especially out there amid the trees and valleys where Mark could be pushed off into a ravine.

Without thinking, Mark revved the engine and spun around. The truck at the back of the pack was approaching him in that lane, possibly attempting to pass the truck between him and Mark. But it might be trying to block him, too. Mark was not about to ask, and he plowed into the ditch and the slightly rising hill next to the road. The driver of the nearing truck watched him go by.

As Mark swerved back onto the road, going the opposite way of the four trucks, he looked through his rear-view mirror. All four trucks had their brake lights on.

"Oh boy," he whispered, and sped on.

$$* \quad * \quad *$$

The rickety old pickup scrambled around turns, up and down hills, even went off-road a couple of times, unintentionally. Mark wasn't much of a driver, but he knew the roads fairly well, and he knew how to push the accelerator to the floor. He knew that if the trucks turned around and chased him, or split up and came at him from several directions, he would need to get away as fast as he could and not spend a lot of time shooting down random paths to escape them. Unfortunately, it was ten minutes and five or six side roads before that thought occurred to him. He drove into ditches on almost every swerving turn and spent more time on the wrong side of the road than the right side, but he somehow managed to only run over two signs. The amount of dust that billowed up in the truck's wake should easily have been seen from a mile away. But he saw only two more vehicles, both cars. Gradually the panic receded from him, and he slowed. It was on the last road before turning into his driveway that he thought he saw another truck, from across a field. He couldn't identify the color, and it didn't turn in his direction when it had the chance. Maybe it wasn't one of them. He stomped on the accelerator and nearly lost control.

His driveway appeared instantly—he didn't usually drive quite so fast—and Mark swerved sideways on the gravel before the back tires caught. From the main road, the driveway was a quarter mile from home. He tried to drive at a leisurely place and even whistled once or twice before he began to feel like an idiot for driving slowly when he was so close to home. The last hundred feet was a long slide that almost pitched the truck onto its side.

"Nathan!" he shouted as he ran around to the back of the house where the lab extended perpendicularly from the house. "Nathan!" Lights were on everywhere, despite the fact that it was still the middle of the afternoon. Mark had to jump over the screen door to the kitchen because it was lying on the ground. He rushed up to the door to the lab and had to push extra hard to get it open because it was off the top hinge and dragging on the floor. It briefly flashed through his thoughts that it was strange that all the doors were in such poor working order. He'd have to get Nathan to have a look at them.

The breezeway between the house and the laboratory was strewn with shoes and lawn chairs, and Mark had to jump over them on his frantic way to the lab. The door into the lab was completely missing...no, it was on the ground too, and he ran over it into the lab, not stopping until he saw Nathan huddled on the floor, leaning against a table, the laser rifle pointed straight at Mark.

He slid to a halt. "Nathan! You wouldn't believe what happened to me! I was coming back from lunch, and these four trucks practically forced me off the road—"

"What the hell are you trying to do, scare me to death?" shrieked Nathan. "I almost blew a hole in you!"

Mark was breathing hard, but he stopped to look at the unfriendly end of the thing pointed at him. "Well, no it wouldn't actually do that. It might knock me across the room, but it fires energy really, so it couldn't—" He frowned suddenly. "Why are you aiming that at me anyway?"

"Have you had a look around yet?" said Nathan, lowering the laser and slouching miserably.

"Yes I have, as a matter of fact. All the doors seem to be falling off their hinges or some such thing. That can't be a coincidence. Now I don't want to point any fingers but it—,"

"How about in here?" Nathan was still talking loudly, his voice high and trembling.

Mark straightened and started to scan the room. He didn't have to go far. The table behind Nathan was a mess. A bin of electronic paraphernalia was overturned and the other bins were pulled out. Copper wiring had been stretched over the table and looked to be in several knots. "Aw," he said in aggravation, "now that wasn't very nice. You invited one of your friends over, didn't you. We've talked and talked about that, Nathan."

Then Mark noticed the table next to the one he'd been looking at. And the next table. And the shelves above them. And the floor in front of the tables. Tools, parts, supplies, experiments, even wall decorations and antiques were everywhere, in various states of destruction, from partial to total. Even a couple of lights overhead had been knocked out.

Mark did a full circle before he returned to facing Nathan. His mouth hung open, and he stared at Nathan in shocked disbelief. "How many of your friends did you invite over?" he shouted.

"I didn't bring any friends over!" Nathan shouted back. "It was like this when I got here. Do you think I got this thing out so I could shoot my friends?"

"*I* would have," replied Mark, then relented. "I'm sorry, Nate. I didn't mean that. Sorry." He looked around the lab again, and a thought occurred to him. "This isn't the act of someone wanting to steal something. Someone's trying to scare us." He started to walk between two rows of tables.

Nathan glared after him. "What brilliant analysis. I'm huddling in awe."

Mark reached the far end of the lab. The table on which he was working with the Tesla coil-cold fusion experiment was untouched. The only table upright and with its contents undamaged. That was very clearly a message from whoever did this. He turned quickly around and looked up at the shelf halfway back to where Nathan was squatting.

It was gone. The pink Barbie Dream House was no longer hovering above the shelf. Mark stepped briskly back to the shelf and looked it over. The table was a mess of broken glass and bent metal. The lower shelves were mostly untouched, and everything above the shelf—the lights and the ceiling joists—was also, for the most part, still intact. He squatted down and looked along the floor to see if the dollhouse had just fallen and rolled under a table. But it was well and truly gone.

"Holy Mother of Christ!" shouted a voice from the lab doorway.

Matthias End stared at the destruction and then bent down to help Nathan up. "They've been here, haven't they?" said End. "Didn't I tell you? We've got to get out of here."

Mark walked slowly toward End. "We're in no danger. 'They' have what they came for. Right now I'd like to know more about these people you're so afraid of. Who exactly is 'they'?"

End looked in the direction of the shelf where the Dream House once was. "They did get it, didn't they." He looked back at Mark. "You can recreate it, can't you?"

Mark's eyes narrowed. "Answer my question."

"'They' is General Micronet. Who else? 'They' is Mr. York and any number of other people who covertly assist General Micronet in either increasing their own profits or decreasing the competition's. Soon, 'they' will be other corporations too. For all we know, 'they' could be your lovely Miss Telfair."

"'They' could be you, too," said Mark, his jaw clenched.

End raised his hands in the air helplessly. "From your point of view, yes I suppose it could. I happen to know that I'm not 'they'."

"Who's 'they' again?" asked Nathan, whining.

Mark began to pace. "That's just swell. It's so reassuring to know that you don't suspect yourself. We, however, do not share your confidence in your innocence."

"I believe him," Nathan said.

Mark glared at him. "Thank you, Nathan. You never fail to be difficult."

"No, I'm pretty sure he didn't do any of this."

"And your deductive reasoning is based on what?"

"He could have done it before this."

"That's true," End said and winked a thanks to Nathan.

"Oh shut up," growled Mark. "That's it? That's the entirety of your defense?"

"Why would I come back if I had the dollhouse?" said End.

Mark had to stop to consider that. "Well…you've always said 'they' need me to make it work. You could be 'they', and you, or rather 'they', are returning to collect me for yourself. Or rather, themselves."

"Theirselves," offered Nathan.

"Thank you."

"Then I could just pull out my gun," said End, pulling out his gun, "and order you to go with me. Isn't that what I'd do?"

Mark's hands went straight up in the air. "Ah…yes." Nathan's hands were also in the air, though he still sat on the ground. He whimpered mournfully.

"Good God, gentlemen," shouted End, "do you think I would spend all this time, day and night, looking after you—not all that well, I admit—just to ransack the place and kidnap you?"

Mark and Nathan looked at each other before Mark hastily said "No, no, I would never have thought that. No."

End realized he was still holding the gun on them. He put it away quickly. "Listen to me. We've just got to get out of here. They could come back any time now."

Mark slowly put his hands down. "I told you, that's not necessary. They've got the Dream House."

"But they haven't got you. Nathan, put your hands down. Please?" Nathan appeared to be about to cry. He covered his head with both arms as if he expected more misfortune at any minute.

Mark considered End and the situation, but mostly End. "You know, frankly, after you—" He stopped and glanced at Nathan. "—did that one thing the other day,"—he flapped his arms like a chicken—"this seems like a logical next step for you."

End cleared his throat uncomfortably. "If it was, I would have…you know…did like I did then. Told you, I mean. So you knew I did it."

Nathan frowned. "You sound just like my parents back home. You guys think you can speak doubletalk, and I won't have any idea what's going on. I'm not stupid, you know. I can figure out what's going on."

"Sorry, Nathan."

Nathan squinted up at them. "So what's going on?"

"Not right now. We'll explain later."

"Well?" End stared intently at Mark. "What now?"

✳ ✳ ✳

"Jenna? Hi! This is Mark Goggin."

"Hi, Mark. Is something wrong?"

"No, no. Well, there may be a problem or two."

"What is it? Shall I come back? I'm only halfway home."

"No, that's okay. It's not an emergency. I just needed to know something."

"What?"

"How bad does your company want my invention?"

"Oh, Mark. I'm sorry, but honestly I don't think they're all that interested."

"But you said—"

"Yeah, I think I encouraged you a little too much, Mark. I'm sorry. It's just...I don't think they see any use for your Tesla fusion device. It's very ingenious, really, but I don't—"

"Oh! Ha! No, no, not that. The dollhouse thing. You know, the floating Barbie..."

"It's terribly important, Mark. I probably shouldn't say that since they're probably going to want me to get you to sell it to me at some point. But it's very, very big."

"How big? Big enough to do whatever it takes to get it? Lie? Steal? Murder?"

"Well, it's business, Mark. There's a lot of lying in business. I think the odds narrow a lot with stealing. And I just don't believe anyone would murder for something like that. Money makes people do crazy things, but not that. At least not at General Micronet."

"Matthias End seems to think otherwise."

"He's been known to lie a time or two himself. What's going on, Mark? Did something happen?"

"It's gone, Jen. Someone stole the Dream House. And they practically destroyed my lab. I've only talked to you, End, and that York guy who came down here with you. Who am I to suspect?"

"I suppose End is blaming Mr. York."

"Yes he did."

"Well, he's not altogether ethical, I have to admit. But General Micronet has always adhered to the highest in ethical behavior and it's only because he brings so much business our way that the company puts up with his, uh, unorthodox behavior."

"Unorthodox? Destroying my lab is not unorthodox behavior. It's ruthless, it's coldblooded. It's against the law!"

"Yes, but you don't know he did it. Matthias End is right there too, isn't he?"

"That's true. And after the chicken thing, I'm tempted to toss him out. It just doesn't make sense that it's him. He could have stolen the dollhouse any number of times before this."

"End is ruthless and coldblooded, too, Mark. And patient. He's certainly capable of stealing it. Believe me. I've heard all about him. From him, no less."

"So what am I supposed to believe then? And who? I'd very much like to believe you, Jen. But you're right; I don't know. And I want to know."

"You could come visit the offices here."

"Really? What, just walk right in? They'd either kill me or be horribly nice to me. And then what would I learn?"

"I haven't told them what you look like. And only Mr. York knows. Pretend you're someone else. A salesman or something. I can get you a pass, and you can snoop around until you're satisfied."

"You'd do that? Give me a pass and all that?"

"I believe in GMN, Mark. But I think I might believe in you more."

"…I…really?…you…I don't know what to say."

"Well figure it out and say it to me when you get here. I'll be waiting. Bye."

"Bye."

Chapter 11

Jenna stared at both men as they entered the grand vestibule of General Micronet's corporate headquarters. She continued to stare as the men scanned the area and removed their sunglasses, then she turned away in absolute astonishment, covering her mouth with an open hand.

She couldn't decide whether to hold her breath or burst out laughing. Gathering herself together, she turned back toward them, glancing anxiously around the lobby to see if anyone else had noticed how ridiculous the two men looked.

Mark Goggin wore a nicely traditional suit, black with a dark red tie. He seemed oddly out of place in the suit, although it may have been because she'd only seen him in ratty jeans and wrinkled shirts. She cocked her head sideways as she watched him survey the room. He was almost dashing, she thought, surprising herself for using the word 'dashing.'

The only trouble was, he had stuck a big hairy mustache under his nose. It was convincing enough, she supposed, but the slightest jostle looked capable of knocking it out of kilter.

Matthias End was the more outrageous of the pair. He wore a double-breasted, dark grey pinstripe suit with a white tie and a pocket square that was so big it looked like a bed sheet had been stuffed in his coat. His fake mustache and beard were light brown and bushy and made him look like a well-dressed Moses, just in town to incite the masses. His height made him all the more intimidating. On the other hand, a small, dark blue felt hat that teetered precariously on top of his head was almost comically inappropriate.

She didn't see any way that this was going to work. Were they dressed up as mobsters or something? Movie stars?

Waiting with her was Justin Cowles, the associate director of marketing. Jenna had tried to get a couple of high level executives to show up, but since she didn't know how Mark and End were going to be making their appearance, who they'd say they were, or why they were visiting, she couldn't convince anyone else to come. Justin had asked her out a dozen times and was only too glad to do her a favor. In a sense, she was acknowledging his existence this way, which was more than he deserved. Still, she didn't think he'd ask her out again after this, so at least something good would come of it. He was already getting impatient with having to wait the ten minutes they'd been standing there.

The receptionist said hello to the two men. Matthias End ignored her and walked around her desk until he was only a foot away from Justin. He glowered down at Justin, who seemed to shrink in height as he peered uncertainly up at End.

"Good morning," said End. "My name is Sachs Lehman. I am the chief strategic economist for Morgan Schwab Stanley Witter Brothers. And you are?"

"Uh, I...uh, Justin Cowles, sir."

"Justin, my dear boy, this is my associate, Goldman Merrill. He's the... what was it again?"

Mark had been staring at the security cameras on all four walls and approached the three people slowly and coolly. "Prime Executive of Financial Stock Analysis," he said without looking at them.

End giggled at Justin. "Have you ever heard a sillier title? Or a longer one?"

"No sir. You...you gentlemen are stock analysts?"

"I prefer Chief Strategic Economist, if you don't mind."

Justin nodded dumbly. "Well, uh, this is kind of a surprise visit. If you'll let us take you to the executive conference room, I'll see if I can get my boss to come see you."

They stepped briskly toward the security doors, which beeped unlocked as they reached them.

"Hey," said Justin, by way of making pleasantries as they stood waiting for an elevator. "Isn't there a company called Goldman Sachs? They have something to do with stocks too, don't they?"

"Please, let's not plunge into the demeaning jokes," said End indignantly. "We get that practically everywhere we go. It makes us feel like we're invisible. 'Oh you're not a person, you're just a *building* somewhere.' It's horrid. Don't you agree, Goldie?"

Mark seemed enthralled with the security cameras. "Uh...what?" he said.

"I frankly don't care to hear any more, little man. Be away." End waved the back of his hand to shoo Justin off.

The young executive reddened. "I'm terribly sorry. Really, I didn't mean anything. I just thought it was——"

"No, you didn't think, did you. Is it any wonder your company is about to lose half its stock value? Oh! I shouldn't have said that."

"Really? Half its value?"

"No. Not really. Now disappear, please and thank you."

Justin gave Jenna a frantic look, and she nodded toward the visitors to indicate she would stay with them. "I'll be right back," he said to them and ran up the stairwell.

"That went pretty well, don't you think?" said End, adjusting his hat.

"Stock analysts?" said Jenna. "You're trying to pass yourselves off as stock analysts?"

"Why do you suppose she has to ask the same question twice?" End asked Mark. Mark grinned at her from beneath his mustache.

Jenna began to giggle. "You two are hysterical!" She covered her mouth again and looked down as someone went past them and disappeared down a long hallway.

An elevator finally opened, and they stepped in. Jenna pushed the button for the twelfth floor, the executive floor. "We'll get there before Justin does," she said. She stifled another giggle as she glanced again at End's hat.

The elevator moved slowly. End flicked at the shoulders of his coat. "Jenna sweetheart, just go along with us, all right? We're improvising here. Not a lot of time to make Goggin happy before York finds us. Nary all the hosts of heaven will help us if he does."

"All right," she agreed dubiously. "You could have picked a quieter way to get in here. But then with security so tight anymore you might not have gotten in any other way. What are you going to do?"

Before they could answer, the doors opened, and Charles McNeill and two directors of marketing stood waiting, smiling politely at them. Mr. McNeill was vice president of Marketing, two positions above Justin, who must have used his cell phone to call ahead as he ran up the stairs. Word had spread faster than Jenna expected if Mr. McNeill had already been notified.

"This is an unexpected pleasure, gentlemen," said McNeill. "We always look forward to talking with professionals like yourselves, people so closely attuned to the pulse of the world's investors. If you'll step this way, we can get acquainted in the executive conference room." They stepped to the right just as Justin whipped open the stairwell door and shot into their midst.

"Oh!" he said, out of breath. "Hello again!"

"Thank you, Mr. Cowles," said McNeill. "I believe you have some reports to finish?"

Justin stared blankly at McNeill, then nodded in sudden gratitude, first at the marketing chief, and then at anyone who looked his way. He glanced uncertainly at the elevator, then spun and disappeared again through the stairwell door.

"I do apologize, gentlemen," said McNeill. "We're in the process of major retooling and didn't properly prepare for visitors. Miss Telfair, I thank you for letting us know about this visit. You may go as well."

"No," said Mark emphatically.

Mr. McNeill raised an eyebrow.

"She's…I've spoken with her several times on the phone, and I like her candid assessment of your various operations. I would…prefer that she stayed with us." Mark lowered his face to level his eyes on McNeill, the desired effect being to compel him to agree.

Mr. McNeill's face registered complete disinterest. "Of course. If you'll please follow me…"

The executive conference room at General Micronet was nothing short of a treasure-trove of luxury. There was a long, curving, ornately-carved conference table, at least twenty chairs also ornately carved all around it, with a dozen more lining the walls. Dark paneling covered the walls, and the floor was a herringbone mix of light and dark wood. The sculpted ceiling gradually rose to a peak, where a monstrously immense gold and crystal chandelier filtered lightly through, its tiny lights making it look like a hovering, glittering, majestic Christmas tree. Jenna had only been in there once, to deliver a note to her boss. They didn't even let the board of directors in there. Something about the board expecting greater compensation if they saw the extravagance the executives treated themselves to. That these same executives would allow two stock analysts—especially ones they couldn't possibly have ever heard of—to enter such hallowed ground said a lot about how they felt about stock analysts.

Seated at the huge table were a dozen more executives. Among those she didn't recognize, Jenna was shocked to see the vice presidents of Finance, Engineering, and Manufacturing, the CEO of GMN's research and development branch, and the chief operations officer himself, Mr. Warner. She couldn't remember his first name, but no one she knew dared to call him by his first name, so it was simply Mr. Warner. Only Mr. York was more terrifying to GMN employees than Mr. Warner.

End made a haughty entrance, ignoring everyone, and introducing himself only to Mr. Warner. He knew who Mr. Warner was, too. And Jenna was sure he knew the significance of Mr. Warner being there. Mark refused to shake hands with anyone, even Mr. Warner, which seemed to surprise him. Mark didn't know the man, nor did he comprehend the significance of his own lack of cordiality. He was still studying security cameras.

After everyone had found a chair, Mr. Warner took charge. "Gentlemen, this is indeed an honor and privilege to have you here with us today. I understand from Mr. McNeill that you were not present at our analyst meeting in February. I'm sure we can provide you with any information you need."

"Really. Then," said Mark, "I'd like to know—"

"Mr. Merrill," interrupted End, "I know you're anxious to be moving on—we're scheduled to meet with Sprint and Aquila ourselves while we're in town. A bit of a rush to get it all done in one day. But I want to find out, gentlemen, why we should upgrade you from 'neutral' to a 'buy', much less a 'strong buy'."

Mr. Warner folded his hands together. "Frankly, Mr. Lehman, yours would be the only securities or brokerage firm *not* to recommend a 'strong buy' on our stocks."

"My, you certainly think highly of yourselves," End commented.

Mr. Warner chuckled. "Well, I don't like to brag—"

With an abrupt and loud backward jerk of his chair, Mark stood. He scrutinized the room, the walls in particular, his eyes intent and his jaw set. The table went silent.

"Hell with this," he said finally. "Let's get out of here."

It looked to Jenna as if Mark was losing his composure, although maybe he saw something that she hadn't. Mr. Warner, on the other hand, completely misunderstood him.

"Please, please Mr. Merrill, I meant no offense. I do sometimes come over a bit heavy-handed. I can assure you that General Micronet very much wants to earn a high rating from your firm, in any way necessary. And I do mean that in the most literal sense possible."

Mark finally looked in a direction other than the walls, staring with the utmost loathing at Mr. Warner. "I would hope so, sir," he said with a whisper.

Tension immediately rose in the room, executives fidgeting with ties and fiddling with paperwork.

"Gentlemen," said Mr. Warner, clearing his throat in unaccustomed discomfort, "we have a primary package of incentives that we offer all stock analysts who watch our company. It includes several vacation options, the use of any of our company jets any time you're in the Midwest, unlimited car rental use worldwide at our expense, as well as special requests such as personal escorts, gambling, and box seats to any sporting event nationwide."

He paused and looked at them as if he were genuinely sizing them up, rather than just pausing so he could toss out a bigger offer. "But I can sense that you two are much more immersed in the ebb and flow of operations here at General Micronet. Men such as yourselves will surely need our 'special' special package."

End smiled devilishly. "I don't know how you could possibly sense that already, but I'm willing to listen."

"Perhaps we can negotiate something to your satisfaction."

"What did you have in mind?" asked End. A garishly decorated condo in the Swiss Alps with a quartet of French models would be his initial demand, he thought. And a Ferrari.

"No," Mark said, and the room again became completely still. "I want some information before I'm going to do anything."

Mr. Warner looked plaintively at End, who shrugged. "Mr. Merrill is the prime executive of our Financial Stock Analysis division," End said. "Perhaps we could obtain a few tidbits of inside information for our investors. It always makes the recommendation more convincing. And Mr. Merrill's fears will at least be assuaged, if not entirely satisfied."

"Yes, of course," replied Mr. Warner, smiling and nodding.

Everyone waited for Mark to set the agenda. He hesitated, then realizing being indecisive wouldn't look very menacing, he frowned. When that seemed to go on too long, he said, "My clients are very interested in what you have in the way of new products."

"Of course, Mr. Merrill," said Mr. Warner enthusiastically. "This year we are coming out with some exciting new items in our polymers and plastics divisions, not to mention three new aircraft engines for the business aviation, turbojet, and regional aircraft groups..."

He went on a bit longer about this and that. Nothing about hovering dollhouses, or hovering anything elses.

When Mr. Warner had finished, he looked expectantly for a response from Mark, who looked at End, who jumped slightly at the sudden attention. All his suave conversation hadn't garnered the same interest Mark's glowering had, so he hadn't expected the ball to land on his side of the net any time soon.

"My thanks, Mr. Merrill," End said. "Mr. Warner, I'm particularly concerned about General Micronet's earnings estimates for the next quarter and, indeed, the rest of the year. Can you give us some assurance that you will meet those estimates?"

"Certainly! How much would you like?"

"How much what?"

"Assurance."

"You think you can quantify a level of assurance for me? Very well, I would like—and I think Mr. Merrill would agree—I would like to have 100 percent assurance."

Mr. Warner seemed puzzled. "How does that translate into dollars? Would, say $100,000 per 10 percent give you 100 percent assurance?"

End was dumbfounded. "I should say it would," he said when he found his voice.

Mr. Warner and his associates smiled and nodded at one another in satisfaction.

"And for my colleague, Mr. Merrill?" asked End.

Mr. Warner was startled, but he recovered quickly. "Why, a million dollars for him as well." The assemblage smiled as one, another negotiation successfully concluded.

Mark scowled in open disgust at the sordid business going on. The assemblage saw this and stopped grinning—End included—and went back to fidgeting.

"What about any promising prototypes you might have in the works?" said Mark with unconcealed loathing in his expression.

The GMN executives did a combined shrug and looked at one another stupidly.

End figured it was once again his turn. "I have a request or two to make, if you don't mind."

"Anything," replied Mr. Warner. "Name it, and it will be done."

"That man right there," he said, pointing to the man he knew was the vice president of new products, "did not answer Mr. Merrill's question."

Mr. Warner eyed the man with sudden suspicion. "No, he didn't, did he."

"I would think you would want someone responsive to investors' needs to be at the helm of your New Products division, wouldn't you?"

"You're most definitely correct, Mr. Lehman. Henderson? You're sacked! Get out." He turned to see what End thought of that. End obliged with a smile and then, once again, the room radiated with smiles, human love, and understanding. Except for the former vice president of new products, Mr. Henderson.

Mark's disgust only grew. "Thank you, Mr. Lehman, you never cease to amaze. I still haven't heard much to give my people so far. I wonder, gentlemen, if you could tell me of any new products or product prototypes you plan for in the next five years?"

The shrugs were less noticeable now as many of the executives became concerned that they might be next to get the axe and hoped instead to become temporarily invisible by responding little or not at all.

"Ah, this is going well so far, I think," said End. "But I'm feeling a tad parched. How about a nice wine? A Burgundy or a claret would do just fine. No Beaujolais, though. I'm working, don't you know. And some Brie, maybe some Stilton too. With crackers. Big ones."

Three-fourths of the executives rose and shuffled for the door. End watched them file out. "Seems to take a lot of executives just to get a light snack. Is this the way you normally utilize your resources, Mr. Warner?"

"Oh, um, ah, no, of course not. McNeill, get them back in here. McNeill?"

Mr. McNeill had fled along with the junior executives.

"Hmm!" said Mr. Warner. "Well, that doesn't bode well for McNeill, does it."

End shook his head in disappointment. "I'll tell you what," he said. "I'd settle for a few dancing girls. You wouldn't happen to have any on the pay-roll, would you?"

"How many—" Mr. Warner began to ask those remaining at the table. Two more executives shot out the door, presumably looking for dancing girls or reasonable substitutes.

"Gentlemen!" Mark said loudly, rising once again to his feet. "I am thoroughly disappointed in the answers we're getting. I'm prepared to make one more attempt at equitable discussion here, and I will base my ratings on my satisfaction as to how that unfolds. Do you or do you not have anything, anything at all, going on in the area of anti-gravitational propulsion?"

Mr. Warner's two remaining lackeys shook their heads and shrank in their seats. Mr. Warner was silent.

"Mr. Warner?" said Mark.

"Leave us," Mr. Warner said to the minor executives, and they were out the door before the echo of his words had dwindled to silence.

Considering both men, Mr. Warner slowly leaned forward. "Gentlemen, this is top secret. Miss Telfair here knows, but few others do. I am simply amazed at the information you analysts are able to dig up about even the most covert operations going on here. But you have uncovered a very big item of business. We are hot on the trail of a new invention that could totally redefine how Americans—hell, how all of humanity—lives."

Mark knew exactly what he was talking about, but found himself leaning forward with keen interest in how favorably his own invention was being lauded.

"I can't tell you a lot," continued Mr. Warner, "but I do know that the prototype is here and is being tested and retested. If all goes according to plan, we could begin mass-producing it by spring."

Mark and End nodded appreciably.

"Will that satisfy your investors?" asked Mr. Warner. "I mean, we'll be more than happy to reshuffle management, implement cutbacks, you name it. Hell, we can lay off another twenty thousand if that's what it takes to earn your blessing."

"That won't be necessary," said Mark. "I think we've heard enough."

"What about the million dollars apiece?" asked End with great interest.

"Not a problem at all. I'll wire it to your bank account as soon as I get your identification."

"I was thinking more of stacks of small bills in a suitcase. Tens and twenties with maybe—"

"Thank you very much, Mr. Warner," Mark interrupted. He didn't want to shake hands with so abominable a creature, and so, what with playing the juicy role of conceited stock analyst, he didn't. Mr. Warner turned his extended—now rejected—hand into a friendly wave.

"One more thing," said End with authority, not wanting to leave with so much power and influence his to have and hold and use.

"Bring me the head of Warren Buffett."

Chapter 12

A man of refinement and quality has possessions that mirror his self-per-ceived station in life. He more than likely owns several fine suits, a handful of European watches, rings, and cuff links, and manages perfectly coiffed hair and capped teeth. He may mingle with the finer sort of people, the jet-set, the wealthy, the famous, and the infamous. But it's guaranteed that he will only drive a car that is the sleekest, the fastest, and the closest to fitting his personal image of himself. A refined school teacher will probably drive a Passat. A refined politician will go for limousines. A refined drug dealer will steer toward a Lincoln. A refined hip-hop singer will settle only for a Bentley. A refined sports athlete will think highly of Mercedes.

But a refined industrial spy? With the financial backing of global con-glomerates, the possibility is certainly there that the refined industrial spy could drive absolutely anything he wanted. Ferrari? Porsche? Lamborghini? Bah! Unworthy! Only the best European luxury sedans will do for the spy of refinement. Aston Martin, BMW, Jaguar.

At least that's the way it's supposed to be.

Mr. York, foremost intelligence operative of General Micronet, was at that moment driving a 1978 Dodge pickup. It may have been another color at one time, but rust now so consumed it that it was a dank and filthy dark orange. It drove as if powered by squirrels, and very old, crippled squirrels at that. There was a hole in the floor on the passenger side.

But it was a necessary evil in order to blend in when they arrived in Brookbury. They had been following Mark Goggin and his companions since they left General Micronet. As if they thought they could waltz around the main offices without being discovered, Mr. York mused sardonically. It had been raining, sleeting, snowing, and otherwise thoroughly damp for the entirety of the trip so far. The heater worked, but it blew damp warmish air that smelled like farm animals.

The cabin of the truck was tiny and the driver-side window had refused to roll all the way up, so that snow and slush and the frozen wind rushed through the four-inch gap. The brakes were suspect, and the backend had no weight and fishtailed on a more or less constant basis.

Worse than all that? He was dressed for the part. His garments consisted of dark jeans with holes in the knees, a checked red shirt missing buttons, and brown work shoes that squished even when he wasn't walking in them.

If all that weren't bad enough, in the passenger seat next to him sat Drake Endicott.

It had taken all of Mr. York's strength not to shove the infuriating little troll through the forward windshield, which was already severely cracked.

He glanced over at Endicott and suppressed a renewed urge to do him mortal injury, for Drake Endicott was not attired in seedy farm wear. He wore a suit that was a perfect medium gray, tailor-made, form-fitting, with a crisp, white shirt and immaculate black tie underneath. He did not appear to be chilled; his door window was closed, and there was far less ice on the windows around him. The heat must also be blowing only through the vents on that side of the truck because he did not appear to be the least bit chilled. Endicott's cologne wafted on the slight internal breeze over to Mr. York's embattled stratosphere, despite the jetstream of harsh cold air coming in the window and the feeble heat drifting up from the vents. The smell made Mr. York more miserable than the heat *or* the cold.

"You're falling too far behind," offered Endicott.

"Have you ever tailed anyone before, Endicott?"

"Of course I have."

"I didn't think so. Save your suggestions for when it's your turn to drive, God help me."

"Yorko, I've paired up with some real bad attitudes, but you win first prize." Endicott looked the driver over. "You smell bad too."

Mr. York felt the revolver in the waistband of his pants dig into his midriff, and he pondered the satisfaction that might be found by firing the entire clip in Endicott's general direction. But no. Then he would have the stench of dead Endicott wafting around with his cologne and that would unquestionably make him retch.

"Man, I don't get it. Why all the hostility?" said Endicott. "Yeah, we've had a bad break here, but we're well on the way to setting things right. If you'd just give the hi-ho to your men, we could take out the collateral targets and get this whole mess done with and have the Goggin guy on the job by tomorrow morning."

"There are too many people in the car," Mr. York replied.

"Well, if we add up all the bullets in all four of these midget trucksters, we gotta have enough to take out more than one person. Right?"

Mr. York did not respond. Endicott folded his arms in resignation and stared ahead.

Normally a man of unbreakable discipline, Mr. York found himself transfixed by the yellow lines dividing the two lanes, staring far up the road until they disappeared over a nearing hill or shrank to invisibility at the far end of a deep valley. He imagined one of the yellow lines was Mr. Endicott, and soon he was weaving over them with disquieting regularity.

"You drive like a drunken orangutan," said Endicott. "The next time they pull over, I'm driving."

"No, you will not," Mr. York said icily. "You drive as if you want to get there before they do."

"And why not? We could lay a trap and catch them and be done with it. Don't you find all this a huge waste of time? We're professionals, baby. Or at least I am. To have to deal with an amateur Edison and a couple of office workers is slumming more than a bit, don't you think?"

"*You* are the amateur if you believe that. Those outside the community may not be as dangerous, but they are more difficult to solve simply because you cannot anticipate their moves. When we were last here, you did not expect Goggin to spin his truck around and drive like a madman all over creation when we had him boxed in. If it had been you who was trapped, you would have tried to go off-road or force one truck into another one." Mr. York paused. "No, on second thought, you would have tried to shoot everyone."

Endicott raised his eyebrows smugly and smiled.

"You are an impulsive idiot with a death wish, Mr. Endicott."

Endicott's smile went south. "That seems a tad unfriendly, Mr. York."

"I could not possibly care less. If you had not destroyed Goggin's lab, he might not have panicked, and we would not be chasing him all over the countryside. I could have brought the dollhouse back to GMN, duplicated it if necessary, and returned it before he even noticed. It would then have been a relatively simple enough thing to capture or neutralize him with his guard still down. Now not only is his guard up, but he is aware that we have stolen the dollhouse and that we know its secrets. You," he said with deadly emphasis, "are a complete imbecile."

Silence followed. "You should watch what you say to certain people," Endicott said eventually.

"Yes, and I suppose you would be dim enough to try to shoot me while I am driving at high speed on an interstate. Frankly, Mr. Endicott, I question whether you truly are a professional. Your methods are not based on logic. They're based on violence and nothing more. The more destruction, the more death, the better. Some day you will find yourself the victim of such tactics."

Endicott laughed. "What, you think you'll be the one to get me?"

"No, you'll do it yourself."

The conversation stalled as Endicott spluttered. Then he began to laugh, loudly and in a manner filled with surprise. "Why, Mr. York, I believe the road has hypnotized you into some kind of suicidal malice toward me. If I were the homicidal maniac you make me out to be, I'd be inclined to take a grudge against you. But it's not in my nature. I enjoy my work, my merry old Yorkster. Maybe I am a little overzealous and maybe a tad too creatively destructive, but I get the job done, and I remain a carefree spirit and a delight to all. Whereas *you* are a fearsome little rattlesnake that slinks in and out of holes, unloved by even your fellow rattlesnakes." Endicott blew a loud raspberry at Mr. York. "I will not allow you to ruin a monotonous but otherwise easy assignment."

He leaned over to Mr. York and said calmly, "But I will not work with you again. You're a mean old poopy-pants."

The journey continued on in renewed silence for another half an hour before they saw Goggin's truck pull off the road and into a rest area.

They stopped just before the exit, and three sets of headlights slowed behind them, also pulling off to the side. They watched as several figures from the truck in the rest area ran through the rain into the shelter of the public restrooms.

"Come on, my turn," said Endicott, getting out and walking around to the driver's door.

Mr. York sneered but realized he was tired enough that it might be for the best. It might be better to risk being noticed if Endicott drove up next to Goggin, waved, and starting spraying bullets everywhere as he was likely to do, than if Mr. York tried to keep going and drove into a cement bridge support. He grudgingly shifted over to the passenger side. At least now he might get warm.

The figures came racing out from the shelter and dove into the truck. There was a long delay before the truck moved again. It merged back onto the interstate before Endicott had even put their own truck in motion. He revved the engine harshly and mashed the accelerator to the floor until they were less than a hundred feet behind their quarry. They were fortunate that the three vehicles keeping pace behind them gave the appearance of many cars being on the road, so Goggin, tired, bleary-eyed, and inattentive as he surely was, might not notice the ignoramus Endicott sitting on his rear bumper.

"Now would be the right time to shoot you, if I were the nut you think I am," said Endicott, trying unsuccessfully to roll the window up as he crept closer to Goggin.

"I would hope you were smarter than that," replied Mr. York. Both of his hands were in his coat pockets, and one was not empty.

Endicott grinned. "I think that may be the closest thing to a compliment I'm liable to get from you, Yorkshire old buddy." The back tires lost grip momentarily as he whipped around a slower car. "Whoa!" he shouted before regaining control. After taking a moment to collect himself, he resumed his grin. "You know, Yorktown, it seems to me that if you were as perfectly professional as you make yourself out to be, you wouldn't have grabbed the dollhouse in the first place. It seems to me that a flawless corporate agent like yourself would have tested it somehow, made sure it really worked as advertised, so he wouldn't have looked like an ass back at the home office."

Mr. York did not respond.

"Of course I'm only a brainless thug," Endicott added and laughed.

Inside his coat pocket, the barrel of the revolver in Mr. York's hand turned in Endicott's direction. To Endicott's everlasting obliviousness, it did not fire. After all, he was right. It made Mr. York seethe with a rage he had not felt in years.

Mr. York had been just as lax in his own way as Endicott had. After he had stolen the dollhouse, he had not checked that it would float once he had removed it from the shelf. He had also conveniently forgotten that when he had taken it down in Goggin's presence and put it on the table, it had not floated either.

No, instead he had stolen the thing and driven it halfway across the state and turned it over to GMN's scientists without so much as a thought of turning it on. It had rested on the passenger seat of the truck—not hovered, rested—for hours without him noticing that anything was amiss.

After all the bad food, poor sleep, repulsive working conditions, and the impossible, ever-present co-worker he had had to endure over the last couple of weeks, he had thought his humiliation could get no worse. But his disgrace did not reach its full crescendo until the scientists had brought him down to their lab, opened the dollhouse, and let him see inside.

It was empty.

Chapter 13

The ride back to Brookbury was long and tiring and punctuated by bickering. The traffic was unusually heavy almost the whole way. Mark was anxious to be home where he felt like he might be able to clear his head. Throughout the drive, End had ranted on a constant and monotonous basis about the evils of General Micronet, to which Jenna had responded defensively at first and then with sarcasm later when she got tired of listening to him. The last fifteen minutes of the trip were silent, to Mark's everlasting relief.

The night was especially dark as they pulled into the drive. The headlights flickered and it was strangely hard going along the path. Must just be tired, Mark thought. He glanced in the mirror and saw End looking behind them. He had done that throughout the trip too, in between his tirades of righteous indignation. Mark looked behind them and saw a set of headlights flash and then disappear. He looked back ahead. He was just too tired to care.

As they rounded the last line of trees, the house came into view. The lights were out, another strange thing. But as they pulled up to the front, Mark saw that a few lights were actually on. The kitchen lights and maybe one in a bedroom or in a hallway upstairs.

The porch lights came on as they got out of the car, and Nathan shot out the door armed to the teeth. He wore an army surplus helmet and his river-wading boots along with his faithful weapon, the pulse laser rifle and its back-breaking pack filled with overcharged capacitors.

He seemed considerably relieved that they were not an invading horde of Nazis or zombies or orcs or whatever it was he had been expecting. He slowed himself down by sliding to the end of the porch. "Hi guys," he said, trying to appear nonchalant.

"Hello, my boy," said End, smiling and knocking on Nathan's helmet as he walked past.

Mark reached the top of the steps, stopped, and looked him over head to toe. "Your friends coming over again?" he said, and shuffled slowly inside.

Jenna followed Nathan in and helped him get the pack off. Mark stepped into a small alcove behind the living room to check for phone messages.

End was there waiting for him. Mark could sense his agitation and braced himself for more wild talk about the looming corporate conquest of the world.

"Why didn't we get the dollhouse while we were there?" asked End instead, his voice shaking with anger.

Mark raised his eyebrows in surprise. "Well, I didn't think it was worth it. Did you like it particularly?"

End glared. "If they have it, they'll eventually figure out how it works. Won't they?"

Mark shook his head. "Naw, I'm pretty sure they won't."

When Mark didn't immediately elaborate, End looked as if he wanted to throttle him. "Why?" he almost shouted.

"Because it doesn't work. It's a dollhouse. Nothing more."

End's jaw hung open. "What?"

"There's nothing in it," Mark said with a mischievous grin, despite his fatigue. "The actual construct that creates the effect is...well, it's elsewhere. I just used the Dream House because it had the right mass and volume for the experiment. It's empty. Not even a Barbie in there. Not that she'd want to go in. No furniture, walls are in bad shape. Should have been torn down and had a new Dream House put up a long time ago."

End's expression turned slowly from frustrated anger to giggly delight. "You son of a bitch," he breathed and shoved Mark into the chair behind him.

"I can't believe you kept that from me all this time." He grinned fiendishly, then turned and danced a little jig out of the room. "They're gonna be so pissed when they look inside!" he shouted from the stairs. "Glory hallelujah!"

Mark watched End romp out of the room, sighed with a quiet satisfaction, and looked for the phone. It was on the table behind a floor lamp where it should be, oddly enough. He reached over for the receiver and noticed a blue piece of paper he hadn't remembered putting on the table. Since they'd last cleaned the place, he had handed down an edict that no one could go in the alcove, hoping that might keep it clean longer.

He unfolded the paper and was immediately alarmed to see the page filled with glued-on letters. It looked just like a ransom note. It also sounded like a ransom note. It read 'Dear Mr. Goggin. We have your mother. If you ever want to see her alive, you will destroy all traces of your experiments involving anti-gravitation. You have two days.'

At any other time, in such a situation Mark would have flown into a tremendous panic and obediently burned his entire lab down. But he was much more tired than he had guessed, and, more importantly, his mother had been up in the Great Inventor's Convention in the Sky for going on nine years. But in his muddled mind he thought maybe he should just make sure.

He pressed buttons on the phone. "Hello, Dad?"

"Dad who?" said a gruff, loud voice. Dad didn't hear so well anymore.

Mark grinned. "How are you, Dad?"

"Is that you, squirt? It can't be. It's not Christmas. Maybe it's my birthday. Just a minute, I'll check."

"No, no! Dad? It's not your birthday. I just wanted to call and see how things are going. It's kind of crazy here and…well, I guess maybe I just wanted to hear your voice. Bring back a little stability to my senses."

"Don't waste your time, boy. You're completely nuts. I should know."

Mark sighed again. It really was good to hear Dad's voice. Dad had never been able to just have a normal conversation with him. He had to throw in zingers and tease and make trouble.

"Got a girlfriend yet?" his dad asked.

"mmm…not yet," Mark said. "I have a possibility though."

"Awww! Son, you're practically fifty! You'll be dead before you get me any grandkids. Just find a woman and marry her, for Pete's sake. No, better yet, just get me some grandkids. That'll do fine. Cut out the middleman, right?"

Mark snickered. "Right, Dad."

"What about that Jenna you always sound so moon-eyed about? Is she your 'possibility', or did she turn tail and run for her life?"

"She hasn't run yet."

"Good. There's hope for you yet. Maybe she'll fix you." His dad cleared his throat. "You…you said things were crazy?"

"Yeah. No big deal."

"Y'sure?"

"Sure, Dad."

"Well, don't go blowing yourself up. Your mother would never forgive me. Damn woman's haunting me as it is. No wonder I can't ever get any sleep."

"Okay, Dad, I'll be careful."

"Take care of yourself, boy."

"Okay."

"And don't call me anymore except on birthdays."

Mark chuckled wearily. "Right, Dad."

"You notice I didn't say whose birthday. Somebody's got a birthday every day."

His dad would have talked for another week if Mark let him. He was tempted to. "I gotta go, Dad. I'll call you soon."

"All right, squirt."

They said goodbye and Mark hung up.

* * *

The sun woke Mark up the next morning. The light streamed in at an angle from a window in the living room and into the small phone room where it lit a long line across the floor and over his face. He was still in the same room as before, except he was lying on the floor. He must have fallen asleep and then fallen out of his chair.

Staring up, he noticed the ceiling needed cobwebs cleared away. And the floor was awfully dusty. Maybe he should take another look at that automated vacuum cleaner he'd been working on.

He sat up slowly, his back stiff from the maple floorboards. Someone had put a blanket on him. Mark grinned. She was just the sweetest thing, his 'possibility'.

Groggy-eyed, he groaned and staggered to his feet, and headed for the kitchen, where there was way too much noise going on at—he looked at a clock—ten in the morning.

"Hello, lazy bones," said Jenna, walking past and grabbing a bowl from a cabinet. Mark smiled and dropped into a chair at the table.

Everyone was eating. "We have food?" he asked.

"Cereal," answered Jenna and put the bowl in front of him.

"We have clean dishes?" he asked. Jenna laughed.

They ate with very little conversation, which was fine because the avalanche of sound from crunching corn flakes shook Mark's nerves from head to toe. The wrinkling of newspaper didn't help either. The morning paper was tormentingly thick that morning.

"I found a blue note last night when I went in to put a blanket on you," said Jenna. "It said someone had kidnapped your mother? But your mother's been gone for years now, hasn't she? What does it mean?"

Mark shrugged. "I don't know. Really stupid kidnappers maybe."

"Aren't you even a little concerned that someone got in the house and put that note there?" asked End.

"Yes." Mark looked over the front page of the paper.

"They must have got in while I was in school," said Nathan and slurped milk at the bottom of his bowl.

More crunching hung in the airspace over the table until the table itself seemed to emit one huge slurp, and Mark thought snakes were burrowing into his brain. Spoons clinked in empty bowls. No one looked at anyone else for a while, preferring the newspaper to conversation, and eventually Nathan got up and retrieved the corn flakes box. Soon the crunch of fresh flakes gnashed anew into Mark's skull.

"We were followed last night," End said. He also refilled his cereal bowl. "From General Micronet all the way here."

That and the rising din of masticated corn flakes made Mark lower his paper. "How do you know?"

"Each time we stopped at the rest areas, four sets of headlights pulled over on the highway behind us. I wouldn't have noticed if we hadn't stopped so often."

"Four?" said Mark, a little nervous now. "There were four trucks after me the other day."

End nodded. "Now does it seem more serious?"

Mark frowned at him. He wasn't wanting to think about global conspiracies so early in the morning. He didn't usually even get up so early. A lifelong nighttime inventor, he was very often up until four or five in the morning. The morning sun was an unidentified flying object to him.

The paper had more of the usual murders, disasters, politicians making promises, debate on bi-state taxes. A heading near the bottom caught his eye: 'Oregon inventor, Archibald Scott, killed in blast.'

Mark leaned forward to read the story. Apparently Scott had been killed when an explosion went off at his laboratory. The police believed foul play was involved. The final paragraph said 'Sources list one of Scott's foremost competitors in the field of antigravity as Mr. Mark Goggin, of Brookbury, Missouri. The Federal Bureau of Investigations will be sending agents to question Mr. Goggin, the only murder suspect uncovered so far.'

Mark lowered the page and jumped a little on seeing that End was looking straight at him.

"Would you say it's serious now?" End said.

"You read it?" Mark asked. End nodded. "Well, I'm sure they just added that to create some excitement in the story," Mark said.

"You don't really believe that, do you?" said End. "How many people know you're working on an anti-gravitational experiment?"

"Just you three...and Mr. York."

"I'm sorry, Mark," Jenna winced. "I told practically the entire board of directors about your dollhouse."

"So the source for that article would probably be...?" End asked.

Mark glared at him. "I think I can take it from here, thank you very much."

"Mark, it should be obvious now. General Micronet is after you. If you want to live, you have to go where they won't find you."

"But you said they'd want me to do the research and development for it."

"I don't think so now. The note told you to stop working on it. I think we can assume that someone from GMN wrote the note, since only they knew about it. So, obviously GMN doesn't want you working on it."

Mark leaned forward, his eyes focused directly on End. "I believe there is someone else, here in this very room, who has been less than honest, and who could also have written the note."

End's eyes became fierce orbs as he also leaned forward. "Nathan, was the note on the table after we left?" he said, still focused on Mark.

"He wouldn't know that because he went to school right after we left. Isn't that right, Nathan?" Mark said, glaring back at End.

Nathan glanced at everyone uncomfortably. "umm...Sure."

"Nathan," said End, "if you lie to save yourself, then Mark will think I wrote the note. He will do nothing about it and his life will be in danger."

Nathan looked at Mark and slouched into a chair. "Okay...I talked with this, um, girl I met at school, after you left. But I went to school right after that, I swear."

"And the note?"

"There wasn't no note."

Mark frowned, but leaned back, still suspicious of End. "If someone's followed us back here and they're really after me, why don't they just come after me now?"

"Who knows? Maybe because there's four people they'd have to deal with now, not just you and Nathan. Maybe they wanted breakfast first. Some corporate operatives think of themselves as being artists in a way. Maybe they've always killed their targets in a certain room or in a specific way. You just haven't walked into the right room yet."

Mark stood up and faced End. "All right. Let's just get this out in the open. Matthias End, I don't believe anything you've said since you got here. Jenna told me you'd say and do whatever you had to, if it fit your own personal agenda. *You*—I'm sorry, Nathan, but I have to say this—it was *you* who put the dead chicken on the door to scare me. It is you, our self-appointed guardian, who has never been around when suspicious cars pulled into the driveway or aircraft flew low over the house. Don't think I haven't noticed how much you like to flash that gun around all the time, just so I'll know what's what. And all you wanted to do was clown around at General Micronet when I was trying to find proof that they—or you—stole the dollhouse. Maybe you didn't put the note there, but that may only be because you had to be with us to keep tabs on me while one of your friends did it."

Mark was red-faced now, his hands balled into fists at his sides. "You're nothing but a two-faced hood out to make yourself rich whether it means killing me or everybody here."

The four sat in silence for a time, leaving corn flakes to get soggy. Eventually Jenna got up and took the bowls to the sink.

Matthias End considered Mark's enraged features and then stood as well, towering over Mark. "I have spent my whole life working to help people," he said, the anger in his voice rising, "Selfish, ungrateful people. I have helped them to be safe and happy, and live full lives. But I have never had someone so determined to ignore me. God Almighty! You're a brainless ass, Goggin. If I wanted to kill you, you'd be dead. You know, I once had a man confess to me that he had been told his boss was out to get him, that he would lose his job, his house, and his savings. But he had been suspicious of the person who told him those things and so he ignored them. And he lost his job and his house and his savings. You remind me of him, Goggin. Stubborn and stupid. Fine, then. Get yourself killed. Maybe I'm not good at it, but I did my best to keep you alive, so the Lord can't condemn me for not trying."

End sat heavily back in his seat. Mark still frowned, but it was more so one of bewilderment.

Nathan screwed up his face. "He *confessed* to you?"

End glanced at him. "That's right. I was a priest. Once."

"What kind of a priest carries a gun and kills chickens?" Mark said, trying to maintain his anger.

"The kind that got pissed off at people who take his advice and spit in his eye," End snarled back.

"Well, your holiness, I—"

"All right, all right, all right!"

Everyone jumped as if cluster bombs were detonating over by the sink. They turned to look at Jenna.

"I've listened to enough of this," she said. "I always try to stay out of things that don't involve me, but this does. For the life of me, I don't know why, but you matter to me. All of you." She stared hard at End, but then her eyes softened. "Even you, Matthias. I may have judged you too harshly. I still think you're looking out for yourself most of the time, but I do think you're trying to help Mark." She said the last words looking at Mark. "Mark, whether you believe he's telling the truth or not, and he probably isn't, he is right that *someone* is after you. We can't stay here."

"We?"

"Of course. If any of us stay here, we're just going to get killed."

"It's a nice thought, sweetheart," said End, "but I'm staying. I need to... have words with Mr. York. At some point." He turned to Nathan, who sensed momentous decisions going on, and it made him nervous. "And Nathan has to show me how to work that incredible laser rifle of his. And he needs to get back to school. Right, Nate?"

"How could you have killed Don?" Nathan asked, his emotions welling up.

"I'm sorry, Nathan. He was intended to serve a greater purpose. If it had worked, you could have called Don a hero for saving Mark. It just didn't work."

"You hate God, *and* you're a chicken killer," Nathan accused.

End waved a warning finger. "That's not true. I quit because I hated people, not God. And the chicken would have been eaten sooner or later."

Nathan folded his hands in his arms, glowering at End.

"I'll make some cookies," End said temptingly. "Your favorite kind."

"With the special ingredient?" Nathan asked, still glowering.

"No," Mark interjected. "No special ingredients."

"Yes, we probably shouldn't," End said and winked at Nathan. Nathan nodded irritably and sniffed and wiped his nose on a sleeve.

Jenna stepped close to Mark. "Then I guess it's just you and me," she said softly.

Mark's eyes widened. "No, Jenna. No, no, no. I'm new to all this corporate espionage insanity, but I'm pretty sure that if you're with me and they kill me, they're probably not going to let you just prance off unharmed."

"Doesn't matter, I'm going."

"No, you're not."

"Yes, I am."

"Nooo, you're not."

"I'll just follow you when you go, then. It amounts to the same thing."

Mark pursed his lips and scowled his worst, but couldn't think of anything to say to change her mind. Truth to tell, he wanted her to go with him.

"Well, if you're going to go," said End, "then I suggest you get packing. They're already in town. They could be heading up the driveway even as we speak."

Any ordinary person who is a murder suspect and who is also being hunted by truckloads of remorseless and lethal company men would have gotten themselves packed and departed with a strong sense of urgency and in short order, to say the least. They would have packed so as to be able to travel quickly, carrying only the essentials. Warm clothing, blankets, rugged boots, that sort of thing. Toothbrush and paste, deodorant, and toilet paper, only if there was time. Two frantic minutes and out the door.

Mark and Jenna, in the span of twenty minutes, had filled three massive suitcases with dress shirts, slacks, dresses, pajamas, leather shoes, and heels. They had also included a hair dryer, a curling iron, an electric razor, towels, facial cream, cologne, pillow cases, sheets, and, accidentally, a bathtub curtain. It took a fourth suitcase to begin packing the actual essentials.

End walked into the upstairs bedroom to find everything lying out and the end nowhere in sight. "What the hell is going on? Don't you understand the meaning of the word 'hurry'?"

Mark appeared from the closet. "Look, your eminence, I'm not leaving my house like a dog with its tail between its legs. If I have to leave, I'm going with some dignity." He dropped a pair of jogging shoes in the fourth suitcase. Jenna came into the room from behind End and dropped a pair of nylons into the same suitcase.

"Have you lost your minds?" shouted End. "This is not a vacation trip! You are escaping from your impending demise!"

Mark pointed a warning finger at him. "I've about had enough of you, your holy worship. One more word and we're not going anywhere!"

End ground his teeth together, his eyes blazing, but Mark didn't budge. "Why don't you just hand them a gun and ask them to shoot you?" roared End. "I swear, you people don't live in the real world." He wrenched the door out of his way and bulldozed down the hallway, raging at the obliviousness of creative minds.

Downstairs, Nathan stood behind a living room curtain, looking out into the front yard. Not so much as a suspicious squirrel had passed through the yard in the ten minutes he'd been standing there. He would have been there longer, only it took him five minutes to throw on the immense power pack he now wore—weighted down with the fully-charged capacitors—strap it around him, and connect all the hookups. His beloved pulse laser rifle, which he'd recently named Spock, hung over his shoulder. He'd held it in firing position for quite a while before the weight became too much.

"Nathan, relax," said End loudly as he entered the room. "You'll have plenty of time to react and fire that thing if they do get in here. And it won't be easy for them with all the stone out there to get through."

Nathan scanned from the left side of the yard to the right and back, over and over again. He realized at some point that someone might be watching and timing his scanning, so he should probably scan randomly. Then no one would catch him by surprise. It also occurred to him that they could be invading from the air too. By the time he had worked it all out in his head, he was trying to look in all directions at once.

Something came crashing down the stairs behind him and Nathan whipped around so quickly that the back of the rifle hit him in the side of the head. As he fell backward, he made a mad grab for the grip, all the while entangling himself in the wires going from the laser to the capacitors. End saw the whole thing unfold and wisely dove between the coffee table and the rocking chair. There was a flash, and a suitcase and part of one stair were black and smoking. Two steps above the suitcase, Jenna was lying prone where she had fallen after tripping over yet another random object, feet toward the top of the steps and arms braced against a step below her, her head down.

"Why don't you turn that down a bit?" suggested End from under the table. "Jenna, are you all right?" he called up the stairs.

Nathan nodded and extricated himself from the wires so he could take the pack off. With that off, he started turning down the dials controlling the capacitors.

As the three other suitcases slid one by one over or past her and followed the remains of the first down the steps, Jenna curled up in a protective ball. Mark appeared above Jenna and helped her up, and they carried the suitcases down the last few steps.

"I told you not to put that at the top of the stairs," said Jenna, huffing with the weight of countless sweaters. "It's just an invitation for me to trip over it."

"And you did," said Mark, grinning. He dropped a suitcase heavily onto two others.

The doorbell rang.

Everyone froze.

Seconds passed. It rang again.

Slowly, very slowly, Mark crept over to the door to look through the spy hole. All he could see was darkness, shadows at best. Whoever it was, was apparently trying to look through the door's smoked glass into the house and was blocking the light.

The figure stepped back to look up at the windows. Mark recognized him instantly, took a huge step backward and fell over Nathan.

From his position lying flat on the floor, he whispered loudly, "It's York!"

Chapter 14

Nathan frantically turned back up the capacitor dials he'd just turned down, then strained, arms flailing wildly, to lift the power pack back onto his shoulders and latch the harness connections together.

End waved violently at him until he stopped.

They listened. The doorbell rang again.

End stepped up to the spy hole and looked out. He'd seen York at General Micronet when he'd worked there, but he'd never connected the face with the name that everyone knew. He'd just thought the brooding man was somebody in operations management or security. They were always looking unhappy about something.

Right now, it looked to End like York was sizing up the house for a full assault. He watched as York looked up, then to the right, then the left. He turned his back on the house and stared at Mark's truck for a second or two. Then he turned back around to face the door.

"Mark Goggin!" Mr. York shouted at the house.

The house didn't answer. Neither did Mark Goggin. Everyone inside stood completely still.

"Mr. Goggin, I know you're in there," continued Mr. York. "I have a proposition for you."

End looked at Mark and motioned at the back of the house. Mark shook his head. "I want to hear what he says," he whispered. He was still on the floor, but was sitting up now.

Mr. York had meandered up close to the door. "Mr. Goggin, I am prepared to offer you a very high, six-figure salary to work for General Micronet and finish your anti-gravity prototype."

Everyone's eyes widened in the room except End's, whose eyes narrowed to a murderous intent.

Mr. York stood on the steps, looking overhead at the top of the house, waiting.

Mark stood up. He stared at the front door, undecided.

"Mr. Goggin, I'm the only one here," said Mr. York. "You have nothing to fear. I assure you, I'm completely harmless. I'd, ah, also like to apologize for my disrespectful behavior on my first visit here. Ah…it was a long trip."

Mark reached for the knob.

"Mr. Goggin is away, Mr. York," said End loudly and suddenly. "But perhaps you could explain where his dollhouse has gone to. I understand you played with it last."

Mark looked through the spy hole again. He could see that Mr. York was weighing what he should say. The man again looked to his left and right, and then turned and looked away from the house in the direction of the driveway as it trailed off into the trees. He turned around again and gave the door a hard stare.

"Matthias End," Mr. York shouted through the door. "I've heard about your recent bit of vandalism on our delivery vehicle, among other damage you've done. Mr. Goggin, I hope you're not going to believe anything a noted miscreant and worthless human being chooses to lie to you about."

"I said Mr. Goggin isn't here," repeated End. "And you haven't answered my question."

"I would not bother telling you anything, End, since you would only twist it in retelling it to the good Mr. Goggin. However, I believe you are lying once again and Mr. Goggin is in fact there. So I will tell you that I do have your dollhouse, Mr. Goggin. It is safe and waiting back at General Micronet. I must grudgingly admit that our scientists have been unable to fathom how it works. It appears to be an empty child's toy to them. That's why I'm here."

Mark looked at End.

"We've been over these accusations about me lying before," said End emphatically, his voice hushed. "I didn't steal it, he did. And clearly I'm not working with him because he says I'm lying about everything."

Mark kept looking at him. "If you've never met him, how does he know who you are?" he asked.

"How should I know? The man stares at security tapes all day long, he's bound to notice me at GMN sooner or later."

Mark still looked at him.

"All right, all right!" End hissed. "Right after I got laid off, I got a little huffy about things and I more or less—with the best of intentions, mind you—broke a delivery man's ribs and tipped his truck over. But he had it coming! York probably saw the tape of me from the truck's video-camera. They have them on all their trucks."

Mark glared at End. "Well, that's just great. You're not a fugitive, are you? What am I supposed to do now? Who am I supposed to believe? He steals things, and you beat people up." Mark looked at End and then looked back out at Mr. York.

Mr. York had his arms folded, waiting again. "Mr. Goggin, your work is very important to the company, but I do have other things besides this I must attend to."

Mark turned back to End and clinched his teeth. "Give me some help here, End, or I'm throwing you to the wolves." He looked again at Mr. York.

Mr. York still waited, albeit with noticeable impatience.

Mark didn't know what to do. Both men lied, both men showed themselves to be ruthless when it was necessary. There didn't appear to be any good choices to be—

"Team three almost in position."

Mark's eyes widened as he squinted through the spyhole. Mr. York reached quickly down to his belt and pressed on something that could either be a cell phone or a walkie-talkie. The voice had come from it.

"What was that?" whispered End.

Mark watched as Mr. York straightened and again looked to the left and right.

From behind him and to the left, someone leaped up onto the steps, vaulted up them three at a time until he reached Mr. York's side. He raised a gun toward the door.

"No, goddamn you!" shouted Mr. York, and he flung his arm out to deflect the gun. The stranger's gun arm went up and the gun went off with a report that made Mark and End jump backward.

There followed a monumental flash and a heavy slam, and they dove for cover.

Outside, something hit the ground heavily, and a truck horn blared away, not stopping.

Mark eased up from behind an overturned chair to see, through blurring vision, Nathan standing in front of the door, the pulse laser trained on a small burnt hole in the door.

He stood and approached Nathan slowly. "You okay, Nathan?"

Nathan was completely immobile, every bit of his remaining senses focused on the pierced door. "Yeah," he said finally. He exhaled slowly and shakily.

Mark looked through the spyhole and saw Mr. York dragging the stranger down the steps toward his pickup. The stranger was unconscious. And smoking. So was the hood of Mr. York's pickup, the source of the deafeningly stuck horn.

The pulse laser's released energy must have been so huge that it had actually obliterated part of the door, passed through and around the stranger, and smashed into the pickup behind him. If the truck started, it would be a miracle. But it did, and Mr. York retreated until he was at least past the nearest tree line and out of sight.

Mark turned around to Nathan. "I guess it can put holes in things after all." He smiled. "Why don't you put that away, Nathan. You handled yourself very well."

Nathan nodded and stepped backward until he could sit on the sofa. He did sit, but his eyes were still staring intently at the door and his laser rifle was still pointed right at it.

End was instantly in Mark's face. "If they're almost in position, then you're almost out of time. Get out! Now!"

Mark and Jenna ran without thinking to the impossibly over packed suitcases, and they struggled to lift even one apiece.

"Leave those!" bellowed End. "Grab a blanket and a heavy coat. Quickly!"

Mark sifted frantically through a suitcase, the wrong one, and flung it aside. Jenna found the blankets and also insisted on shoving matches, a hat, forks and spoons, a hammer, and a clothesline into a gym bag. Together they ran after End, who moved quickly to the back of the house.

"Head toward the south. Keep alongside the river as you go," ordered End. "Stay with it as much as you can, and I'll try to meet up with you as soon as I can." He pushed them in the direction of the trees that concealed the near side of the river.

Instead, Mark ran to the lab, followed by Jenna and End. "What are you doing?" End shouted.

Inside, Mark ran first for a table piled with debris. He grabbed what appeared to be a pizza tray, wedged among a stack of metal sheets, as well as an altimeter gauge, several feet of heavy duty electrical wire, and some cable. They were all sitting on the table together as if he'd intended to use them together for something. Mark stuffed everything into a backpack that he pulled from under a nearby table.

Then he went to the shelf where the Barbie Dream House had hovered. He climbed up on the table and up the shelves until he could reach the rafters above.

"Hurry up!" whispered Jenna as if she thought someone might hear them in the lab.

Mark bent aside a piece of wood attached perpendicularly to two rafters. A fist-sized object fell and he almost dropped it. The shelf teetered momentarily and then Mark jumped to the table and slid off it to the floor.

End looked at the object in Mark's hands and nodded to him. The object went in Mark's backpack as well, and he and Jenna ran out the lab door and out into the backyard.

As he ran, Mark fully expected to hear gunshots. He had seen plenty of movies where the ground explodes all around the good guys as they dodge bullets while running for cover. He didn't see how that could possibly work in real life. He thought it rather more likely that the hero would catch at least every twentieth or thirtieth bullet coming his way.

After racing across an agonizingly long stretch of open land, they reached the tree line obscuring the river. Mark jumped between two trees and dropped to the ground. Jenna tried to do the same and succeeded, but then had the unfortunate happenstance to land in a pile of leaves. She slid all the way to the very banks of the silently flowing Pomme de Terre River.

Mark saw her stop short of the water and turned back to survey the house and the land visible from where he was. If the people after them were in position, they should be surrounding the house and maybe even hiding near the same copse of trees and shrubs he and Jenna were in.

He was reluctant to abandon End and Nathan, but they certainly seemed to be able to take care of themselves. He turned to face the Pomme and saw no one. No motion, no movement, none of the litter of leaves and twigs disturbed, at least nearby. Surely that meant no one had been here yet. It wouldn't be that way for long.

Jenna sat huddled right at the edge of the water.

Mark slid down the leafy bank until he reached her. She tried to smile. He smiled back with a confidence he wasn't in the least bit feeling.

"Come on."

Chapter 15

Matthias End watched Mark and Jenna zigzag toward the trees. He saw no movement elsewhere in the huge undulating meadow behind the house. The trees where the forest began were mostly still, except for an occasional swaying in a mild breeze. If any of York's men really were positioned back there, they were either incompetently placed, or collectively blind.

End turned to Nathan, who continued to look out the window as if he wished he were going with them. "Don't worry, Nate. Believe me, we're safer than they're going to be." He headed back for the front of the house. "All we have to do is hold tight, keep the bad guys out of the house, and they'll go away."

"Ha. I'm not that stupid," replied Nathan, wandering over to a lamp table. "They won't leave without Mark." He reached under the table and yanked a plastic bag out from under it.

End frowned.

"Hey, I went as long as I could," said Nathan, picking at the contents until he found a long, tightly-wrapped joint. "Want one?"

"Normally, I might," End said. "But in our present situation I think only one of us can afford to be floating up in the clouds. See if you can see where York's men are hiding while you're up there."

"Gotcha," said Nathan. He'd already lit up and took a long drag that impressed even End.

Opening the front door, End stood boldly looking out at the wide dreary expanse of land at the front of the house. There were not a lot of trees near the house, but there were enough to provide cover for them to get to the woods if they had to. As soon as York's men had completely encircled the house, it was really going to be the only way of escape, unless he decided to join Nathan up in the clouds. He did join Nathan on the couch looking out the front windows.

They'd just have to wait.

The sun must be just overhead. Except for darkness, and sunset, when the sun would be shining onto the front of the house, now was a prime opportunity for an assault. It just depended on the patience level of the men outside.

When nothing continued to happen, and for quite a while, it occurred to End that maybe York and his men weren't doing anything because they were all chasing Mark and Jenna instead. No, he thought again, he'd have seen movement from somewhere.

"How many men would you guess are out there?" End said to Nathan, by way of making conversation.

Nathan considered the possibilities, already a challenging thing for him. "Got to be billions," he said finally. "I mean India's got five billion people alone, don't they? And that's just one country. Why?"

End smiled. "Just curious."

Okay, Nathan would be completely unreliable for any constructive thinking for the rest of the day. At least he could bounce a few thoughts of his own off the boy. "I was thinking. If there were four trucks, then there isn't likely to be more than eight people total. Two to a truck. Right?"

Nathan slowly turned to End and jumped when he saw that End was looking at him. "What?"

"Right," continued End. "Now if they've got two singed guys laying on some salve out front and, say, two guys out back, that's really just four more guys, probably on the sides. Is there any way to get in from either side of the house?"

Nathan stared at End's mouth, then made a face. "Have you been talking to me?"

End smirked. "Watch for unwelcome guests while I check things out."

"Okie-dokie," Nathan said cheerfully.

End pulled his revolver from the waist of his trousers and left the room. A long hallway went down the northerly portion of the house, ending at a huge wall with clusters of portraits of people he didn't recognize, Mark's family presumably. He went very slowly into the room on the right and slid even more slowly up to the windows. One faced north, and the other faced east and showed the back yard of the house and the north side of the lab. It was a great vantage point to see anyone sneaking around there, and End could still see a fair amount of the meadow in the back. He glanced up to find the locks on the windows and panicked when he couldn't immediately spot them. He slid against the wall and stood up until he could see that they were both locked. With so many rooms in the house, defending it was going to be difficult anyway, and having open, inviting windows would not help.

End waited for a few minutes to see if he could spot any movement. Nothing but trees slowly shedding leaves and shivering in the wind. He went quickly to the door, ducking under windows and easy view from outside, and headed back up the hall he had come from. As he passed the living room area he saw that Nathan was marching, guard-like, back and forth in front of the door. The pulse laser leaned against his shoulder and wobbled unsteadily whenever he pivoted to go back in the other direction. He didn't notice End at all. His keen, well-honed senses must all be trained on the front yard.

At the far southerly end of the house, the rooms were configured the same as the north wing. He checked the room to the right so he could see the side and the front of the house. Everything was the same. Windows were locked, no movement outside, more trees shedding leaves.

An idea came to him, and he looked around for some wire. It took quite a while and he had to go up the hall a couple of rooms before he found a stack of coat hangers that might work just as well. In that southern-most room, he unwound the hangers and looped them back and forth along the curtain rods over both windows so they dangled down, tangling with each other. There was still plenty left over when he was done, and he joined several together and looped them around the bedposts and the doorknobs and whatever else he could hook or tie them to. It took less than he had expected, and he used the rest on the room just across the hall. That should make things interesting.

Just to be sure, End checked around the back of the house. It had only been half an hour since Mark and Jenna had left. York's men had to be in position by now. When he reached the kitchen, he thought he saw bushes at the tree line snapping back into place. He squatted down immediately and watched. His was not a safe place or a good position to see everything. He scanned the tree line a minute or two longer and returned to the living room to rejoin Nathan.

"Any sign of York or his friend?" asked End.

"Nope," Nathan said. "Not so much as an armed cow." He giggled at the thought.

End nodded down at the laser rifle. "That thing all charged up?"

"What thing? Oh this," said Nathan patting the rifle. "Not fully. But it's still got enough juice to take out an armed cow." He giggled again.

"Fire it, then. At those trees York ran around." End pointed at them. "Will it go that far?"

Nathan's sneer looked more like a facial tic. "No problem." He twisted a small dial at the barrel end and stepped up to the doorway.

"Be careful," said End.

"Yeah, okay, Mom."

Nathan sighted along the barrel at the clump of trees, took a deep breath so he could hold it while he fired, and instead fired as he was still breathing in.

A loud whoosh sound assaulted their ears and a blue bolt of something very close to lightning zapped out the door and across fifty yards of grassland. It veered toward a number of trees as it neared them but stuck more or less to its intended target. That target shook violently when it was struck and burst into flames. It wasn't a massive inferno, but it lit up the area quite nicely. The shadows of two men could be seen some distance behind the flaming tree, running farther away.

"That'll work," End said, satisfied.

* * *

"You are the biggest fuckup on the face of the Earth!" Mr. York screamed as he and Endicott staggered away from the burning tree.

He had already said it ten or twelve times since Endicott had regained consciousness. The exploding tree forced them to retreat farther away from the house, and this afforded him the opportunity to say it again. Possibly the worst part of it was that Mr. York was just getting his men in position. If they were doing their jobs, unfortunately, the two men in the back would have held their positions while the other four in front, seeing the flames, would have come to his aid.

Sure enough, the four men vaulted through the trees and into the clearing, weapons at the ready. Mr. York pondered how they possibly thought they would be aiding him by doing that.

"Shoot him," he told them in aggravation, pointing at Endicott.

Three of the four aimed their guns obediently, but confusion then reigned over discipline, and they stood there, awkwardly shifting from one foot to the other and looking at each other, pistols eventually pointing impotently at the ground.

Mr. York leaped to his feet and advanced on his men. "Dammit! You damn, stupid…" He howled and insulted and berated them long enough that the tree was totally engulfed in flames when he finished. When he turned around, Endicott was standing, but not very well.

"Feeling better?" said Mr. York.

"What do you think, man? No, I do not feel any better. Not at all."

Mr. York then leaned back and let go a punch that dropped Endicott instantly. "Then that probably didn't help," he said, rubbing his knuckles.

He turned again and ducked down so that he could move over just enough to see the inside of the house. "Somebody get me some binoculars," he said. The blast that torched the tree and knocked him down apparently flung his pair into the brush.

He scanned the windows on the front, starting at the ground level. Whoever was inside was being very smart. He hadn't seen any movement near the windows to tell him where anyone was, nor even how many there were. It was reasonable to think all four people were still in there, although there had probably been enough time for them to escape after Endicott had gotten himself and Mr. York's truck fried. The tree now in flames told him that at least one person was still in there.

The source of the blast could only have been that lethal-looking laser-beam weapon that Goggin's apprentice had been hefting when he'd first visited. Which meant that either he or Goggin himself was still inside. If it had been Mr. York in there, he would have sent Goggin out to escape and left the rest of them to distract Mr. York and his men. Of course, he'd noticed the kissy-face going on between Goggin and Jenna Telfair, so she could have fled with Goggin too. That meant that if the boy stayed, then that lunatic End would probably be there as well. He wouldn't have left the boy to fight grown men by himself. Mr. York had profiled Matthias End, and, although the man was definitely an amateur, without a doubt he had the brawn and the cunning to make things difficult.

On the other hand, his men had gotten to the back fairly quickly and hadn't seen anyone. So it was certainly possible all four were still in there.

He ought to take Endicott's advice and just demolish the place. It would be so easy. He could get out of these blue denim jeans that made him gag, clean his pores thoroughly of this dank region, and actually fly—fly!—back to the office. He could even blow up that damnable pickup truck he had been cursed with for so long.

But to agree with anything that pin-headed troglodyte had suggested went against every kind of self-respect he had for himself. If he could just ensnare Goggin, a little sodium pentathol applied in strategically-timed doses might just get the answers they desperately needed.

The business was in trouble.

General Micronet's profits were down world-wide. So it was time for the cutthroats to step in. The clandestine operatives. People like himself. Business was business, after all. It was a new decade and time for the next great product to come out, something to call the Product of the Decade or some such nonsense. This one would be Product of the Next Millennium, easily. Everyone was convinced, not just at General Micronet. But it was General Micronet that had to unveil something spectacular for the public, and do it quickly, and whatever it took to do that was whatever it took.

Mr. York glanced morosely back at his staff. "If you're all through milling around, perhaps you'd like to help me get this piece of business settled." He sent two of them to either side of the house, basically in the same positions they had been before the fire, but with different orders. The other two he sent around back to look for any sign that anyone had escaped.

He intended to step up closer and distract whoever really was inside, so his men could do their jobs. With as much power as the boy had unleashed, that laser surely could not have recharged enough to——

"Perhaps you could wait just one moment."

Mr. York knew exactly who it was. "Up so soon?" he said sarcastically. He turned around to see Endicott, staggering but on his feet, waving a revolver that veered off target as often as it was on target.

"You know," said Endicott, "I'm getting a little tired of people knocking me out all the time. I'll grant you I expected it from them, but I thought you might suppress your baser instincts long enough for us to get this business concluded. I see I was wrong."

Endicott reached into his coat and withdrew a small box with a button that he pushed. Mr. York waited for something to happen, an explosion, gunfire, jet aircraft powering overhead. Endicott must have expected something similar because he pushed the button again and again, until five black Hummers crashed through the trees, coming up the drive toward them. They mostly missed driving on the drive itself, obliterating bushes and saplings and half the fencing in the front yard, and slid to a halt in an imposing line. The men inside, all dressed in formidable black, piled out of the vehicles.

"That is so cool," mumbled Endicott.

Mr. York nodded. "They are impressive," he admitted. "So you're just going to kill them?"

Endicott opened his mouth in feigned horror, then blandly said, "Yes." He continued to point the gun at Mr. York while he waved over a huge man who had emerged from the first Hummer. The other men were squatting on a knee to the side of their vehicles, as if they were huddling up before the big game. "Keep track of Yorkenheimer here, wouldya please?" The solid fellow frowned, folded his arms, and settled into an unblinking stare at Mr. York's nostrils.

More delays, Mr. York thought with a sigh. He watched as Endicott sent six other men back into three of the Hummers. The rest followed him up to where they were just out of sight of the front of the house. He issued orders and waved his arms in circles and pointed at imaginary spots.

"I'd hit them from the sides, if I were you," Mr. York said loudly from where he stood. "I was watching them while you were asleep, and they seem to be mostly at the front."

Endicott sneered in contempt. "Thank you, Old York. Appreciate your input, but I'll just ignore you if you don't mind."

"Suit yourself."

Mr. York watched as Endicott ordered the foot soldiers on and turned away to survey the house. Suddenly he yelled out "Stop!" The men returned and he issued new orders. A couple of the men glanced at Mr. York, who smiled. The moron had taken the bait. One man said something back to Endicott and he became strongly animated and even poked at the man's chest. The man's face was expressionless, and the lack of warmth was obvious. He pointed at the front of the house and spoke again. Endicott poked again at the man's chest and also pointed at the house. The man said one more thing, this time with clear menace in his eyes. He must not have liked getting poked. But he said nothing more.

Endicott shouted "Now! Move out!" to the men and they stared at him with something not far off from the same contempt Endicott had shown for Mr. York, and vice versa. They were obviously professionals, or at least thought they were, and viewed Endicott as some kind of ignorant paper-pusher. But he had the bankroll, so he gave the orders. They moved out.

Turning to Mr. York with something of a sweat beginning, Endicott tried to grin with the same arrogance he'd come into the project with. But he wasn't feeling it.

The men fanned out in threes to the left and right of the building, heading in the vicinity of where Mr. York had positioned his own men. He expected that his men would move well away so they wouldn't be noticed. Endicott's men had just about reached the sides of the house when they banked sharply and ran along the front of the house, stopping until they were about twenty feet from the front door on each side of it. They dropped to a knee and waited.

The three occupied Hummers howled to life and leaped forward. The massively treaded tires tore up the ground as they spun around the burnt tree, heading directly for the front, just as Mr. York had expected. He knew Endicott wouldn't take a suggestion from him, even if it meant doing something totally idiotic. His thugs must have thought it was idiotic too.

Mr. York watched as the three Hummers raced across the yard. They separated to go around trees but joined when they finally reached the steps.

Endicott screamed "Go, go, go!" Then he watched as the three Hummers parted ways. The one on the left and the one on the right seemed to falter, accelerated uncertainly and rammed straight into the heavy stone pillars on either side of the steps going up to the entrance. The one in the center roared up the steps quite impressively at first, then quickly lost momentum on the very steep incline, and finally came to a stop, wedged between two matching heavy stone pillars at the top of the steps.

"What the hell?" was all Endicott could say.

Of the two vehicles at the bottom of the steps, only one person staggered out, the others presumably unconscious or worse. Both occupants in the lone Hummer that had made it to the top were awake and trying to climb out. With both doors jammed, they were forced to climb out the back. The six men waiting to the side joined up with the three survivors, and they began to climb over the Hummer to get at the entrance. They made good progress despite the steepness of the vehicle and its high clearance above the steps.

But just as they reached the front of the roof, two figures came out the front door of the house with long objects that looked like they might be metal, like crowbars. In a matter of seconds they freed the Hummer from its imprisonment, and it began to roll. It rolled quickly and with precision straightness, as finely engineered automobiles do. As it reached the bottom of the steps, a familiar blue bolt of lightning arced out from the front door and zapped a large portion of the nine men. Half fell off as the Hummer veered this way and that, running backward over the uneven ground. It continued to roll until it was halfway back to where the bankroll waited.

"Goddammit!" screamed Endicott. He stomped and kicked at the ground and shook his fists at his cooked hired guns. He spun violently around and headed in the direction of the two remaining Hummers.

"Good thing you didn't listen to me," said Mr. York as Endicott huffed briskly by. Even his brutish guard snickered as Endicott climbed up and yanked closed the door of one of the monstrous trucks. He sat inside and sulked as his men staggered and carried one another back to their launching point behind the charred tree.

Mr. York looked back at the house. The Hummer that was halfway back to them had its hood and roof smoking lightly in the breeze. He half-smiled as he watched his men approach one of the Hummers still near the house. In just seconds they had started it, and in the same amount of time it disappeared behind trees on the north end of the house.

Mr. York turned to watch the burnt mercenaries one by one sink beaten to the ground. Their fine black clothes were dirty and torn and smoked noticeably. His appointed guard left him to help his comrades, or at least lend moral support to their grievances, as they checked for broken bones and dislodged fillings, and growled about additional compensation due to unusually adverse working conditions.

Mr. York disappeared.

Chapter 16

Running. And running. And more running. It seemed to Mark as if they had been running for years. He checked his watch. It had been half an hour. Crap. At this rate they wouldn't get a mile away before they were caught. He looked back at Jenna, who had stopped to sit on a rock, breathing in huge gulps of air. He went back to sit beside her.

"Are you all right?" he asked, breathing hard himself.

"Yeah, yeah. Just shook me...that last fall."

Mark nodded. In the half hour they had been fleeing for their lives, she had fallen down a hill, tripped three times—once so badly that she was sure she'd broken something—and gotten her hair caught in branches, well, pretty much constantly. Mark never became impatient with her, first because he was far too enamored with every pore of her being, and second, because he himself had run into a tree. In fact, all of her mishaps combined hadn't delayed them any longer than the time it took him to collect his wits after losing the game of chicken with the very beefy oak.

"Okay," said Jenna and she started off again. Mark followed.

They had run along the river the whole way, hoping to come along to a boat or, better still, the police. But nothing nearly so helpful had appeared so far. Just more river. It wound so often it was hard to stay alongside, and the banks became steep or muddy very suddenly. Mark had suggested they stay away from the paths that had been worn away by tourists and wildlife, on the theory that they wouldn't be noticed as easily. Jenna had thought that a little silly since she hadn't seen a house in any direction, and the leaves were falling at such a pace now that the trees weren't likely to give them any cover at all. And it slowed them down immensely having to wade through the heavy brush and ground cover. Tree limbs whipped at them, and spider webs clung to their faces, until Jenna decided she would rather be captured than endure another minute getting beaten up by the flora and fauna. Mark was perfectly content to do the same.

They had gone only a dozen steps or so from the rock when a colossal whoosh came from behind them. Both ducked instantly. Jenna looked around quizzically, then got back up and started forward. She stopped when Mark didn't move. "That was the pulse laser," he said, looking back in the direction of the house. "The dumb kid turned it up too high. That kind of discharge will do worse than just stand their hair on end." He grinned at Jenna. "I'd hate to see what got hit." Then he frowned. "As long as it wasn't my house."

Jenna smiled, and they were off again. For another half an hour they tried to keep to a consistent pace, which was similar to that of a fit and trim eighty-year-old couple. Jenna slipped on piles of leaves, and Mark tripped over a tree root. It helped that they stuck to the path. Until the path ended at the banks of the river.

Mark was startled to see how much the Pomme had widened. It had become almost three times its size back at his house. It flowed serenely and quietly, the occasional rocks to tumble over or fallen trees to work around.

"Now what?" asked Jenna.

"See any boats?"

They looked up and down the banks. Jenna jumped suddenly and pointed at the other side of the river, a hundred feet away. An actual boat, as ordered. Only it was upside down with a gaping hole in the hull. "Yep," Mark nodded, "that's a boat. You wanna go get it or shall I?"

Jenna glared.

They traced back up the path and then left it, still travelling parallel to the river, fighting through trees and the heavy undergrowth. As they traveled, a sizable hill began to take shape to their right, running alongside the river and sandwiching Mark and Jenna between hill and river.

Minutes passed, the going agonizingly slow, when a hawk squealed from some distance to the north. Mark dropped like a rock to the ground. "What was that?" he said, an ear cocked.

Jenna listened. "I don't hear anything."

"The bird, the bird, didn't you hear a bird caw or twitter or screech or…something?"

"Yeah, so?"

"It came from the north."

"Right. So what?"

"That could be a signal to someone."

"Yes, Mark. Another bird. Can we go?"

"Not a bird. Someone with Mr. York."

"How do you know that?"

"I don't know, but it could be." The bird squealed again, this time to the east, directly over the river. "Did you hear that?" he ducked again.

"Yes, Mark, it's the same bird. Flying over the river. Come on. The nice little birdie is not going to attack you."

It was Mark's turn to glare. Maybe he wasn't as enamored with her as he thought. In fact she was getting irritating.

The battle with the trees and brush resumed for several more minutes before they came to a path. It meandered behind them and up the now towering hill that had neared to within thirty feet of where they stood. The path wound halfway up, then down, doubled back briefly, and ended up very close to where their earlier path had ended.

"This is the same path we just left!" Jenna shouted.

Mark just looked at her.

"We could have taken it and gotten to this spot in half the time."

"Wandering around all over the place like that?" replied Mark. "I hardly think so."

Jenna put her fists on her hips. "I bet if we went back to the earlier path and raced I'd get here on the path faster than you could through the trees."

Mark leaned forward. "Go right ahead. I'm not particularly interested in conducting pointless and time-consuming experiments when someone's trying to kill us."

They glared unblinkingly at one another until they both realized that Mark might be right. Looking north one more time, they took off running down the path.

After what seemed surely to have been several hours of running, the river steadily growing bigger and louder, the trees thickening some and the hill rising taller and nearer, Mark was disappointed to see by his watch that it had been only another half an hour.

"Let's rest a second," he said, slumping to the ground. Jenna was only too glad to go along, immediately collapsing. Both gradually leaned back to lie on their backs, breathing heavily.

It was not fit work for two unfit people, a desk jockey and a lab rat.

Some minutes later, the rush of water over rocks came to their ears and brought them a much-needed calm. The trees rustled, and leaves in oranges and yellows fell around them. Though the hill blotted out much of it, the sky was clear as they looked overhead. Only three clouds crossed an otherwise clear, bright blue day.

Another bird flew by and Mark tensed.

Jenna glanced over at him. "Was that one spying on us too?"

"Okay, okay, it's a little ridiculous. I know it. There's no way birds are spying on us. It's completely paranoid." He thought a second. "You know though? A multinational conglomerate would use remote controlled airplanes or helicopters or even those scaled-down dirigibles they fly around in sports arenas. Or—"

Mark abruptly stopped talking and looked straight up. His mouth hung open momentarily and then he shouted, "My God, we've got to get to cover!"

He scrambled over to a tree and hid under it. Jenna crawled over next to him.

"No, not next to the tree," he said, "under it. Under it!"

"What? Why?"

"Satellites! I should have thought of that before. General Micronet has control of weather satellites, don't they? Don't they do some surveillance for Egypt or Israel or somebody in the Middle East?"

"I've never heard that."

"Of course they do. Don't you read stuff on the Internet? Every subversive site on the web talks about it. That's how they do that pin-point bombing." He licked his lips and peered up through the treetops, as if expecting to see a great eye in the sky. "They'll find us. Any minute now—"

Jenna stood up and fought with him as he tried to pull her back under the tree. "What's the matter with you?" she said. "I thought scientists were supposed to use logic now and then. They're not going to bomb us. They aren't even going to use satellites. You know why?"

Mark shook his head, no. But he was terribly hopeful she might know something he didn't.

"Because most satellites are geostationary. It would take hours to adjust them enough to put them over us. Maybe even days. And the ones that move around have to have their momentum slowed or accelerated and that takes a whole lot of time."

Mark frowned. "I knew that."

"Oh, of course." Jenna frowned in mock exaggeration. "And you call yourself a man of science. My cell phone knows more about satellites than you do."

"I have a very focused area of expertise," Mark said, standing but still eyeing the suspect sky. "Everything else just has to take a lower priority. You see, Jenna, not every—"

"Please. I've seen your lab. You have no area of expertise. You dream something up and then you build it. What you have is the most exceptional persistence and ingenuity of anyone I've ever met." She smiled at him. "And that'll get you farther than half the MIT grads on the planet."

He grinned awkwardly and looked down. "Well, it's nothing really. I—"

"Why haven't you ever tried to kiss me?" she said suddenly.

"What?" Mark stared at her, thrown by the sudden end to the insults and compliments and the start of this new...topic. "Uh, well, I didn't want to ruin...I mean, I...You always seem so professional about things...I just...I didn't want to mess up our professional relationship...you know...in case you didn't want to kiss me back."

Jenna stood as well, and they gazed at one another for what seemed like a very long time, though it was still much less than the half an hour Mark was so bad at estimating. "Shall we get going?" he said finally, vaguely.

She nodded, lost in those uncomplicated eyes masking the mad genius that might well change the future of civilization. Or get the two of them lost.

As they trotted along the path now, Mark periodically went over toward the banks of the Pomme, looking for a canoe or a boat or a raft. At this point, a simple inner tube or floating tree limb would do. The hill—was it a mountain now?—had shifted so that it was almost directly in front of them, and at any point they could well come face to face with an impassible vertical cliff. The river was the only realistic way around it, without losing time doubling back to look for a way over or around the hill.

Up ahead—difficult to tell how far because they couldn't see it—was a road. They'd heard a car horn not long ago, and from time to time, the vibrational hum of vehicles passing across a bridge carried over the water to them.

The next time Mark jumped over to check the banks of the river, he didn't immediately jump back. Twenty yards down the way he spotted a beach of sorts. Not altogether big, but big enough to have a family, their dog, and a canoe enjoying the afternoon together.

When he returned, he had an expression that Jenna found worrisome. "Did you find anything?" she asked.

"Follow me," he said and walked along, quickly but calmly, toward the family.

The path connected briefly with the beach before continuing on. Mark walked smartly up to the family. "Good afternoon, folks, I'm a ranger for this park…uh, this is another ranger." He pointed at Jenna. "I'm terribly sorry, but I'm going to have to ask you to leave right now. We're going to have to close off this beach and the surrounding waterway."

The father stepped forward uncertainly. "What's wrong?"

Mark blinked. "Ah, well, we have a water moccasin infestation upriver, and we expect it to reach here within the next five minutes or so. We'd have notified you sooner, but most of the rangers have been busy trying to contain the infestation. Very iffy proposition wading in after the little buggers. So if you'll just pick up your things very quickly and leave, we'll get this thing taken care of."

The family was quite swift, panicky in fact, in throwing its things into two wicker baskets. The father started toward the canoe when Mark stopped him. "Just leave that, sir. We'll have someone take it to the entrance to the park. You can pick it up later this evening if you like."

The father nodded agreeably, no doubt not wanting to drag the thing all the way back to wherever they came from. "Where do we go?" he asked.

"Just follow the path."

As the family disappeared around a corner, the mother said, "Weren't they nice? I didn't know this was a park."

Mark and Jenna stood at attention, trying to act like police officers in a forest—they didn't know how forest rangers acted—until they judged the family well gone. The canoe took some doing to get through the sand and into the water. "Would this be our first illegal act as fugitives? Stealing someone's canoe?" said Jenna as she pulled at a seat.

"No, impersonating a park ranger is probably illegal too. The canoe would be second."

The Pomme de Terre was still very wide, and the current didn't jerk the canoe too much as they climbed in. It slid out into the center where a more brisk channel caught it and sent it downstream.

Mark sat down immediately, found an oar, and started paddling, leaning forward, rapid strokes, two left, two right. He hadn't been canoeing in years, but it came quickly back to him. The pace of the current was a little strange though. He expected to go much faster than——

He stopped paddling. At the other end of the canoe sat Jenna, paddling hard as well, leaning forward. She flailed away and slapped the surface a little more than was to his taste, and she had no hesitancy in paddling on her left side for seven or eight strokes and then switching to her right side for three or four more before returning to the left for one or two.

It was how she sat that bothered him. "Would you turn around please?" he said as patiently as the situation could possibly allow. "Downstream is behind you."

"I know that! I was trying to turn us around."

"We don't need to turn around. Just you."

"I can't steer from the front of the boat."

"Good, because I'm steering."

"You?" Jenna laughed. "You, the great inventor, are going to steer? Do you even know what this is? I'm surprised you haven't fallen out already."

"Is that so? That back there is my land from birth, Telfair. Do you think I ignored a whole bunch of water pouring through it every day for three decades?"

"Yes! In fact, I'm surprised you haven't crashed into more trees than just one."

"Oh no, I think the monopoly on graceless klutzery in this canoe is yours, miss nine-to-five cubical inmate."

"Mr. Cold-Fusion-Fanatic!"

"Miss Menace-to-Restaurants!"

"Mr. Lab-Jerk!"

As they discussed their differences and minor shortcomings and exchanged witticisms, the river widened still further for a short interval, the current slowing to a meandering pace, and the canoe began to turn sideways. Neither occupant could say they were steering any longer.

"This is ridiculous!" shouted Jenna. "They could be right behind us."

"Exactly. So turn around and let's get going."

"I've steered canoes before," Jenna insisted. "I've gone through rivers a tenth of this size with ten times the current." She noticed their sideways position, which was circling with no one steering. "Now look what you did!"

"Me? We'd be fine if you'd just let me steer."

"Oh, a woman isn't capable of steering, is that it?"

"Why is it that every time women don't get their way, they have to make it a gender thing?"

"Because it is! You yourself just said 'every time *women* blah blah blah.' You just made it an issue."

"It wouldn't even have come up if you hadn't said anything!"

"Oh, I'm sure it would have come up. You're just like every other man. Dim and always preoccupied with breasts."

The last comment threw Mark off his prepared response, and he sat there with his eyes narrowed and his mouth open, ready to speak but with nothing to say.

Meanwhile, the Pomme was beginning to narrow again as the canoe continued going sideways. Breaks in the water began to appear where obstructions—rocks, tree trunks, and lodged debris—hid just under the surface. The current gradually separated into three channels.

"A bridge," Mark said, pointing downstream a couple hundred feet away. "I'd have seen it earlier if you weren't pestering me. You're the bane of my existence, woman!"

"Thank you."

"We've got to get to the side."

"What for?"

"So we can get help on the road."

"We don't want people to see us on the road, Mark."

"Yes we do, Jenna."

"No, we don't. It could be them."

"Now who's paranoid?"

The canoe crashed into obstructions with a jarring regularity. The river continued to narrow. Fortunately, where they were in the center had the slowest current of the channels. Mark began paddling furiously, trying to at least get one end of the canoe pointed downstream. Jenna did the same.

Mark and Jenna both suddenly jerked sideways and almost lost their oars as the canoe slammed into a pile of rocks. It slid around the side of the rocks so that Mark's back was facing downstream. He growled but spun around so he could see where they were going as the canoe ground into the shallows. It became stuck and water poured powerfully against either side. Mark pushed down on the rocks with his oar and the force of the water behind propelled them on. The current was swift enough that it became more of a concern to aim the canoe than to make it go fast.

The bridge had become very close, but the river was now extremely narrow, the water hurling along, vying for the very small space.

"Head for the bank on the left," Mark shouted above the roar of water crashing over a growing number of rocks. He paddled hard on the canoe's right side, stroke after stroke.

Gradually the front headed for the left side. But the bridge was practically overhead.

"What are you doing?" Jenna shouted.

Water foamed everywhere and splashed over everything in its path. The canoe was turning sideways again, despite the force of the current.

"You're heading for the wrong side!" she shouted again.

"The left!" He shouted as well. "On the left!"

Jenna must have agreed, because the boat leveled to running along with the flow of the channel. They slid into an even faster channel and the canoe leaped over rocks, scraping the aluminum as it went with mad enthusiasm.

The bank neared to within ten feet of them, but the rocks and spitting whitewater were everywhere. Mark paddled short rapid strokes in a last ditch effort. But he could feel them leaving the bridge behind.

"Look out!" screamed Jenna.

Directly in front of them waited a monstrous tree, broken by lightning or age, leaning out over the water, and lodged precisely in the line of their path. Mark paddled in blind panic and succeeded in angling the canoe all wrong once again.

They hit the tree with a fairly square impact, and the force merely knocked both paddlers sideways. The level of the river dropped in the next instant and they shot out like a jet ski into the center of the river.

The bridge was now a couple hundred feet behind them.

Jenna sat up from the bottom of the boat and peered over the side. "Did we make it?"

As the canoe shot through more rapids, and wrenched over and around rocks that jutted up out of the water, Mark stared glumly ahead. "What do you think?"

Chapter 17

The afternoon was winding down. The sun angled in the direction of sleep, and not a minute too soon. The great star had shone on the pathetic goings-on of human beings near the town of Brookbury for the span of half a day. It had tried to brighten the appalling behavior of a band of men in a very tiny area of a very tiny world, when it could very probably have made better use of the light elsewhere. It had even made a last-ditch effort to warm the countenances of all involved, despite its ever-growing orbital distance, but the fools just kept at it. 'So let them fight amongst themselves in the dark' about summed up the sun's feelings on the matter.

Matthias End could not have agreed more. Ordinarily, the cover of darkness worked to the advantage of the smaller forces in a battle. They could come and go at will, darting into enemy encampments, wreaking havoc in their ranks, then darting out like a bad dream. Unless of course, the smaller force was stuck in a house surrounded by the enemy encampment, outnumbered ten to one, facing soldiers all looking in their direction.

The excitement from the last assault had died down hours ago. Windows had been shot out, and smoke and tear gas had been fired. Nathan's ingenuity had saved them again when he had turned on a fan and aimed it at the gas canisters until the air cleared enough for End to find them and throw them back out the window. The majority of the men outside were unable to find any windows with gas everywhere outside, and those who got close received a jolt from the now highly respected pulse laser rifle.

End returned from another stroll around the house, looking for infiltrators. The house's thick stone walls were proving to be a boon. York's men couldn't crash through it with trucks, or blow holes in it, and the smooth surface of the walls coupled with the slate roof made it impossible to climb up or rappel down. The windows were higher above the ground than End had realized, and apparently York hadn't figured out how to get to them.

As a result, End and Nathan had remained safe, the siege still held at bay.

Nathan had been asleep when End left to roam the house, but he was awake when End returned to the living room. Nathan's eyes were hazy, both from sleep and from the marijuana he'd consumed, smoked, and otherwise soaked into his pores all day. It had seemed prudent for End to stand well away when Nathan next unleashed the energy of the pulse laser. The seventeen-year-old was smart and capable, but still young. And no child that skinny could retain his faculties after devouring as much weed as he had.

End dropped into a chair and watched out front. An occasional flashlight shot across the open space, illuminating tall weeds and tree limbs. The constant flickering light of a fire on the other side of the charred tree meant York had decided to slow things down, and think things through a little more carefully. Remembering the impetuous stooge who had leaped up next to York and triggered Nathan's response made End consider the possibility of dissension in the enemy ranks. That could be something worth making use of in the future.

He looked over at Nathan and was surprised to see the boy staring at him.

"So you're a devil-worshipper now, huh?" said Nathan, enunciating the word 'devil' with distinct dislike. The drugs had made him moody now, it seemed.

End smiled and went back to scanning the front of the house. "It's possible to no longer be a clergyman, and still believe in God, isn't it?"

"No," said Nathan.

End looked at Nathan, but didn't reply. Out front, he noticed the flashlights were all moving toward the fire. A meeting about to start.

"Why'd you quit?"

End sighed and didn't look back. "A number of reasons, mostly stemming from my inability to deal with the down side of the job."

"Down side? What down side?"

"The congregation."

"What, the whole congregation?"

"Most of it."

"What did they do?"

"Be themselves, I suppose. I'd rather not talk about it, Nathan."

"Well, I want to. I'm pretty religious, you know. Sort of. Mom is, anyway. I'm not up on all the lines and stories and things, but I do know when you get the call, you don't turn away."

"You don't know the first thing about it."

"So what was the matter? Didn't like not being able to have sex? Or are you one of those anti-lifers? Or you liked to marry guys to each other?"

End laughed. Outside, the air was still. The fire burned bright. The sunlight was weakening to a distant red burst, half-covered by the trees.

"What was it?" Nathan persisted.

End looked intently at Nathan, ready to cut the whole conversation short. Instead he sighed again. "I found the two-faced insincerity of most people to be too much to bear. I bore it for ten years, which is not a short time for the average priest. I just couldn't do it any longer." He slouched a little in the chair, closed his eyes, and leaned his head back. "People do things that are not good. They lie that they are good. They confess anonymously for being bad only when they absolutely have to. They gain a meaningless forgiveness from a priest who has no understanding what the person has done or why they did it. And then, with a clear conscience, that person goes off and does the same bad thing all over again."

"But they're supposed to be forgiven, aren't they?"

"Sure, but they're supposed to at least make a token effort not to do it again."

"How do you know they didn't?"

End straightened uncomfortably. "Being a priest means hearing about all sorts of things from all sorts of people. In a small parish like I was in, you find out a lot. When a man confesses to hitting his neighbor with a shovel and another man confesses to hitting his neighbor with a hedge trimmer because the neighbor hit him with a shovel, you can figure out what is going on. After a while you recognize voices and put them with faces. They tell you all the wonderful things they do, to your face, then hide behind a screen and admit they lied about the whole thing."

He sat up and leaned forward to see more of the yard. The flashlights were on again and pointed everywhere like spotlights at the opening of a new movie theater. He looked back at Nathan, who had folded his arms and was unhappily staring out the window.

"Hey, junior," said End, "it ain't no big thing. People change jobs all the time."

"Not when you work for God."

"I didn't work for God. I worked for the Church. There's a huge difference, believe me. I don't get paid by the Church now, but I get paid a whole lot more from God, I'm hoping anyway. If I can survive this and get back to Goggin."

"What do you mean?" Nathan's face screwed up in bewilderment.

"Goggin's my test," said End. "He's going to bring me back. I didn't see it at first, but I do now."

If such a thing was possible, Nathan's face scrunched up even more. "What? What in the world does that mean?"

"You know what? You ask too damn many questions."

"You shouldn't say 'damn'."

"Damn, I'm sorry. I feel damn awful." End stood up and headed to the kitchen. "Damn. Which way is the damn kitchen?"

Nathan smirked and shouted "It's down the damn hallway, you damn ass." The grass wasn't even remotely out of his system yet. He could hear End rummaging around the kitchen for something. He took the opportunity to light up and take another hit or two.

Just as he exhaled the sweet fumes, an explosion went off on the south end of the house. "Nathan! Watch the front!" End shouted at him from the kitchen.

Seconds later an explosion went off on the north end of the house.

"Do you see anything?" Nathan shouted. He grunted as he struggled to get the backpack for the laser rifle on.

"No," End shouted back. "They could just be feeling us out."

"Sounds kinky," Nathan shouted and giggled almost to hysterics. After he calmed down, he decided it wasn't all that funny. He really needed to kick this habit.

He was about to stand in front of the house and scare everybody when automatic weapons went off from the back of the house, and glass shattered so loudly that he was sure every window must have been hit. Nathan was on the floor before the bullets exploded through the windows in the living room and ripped across the furniture and far wall.

From his hiding position, he could hear trucks—those Hummers probably—moving toward the house, away from the house, and around the house. More explosions went off directly over his head.

It was like a war, he thought.

Nathan sat up when the bullets stopped flying into the living room. He could hear them still hitting the walls and everything else in the back of the house. He could also hear what sounded like a struggle. He eased up over the sofa but couldn't see anything. The kitchen was dark, and the night was even darker through the kitchen windows.

Glass cracked behind him. Nathan froze, hoping he might not be seen in the shadows, then realized that was pointless because a lamp was still lit, and whoever it was could see him plain as day. He turned slowly.

Standing in the front doorway was Mr. York, looking directly at Nathan. Without thinking, Nathan dove to the floor and scrambled around trying to find the laser rifle. The pack was still only half on and it clanked against chair legs and eventually flipped off his back and onto the ground. Nathan couldn't think of anything else to do but lie there and pretend to be dead.

"Are you all right, Nathan?" said Mr. York pleasantly, his voice calm and friendly even with explosions and roaring truck engines working to drown him out.

That surely couldn't be the voice of the same person who was so evil the last time he was here. Nathan peered up over the seat of a chair. "Yes," he ventured.

"Let me help you up," said Mr. York and he lifted Nathan up to a squatting position. Nathan noticed the laser rifle lying at Mr. York's feet. Mr. York also saw it, but didn't move to grab at it. Even after all the searing pain and havoc Nathan had caused. Frankly he was dumbfounded.

"Thanks," he said uncertainly. Mr. York grabbed his hand and hauled him up onto the sofa.

"There's not much time, Nathan. I need to know where Mark is. I'm sure you have doubts about my character, but I swear to you that I didn't start this. There is a group of people who do similar work to what I do and they are firing all the bullets and crashing trucks into the house. They're after Mark, Nathan."

Nathan was plainly not inclined to believe him and Mr. York knew it.

"Nathan, I could easily grab this fine weapon of yours and shoot you with it, or shoot you with my own gun. But I haven't done that, have I? Didn't you hear me offer Mark a job? It was my idiotic associate who jumped out of nowhere and attacked you, not me. All I want is to bring Mark back to my company and get him to work on that miraculous invention of his. I will do everything in my power to accomplish that. Obviously that means I don't want to kill him. Do you understand me, Nathan? I don't want to kill him. And I don't want to kill you, either. I don't even want to kill Mr. End. Now I need your help. Where is Mark?"

What Nathan had thought were sounds of struggle became very clearly a huge brawl going on in the kitchen or somewhere near there. The bullets were not going off inside the house anymore, remaining instead outside with the Hummers racing around the house. End was not going to help him with this sticky little problem. Not that he was ever around to deal with any other problems.

"Nathan? Is Mark here?"

Nathan finally relented. "No."

Mr. York smiled. "Okay, great. Where is he?"

Nathan looked at him and then looked back in the kitchen.

"Nathan, please. These men will find him, and someone has to be there to protect him."

Nathan bit his lip.

✳ ✳ ✳

Night had come to Brookbury, and the trucks circled Mark Goggin's house like buzzards. The Hummers' headlights beamed across the house and through windows, into the trees and at each other. More than once, a Hummer sideswiped the house or another Hummer. Rifles, shotguns, and pistols fired bullets into the house intermittently with little effect.

In the shadows just outside the front door, Mr. York waited for the right moment and trotted through a gap between two of the wildly careening vehicles. He was in the trees before the next one had come around the house. The house still stood, despite who knew how many sticks of dynamite Endicott had thrown at it or how many times the Hummers had rammed it.

He turned away in aggravation. There were a lot quieter ways than this to accomplish what was needed. No amount of money paid to the sheriff or the state police would keep them away if Endicott blew up the house, although that seemed an impossibility at this point, even for him.

Mr. York glanced at his men. "I know where Goggin's headed. Let's go."

✳ ✳ ✳

Drake Endicott watched as his men pummeled away at some unfortunate fool in the back of the house. Oh, what a glorious way of life! No other job could compare to the thrills and excitement and never-ending surprises that came with what he did. And it happened practically every day! In his opinion, people like him should be celebrated as heroes of the country. What he did was just like all the stuff the CIA says: 'People don't want to know how it is that they have all the perks and live the good life. They just want it. And it's the CIA that gives it to them.'

Well, it took people like Drake Endicott to make sure people got all the really good perks. The CIA could only make sure Americans got diamonds relatively cheap. Just any old diamonds. It was Drake Endicott who could make sure the diamonds were the finest in the world and cost next to nothing. But no one knew all the hard work he did to bring those diamonds to the wallets of the adoring consumer.

So it was a good thing he enjoyed what he did.

The unfortunate fool, Endicott had been told by one of his men, was Matthias End. He was actually putting up a good fight. A couple of Endicott's wimpier men had been thrown out of the windows, landing with a thud or a crunch on the ground. He snarled gloomily. Attrition was playing hell on his team. He'd already lost eight of the twenty he'd come with. The two shown to the window by End were definitely out of the picture. Two others had staggered back from the ill-fated Hummer-ramming with broken ribs. Three had met unpleasant fates wading through clothes-hanger booby traps in a couple of the rooms in the house. The last one had completely disappeared, along with his vehicle. A chicken-ass turncoat, no doubt. Never mind. Endicott would hunt him down when this was over. Loyalty was prime in the corporate intelligence community.

In the meantime, he'd have to get hold of the coalition and get some more men. These twenty had come from twenty different corporations, and none of them could agree on anything. Maybe he could just request employees from his own firm. At least he could fire those when they screwed up.

Endicott watched the battle going on in the house until a Hummer pulled up next to him. The driver leaned out. "Endicott! That missing Hummer! It's heading out the front driveway. It's got half a dozen men in it."

"What?"

The joy of the moment quickly disappeared. He had managed to avoid putting all the facts together so he could enjoy obliterating the house, which hadn't worked out all that well. But now there was no getting around the fact that there were only two people in the house. They knew about the boy guarding the front from the moment he opened fire on them with that probably very illegal thing that threw lightning bolts. No one was upstairs. And with End identified, that meant Goggin and his girlfriend were gone. The Hummer getting away had to be York and his men.

And if he was leaving, then he must know where Goggin was.

Endicott rolled the same facts back through his head twice more and came up with two other possibilities. He growled in aggravation. Hell with it. When in doubt, go with the aggressive thought.

"Everybody into the trucks!" he shouted. "Move it, move it, move it!" He pointed at End. "Shoot him or leave him." Endicott stepped into the truck that was next to him.

The last remaining man in the kitchen looked at End and jumped out the window. He had to run hard to catch the last Hummer as it rumbled away from the house, following the others over the trees in the direction of the main road.

Chapter 18

"Are we there yet?" said Jenna Telfair. She suppressed a giggle for a second then burst into laughter.

Mark Goggin didn't see anything funny about it. He leaned his head up to look at her. "Where? Were we trying to get to some place specific?" He was awfully afraid he hadn't been paying attention if that particular detail had been discussed.

Jenna leaned her head up to look at him as well. "It was a joke."

"Oh. Well then…ha, ha ha," said Mark blandly.

Mutually aggravated, they both sank their heads back down and stared up into the sky. It being dark, there wasn't much to see. Clouds had obscured the heavens for a short time after the sun disappeared behind the trees, but they had cleared away not long afterward, and now the stars were out for all to see. Even the moon was shining, boldly white and nearly full.

Shortly after the excitement back at the bridge had died down, they had vented their wrath at one another until both were emotionally drained, and then they paddled furiously for a while longer before it became hard to see. That was a good enough excuse to rest. They'd done the best they could. If they were meant to be caught, so be it.

Now they sat at either end of the canoe, facing one another and lying on their backs. It wasn't that they were arguing again over who should steer, it was just where they had collapsed after one last argument over when to rest. Both wanted to stop, but neither wanted to be blamed if they were caught because they had been the one to suggest stopping. In the end, the decision was made simply because they could no longer lift their oars.

They had been resting for the past ten minutes. Jenna still wasn't sure she'd be able to lift her oar to go any farther. She was so tired. If a snake jumped into the boat, it would just have to eat her without bothering her about it.

The current was almost nonexistent in the center of the river where they were. The Pomme de Terre at present took a wide, plodding course through the forest. If they hadn't been so tired, they'd have been alarmed by how little they were progressing. Tired as they were, though, they could probably have ignored anything they came upon, short of Niagara Falls.

It was a warm evening for autumn. Gnats and dragonflies circled overhead, and the crickets were in full chorus and in stereo, coming from both banks of the river. Trees on both sides took turns leaning out over the water, dropping leaves that floated slowly down. The stars twinkled on the water and nary a rock could be found to jostle the canoe in its path.

For most any other new couple, meandering down such a river as Mark and Jenna did would have been exceedingly romantic. For at least as many, such a moment might never happen even once in their lifetimes. But for these two, it wasn't even an afterthought. They were much more inclined to dump each other overboard. Romance be hanged.

After an hour of rest and trying to pretend the other person didn't exist, it was time for them to get on with things. Mark sat up gingerly, rubbing where the sides of the canoe had dug into his back. Jenna stubbornly continued to pretend that he didn't exist, remaining on her back, and staring upside down in the opposite direction.

Mark watched her working hard to make him invisible. Eventually, the silence between them became too long. Someone had to break it, he thought.

"You've never steered a canoe in your life, have you," he said.

Jenna raised her head very slowly and fixed him with a spiteful glare. "What did you say?"

"You heard me."

She sat up and gasped "Oww!" Terrible kinks in her muscles had knotted up and down her back. "I did as good a job as you could have," she said, trying to rub knots she couldn't reach.

Mark started to unleash a savage retort regarding the unfortunate bridge incident, but they'd been through that already. Instead, he looked down and watched the canoe flow through the water. "This is the farthest I've ever been down this river. My family usually stopped at the, uh, bridge."

Jenna eyed him warily, expecting to hear another negative appraisal on her rowing skills. She found herself looking down at the water too. It was mesmerizing to watch the ripples carry away from the canoe's hull. Even at night, everything around them glistened and shined.

"I've never steered a canoe before," she finally admitted.

"Really?" he grinned, and she started to erupt at him again but didn't.

"Actually, this is my first time in a canoe," she added.

Mark stopped smiling. "Really? I mean…I'm sorry to hear that. Your parents never took you camping or hiking?"

Jenna laughed derisively. "My father is a corporate attorney, and my mother hates the outdoors. It ruins her hair." She leaned down to brush at the water and a yellow maple leaf floated into her cupped hand. She brought it up to see it better in the moonlight. "I always wanted to go. Sleeping in tents and walking through forests and riding horses. It sounded kind of like living in a fairy tale. You know, knights and princesses and scary wild creatures." She glanced at him. "Maybe the tents wouldn't fit in that."

"It is nice, don't you think?" said Mark. "Canoeing, I mean. Once you stop paddling so hard."

She looked behind him, in the direction they had been heading away from for hours. "Yeah. You know, in a way this is a fairy tale. We're being chased by evil wizards who have taken over the castle. I could still be a princess."

"That makes me a scary wild creature then."

She finally smiled. "No, you're a wizard too. Just not as evil."

Mark nodded as if that seemed reasonable and looked up to watch tree limbs dangling down just over their heads.

Jenna watched him for a bit. "I'm cold." She put her arms around herself.

"Yeah, me too," Mark agreed, still looking at the tree branches. Comprehension of what she had meant pummeled his brain and he looked at Jenna. She patted the seat next to her.

Mark hastily grabbed the blankets and stood up. The canoe rocked back and forth as he stepped over seats to reach her. Jenna gripped the sides in momentary panic, until he squatted down in front of her.

The seat was a wonderful romantic notion, but it was too small for both of them, so they worked their way back to the middle of the canoe where it was widest. Mark spread a blanket, and they sat on it and covered themselves with another one. They leaned against the seat behind them, his arm around her, gazing together up at the stars, the moon, and the lonely thin translucent clouds that passed between them.

"I wonder what's happening," Jenna said when they'd both been silent for some time.

"Back home?" said Mark. "Oh, if I know Matthias End—and I don't, at least not as well as I'd like—I'd say he disappeared sometime after we left, and Nathan is capably protecting home and hearth all by himself."

"If End hasn't changed sides and started helping them," said Jenna. "Poor Nathan."

"Poor Nathan nothing. I'd bet money he's high on marijuana or something worse and is destroying everything that crosses his path. End had better watch himself." Mark laughed. "I don't really think he's turned on us, though. He seems like he really cares. And he's certainly had plenty of opportunities when he could have killed me if he'd wanted to."

Jenna's eyes narrowed. "You haven't worked with him as long as I have. He's a self-motivated ruthless human being."

"Well, how would you be after getting laid off?"

"Self-motivated and ruthless," Jenna admitted after some thought. "I'd have probably shot the whole place up."

Mark looked strangely at her. "You would?"

She grinned. "Yeah! Didn't you know? They call me the praying mantis of Product Development. I kill all the men around me! Yeee ha ha ha ha!"

He gave her a sour expression.

Jenna sighed. "We really shouldn't be doing this, you know."

"Doing what? I haven't done anything," Mark said, suddenly feeling guilty. For what, he didn't know.

"Just sitting. They could catch us any time now."

"That's true. Shall we row some more?"

"No. We'd just flounder around anyway."

"Right. Lots of floundering."

Jenna looked overhead. "Sure is beautiful out."

Mark looked up as well. "Sure is. Beautiful."

She leaned away and stared at him. "Are you making fun of me?"

Mark was surprised. "Me? No! I'm just...well this is not something I excel at, and I frankly don't have any idea what one is supposed to say. You seem to be doing well, so I guess I was just...following along."

"Well, stop it."

"Right, stop— Right. Okay."

The canoe came upon an unexpectedly swift-moving eddy and slid up against piled stones that nudged at the hull, making the sides rock gently. Jenna grabbed the rail of the boat with a hand.

"It's all right," Mark said. "Just a very small tidal wave."

Jenna slowly took her hand away from the side as the rocking subsided and instead gripped the blanket tightly around her. Mark tried to hold her closer.

"Isn't this awful?" she said suddenly. "I just can't believe we're out here like this. Fleeing for our lives. This is America. I mean, I know the reality of how things work. There are plenty of amoral conscienceless people out there. I can accept that. But I didn't expect to ever meet one, much less a whole army of them."

"I'm not sure what you mean."

"This whole thing over a stupid invention. I mean, it's great; it'll do a lot of great things. Eventually. But someone will do better someday. I mean, that's just the way things work. Why do they have to go around destroying houses and stealing things and killing people?"

Mark shrugged. "Everybody has a job to do, I guess."

"That's your answer? It's just a job?"

He opened his mouth, but decided it might be better to keep quiet.

Jenna watched the trees shake as a gust of wind blew over the river. "Is this the way business innovation really works? Is this the way *life* works?" she said, weariness making her feel suddenly very sad. "Have I been going about it all wrong all this time?"

Mark didn't want to talk, but he needed to. "Life is a struggle, sure. But I believe those who work the hardest will win out in the end. Survival of the fittest, after all."

"They're fitter than we are," Jenna pointed out.

Mark glanced at her and then looked quickly away.

She smiled. "It's a nice thought though." She studied his face. "You don't think they'll have destroyed your house, do you? It's just about the most amazing place I've ever seen."

"My house? Big whoop. I just hope they don't destroy my equipment. I've got a couple of scopes I couldn't possibly replace."

"You couldn't replace the house either."

"Oh sure, I could. An old warehouse would do just as well. And probably leak less."

Jenna shook her head in wonder and nestled closer to Mark.

They listened for a while to the silence of the water as the canoe glided along. The forest around them was eerie for its noise, in comparison. Maybe it was the constant breeze blowing through the upper branches and the falling leaves, or maybe the collective chatter of thousands of creatures settling in for the evening—or coming out for the evening. To Jenna, it reminded her of a ride in an amusement park, floating along, listening to scary noises, waiting for the inevitable scary thing to jump out at them.

"Hey! Look at that!" Mark said suddenly, his voice animated but hushed.

Jenna jumped up almost onto the seat they were leaning against. "What? What?" Just as quickly, she shot down to where only her eyes peeked over the side of the canoe.

"See?" Mark pointed somewhere in the trees. He looked down at her, puzzled. "What's the matter?" Seeing how frightened she was, he grew alarmed too and dropped down so that he was almost lying on his back. "What is it?" he hissed, trying to see over her head.

"How should I know?"

"Well what are you hiding from?"

"Whatever you were pointing at? What was it?"

Mark stared at the back of her head. "Uh. Well…it was an owl."

"A what? An owl?" Jenna sat up and pounded on his arms and chest. "You scared me out of my wits!"

"I thought…ow!…I thought you'd like…ow! Hey stop that…I thought you'd like to see an owl!"

Jenna stopped and wrenched the blankets violently around herself. "You could have said it a little less excitably." She brushed her hair back and looked away from him.

"I'm sorry!" He looked at her in surprise.

She glanced at him and looked away again.

Mark stared at her. "Hey," he whispered, "there was an owl back there. Is that better? Not so loud?" His grin was tentative at best.

She whipped around and pounded him some more until he was pleading again for mercy. "I'll show you some wildlife, Goggin!" she shouted, although there was a giggle that followed.

It seemed sensible at that point for Mark to defend himself before he became seriously injured. Girls were wonderful, but there was a certain element of danger to them that he hadn't anticipated. He grabbed at her arms, their combined weight shifted all to one side, and the canoe rocked precariously close to capsizing. Panicked, Jenna grabbed for him and they clung to each other as the canoe rocked back and forth.

When it regained its equilibrium, there they were, much as they were in the stairway back home. Very close, face to face, holding each other. But there was no one to interrupt—

Mark looked up out of the canoe. "Did you hear anything?"

Jenna tensed but didn't sit up. "No," she whispered.

"Good," he said, lying down close to her again. Before he could rethink the risks, he pulled her close and kissed her. It was awkward, at first. At least it seemed to be to Mark. But Jenna didn't pull away in revulsion or knee him in the groin, so he thought he'd kiss her longer than the second or so he'd originally planned.

It seemed like they had kissed forever when they finally parted lips. Mark wasn't sure that was long enough though, and he looked again at those lips he'd seen almost everywhere since he'd first met her.

Before he did, she said: "What did you hear?" Her voice was calm and filled with warmth.

He smiled. "Oh, I was just checking for owls."

She swatted lightly at him, and they kissed again, for a long time. The embrace that followed was not just one of attraction but one of comfort as well, a need to cling and cling hard. When they loosed their fearful grip on one another, both seemed suddenly tired, more so than before they had rested.

Jenna looked into Mark's eyes, searching for his thoughts and emotions somewhere in them. "Are we going to make it?" she asked.

"Probably not," Mark said.

Jenna pressed her lips and punched him. "I'm serious."

"I know! That hurt, you know. It's a good thing girls beating me up turns me on—since kindergarten, I think."

She hit him again.

"Okay! Come on. Of course we're going to make it." Mark pointed up ahead. "The only thing we have to worry about is the falls we'll get to right around this corner up here.

"What?" Jenna shouted. She tried to get up to the seat to row but Mark wouldn't let her up.

"Might be the next corner," Mark said, grinning.

"I'm going to push you right out of this boat in a minute."

"It's a canoe."

"That's it!"

More wrestling ensued, neither one gaining or wanting to gain the upper hand. After a time they settled again on the bottom of the boat, clinging to one another, watching the stars twinkle down on them, as their breath wafted up and dispersed in the cooling night air.

The only thing that could have made it more perfect for either of them was if they weren't being chased by unknown assailants whose motives and ultimate intent were still mostly unknown.

"You didn't even camp out in the back yard?" asked Mark.

"No, all right?"

"How about making a tent out of the dining room table?"

Chapter 19

Ah, the sweet taste of life. Expensive and soon at an end. But still, for the moment, life.

Nathan Hamper breathed in the smoke of his third twisted boo since those crazy fucks had scrambled out of there. This last one he inhaled until he thought his lungs would burst.

The instant the Hummers had disappeared from view, he had grabbed a joint out of his sock. He wanted nothing more than to envelop and suffocate the day's terrible memories in the numbing nothingness of his carefully rolled grass, and the sooner the better.

It wasn't until the second joint had fallen apart in his hands that he had stopped shaking.

So now all was fine again in the land of the brave and the home of the free. Except, he'd noticed on looking at his bare right foot, that he'd lost his shoe somewhere. And a sock as well, it now occurred to him. Damn. His remaining stash was in that sock. Unless it was the other sock. It was a wonder his feet weren't permanently stoned, what with all the hemp he kept in them. The thought made him giggle. He stood up to look for his shoe and sock and kept on giggling.

A long, low, deep-voiced groan came from the kitchen. Nathan turned to listen carefully. The groan came again, louder. Unless there was a cow in there mooing to get out, he thought with another half-giggle, someone was in there. Strange that they hadn't left with their friends in the Hummers. Never mind, he thought, shrugging carelessly.

Nathan tracked down the missing shoe and sock—he'd been sitting on them—and commenced hunting for the pulse laser rifle and its backpack. It didn't turn out to be difficult because the pack was sitting comfortably on the sofa and the rifle leaned against it, with a half-smoked joint in the muzzle.

He pointed at it and giggled uncontrollably. "That's bad for you!" he gurgled out and fell on the ground in hysterics. While he rolled around in his mirth, he nudged the sofa enough for the rifle to fall off and clank against his forehead. That ended the hysterics, if not the giggling entirely.

Rubbing his forehead, Nathan held the barrel of the laser rifle and let the gun stock and the backpack drag behind him, the many wrapped cables some-how still holding the two together. He stood at the entrance to the kitchen and surveyed the damage. There was no glass left in the windows. The kitchen table was seriously cracked and a corner broken. Oh man! he thought unhappily. Every last cereal box had been shot full of holes. He hated to eat cereal crumbs.

The mooing sound happened again under the table next to the windows. Whoever it was, was trying to move. Nathan hastily stuck his joint between his lips and grabbed at the rifle, looking for the trigger and grip. The man was having a difficult time of things, and Nathan aimed the weapon, relishing the anticipation. Over the course of the day, he had grown to enjoy listening to men yelp when he zapped them. This guy was in closer range than most of the others had been, and the pack had not been fired for hours. He'd get zapped right out the window if Nathan could angle it right.

He pulled the trigger and raised his eyebrows to see what would hap-pen. But nothing did. Nathan frowned and took a hit from his joint. He looked down at the pack. It was humming at least. A little too loud maybe, like when the radio was just off an AM station.

"Ow!" he said suddenly and quickly took his hand away from the barrel. It was hot. Really hot.

The man was still getting up while Nathan tried to puzzle the whole thing out. "Hang on a minute, man," Nathan said to the man. "This thing's messed up." He stared at the pack a moment longer before he began to feel heat again.

"Ow! Shit!" he said, grimacing in pain despite the numbed state of the majority of his nerve endings. The trigger and grip had become too hot as well. He dropped the rifle to the floor and rubbed his hands together.

The man, finally in a sitting position, put his chin onto the tabletop. "Perhaps you should look down the muzzle," he said.

Nathan turned to look at him. "No, man, it's got some kind of short somewhere." He looked back at the gun and, slowly, ever so slowly, a new awareness came to him.

"Oh, hey, dude," he said, looking back at Matthias End's head. "How's it going?"

"Just great. Dude," replied End. He sank back to the floor, totally exhausted.

After a minute of tracing cables and connections, Nathan gave up and walked around the table to where End was lying. "Ha! Man, you're wrecked."

"Very much so, yes," End agreed.

End leaned against the wall and moved limbs cautiously. Nothing felt broken, although everything felt bruised. Most of his clothes had been either torn or spattered with blood. He wondered how his face looked. He prodded at swollen cheeks and a battered nose.

The fight had been better than any bar brawl he'd ever been in. The fellows who had attacked them were most definitely not just another bunch of drunks. They knew how to fight. End was fortunate that he'd been in so many fights. He could take a punch with the best of them and he'd taken quite a few in this melee. He was also lucky that the men who had gotten inside the house had jumped him when they did, otherwise the men outside would simply have riddled him with bullets.

"So, did you kick some ass?" Nathan asked.

"I probably gave as well as I got," End said, grabbing at a windowsill in an effort to stand. "But not much better."

"Yeah, I heard," said Nathan. "It was loud. They must be pretty good, huh? Soldiers or something."

Finally standing, though unsteadily, End leaned against a wall and surveyed the room. He turned to look out a window, but carefully so as not to be seen. "Maybe," he said. "They're just paid company men now." He looked around the yard, a mostly fruitless effort since it was now almost completely dark outside. "Did you see where they went?" he asked.

"Oh, sure. They all got in the Hummers and drove out of here."

"Strange." End said, then looked Nathan over. "You look unscathed. How many joints have you smoked so far?"

Nathan shrugged. "Twenty. Thirty. I don't know."

"You must have had quite a scare in there," said End.

"Oh yeah, there were bullets flying all over the place. All the windows are shot out. I was scared, but I was cool. Mr. York surprised me there for a second, but I took care of him. No problem."

"York?" End raised an eyebrow. "What happened?"

"Oh, he snuck in the front door when I was ducking the bullets. He pretended to be my buddy, blamed the whole thing on that other guy that jumped up on the porch with him. He said he just wanted to protect Mark from the other guy. I could sure believe that! That guy was nuts, huh?" Nathan dropped the tiny remains of his smoke on the kitchen floor. He didn't think it likely he'd get in trouble since the floor was mostly ashes and pieces of chairs and broken glass. Still, somehow Mark would probably notice it and yell at him, he thought.

"So what did you say?" asked End.

"Hmm?"

"To York."

"Oh. Well, first I tried to shoot him with the pulse laser. It didn't work. All shorted out. Then I wailed on him. You know, karate kicks, judo chops, stuff like that. Learned it in gym. Then! Then, he's, like, about to go down for the count, right? So he pulls out some way cool big black gun and, like, blasts a lamp with it. He must not be a very good shot, which is why he's got all those men around. Although," he grinned and looked around the kitchen, "they must not be great shots either." He giggled and shook his head at the insanity of adults everywhere as he lit up another joint.

"Anyway. I'm too far away to kick the gun out of his hand and there's nothing to throw at him and, like, my mind rays were too fried to make him think I'm invisible or anything, so I pretended to cry and plead like a little kid. Worked too. He's all "Oh, don't cry Nathan, you know I wouldn't really shoot you, I—"

"Nathan," said End. "Did you tell him where Mark is?"

"I'm getting to that."

"If you've told him, we don't have time—"

"Hey, this is my story and I'm gonna tell it! If I can hold off four thousand armed soldiers single-handed, then so can Mark. He's the *genius* after all." Nathan said 'genius' with a plethora of sarcastic expressions, a waving of hands in the air, and a rolling of the eyes for the benefit of the ceiling.

End put his hands on his hips and glared at Nathan, but he didn't say anything.

"Anyway," continued Nathan. "He's starting to get all weepy himself and not paying much attention to me, right? So I kick the gun out of his hand and it flies out the window. You can probably still see it out there. Unless maybe they picked it up before they left."

"And then?" said End.

"Oh, well then I'm about to wail on him some more when he gets really weepy. Like when Mom's having her period? It was embarrassing. I mean a grown man acting like that. So I say, like, 'You're pitiful, man', and I'm about to stomp him when he says 'Better not!' I'm, like, 'Hey, dude, I'll kick your ass any time I want.' And he's, like, 'My men'll kill that guy in there.' Meaning you, right?"

"And? And?"

"So what could I do, man? I can beat the guy every which way but then you get killed. So I told him."

End's eyes widened. "You told him?"

"Well yeah…had to." Nathan became absorbed in his joint, which had fizzled out while he told his story.

"Great God Almighty!" bellowed End. "We've got to go!"

"Hmm?" mumbled Nathan, looking up. "Yeah sure, hang on."

"Where's my gun?" End yelled and yanked out drawers left and right, then ran into the living room. "Doesn't Mark keep a gun?" he yelled from there.

Nathan didn't move. "Mark? Course not!" He tried to steady his hand as the lighter approached the umpteenth smoke.

End ran back into the kitchen, loading his revolver. "Come on! Where's the key to the truck?"

Nathan was unable to steady the lighter enough to light up, and he dropped his hands huffily. "Do I have to do everything?" He pulled the keys out of his jean pocket.

End grabbed him by the shirt, lifted him off his feet, and ran out the back door. They reached the side of the house and stopped in front of the truck.

Mark's truck had never been in good shape, with rust and general neglect the most obvious reasons. However, the scorch marks and bullets holes that now decorated the surface did nothing to improve its appearance.

"Cool," leered Nathan from mid-air.

"Never mind!" shouted End and he tossed Nathan into the truck and leaped into the driver's seat.

"Not wise, Mr. End. Or should I say 'Father'?" said Nathan. "It's too shot up. Too much lead." He started to giggle. "Uses leaded gasoline, you know." He howled with laughter and slobbered on himself.

End ignored him and turned the key. The truck made a valiant effort to start, but only a couple of cylinders had been working before it was shot at. Now nothing moved.

"Damn it all!" roared End and he dragged Nathan from the truck. 'There must be something else we can use."

"You say dirty words a lot, there, Reverend," Nathan commented.

"Nathan, if you don't try to clear your head right now and help me, I swear to the Virgin Mother herself I'm going to break every bone in your body."

"Shit, padre, take it easy. There's an old motorcycle we can use." Nathan pulled himself free of End and stumbled toward the open meadow behind the house, where nothing but trees and grass was in sight. "I'm a virgin. Did you know that?" said Nathan walking quickly and hopping over obstacles. He took a couple steps and stopped. "No wait. I'm *not* a virgin. That's what I meant to say."

"No one cares," End said and nudged Nathan to go on.

"Oh, plenty of girls care, let me tell you," Nathan said as he hopped over the broken remains of an old wood fence and rounded a thicket of trees and wild bushes. "Actually I think they're just looking for an excuse not to go out with me."

They wove between bunched trees until they reached a monstrously canopied willow. The tree's limbs hung down from some forty feet up, cloaking all within in mystery. Its leaves had fallen quite rapidly so that it wasn't too difficult to peer through the branches and spot a small cabin. It was almost an outhouse, in fact, and, judging by its hidden position, that seemed very possibly its original identity. Nathan pushed through the dangling tree limbs and opened the cabin door. "There it is," he said, pointing into the darkness.

End couldn't see a thing, but he was anxious to get going. Every second counted, and even though York might have considerable trouble following the course of the river Mark was hopefully keeping to, if they wasted much more time here, the odds against Mark would grow steadily worse. He forced his way through objects he couldn't distinguish from just feeling, and came to what must be the motorcycle. He grabbed at the hydraulic fork in the front and pulled. The bike moved grudgingly and then caught on something. He pulled harder, and Nathan moved around to push. By strains and groans, they managed to wedge it in the doorway.

"Bloody Christ!" raged End. "Is this thing chained to the cabin?"

Nathan frowned. "Father, I'm gonna have to ask you not to put those two words together. There's a reason my family never could hang up those little crosses with Jesus on them in our house. Gave me nightmares. Oh!" he yelped suddenly. "Shit! I dropped my joint. Hang on a minute."

Nathan flipped his lighter on and ran it low over the ground inside the cabin. The light illuminated enough of the motorcycle for End to see it for what it was.

"This isn't a motorcycle! It's a scooter, for God's sake," End seethed. "With a sidecar? God save us!" He dropped the front end and disappeared outside.

The joint proved elusive amid the piles of dirt, unidentifiable rusted metal fragments, old decaying pieces of newspaper, and crumbling leaves that suggested a hole was in the roof. Nathan gave up in disgust. He climbed over the wedged bike and out the doorway, and looked around for End.

Matthias End had his head in his hands, standing around the corner from the cabin door when Nathan found him. "It'll go, man," Nathan insisted. "I've ridden it around a bunch of times, and it'll get us where we gotta go, faster than running. It *is* a motorcycle. It's just small."

End forced himself to smile. "It will be fine, Nathan. Thank you."

With renewed vigor, End applied his strength to the bike and, gradually, with a lot of scraping metal and snapped timber, he and Nathan freed the bike from the cabin.

It was in dismal shape. The frame was bent as if the bike had been hit from both sides at once so that somehow the wheels still went in their proper directions. The forks on front and back were also bent. The seat was an old leather banana thing that was torn, and the padding was mostly absent. A brake cable was completely disconnected. And both wheels wobbled when they rolled, probably having something to do with whatever or whoever had twisted the frame.

"There wouldn't happen to be any helmets lying about, would there?" asked End.

"Sure! Just a second." Nathan jumped into the cabin, rummaged about, and reappeared with a football helmet and a hockey helmet. He waved them happily in the air.

"That'll be fine," End said tolerantly, pointing at the hockey helmet.

Helmets on, they got on the machine and End pulled out the choke, flicked the fuel valve on, pumped the kick-start ten or twelve times, and violently kick-started it.

Not so much as a sputter. Not even a click. Their nostrils were soon filled with the fumes of a flooded engine.

Such a torrent of vile oaths gushed from End's lips that it would have been a surprise even to him, had he not been consumed with equally vile thoughts. He crashed his fists down on the fuel tank and the handlebars, and kicked at the gear shift and anything else within range.

"The key's right there," Nathan said when he'd finished. "You just…" Nathan twisted it to the 'on' position. "Like that," he said, smiling pleasantly. As End leaned away to sight the kick-start again for another try, Nathan deftly popped the choke back down. It didn't work anyway.

End gave the local airspace exactly five seconds to clear of combustive fumes before he crashed a boot down on the kick-starter so hard Nathan expected the entire bike to crumble to pieces. Instead it slowly spluttered to life. The excessive amount of gas pumped in caused the tachometer to fluctuate drastically and the entire motorcycle to tremble ferociously.

End twisted the throttle handle, and the machine bent from the torque so badly that he almost jumped off it in panic. "How far can we get on the gas in this thing?" he shouted at Nathan.

"The way you handle it, maybe all the way to the house. Ease up, there, your holiness. It's vintage Bronze Age, man, not a rice rocket."

End revved the motor and grinned. He found the gear shift, popped the clutch, and the rolling rattletrap lurched forward. In fits and starts they rolled forward, veered crazily through the hanging willow branches, and accelerated over or around unsuspecting saplings and astonished shrubbery. The underbrush retaliated as best it could by swatting and slapping at Nathan, who ducked and otherwise huddled in the sidecar.

The house appeared and disappeared behind them, and they did not in fact run out of gas. The machine shot over the gravel impressively and flipped up onto the main road more by sheer momentum than power. End turned left, heading south, and wrenched the throttle as far as it would go. Overwhelmed, the bike almost stalled. Thankfully the inner workings were slow in reacting to its driver's mad demands, and gradually the bike gained speed.

The next fifteen minutes were spent in the saddle, in growing darkness, going as hard as the motorcycle would allow. It didn't last long. The machine began to sputter and wheeze and End coasted into a graveled area to the side of the road. As soon as they stopped, the engine went into a terrifying spasmodic fit, and End thought again of abandoning it in favor of preserving his life.

"It's all right," Nathan reassured him above the sound of the gasping machine, "it does this all the time. Try not to crank the gas so hard."

End responded by twisting the throttle hard once again and the bike jolted forward, slowed, jolted forward again, almost stalled, then somehow got control of itself and continued on.

They drove on for another fifteen minutes when End inexplicably pulled over again. "The headlights don't work," he shouted at Nathan.

"What?"

"The headlights!"

Nathan shook his head. "You can't use those! They don't work!"

"I know they don't work!"

"Then why are you asking me if they work?"

End gripped the handles to steady his aggravation. "How are we supposed to find them without headlights?"

"Wait until morning?" replied Nathan carelessly. He had his hands folded and had long ago resigned himself to waiting to light up until the wind stopped blowing his smokes out of his hands.

End sneered with a burgeoning loathing for the potted teenager and gunned the beleaguered machine once more.

By the dying light, they could just see the river as they continued south, although only sporadically. Then the road would twist away or dive into a deeper part of the forest. When they did see the river, it certainly seemed navigable. If Mark and Jenna were able to find a boat, they should have been able to navigate through it. Assuming either had any clue how to. There were a surprising number of streams and creeks that branched off from the main artery, and for a minute, End was unsure if he was doing the right thing in following this road. Had he gone too far south? Could they have drifted down one of the diverging streams? They needed a helicopter, that's what they needed.

This was all so damn maddening!

It was not long before it was too dark to see well enough for proper tracking. End continued stubbornly on, and it was the motorcycle that dictated when it was time to halt the search. The spasmodic fits shook the thing to its exhaust pipes and it wobbled to a stop.

"Don't feed any gas—" Nathan started to say.

End throttled the accelerator with his usual defiance and the engine died instantly.

Nathan shrugged and pulled a joint out of his sock, checked for crosswinds, and lit up.

End responded with more expletives unflattering toward two-wheeled motorized apparati. When he had calmed, he watched Nathan roll the joint between his lips and stare off into the trees. Even given the effect of the drugs, this cavalier attitude seemed uncharacteristic for Nathan. York could have killed both Mark and Jenna by now. Or at least effectively removed them from the face of the earth.

"What the hell is wrong with you!" he roared at Nathan. It felt much better to seethe and yell and generally throw a tantrum at people than to try to reason with them.

"Grass withdrawal," Nathan answered, pointing to the lit butt.

End stood up, determined to at long last strangle the infuriating boil once and for all, or at least stomp his stash into pricey mulch.

"I don't know why you're so worked up, your holiness," said Nathan. "It'll take them, what, four or five hours just to get to where we are. We're light years ahead, dude. We can go on impulse power from here, Captain Spock." He giggled for half a second and stopped as if he'd forgotten what he'd just said.

"That's Captain *Kirk,* you stupid fucking wasted child!" End screamed. "Why wouldn't I be 'worked up'? You've gift wrapped your own friend for these people and you say 'don't get worked up'? Give me that!" End lunged for the latest of Nathan's wrapped weed, falling into the sidecar, which had already had too much to contend with, trying to keep up with the motorcycle. This additional weight allowed it to readily concede defeat. It unhitched from the cycle and pitched sideways.

"Psychotic priest! Psychotic priest!" Nathan yelped from inside the sidecar. "Let go, asshole! You guys are all perverts, aren't you."

"Boy, you have demeaned me for the last time!" End bellowed. He rolled over and bounded up nimbly to his feet. Reaching down, he grabbed a handful of teenager and hoisted him two feet off the ground. A foot kicked out, and End caught the ankle and turned the boy upside down. Three great shakes and out dropped a lighter, some change, five keys, a picture of a girl Nathan's age, and a baggie with something in it. End lowered Nathan until his head thudded against the ground. The boy grabbed at the baggie, then clutched the top of his head to protect himself, groaning and cursing the whole time. The baggie contained four rolled cigarettes.

End inspected the bag and smiled. "Fakes. Pencil shavings, right? Maybe crumpled leaves? You're a clever little drug addict." Still gripping his ankle, End pulled out the real stash from within Nathan's sock. There were more than a dozen joints still waiting to deliver their deluded pleasure. He released Nathan's leg and the boy fell in a heap at End's feet. "You won't be needing these anymore." End squashed the baggie in his fist and dumped the contents onto the ground. Nathan watched morosely as End kicked and rearranged the dirt around until the joints were effectively no more.

"Son of a bitch," Nathan said under his breath. "I had no idea you could be so unholy."

"Shocking, isn't it?" replied End with relish. "Now I don't care to hear any more sarcasm or any of that witty banter of yours. We've got to find them before York or anyone else does. I've told you how important Goggin is to me."

"I still don't see what the rush is," Nathan said. "Mark can't have gotten more than ten or twenty miles from home. We've gone that far already. Probably twice that far."

"Your point being?"

"You're assuming they knew I was lying to them, right? We should've spotted them by now. But we haven't. So they must be headed back to Kansas City."

Something wasn't coming together for End. "Wait a minute. You lied to them? About what?"

"About where Mark and Jenna went."

"What did you tell them?"

"I said they were meeting some friends of Jenna's in Kansas City. At General Micronet. Big, high-falutin' important-type people. Executives. I told York his ass would be grass then. I pretended to be real scared and panicky. He bought it, no question about it."

End's mouth hung open in complete dismay. "All this time I've had us running like frightened rabbits? All this time you let me stew and worry?"

"Hey, I told you I took care of it. You just figured I wussed out."

End sat hard on the motorcycle seat. "So they're..."

"On their way to KC, man. Can't you hear anything? I fuckin' swear, adults are complete dinks."

"Little man," End laughed, picking Nathan up and setting him on his feet, "you are something other than usual. I do hereby profusely apologize for thinking you were dead space." He brushed away the dirt and leaves and happily straightened any unseemly creases.

Nathan scowled. "Yeah? And what about my herbs and spices there, dude?"

"Oh, no, I don't regret that at all. The whole purple haze thing of yours was getting old."

"Dickhead," Nathan said under his breath. He dropped moodily into the sidecar.

End stared after him. "Nathan, I understand you have some...animosity toward me, now that you know something about my past. Maybe I did wrong by leaving the church. I don't really know. I certainly feel the guilt of it occasionally. But I know I'd feel worse if I stayed. And it seems to me that if you can hear God's call to ministry, why can't you hear God calling you elsewhere?"

"Because it doesn't work that way."

"Who says? You? You said yourself you aren't all that religious."

"That's just the way it is. Father Jorgensen says once you're called, you're called. There's no quitting."

"Well, your Father Jorgensen only says that, because he was told to. I'm not going to debate a system that has existed for thousands of years. But I'm not going to put up with it any longer, either. That goes for you as well. Knock it off with the sarcasm or I'm going to be dumping you on your head a lot more often. Got it?"

Nathan didn't respond.

"Got it?" End said louder.

Nathan nodded, still not having turned to look at him. End waited a moment longer, unsure whether to pursue it further. Finally, thanking the Lord above that he had not been blessed with a teenager of his own, End sighed and got onto the motorcycle.

The darkness of night had vanquished the weakening daylight. They sat in the darkness and in the silence between them. End was disappointed to think that the respect Nathan once had for him was gone simply because of a vocational decision. But there it was.

"Where now?" he asked, looking up and down the road. Neither way seemed the right way.

"I'd go along the path next to the Pomme," Nathan said quietly.

"The Pomme?"

"The river."

"There's a path?"

"Every river has a path."

"How do you know that?" End asked.

"I'm a kid. Kids get into everything."

"Fair enough." End kick-started the bike to life, turned the throttle, this time ever so gently, and drove slowly along the road until he spotted a promising break in the trees. The bike turned there, bouncing and careening over rocks and brush.

Chapter 20

Light. Tremendous light.

And warmth. Warmth that enveloped him from somewhere above.

Was he dead? He couldn't be outside or in the canoe anymore. It hadn't been warm in the canoe, and last time he'd checked there was no light.

Mark Goggin had never particularly cared to know what death was like. It's not something a good inventor wants to think about when radiation and balls of electricity are all around him. Still he'd heard all the stories of near death experiences. Darkness and then a long tunnel. Brilliant light. Angels.

If this was it, it certainly came suddenly. And painlessly, which might be the best part. Being a man of science, or at least a man working in infrequent harmony with science, Mark had never been altogether comfortable about God, man made in God's image, the afterlife, Heaven, all that. The whole thing smacked of mindless belief, a trait abhorrent to any respectable man of science. To do his work, he had to have the consistency of scientific law. Everything had to happen the way the laws of science predicted, every time. Of course, the uncomfortable thing was, it didn't always happen the way it should. Most scientists under those circumstances chalked it up to their own imperfections in how they conducted a given experiment. They may have used a different amount of some chemical than they had in an earlier experiment, or they may have built a longer lever for a device, even if only by a millimeter.

Was there a Heaven? If there was any reason Mark wanted there to be a Heaven, it was so he could meet his lifelong inspirations. His heroes. To meet Thomas Edison, Alexander Bell, Albert Einstein, and Nikola Tesla. To sit down and have coffee with them, to listen to them think out loud about some new idea of theirs. To hear in their own words how they had figured out why something wasn't working and made it work right. To have them critique his own experiments and inventions. That would be something.

Of course, since there was some suggestion of infidelity in Einstein's behavior and possibly unlawful ruthlessness in Edison's business machinations, it wasn't entirely certain all of them had been invited to the Mad Scientists' Ball in the Hereafter. Would he go to Hell to meet Einstein and Edison? No, probably not. If there really was a Hell, then one could reasonably assume the people there were doing what had always been said people did in Hell. It would be gruesome and tortuous, mentally and physically. In Hell, Einstein would certainly not have been in the mood for chitchat what with the devil making him flirt with ugly, old biker chicks, and an enraged Edison would have been too busy throwing phonograph records while George Westinghouse got all the credit for his inventions.

Something swayed back and forth in Mark's clearing reality.

Light dimmed when the swaying went one way, then brightened when it swayed out of his peripheral vision. If it could be called vision. If this was Heaven—or Hell—he was sure going to have an awful time getting around.

Speaking of Heaven and the dead, Mark recalled his erstwhile competitor, Archibald Scott. The now *deceased* Archibald Scott. No doubt Scott wasn't among those in Heaven. Mark wondered how he had really been killed. An explosion going off in Scott's lab wouldn't have surprised Mark. The man blew things up like nitroglycerin was in his veins. No regard for anyone but himself. At least five assistants of his had been hospitalized, Mark had heard. Scott should have experimented in a bunker, not a laboratory. Well, he'd get all the fire and horrific detonations he wanted in Hell.

A sensation of bobbing started now.

Mark saw the swaying taking a more energetic and aggressive stance in his still clearing vision. Frankly, spending eternity dizzy and half-blind didn't sound like Heaven to him either.

Without warning, a loud grating noise erupted all around him. He jerked up to a sitting position, and reality took firm hold of his vision and his faculties.

He was still in the canoe, sitting in the bottom. Jenna slept next to him. It was morning. The sun was out, somewhere out of direct sight behind the trees, brightening everything. Too bright. It was either early, or there had been a rain because everything on the banks—trees, grass, leaves—glistened with moisture. Their blankets felt dry, so it must be early in the morning and the moisture was the morning dew.

The Pomme de Terre River had become considerably narrower than the night before. He looked over the side and saw that the river had also become shallow. It was no deeper than a couple of feet now, and small sandy and rocky islands poked up above the surface now and then. The water rippled over the rocks and deposited more sand on the tiny islands. On the river bottom, Mark spotted some of the most beautiful, smoothest stones he'd ever seen.

They ran up onto one of the islands, one barely keeping its sand above water, and the canoe made another grating noise as the current forced it over the sand and on past it.

This could be Heaven, he thought. A beautiful girl, out in the wilds of nature, no other human being within miles. The only thing that could possibly make it better would have been if there was hot coffee, a cherry Danish, and the day's newspaper hiding behind a tree somewhere. A heater would have been pleasant as well.

Beside him, Jenna was stirring. "What's going on?" she said, yawning and looking at him with one eye.

"Heaven," he said.

She opened the other eye and looked around. "No, this is a canoe. Heaven is not surrounded by metal."

"And how do you know that?"

Jenna sat up and rubbed her eyes. "My Aunt Sylvia. She had a near-death experience when Uncle Ralph's electric razor fell in her bath. She mentioned seeing a lot of things. Angels, Humphrey Bogart, Abraham Lincoln, James Dean. Maybe Elvis. She wasn't sure because he had sunglasses on. But she never mentioned seeing a lot of metal."

"Did Uncle Ralph try again?"

"Yes, the old coot— How did you know?"

Mark shrugged. "I've never seen an electric razor with a cord long enough to reach the bath. That kind of thing would take a special effort."

"He denied it, but he was always trying to get rid of her," Jenna said. "They made him use a regular razor and shaving cream after the second time. Even so, Aunt Sylvia was convinced he had tossed the shaver in on purpose. She divorced him and got his Olympic coin collection."

"Is there *anyone* likeable in your family?"

Jenna closed her eyes. "My cat. I had a great old alley cat that ran away when I was seventeen. He was light brown and gold and white. He always waited in the front yard for me to come home from school. I think Mom chased him away. She likes dogs."

"I never had a pet," Mark said. "My parents were afraid I'd electrocute one or launch it into orbit. I always wanted an owl."

"An owl?"

"Sure. They look so intelligent, like they know something you don't, and they haven't decided whether to trust you enough to share the information."

"Like that owl you saw back there?"

"No, a snow owl. Pure white, regal and majestic. The Rolls Royce of birds."

The river was now less than a foot deep. The smooth stones were easy to spot, amplified by the water so that the river looked like a cobblestone street submerged underwater. The canoe grated along the rocks more often than not.

"I don't remember it ever being this shallow," Mark commented. "You know, now that I think about it, I'm almost sure there was a second bridge that we'd float down to when I was a kid. We must be past it because I don't recognize anything. It was never this shallow. Definitely not after being so high last night."

"Maybe we've left the big river," said Jenna. "This could be a quiet little brook that came off the big river and just flutters away into nothing. It's beautiful, isn't it?" She stood up, the canoe swaying unsteadily, and stepped into the water. "Ooooohhhh!" she screamed. "It's cold!"

"Next time maybe you should just dip a finger in," Mark suggested.

She kicked water at him, the spray getting her as much as him.

The canoe ground to a stop. The rushing water pushed at it, and the canoe moved forward, but only so it could wedge itself into the stones more thoroughly. All around them, the water was noisily crashing over stones and larger rocks.

"You wouldn't want to pull me to shore, would you?" Mark called out as Jenna waded farther away.

She ignored him. Her neck had felt tight, and her back ached from sleeping on the hard metal of the canoe. For some reason—maybe it was the frigid temperature of the water, or maybe the roar of the torrent of clean, clear river rushing over polished rock. Maybe it was just the clarity of the outdoors—whatever it was, her back no longer ached, and the tension in her neck was gone. In fact, she almost wanted to run around in the water, kicking it and throwing the small stones, and maybe even lying in it and letting the water pour over her. It was much too cold, but the thought was hard to resist.

"So I guess I have to get out then?" Mark called out again from the distance between them.

Jenna kept moving farther downriver, so Mark stood and took a step out of the canoe. Because there was no other weight in the boat, it did two things. First it wobbled very quickly and then it took off down the shallow channel. Mark was thrown off-balance, and it was only because he'd been leaning the way he should have, that he didn't fall face-first into the water. Instead, he landed on his rear. The water ran into his pants and up and around his waist, even as he leaped up out of the water the instant he felt the cold.

When he looked downriver, he saw Jenna watching him. The river was too noisy to be sure, but he thought he heard her giggling. The canoe reached her and cooperatively ground to a halt in what was ankle-deep water.

Mark spent the next few minutes pointlessly shaking his legs and trying to wring the water from the seat of his soaked jeans. The bank was close, and he waded over and sat down on the ground with a splat. He took his shoes and socks off and at least was able to extract most of the water from them.

His only solace, as the cold, cold water squished in his boxers, was that he was better positioned to watch Jenna try to force the canoe over to where he waited. Not only did she have to push it sideways, which is not what any self-respecting boat wants to do, but she was also trying to make it go back upriver, which both the boat *and* the river were decidedly against. By the time she had wrestled it over, she had fallen to her knees in the water more than once and splashed herself enough so that she was at least as wet as Mark.

"That went pretty well, don't you think?" he said.

Jenna only glared at him as she removed her own shoes and socks.

They were fortunate that the day was so unseasonably warm or they would have spent the next few hours getting used to cold, damp clothing. As it was, the sun beat down, and in the time it took them to calm down from their traumatic mishaps, their clothes were no longer cold, only damp.

"What now, o man of the woods?" Jenna asked.

Mark looked down the river as far as he could, but it was impossible to tell whether it became deeper any time soon. The woods seemed far more hospitable. "Let's take the canoe along the water for a bit. Maybe it's deeper farther down."

The plan was not unsound, but they soon discovered its critical flaw: a canoe is surprisingly heavy. They first tried just lifting and carrying it. Jenna started in front, but quickly became suspicious that Mark was not carrying his share of the load. They then tried putting the thing over their heads, but Jenna found it impossible to lift that high without help, and every time they rounded a corner, the weight threw her off. Finally, they resorted to dragging it along the grass and dirt.

"This is hopeless," Jenna whimpered, her arms tired and complaining about lifting something heavier than the demographics reports they were used to lugging around.

"Completely," Mark agreed. "We're still nowhere near deeper water."

They decided to press on without the canoe and hope that they might come upon traversable water and then return for the canoe if it wasn't too far away.

It was an amazing day for autumn, warm with a mild wind blowing across the river. The trees and grass and birds all seemed uncaring to the incongruity of the weather. Mark recognized the twitter of a nuthatch and a duet of loud wrens fluttering about amid the tree trunks, and he even spotted a cardinal through the slowly shedding trees, and kingfishers shooting in and out of the branches and over the riverbank. Jenna thought she saw a hawk circling overhead—"Are there vultures in Missouri?" she asked—and could have sworn she spotted snakes several times, although they may have been sticks.

They stuck to a path that was barely a path, breaking off for fallen trees or undergrowth too thick to get past. The forest was becoming wilder now, the ground-level vegetation easily the dominant inhabitant. Occasionally they would have to backtrack to get around a small stream or a deep cavity in the ground.

"This is cave country, did you know that?" said Mark.

"No, I've managed to ignore all the billboards about caves when I drive through Missoura," Jenna said sarcastically.

"All right, then I don't need to warn you about the holes you'll probably fall into."

"Holes?"

"Big empty spaces with no ground in them."

"There are holes? What, like a bottomless pit? Just anywhere?"

Mark couldn't tell if she was making fun of him again, but it wouldn't do to not explain the holes, in case she was genuinely frightened.

"Yes, there are holes," he said. "No, not like a bottomless pit. Technically, there is no such thing. Yes, they could be anywhere. Usually they're near hills and cliffs. But you never know."

"Are there bats in them?" she asked with trepidation.

Mark frowned. "Bats? I suppose. But if you fall in, the bats are the least of your problems."

"Why?"

He had a strong feeling he shouldn't be continuing this topic in the morbid direction it was heading. "Well, it's pretty cold in caves. And wet. Lots of mold and mildew. Not good for allergies."

"Oh," Jenna sighed and smiled. "I thought you were going to say there were bears and mountain lions and rattlesnakes and spiders and scorpions and—"

"Naaw," Mark said, grinning half-heartedly. "In Missoura? Not a chance."

Her worried expression lightened with the strength of her relief.

Mark smiled in reply but not with the same joy. "You might just stick close to me, though," he said awkwardly. "Wouldn't do to fall in a hole and get the sniffles."

Jenna leaped forward and grasped his right hand in her left. The suddenness of it made Mark jump, but the feel of her hand in his sent jolts of excitement ricocheting all over him. This was almost like having a girlfriend, he thought. Of course that was only speculation. He'd never had a girlfriend, unless he counted the three little girls he'd liked in fifth grade and told everyone were his girlfriends. He wasn't sure he'd ever even spoken to them.

The river banked slowly to the left as they continued walking alongside. It had narrowed in the last hour or so, but the tumble of water over stones was impossible to miss. The sun was difficult to pinpoint for all the trees, but Mark guessed it must still not quite be midday.

"Are you hungry?" he asked.

"Very," said Jenna.

"I wonder what we can eat around here. You didn't pack anything, did you?"

"No."

"Me neither. I've seen all sorts of berries, but I don't know how to tell if they're poisonous or not. You ever killed anything?"

"Me? No! Never! What an awful thing to ask."

"It's not so awful," Mark said. "Where do you think a ham sandwich comes from?"

"A deli."

"Yeah, well, somebody has to kill the ham sandwich before it can go into a deli."

"Well, it's not going to be me."

Mark regarded the immediate vicinity. "We could set a trap."

"For what?"

"I don't know. A rabbit, maybe. If we catch one, I'll kill it if you'll cook it."

Jenna made a disgusted face. "I'm not that hungry anymore."

"Well, I am."

Mark walked in an ever-widening circle around Jenna, scouring the ground for what, she didn't care to guess. He picked up broken tree limbs and lifted rocks but always dropped them where they'd been. Jenna folded her arms, prepared to argue against him killing something small and helpless that she would refuse to cook anyway.

He approached her, finally. "How about fish?" he asked.

She smiled. "I'd cook a fish. Do you know how to catch them without a fishing pole?"

"No. But I'll wing it like everything else."

Jenna followed Mark over to the riverbank, the water still no higher than their ankles. Mark stared down into the water for a long time. But not so much as a minnow showed itself through the cloudless water.

"How big a fish do you expect to catch?" she asked after a time.

"Something pretty damn small, I'd expect."

"Why don't we just keep going?" Jenna rubbed his hand, which was again in hers, while he stared unhappily at the fish-challenged river. "We don't really know how far behind us they might be."

Mark nodded, and this time she led them through the dense woodlands. It was a fortunate thing that so many of the trees had lost their leaves, allowing them to see the way ahead easier, because it was difficult enough to determine where to go. Being able to see a long hill or a steep cliff blocking their path well before they reached it, helped them adjust. Still, the spiderwebs and the whippings delivered by tree branches they passed made the going far from easy.

A deep brook, on the other hand, was a total surprise when they almost fell into it. Looking across it, the far bank was not quite close enough for them to safely jump over. They would have to find a way around it.

What interested Mark was the profusion of fish-like objects floating just below the surface. "Lunch," he said.

They were small but they were still fish, he thought, as his stomach gurgled agreeably. He turned away and began shuffling his feet around, sifting through leaves and lifting rocks out of the way.

"You're not going to drop rocks on them, are you?" Jenna asked in dismay.

Mark looked up. "Why yes, I thought a big huge rock would kill several at a time, and the rest could just mill around waiting to have rocks dropped on them too." He went back to his search. "As a matter of fact, I'm looking for a long stick so I can try to spear a few. They're small so I'm trying to find a stick with a bunch of branches so I can make something like a pitchfork. Do you know what a pitchfork is?"

Jenna didn't respond, instead making an ugly face at him behind his back.

"That's what I thought," Mark said. He wandered farther away, sloshing his feet so that leaves billowed up, and he could see branches under the leaf bed. Yellow and red and orange foliage floated back down where he had been.

Jenna sat down at the edge of the brook, her feet dangling over the side. The water's surface was at least three feet down, otherwise she could have just reached out and grabbed one of the fish. That would have served him right. Leaning closer, she tried to focus on the objects swimming around. If they were fish, they looked awfully small. And wasn't the water supposed to make them look bigger than they really were? Well, she was certainly not going to cook a bunch of bones.

Mark returned with two sticks. One was long and curved, the other shorter but straighter. Both had smaller branches protruding on the ends like he'd wanted, but they weren't all pointing in the same direction and seemed too fat and blunt to do the job properly. Nevertheless, he positioned himself on his stomach and began jabbing at the water, a stick in each hand. That quickly scared away every living aquatic creature within forty feet, and he had to wait for them to return.

"Wasn't there a movie where some guy stood in the water with his hands in it and let the fish come to him?" said Jenna. "Then all he had to do was swoosh his hands up and throw the fish up onto the land."

Mark turned to regard her. "Do you mind? You're scaring the fish away."

He jabbed at the water again before having to sit once more to wait for them to come back.

Jenna leaned down next to him. "Just stand in the water," she said. "They'll come to you."

Mark didn't answer. The largest fish he'd seen so far was moving under one of his sticks. It was darting and stopping so much that he couldn't get the timing right when to jab at it.

He felt Jenna touch his arm. She must have seen it too. He concentrated again on the big fish, which seemed as if it had found lunch itself and had slowed to inspect its find. Mark leaned out so that his stick almost touched the surface of the water. The fish had almost completely stopped moving. He eased back for the fatal thrust.

"Hey there!" said a loud voice.

Startled, Mark thrust his stick into the water with such force that it stabbed the stones at the bottom of the stream and snapped. Jenna fell sideways and almost rolled into the water herself.

A massive figure of a man stood over them. He was of medium height, but extremely stout. His hair and beard were consistent with someone who hadn't had a bath in several years, or else he had recently survived a powerful concussive blast and had forgotten to comb himself afterward. His clothes negated the blast theory, as they were entirely intact, backing instead the unwashed theory from his head to his shoeless feet. His expression was one of affable confusion, as if he didn't know why they would want to be out in the middle of nowhere, but he was pleased to see them nonetheless.

The man surveyed Mark's activities with a critical eye. "You realize," said the man, "that that will never work. Your stick is too blunt, and the fish are not close enough to the surface. These are also the smartest fish, relatively speaking, in this vicinity. Believe me, I know."

Mark sat up on his knees and disgustedly brushed leaves and mud from his coat. "I would have liked to find that out for myself," he said brusquely.

"Entirely up to you," said the man. "I've only been out here for six years. What do I know?"

"Six years?" Jenna said in amazement. "You've lived outdoors for six years?"

The man regarded Jenna with a smile that grew into a leer. "Well," he said, licking his lips, "not exactly outdoors."

"Yeah, I didn't think so," Mark mumbled in aggravation.

The man wiped his hands on his coat—which could only have made them dirtier—while he stared at Jenna. "I have a little place that I've used for shelter on occasion. Haven't been there in a month, though. At least. I don't have a watch, but I keep very close track of the days. That way I know when Christmas is. And New Year's. Birthdays. That sort of thing."

Mark stood and brushed leaves from his knees. Mud had caked them on and he had to scrape the leaves and mud off with his broken stick. He'd thrown the bent one at the other fish he kept missing, who were no doubt even now chortling at him from under the water.

"Still, to be able to live off the land for that long," said Jenna, trying not to take offense at being stared at. After all, the man probably hadn't seen a woman the whole six years he'd been out there. "I just don't think I could possibly have made it," she said. "I've only been out here a day," she said and laughed.

Brushing the last leaf off, Mark said "Well, it's been a pleasure, mister, but—"

"Oh! Where are my manners?" said the man. "I'm Brad. Brad Granger. My friends call me Bradley." He stuck out his hand to Jenna, who hesitated, but eventually managed a smile and grasped his hand.

Mark was nonplussed and looked at Jenna as if she were shaking hands with a contagious disease and should know better. "Okay, well," he said, "Great to meet you, terribly sorry to run off like this, but we've got to be going."

"I've got fresh fish cooking about a hundred yards from here if you'd like to join me," said Bradley.

"Fresh fish?" Mark said with a start.

"We really should be going, shouldn't we, Mark?" said Jenna.

"Nonsense!" Mark replied. "It wouldn't be polite. Isn't that right, Brad?"

Bradley smiled and nodded, but he only had eyes for Jenna. She nodded as pleasantly as she could and motioned for him to lead them.

Mark and Jenna argued in loud whispers and made ugly and disagreeable faces at one another as they followed Bradley along the brook and up a hill that they had worked very hard to avoid climbing all morning. As they labored up the steep hill, the smell of cooking fish surrounded them and lent energy to their steps. It wasn't until they saw the smoke of the fire and their hunger pangs were at their worst that the smell took on a more charred sensation. Bradley gave forth an "Oh no!" and walked quickly to rescue his lunch.

As soon as they reached him, Bradley was again all smiles. He scraped the fish from the skillet onto two plates.

"A little burnt?" asked Jenna.

"Uh, yes, ma'am! That's the only way to do it. You see, we're not far off from a toxic landfill that was closed down in the seventies. If I don't get this carcass thoroughly cooked, the toxicity could potentially be lethal. Here you are." Bradley handed a plate to Jenna. He started to eat from the other plate, then realized Mark was standing empty-handed. "Oh, help yourself. Have to use the skillet, I'm afraid. Only got two plates." He leered again at Jenna. "Kind of a his and hers set, you know?" He laughed, and the sound of it came out like a sneezing fit.

The fish on Jenna's plate looked more like a raw frog, dressed up with the shredded leaves of a water lily. The frog, or whatever it was, must have been dead long before Bradley had scooped it out of the muck it was decaying in. She might almost have thrown up except that her stomach was empty.

Mark, however, stabbed at the thing in the skillet, broke off a piece, and tossed it in his mouth before ever questioning the wisdom of it. The glob rolled over his tongue and took on a puffier and slimier aspect as he tried to decide what to do with it. He elected to take a stroll around the campsite and surreptitiously spit the nasty glob out of his mouth while his back was turned.

"So," said Bradley, his mouth full of the repulsive frog globs, "what brings you to my neck of the woods, so to speak." He chuckled at his witty turn of phrase.

"We're being chased by ruthless thieves and murderers," Mark replied. "You wouldn't happen to have anything else to eat, would you?" He set the skillet onto the makeshift grill and held his stomach. "I'd forgotten I can't eat fried foods."

"Uh, I've got a can of green beans left," Bradley stammered, tossing him a rusty, bent can opener. "You're...you're being chased? Why?"

Jenna laughed and waved him off. "It's a long, silly story."

202

"I built a device that could quite possibly remake society as it exists, and they want to either steal my invention or kill me, or both." Mark twisted the can opener around the can. "Do you have a clean fork? That one has grease all over it."

"What sort of device?" asked Bradley.

"It's not nearly as fantastic as it sounds," Jenna exclaimed. She put her finger up to her lips to shush Mark, who was too absorbed in the green beans.

"Not nearly as fantastic? Ha! Listen to me, Mr. Granger. Every business on this planet would kill to get my invention. And that is in fact the case, because most of them have sent their stooges out after me, and that's who we're running from."

Jenna mouthed 'Shut up' at Mark, who mouthed back 'What?'

Bradley raised his eyebrows. "Must be an antigravity device," he said between mouthfuls of roasted amphibian.

Both Mark and Jenna stopped their silent shouting at one another to stare at their host. "Antigravity?" said Mark tentatively.

"Sure," said Bradley. "That's the next great discovery of science. Oh, you'll hear people talk about forms of nuclear propulsion and even antimatter warp cores, but those are a bit down the line. Antigravity's next."

"You sound like someone who has quite an interest in science," Jenna said.

"I should. I was an aerospace propulsion engineer for five years at NASA. We built an antigravity-propelled vehicle ten years ago."

"No way," said Mark in disbelief.

"Oh yes," Bradley replied. "We had all the bugs worked out; everything was a go for mass production. NASA figured they could fund the space program for the next thousand years. But then the budget cuts hit so bad, they had to shift all the engineers to the electromagnetic solar sails project so we could get to Mars. Congress and the president were really big on Mars."

"You mean to tell me you've worked on creating solar sails?" Mark was almost in awe of the dirty, foul-smelling man.

"Yeah, but I quit before it got very far. Now they're dead in the water. The idiots."

Jenna eyed him with suspicion.

Mark was feeling severely challenged in his self-crowned role as the smartest person in the Midwest. Or at least central Missouri. "Ever tried building a perpetual motion machine?"

Bradley laughed, swallowing the last of his fried and bloated meal. "The government has had three of those running since the fifties."

Mark gaped.

Jenna smirked. "I've heard NASA has taken a serious look at powering their new shuttles with a form of cold fusion. Is that true?"

Bradley leaned forward and smiled. "Way past that, miss...uh, I don't believe I got your name."

"Trixie."

He smiled again, only bigger. "I love that name, Trixie. Anyway. I did my thesis at UC Berkley on cold fusion, and I can tell you, NASA and the Tibetans both are using cold fusion practically everywhere now."

"Tibetans?" Mark asked.

"Of course! How do you think they keep the Chinese army at bay? They've been dropping cold fusion-catalyzed cobalt bombs out of their little caves in the Himalayas for decades."

"You don't say," Mark mumbled.

Jenna giggled, and both men looked at her. "Excuse me," she said. "So, Mr. Granger, you'd refute all of your esteemed colleagues in the scientific community who say cold fusion is a fool's dream?"

That hit Mark where it hurt.

"Please, please, Trixie. Call me Bradley. As a matter of fact, I do. The problem with all those experiments the amateurs have done is that they aren't thinking big enough. You need to make at least a hundred times the ingredients that most experiments use."

"Ingredients?" asked Mark.

"That is correct. The principle is universal. For bigger buildings, you need more titanium. For bigger explosions, more uranium. For quicker escape from the earth's pull, more thrust." He smiled and winked at Jenna in a way that was much too suggestive for her empty stomach.

Mark shook his head. "I don't see how that would work with cold fusion. You've just got more heavy water and more—"

"Hey, professor, I know what I know. Okay?"

Jenna could almost see the gears in Mark's head grinding away and having a difficult time extricating the monkey wrench lodged in it.

"May I ask you, Bradley, what brought you out here, and kept you out here, for six years?"

Bradley settled himself more comfortably on the jagged boulder he'd been sitting on. "Very nice of you to ask, Trixie. As a matter of fact, my problem is very similar to your friend's here. Only much, much worse. See, I had been part of a team of government agents who had uncovered the truth about the alien landings in New Mexico."

"A complete hoax," Mark replied, trying to reassert himself in the intellectual pecking order.

"Far from it," Bradley shot back. "The government had locked up and isolated the entire area back in the fifties. It was so top secret, the president couldn't have gotten in there. My team had been created by a group called...well, I don't know what it was called. It was so secret that no one wanted to give it a name for fear of giving everyone away. Even the top, top secret agencies, the ones the CIA and the FBI don't know about, didn't know about us."

"Sounds very hush-hush," Jenna said, humoring Bradley. She liked a good story.

"Oh yeah, Trixie. And we knew everything about everyone. All the great mysteries, we had to figure out. Who stole the Lindbergh baby. What's going on at the Bermuda Triangle. Is there really a Big Foot. Who shot JFK. What happened to Jimmy Hoffa. And, why can't you just fly a regular jet into space instead of paying for something huge and expensive like a space shuttle."

"You must have been very busy," said Jenna, trying to quell the urge to laugh.

"Well, there were twenty of us, so we more or less took one or two problems apiece. Didn't want to burn anyone out."

"I'm having a little trouble believing any of this," Mark said.

Bradley nodded sympathetically. "Of course you are. The government wants you to believe those mysteries are all so complicated that they can never be solved."

"Why?"

"To divert your attention from the real problems of the country: subverting our freedom, unnecessary taxation, needless starvation, fluoridation in our drinking water, subliminal suggestions over the public media."

"Why didn't you just solve those things instead?"

"No funding. Could have done it in our sleep if they'd just paid us."

Mark looked at Jenna, who shrugged and smiled. "That still doesn't explain why you've been hiding for so long," she said.

Bradley leaned forward and stared at both Mark and Jenna for a moment or two. Finally, he said, "I haven't told this to anyone, but since you're on the lam as well, you'll probably be dead in a matter of hours. So I'll tell you. You've heard of the Grand Unification Theory?"

Mark was only now beginning to get irritated. "No. What's that?"

"It's the theory that Einstein and everyone else has been trying to solve since— Oh. Ha ha ha! I thought you were serious. You're a scientist, of course you know...I'm terribly sorry. Anyway, I'd been stumbling around with a summation on my theories on quantum gravity, as part of the anti-gravity vehicle we built some years ago. I had an old chum from Berkeley working with me who knew a thing or two about quantum physics at the sub-subatomic levels. You know, muons, gluons, gravitons, and all that. So we're, just on a lark, working up our own Grand Theory. Too much to drink, late at night, lots of spicy foods. But you know what? We figured it out. It took the whole night, but we got it.

"Well, you can imagine how excited we were. It's not everyone who outthinks Einstein. So we called practically everyone we knew. And they called everyone they knew. And the people they called, called everyone they knew. Pretty soon we had Central Intelligence on us. And after that they brought up the Seals, the Rangers, and some Special Forces teams.

"We freaked. Let me tell you. My pal went one way, and I went the other. I haven't heard from him since. In fact, I haven't heard from anyone since that awful day. Six years. All alone." He looked meaningfully at Jenna, and turned away as if he were trying to keep from breaking into tears.

There was a hushed moment where possibly the greatest achievement of man was being contemplated by all three people present.

"That has got to be the single largest load of bull shoved in my ears since I can't remember when," Mark said loudly, leaping up and pointing an unfriendly finger at Bradley.

"Mark," Jenna said, trying to warn him off. She wasn't sure of Bradley's mental stability in the face of any kind of derision.

"No, I'm sorry. The Grand Unification Theory? Pulease! Even if I were to buy into your malarkey about solving quantum gravity and all that, you couldn't devise a theory on Grand Unification if you had cloned yourself a thousand times. And...And! Even if, say, God himself was standing over your shoulder feeding you the Theory, why in the world would the United States government care about it?"

Bradley sat speechless. He had thought they were eating out of the palm of his hand, but that was obviously not the case. Still he had the convictions of his cause behind him, and he would not be deterred. "Don't you see?" he persisted. "If you knew the Grand Theory, you would evolve to a hundred times, a thousand times, the intellect of the average human being. In an instant! Your charisma, your sheer intellectual might would bring people to worship you by the millions. You'd only have to march to Washington, DC, and the government would fall the instant you got there."

Mark stared at Bradley for a moment, then glanced at Jenna, who had a hand covering her face. He looked once more at Bradley. "Well, okay, I guess that's an entirely plausible explanation from someone who believes in little green men and Big Foot. Shall we be going, Jenna?"

Jenna nodded and rose.

"That's Trixie," Bradley said.

"Ah yes, of course. After you, Trixie."

Bradley watched them walk away, and then called out "You're going the wrong way."

"Okay thanks," Mark replied from a distance as he continued in the same direction.

Bradley again waited for dramatic effect. "You're going to run into the wrong stream," he said casually and reached for the can of green beans.

He finished the can as Mark and Jenna returned to the camp two minutes later.

"All right, so which way is the right way," Mark said huffily.

"I'll take you there," Bradley said with sudden animation. He quickly doused his fire, closed up the flaps of the burlap and canvas mound that was apparently where he slept, and heaved on a backpack that would have pinned Jenna to the ground. "Okay, I'm ready."

"You're not staying with us that long." Mark pointed at the backpack.

"I never go anywhere without being prepared for anything. I've got food for a week, utensils, spare clothing, flares, a fire extinguisher, and my twenty-two."

Jenna glanced at Mark with concern, but maintained her cordial demeanor. "A gun, huh? That'll come in handy with bears and wolves, I imagine."

Bradley shook his head. "I haven't seen any bears. Or wolves. The twenty-two is for small game. And when snakes get too close. Might have to use it on those friends of yours that are after you." Bradley laughed at that.

"Ha ha," Mark forced a meager laugh and glowered meaningfully at Jenna. "Look, honey, we've got Wyatt Earp himself helping us," he mumbled to her from between clenched teeth.

The sun shone through the treetops as they stepped over roots and under low branches, and clambered over rocks on their way to the summit of the hill, the only part of the hill left that they had successfully avoided. Mark and Jenna were surprised to find themselves falling behind as they approached the top.

"I think in his own way he's trying to be nice," said Jenna between labored breaths.

"Yeah, well, this guy thinks he's evolved to a much higher hilltop than this one. Anyone that almighty ought to at least be able to conjure up something decent to eat. Do you think he can walk on water too?"

They came to an abrupt stop. Bradley was standing in their path, looking at both of them with what must stand for him as irritation.

"I'm not so far ahead that I can't hear every word you're saying," he said, his chin jutting out, working his jawbone around tensely. "If you're going to say unflattering things about me, please try a little harder not to let me hear it. All right?"

Mark smiled weakly. "Oh, I was just joking. Ha ha ha ha!"

"Uh-huh. Try to keep up."

Jenna socked Mark in the arm.

Chapter 21

Gibson Lucy stood at the head of the table, swaying unsteadily but buoyed by his rage at those assembled before him. The ancient CEO of General Micronet scanned from face to face, looking for a reason to fire any one of them, but knowing, even in his own rapidly weakening mind, that he needed them all.

"I don't like in the least that I have to be here," he began with a rasp in his voice. Since his last stroke he'd not been half as articulate or charismatic as before. His mind was still lucid enough to be aware of that. And it left him with only intimidation to bring his point home.

"I have said many times that I cannot afford to be associated with any of you in any way," he continued. "In your line of work, I'm sure you understand why. But it seems that I must be here today in order to make it perfectly clear to you the stakes involved in this situation."

Lucy took another moment to register the expressions on the faces of his audience. "I don't mind telling you, gentlemen, that I am shocked—shocked!—at how pitiful your efforts have been to date. General Micronet and dozens of other major—and I mean major as in power on a world-wide scale!—corporations have provided you with the funding and the backing to handle this…person…in a quick, clean way. Instead you have fought amongst yourselves and squandered easy opportunities."

Hobbling around the long table, Lucy scowled his worst at both those facing him and those who hadn't the nerve to face him. Gnarled hands gripped the backs of the two chairs in front of him. "Let me tell you the stakes that are in play at this moment. For General Micronet alone, we have committed 45 percent of our factory space to the production of this new device. A device that hasn't even had a prototype built yet. We have set up our research and development divisions with all the latest equipment—atrociously expensive equipment, I might add— so that we can get that prototype built the instant we have a clue how to build it. We are leveraged beyond the means of even a corporation of our size to climb out from under. If you fail to acquire the real device and not some goddamn girl's toy, or you fail to deal with this Goggin fellow, General Micronet will very possibly be forced to disintegrate into hundreds of smaller businesses that must be quickly liquidated just for us to stay alive. And I won't even get into the creative accounting that will be necessary to pull that off."

"I want this to be perfectly clear." Gibson Lucy turned and stared directly at Mr. York. "I want this project completed immediately. Your deadline is now. To hell with the expense or any other excuse. Get it done now."

With the help of his attractive and always present assistants, Lucy shuffled through a pair of doors and was gone.

Mr. York, standing behind Mr. Lucy at the front of the table when he first spoke, remained there after he had left, in full view of his fellow operatives, recognized as the focus for good or ill of the future of this campaign. For the first time in many years he wondered, not whether he would be able to carry it through, but whether he *wanted* to carry it through.

The previous night had been an arduous, professionally humiliating ordeal that Mr. York would just as soon forget. The state highways and the interstate back to General Micronet's corporate office in Kansas City had been slowed by heavy traffic virtually the entire way. Chasing the elusive Mark Goggin, Mr. York had driven as hard as the Hummer and the idiotic drivers around him had allowed. But the massive vehicle was too wide to easily slip around the other motorists, and it grew dark soon enough that it became next to impossible to check every truck he passed to see if Goggin was in it.

Worse, doubt crept into his thoughts the farther they went from Goggin's house. Mr. York was an expert driver, all modesty aside, and it didn't seem at all possible that someone like Goggin could have driven a beat-up pickup well enough to elude both him and Drake Endicott and his entourage. Endicott and his fools had followed Mr. York the entire way, cruising with uncharacteristic patience behind him. They weren't expert in anything, he knew, but they had the advantage in numbers, and in the gathering darkness that counted for something.

But they hadn't found Goggin, either. That was probably the only positive thing to happen all night. At least he wouldn't have to listen to endless derision spewing from Endicott regarding the whole sordid issue.

On returning to the metropolitan area, Mr. York was dismayed to now learn from Mr. Lucy himself that he must find Goggin at all costs. In point of fact, that was not the dismaying part. The dismaying part was being told that he must 'bury the hatchet' with Drake Endicott. The consortium of businesses working in concert on this particular problem was unanimous that nothing was more important than taking possession of the knowledge behind the floating dollhouse. Money, properties, even lives were unimportant in the face of such a monumental risk to the futures of their respective businesses. And certainly, professional animosity must be forgotten and the job brought to its successful conclusion.

When this job was all over, Mr. York mused, he intended to bring Mr. Endicott to a successful conclusion.

It was early, the morning after their tear across the state of Missouri. In the branch offices of another member of the consortium, Mr. York and Mr. Endicott, together with the survivors of the ill-fated assault on Mark Goggin's home, met to regroup and plan their next course of action.

The animosity in their ranks was still palpable, and no one seemed interested in clearing the air. Mr. York could well imagine that Endicott would like nothing better than to toss him through a window to fall forty-eight stories to the street below. He had no doubt Endicott remembered that Mr. York clubbed him unconscious. Twice.

"There's one thing I'm very curious about, Mr. York," said Drake Endicott. "How is it that you thought Goggin would be coming back here?"

There was the source of Mr. York's self-recriminations— Goggin's teen-age stooge had fooled him. He had replayed it over in his head countless times, and he was appalled that he had fallen so easily for the child's whimpering and pleading. Reeking of drugs, the boy had still put on a convincing performance.

"I was...misinformed."

"That's pretty obvious, there York-York. I would have sacked the ass responsible right then and there. Before it even happened, in fact."

"Would that I were surprised, Endicott." Mr. York turned to address the assemblage. "Gentlemen, let us face facts. We are temporary allies, but we have not acted in a very professional way. Rather than waste time trying to kiss and make up, let's just leave our mutual dislike and distrust intact and carry on with the task at hand. Mark Goggin could be virtually anywhere. If he has been fortunate, he will have traveled on foot only a short distance and gained swifter transportation within minutes. However, we all know that country well enough now to say it is unlikely. What is more likely is that he has been on foot for some time and may continue to be on foot even now. The unfortunate result of our being here is that Matthias End may have already found Goggin and helped him reach relative safety.

"Given those facts, we have no option but to call out some IOUs and track Goggin with geostationary satellites. At the same time, we can make use of military helicopters our friends in the defense industry can provide us." He motioned to certain men in the group, who nodded importantly. "We can fly down and be there within an hour. Are we agreed?"

"One moment, good Sir York," said Drake Endicott. "Your schemes are to die for, but your tactical sense sucks canal water big time. We show up with helicopters, and they'll shoot into a hiding space like field mice."

"There is such a thing as stealth mode on the latest models," Mr. York pointed out politely.

"No doubt, no doubt. And I'm not against helicopters for herding them into a few square miles. But we've got to be a tad more mobile than that. And a tad more on the ground, you know?"

Mr. York made an effort to suppress his less civilized urges. "Naturally, Mr. Endicott, we will not be able to capture them with helicopters. I would sugg—"

"I would suggest that we hit them with a bit of everything," Endicott interrupted, turning to the group at large. "We can cover lots of territory and get through the heavy brush with the Hummers. We can cut through the open paths with half a dozen dirt bikes. Yamahas probably. And we'll smoke 'em out of the water with airboats. We've got infrared night goggles for everybody and enough ammo to take Whiteman Air Force base. Whadd-ayasay?"

It sounded like a pep rally, but these were professionals. Nevertheless, they nodded approval, or at least they did not object.

"All right!" Endicott said with enthusiasm. "I propose we have a team leader for each group, and the Yorktown here and I will handle the recon-naissance on the airboats. After all, we're more familiar with the prey, so to speak. Right?"

That was met with more indifference.

Endicott turned to Mr. York. "Any new business, el Yorko?"

Mr. York didn't reply.

"All right! Then let's catch some meat!"

The gathering began to disperse.

Endicott approached Mr. York with a strut and a grin. "That went pretty well, huh?"

"I don't do reconnaissance," Mr. York replied flatly.

"No, no of course not, my man. You're the head dude here, like I've always said. But the guys out front will be the first ones to get to the goods." Endicott looked around and then leaned closer. "That means you and I will be up close and personal with the Goggin guy. Before anyone else. You get-tin' it?"

Mr. York would rather not be teamed up with Endicott, but he had to admit it was a good idea to be on the point. And if he'd suggested it rather than Endicott, the others would have become suspicious. Most considered

Endicott to be an overly violent but otherwise predictable agent. They could tolerate him just as long as he wasn't calling the shots. On the other hand, they knew that Mr. York, almost as standard protocol, had agendas within agendas within agendas. They knew him to be a superior strategist who could be counted on to behave professionally. But they would not have agreed nearly so easily if he'd made the suggestion.

It would therefore be the cool, dangerous Mr. York in charge, with the hot-headed, dangerous Mr. Endicott at his side.

And no one would rest until the job was done.

Chapter 22

Matthias End and Nathan Hamper had driven all night. And not just twelve hours of regular road travel. This was driving on every kind of terrain and in every possible place on the map. Or at least, so it seemed to them. They had driven north along the river, hoping to spot Mark and Jenna and whisk them away to safety. But the way was beyond impossible for a sidecar-laden motorcycle with no headlight. Obstacles too wide or large to zip past seemed to appear every ten feet. After driving for an hour through trees they were convinced someone had intentionally planted in pairs and three feet apart just to foul them up, they gave up driving along the river altogether.

It was not long after they had rejoined the road and paused to look somewhere else that the complaining began.

"…I'm tired…"

"…I need to go to the bathroom…"

"…Let's just quit…Shouldn't they be dead by now?…"

End had ignored it easily enough. It was not unlike the typical whining that every three-year-old or twenty-three-year-old said when driving for more than ten minutes to somewhere they didn't want to go to in the first place.

Not wanting to retrace their steps south down the same road, End had decided to cross the river if it was possible and search from the other side. Nathan had advised against it in his own whiny, sarcastic way. Not only was there not a serviceable bridge across the river within twenty miles in either direction, he said, but even if they did get over to the other side, there were so many streams and ponds and hills and very large trees that they would move faster if they just walked.

"Then how about an *un*-serviceable bridge?" End had asked.

"There's probably a fallen tree every hundred yards. You might get half-way across one of 'em before you fall in."

"Rocks?"

"There's rocks everywhere, man."

"Ones we can go across."

"Oh."

They drove south for a mile or so before Nathan recognized a spot that showed promise. In his relatively unfettered childhood, Nathan had gone as far as he'd wanted to along the Pomme de Terre and everywhere else. He and his friends had traveled almost to Branson to the south, to the Kansas border to the west, and to the Mississippi River to the east. They never went north. Nothing but grass and flat prairie, or at least that's what they'd heard. The result of their frequent and wide-ranging travel was that they knew a lot of places. This particular river they had floated down, swam in, partied in, and thrown up in so many times, they could have recognized favorite spots with their eyes crossed. And probably had.

End came to a stop to eyeball the descent from the hill where they sat, to the banks of the river, the zigzag of flat rocks rising up above the water's surface, to the steep bank on the other side.

Nathan eyeballed it too. "I'd like to go home now."

End ignored him and gunned the engine. They roared through the tall grass and brush and clanked against saplings that had grown in imprudent locations. The rocks had luckily been stable enough that they didn't immediately sink as they crossed the river. Instead, they mostly twisted sideways so that the crossing was done seesawing and hydroplaning through half a foot of water.

"I don't feel so good!" Nathan had shouted as they crashed into the far bank and shot up the steep incline onto dry land.

They spent the next several hours dodging just about exactly what Nathan had warned would be there. Small creeks and streams popped up nearly everywhere, and trees popped up everywhere else. The hills weren't always just hills; many times they were sheer cliffs shooting straight up.

They spent as much time driving east and west to get around the obstacles as they did heading south.

The up-down-left-right motion coupled with a growing exhaustion slowly began to wear on Nathan, hunched down in the sidecar. "I've gotta smoke somethin', man, or my head's gonna explode!" he had shouted while they bounced over tree roots that felt like railroad tracks.

With a determination Matthias End had never felt before in all his misbegotten life, he continued relentlessly on. The motorcycle and sidecar took a terrific battering, and Nathan's head slowly began to roll less adeptly with the jolts as he grew more tired.

Finally, End could see that they were gaining little ground and taking too much time doing it.

"All right," he said after bringing the bike to a stop. "How do we get back over again?"

Nathan stared up at him from within the protective shell of the sidecar. "You know what, dude, maybe I should just unhook this thing. You can go your way, and I'll go mine."

After much gentle persuasion from End, Nathan suggested they keep going south for a while longer. There might be another line of rocks somewhere around there.

So they continued with the same tacking motion they had followed for the last untold number of hours. As they veered left and right or sped up and slowed down, Nathan thought he might try to doze.

"Statistics show that children who don't get sleep do less well in school," he pointed out while End gunned the bike up a hill. Nathan wondered whether he had school that day, and also what day it was.

Shooting through a clearing, they came upon the rocks he had spoken of.

"That?" said End in disbelief. "That?!"

The way was straight and, End supposed, not unreasonably narrow. A solid acceleration and maybe if they had a long ramp on this bank, it might see them through the air and over to the other side —into a tree more than likely, since they could barely see the far bank for the long, dense line of trees. It was nevertheless a moot point, since there was no ramp. There also were no rocks, at least none that could easily be seen peeking up through the surface of the river. And the water was deep —deeper than the river had been for miles.

"It's not as deep as it looks," Nathan said from the floor of the sidecar. He was lying on his side, curled up in a tight ball.

"All right," End agreed. He revved the throttle twice and popped the clutch and twisted the throttle for all it was worth. The rear tire spun, digging into the dirt for half a second, and then the front tire left the ground as the bike leaped forward. They were fortunate that the near bank was high enough above the water level so that when they entered the water, they were already a quarter of the way across. But it was, in fact, much too deep.

The motorcycle was caught by the water and brought to a near stop. End was almost thrown over the handlebars. Instead, his weight carried him over the sidecar, and by some miracle, the sidecar kept them afloat long enough for the bike to reach the shallows just shy of the far bank. End kept the engine revving so that they were able to climb up out of the water with relative ease.

"No problem," Nathan murmured.

The line of trees was relatively easy to negotiate as they were now well-accustomed to having to wind around close-knit trees. They pulled back up to the road they had been on however long ago.

Where to go now? End wondered. Maybe the next thing to do was to keep driving south until they found someplace where they could somehow acquire a boat or an airboat to travel on the water itself. And there was always a chance that someone had spotted Mark and Jenna.

It might not be the best plan of action, but it was the best his muddled brain could come up with at the moment. Turning south once more, End accelerated down the road, the glow of dawn arising in the east.

By the time sunlight began to shoot through the trees with a warm-ing intensity and the world began to wake up, Nathan was all but asleep. He mumbled vaguely coherent threats of teenage retribution against the oppressive adult population, but for all intents and purposes, he was talking in his sleep.

All night End had doggedly pursued his quest to rescue the unknowing subject of his great experiment, but after fighting off half a dozen men back at Mark's house and tearing through most of central Missouri all night, even he couldn't keep up the pace. The motorcycle veered this way and that as End's eyes blurred, and he realized he would have to slow down at least a lit-tle. Trouble was, even going slower, the bike continued to veer and his eyes continued to blur. Okay, he thought, maybe he could stop just long enough for the bike and his eyes to get themselves together.

The strange thing was that the cycle still felt like it was veering, and his eyes still couldn't focus, five minutes after he had already stopped.

"Maybe if I close my eyes and rest a bit," he said out loud.

"Okay," Nathan responded in his sleep.

End folded his arms on the handlebars and put his head down on his arms. Just for a short rest.

Ten minutes later the motorcycle began to sputter and choke.

"Turn it off if you're going to bed," Nathan said, again in his sleep.

End turned the key.

The forest gradually came to life as End and Nathan drifted off to exhausted impenetrable slumber.

* * *

Matthias End's vision blurred when his eyelids first opened. Everything was blue and green and smelled like gravel. He blinked rapidly, panicking for a reason he couldn't immediately identify. Sitting up almost as quickly as he had blinked, he noticed the motorcycle next to him. He rubbed his eyes and blinked a few more times before his whereabouts unfolded before him. He had fallen asleep.

"Dammit!" he growled under his breath.

The sun was overhead so it must not be too far past noon, he thought. He must have fallen off the cycle. They couldn't have slept more than five hours. Still, that was plenty of time for York to have driven all the way down here. And he'd have been here in an hour if he had the better sense to fly. Still, unless York had some kind of advanced tracking like satellites or ten thousand FBI agents at his disposal, he'd be searching for Mark and Jenna forever just like End was having to. He had the sick feeling, though, that General Micronet did have satellites at their disposal.

Well, he didn't. He'd just have to work ten times as hard, that was all. The problem was that Mark and Jenna could be anywhere in fifty square miles. How would he find them? It seemed entirely possible now, that they weren't along the main river way They might be and he had just missed them, but if Mark was smart, he wouldn't be sticking to the main water. Actually, if he'd been smart he'd have seen the road and hitched a ride to Rio. If that was the case, he and Jenna would be safe, and End wouldn't need to worry about them. On the other hand, if End was to discern his own ultimate destiny from this mission and gain the answers he sought, he needed to assume that Mark hadn't found a ride, that he was actually somewhere out in this wilderness.

The clincher was that End had told Mark to follow the river and wait for End to reach them. Mark and Jenna were both intelligent and capable under life's normal crises, but neither had ever been under such life and death circumstances as they were now likely encountering. Given that, End decided that they had not taken the road to Rio.

So. If they hadn't taken the road and they weren't along the main river, they couldn't be far off. There were dozens of smaller streams that were fed by this main body, but only a few that were large enough for a boat to float along. Nathan would know where they were. Grimacing and grumbling to himself, End staggered to his feet and looked over the motorcycle to the sidecar on the other side.

Nathan still lay curled at the bottom of the sidecar, his coat pulled up covering his neck.

"Nathan!" End shouted down into the small space and was rewarded by seeing Nathan jerk and whack the back of his head against the sidecar's metal insides. It wasn't kind, of course, but he'd grown tired of Nathan's irreverent—so to speak—bashing of his past. Not to mention his mostly unhelpful advice and general uselessness so far. "Get up. We've got to figure out where to go from here."

A low moan emitted from the bowels of the sidecar, which made End grin, and then a couple of words even teenagers weren't supposed to say. Nathan flung his coat back from his head with his usual early morning bad temper.

"I was sleeping," he whined resentfully. "I don't go waking you up, do I?"

"You'd have to wake up before me to do that. That's none too likely. Now, we need to find those three or four smaller streams that left this river. We saw them yesterday on the other side. Big streams. Big enough to take a small boat through."

Nathan squatted on the sidecar and frowned in aggravation at everything he saw.

"Nathan?"

"What."

"Come on, we're out of time. Where are they?"

"Why do you want to go there again? Let's just go farther south."

"No. We've been farther south than they could have reached by boat. I told Mark we'd meet him downriver. So he's going to stick close to the river. This road diverts away from the river just a little south of here. We haven't seen him on this river or wandering around near it, so he has to be on one of those smaller streams." He paused for Nathan to take it all in.

"What?" Nathan said, screwing up his face in incomprehension.

End sighed. "Want some breakfast?"

Nathan's eyes brightened. "Yeah, what are we having?"

"What's your favorite?"

222

Nathan straightened, his eyes twinkling and his hands imagining holding a plate in front of him. "Eggs, bacon, hash browns, juice, sausages, and milk."

"Okay. And will you smoke a joint before or afterward?"

"Definitely after. I—" Nathan frowned and glared at End. "Fuck you. I got no joints. You took care of that yourself."

"At least I got your attention. Where are the smaller streams that flow out of this river?"

Nathan eyed him and became suddenly sly. "I want a joint first."

"No problem. Make it out of oak leaves if you like. Find some marijuana plants and make the real thing, for all I care. But not until after we find Mark."

"No, now." Nathan leaned over and flipped the motorcycle's seat up. Inside were a map, a screwdriver, thirty-nine cents in change, and another bag full of the damnable wrapped weed.

"Good God, boy, you'd put half the pot-smokers in the sixties to shame. You haven't hidden any on me, have you?"

Nathan grinned. He lit up and was puffing away before End took another breath. That breath was filled with the smoke's unique aroma.

End pulled the last of the reserve tanks loose from the back of the bike and refilled the gas tank while Nathan described, with decreasing clarity as he sucked on the joint, where the smaller streams might be located.

"That's the best you can do?" End said in disappointment.

"Yes," Nathan replied simply.

The engine started on End's first try—he couldn't resist a smug glance in Nathan's direction—and they were off again.

Nathan's directions consisted of backtracking north for a few miles until they spotted a side road that went west. Somewhere around there, was another shallow spot in the river where they could cross again, heading east. The southernmost stream branching off from the main river was north of there. Or maybe south.

Driving north again, End noticed that the hills had finally surrounded them. They couldn't have noticed last night because it was dark. But they were looming on all sides around them; in fact they were so high he began to worry that they were about to search in the wrong area.

"Are there a lot of caves around here?" he shouted at Nathan as they drove swiftly along.

"Babes? No, not many," Nathan shouted back.

"No, 'caves'."

"What?"

"A lot of caves!"

"I said 'no'!"

End gave up.

With the sun out and shining under what appeared to be a clear sky—he caught only an occasional glimpse of the sky for all the trees—it was startling how deep inside another world they had found themselves. The road wound around constantly and must have had to be built with relentless patience to cope with the high steep hills and the sudden appearance and disappearance of bodies of water or valleys that sloped away so unexpectedly. The trees were the most astonishing of all. They were so densely packed everywhere that they blotted out the sun at times. This must be what it's like traveling through a jungle, he thought.

They came to the road and End turned away from it and onto a path that was plenty wide enough for them. In fact it looked like a perfect place to launch a boat into the river. As they approached the water, he saw that it was not a perfect place after all. The breadth of the river was quite narrow and winding. The current was fierce and made a terrific noise as it crashed over the pitiful collection of rocks that Nathan thought they would somehow make it over.

"No. No, no, this is way too deep and way too fast," End said, shaking his head emphatically.

"It's nothing," Nathan insisted. "Just get a running start like you did the last time. You'll jump out there, and we'll maybe skip a couple of times and we're over."

No, End thought. No, no, no, no, no. This won't work. This is doomed. But he wrenched the throttle all the way, and the motorcycle lurched forward for what was to be, to its momentary dismay and eternal relief, its very last time.

The bank leading down to the water's edge fell away much more suddenly than End had anticipated, and he, Nathan, and the bike fell away along with it. When they reached the waterline, they didn't leap into the air so they could skip over the water, but instead they drove straight into the water, spraying it everywhere. The momentum of the bike and what rocks there were, succeeded in providing the bike with enough steam to get to the exact center of the river before it came to a tragic stop. And then all was lost. The tremendous current there in the center spun the bike around several times and then capsized it, tossing its occupants into the chilly water.

End tumbled over more rocks as the current dragged him along. He tried to stand but couldn't get his footing long enough before the waist-deep current knocked him down again. Nathan was just a few feet farther downriver and seemed to be doing all right. The bike was nowhere to be found. The sidecar was floating a good twenty feet downriver from them, gaining distance rapidly.

The river rounded a bend a bit too abruptly and End and Nathan both twisted around uncontrollably as three different currents contested for control of them.

Then the water dropped away.

It wasn't a particularly high fall, but the rocks at the bottom were memorable. Nathan somehow avoided the worst of it and landed with a loud smack in deeper water. End found nothing but rock. He crashed onto his back, lost his sense of direction, and careened wildly around in the grip of dueling currents. At some point he hit his head on something and couldn't remember anything for a dizzying amount of time.

When End came to his senses, he found himself swimming. Was it possible to black out and yet still be swimming? That didn't seem possible. Still, there he was.

On a bank to his left and just a bit downriver sat Nathan, wringing water out of his shirt.

End saw him and swam with a sudden energy. He felt the ground with his feet and pushed furiously through the water until he was standing in ankle-deep water.

"That was three feet of water back there! There were no rocks!" he bellowed wrathfully. "We weren't going to skip over anything!" He spit something slimy and awful out of his mouth and hoped it landed on Nathan.

Nathan stood up to his full height, still nearly a foot shorter than End, and screamed back "Yeah, it was. But you tried to go over it anyway, didn't you. You goddamn stupid fucking welder."

End pondered his options with an amazing calm. Then he calmly waited for Nathan to have wrung as much water out of his clothes as he could, picked him up by the backs of his shirt and jeans, and tossed him back into the river.

Nathan came up spluttering and furious again and even stomped back toward shore looking for retribution before he saw End's lethal glare. Instead, he sat on a grassy patch of ground and started wringing water out of his clothes all over again, grumbling as he did.

After a time, End sat next to him and began wringing his own clothes out. The water was much quieter there, the river's span much wider and deeper. When they gave up trying to wring out more water, End pointed something out passing by them in the water. It was one of the motorcycle's spare tanks.

"It was about out of gas anyway," Nathan said.

Twenty feet or so behind it was the motorcycle's seat. That gave Nathan a nasty turn because it meant that his secret stash was drenched and not even remotely smoke-worthy.

Nothing else washed by, which meant the bike was probably still upriver, submerged somewhere it could take them hours or even days to find.

"What do we do now?" Nathan asked. For the first time since they'd left the house, he'd sounded more like the young boy he still was. The river had shaken him.

"Well," End said, slapping him on the back and making a loud slurping noise when that squeezed out more water from his shirt and coat. "We go north."

"And then?"

"We go east when we find that smaller stream I asked you about."

"And then?"

"Oh, I thought maybe we'd stop for lunch. I know this fabulous little bistro under a big oak right next to the Meramec caverns."

"That's practically all the way to St. Louis," Nathan said, scowling.

"Yeah," End grinned, offering another wet slap. "I know."

Chapter 23

"Reagan asked me to build him a floating pedestal right before he ran for office for his second term. He had plenty of funding, millions of dollars from all these pharmaceutical and defense companies, and he thought it'd look good, inspiring or something, to float in the air like he was God."

Bradley Granger crested another hill, the fourth, or maybe fifth, or possibly sixth hill they'd climbed since they left his camp. He stopped to scan the area, took a deep breath of the fresh air, and let loose a fishy belch. Looking behind him, he called out "Get it in gear, people. The river isn't running to us."

Mark Goggin stopped climbing to look up. "Ha ha, okay Brad. Be there in a minute, you arrogant walrus." He said the last for the benefit of Jenna Telfair, who was not suffering quite as badly with the hills as Mark, but she was not enjoying it any better, either.

Jenna looked up to see Brad turn away and continue on. "You know if you were to sneak up there and shove him down the hill, I bet he'd roll all the way to Illinois."

"How about I just throw rocks at him?"

"I don't think you can throw it that far."

"Oh ha ha."

They reached the top of the hill several minutes after Brad had begun his descent down the other side. It seemed a good time to stop for a drink and a rest and hope they lost Brad. Of course, with Brad being their guide, that would mean becoming lost themselves. But better to be lost for centuries than to hear another one of his tall tales.

At the summit, the hill stretched north and south, and the mass of trees blocked their view in that direction, but they could see east and west for miles. The sun was on its downward course, but the treetops were still glowing yellows and reds and oranges and even a little green. Back home the trees were virtually naked, but here they protected each other from the wind and the other elements and clung defiantly to their foliage.

"It's so beautiful," Jenna said. "You know, we could have a house right here, or maybe just a bit off the path. And maybe downhill enough to stay out of the wind. Just a little cottage, a Tudor maybe."

"We?" Mark said.

Jenna glared. "Okay, just me then." She shoved him enough that he slid down the hill a couple of feet. "Don't you think it's pretty?" she demanded.

He stared at her, a half-smile playing across his face. "Yes, very much so."

"Are you having any trouble?" said Brad, bursting from between the trees.

Mark and Jenna both jumped and immediately fed him excuses. Thirst, fatigue, rock in a shoe, diving birds, heard a bear, whatever came to mind.

Brad seemed skeptical. "Well, if everything's all right now, let's keep moving."

It was probably a good thing that he'd come back to them because he hadn't actually gone downhill but more sideways, moving downhill but also along the slope of the hill. They'd have lost him for sure, damn the luck.

Maybe it was quicker this way, but the footing was five times more difficult than just going downhill and turning left at the bottom. The only plus—or minus—was that they were able to keep up with Brad more easily. There being no real path, the person in front was the one who made the path, slowing them considerably.

"So anyway." Brad was breathing hard, but wasn't letting that stop him. "I told Hawking that I didn't care for his conclusions. Too much like watching Star Trek or, worse, Lost in Space. He kinda got offended. Stephen's pretty sensitive about his work."

After a couple of hours of this, Mark had quit trying to refute or even follow Brad's stories. The man had probably admired a physics teacher in high school and read a lot of the science section of the newspaper. More than likely, what he was really doing out here was hiding from everyone tired of hearing his claims as savior of the world and name-dropper extraordinaire.

Jenna tried a more subtle approach to quiet him. "Bradley, aren't the birds sounding beautiful? Let's listen to them."

Brad waited just long enough for the first unsuspecting bird to sound off, before he did too. "Ah, that would probably sound to the layman like a robin. The full tweet followed by some rather suggestive whistling," he said, leering at Jenna. "But it is in fact the call to her young of the female striped American chipmunk."

"All right, all right," Mark came to a stop next to Jenna. Brad had to slow his momentum before he could turn and look back.

"Chipmunks do not sound like birds," said Mark firmly. "I'm not an expert, but even I know that. I'm sure you know a lot of things, and you'll get to them all at some point, but let's not delve into alternate realities and pretend like you were born there. You know, actually, you do sound as if you've spent most of your time in an alternate reality now, so why shouldn't you know everything about it? Terribly sorry. Please, do continue."

Brad squinted at him from behind a bunched trio of saplings. It was obvious he was trying to decide if he might have just been insulted again. Expressions appeared and morphed from one to the next on his face, before a final look which was clearly back to thinking about chipmunks. "All right. Thank you," he said. "Now, the Asian striped chipmunk whistles suggestively in double-time..." Another story began thereafter, and neither Mark nor Jenna listened to any of it.

The hill they marched across was higher than the others they had scaled so far, or at least the descent to this point was the longest. Mark could feel his wind returning to him as they went on. The trees were farther apart there and mostly bare of leaves. Pine trees sprouted up in fewer numbers but with greater size and density.

While Brad reenacted the approximate and theoretical sound of Asian and American striped chipmunks fighting to the death, the threesome walked between two tall, fat pines into a clearing.

Brad stopped in his tracks.

An older fellow sat in the center of the clearing on a tree trunk that had been cut for just such a purpose. Next to him was a burlier man who was trying to get a fire going.

"Hello there, Brad. How are you?" said the older man.

Brad glanced nervously at Mark and Jenna before acknowledging the older gentleman. "Mr. Hamilton, good to see you again, sir."

The older gentleman regarded Mark and Jenna with considerable intensity.

"Word, you're gonna bore a hole through the both of them," said the burly man. He stood up and approached them, extending a hand. "I'm Mike Abram," he said pleasantly but without a smile. Mark and Jenna shook it easily enough. Surely, he couldn't possibly be any stranger than Brad. "This is Word Hamilton." Abram indicated the older gentleman. "Regardless of how tactless he may be, Word is a good man. He's just been itching to ask you a whole pile of questions."

"Why is that?" Jenna asked.

"I'm a journalist," Hamilton said simply. "Asking piles of questions is a professional habit, I'm afraid. I'm anxious to hear what you have to say, Mr. Goggin." He turned to Jenna and nodded politely. "And you as well, Miss Telfair."

Immediate alarm registered on Mark's face.

"Now, now, don't worry," said Hamilton. "I told you, I'm a journalist. You don't have to be afraid of anything but what I write about you."

"How do you know our names?" asked Jenna.

Hamilton grinned. "You're only two of the more newsworthy fugitives in the country. By the way, did you know that you're fugitives?"

Mark glanced at Jenna. "Is this about Archibald Scott's death?"

"Naturally. What else would it be? Oh, I'm personally curious about who it is that's chasing you. Doesn't seem to be anyone related to actual law enforcement, does it?"

"You knew that?"

Hamilton smirked. "I have my sources."

"Are you a reporter too?" Jenna asked Abram.

"No, no way. I'm a cabinetmaker," Abram said, returning to his fire-building effort.

"He's much more than that," said Hamilton with a chuckle.

"Well, we don't have time for an interview," said Mark. "There's an army after us, and we've got to get a long way from here."

"Oh, no. You've got plenty of time. Your hunters are still way upstate. They won't be here for at least an hour or two."

"That's an hour or two we can get farther away. Sorry to disappoint you." Mark started to leave.

"I *could* tell them where you are," Hamilton pointed out. "Or at least inform the local police. You are wanted for questioning, after all. And you're on the A-list of suspects for Scott's murder."

"All right, enough of this," Jenna said suddenly.

Hamilton and Abram regarded her.

She straightened and put her hands on her hips. "Gentlemen, I'm going to have to ask you to allow us to leave and to keep this quiet. I am an undercover agent for the Securities and Exchange Commission. I know that sounds strange. I don't believe it myself sometimes. But it's true." Jenna then crossed her arms importantly. "The SEC has been following the activities of a number of companies thought to be illegally acquiring products and padding their books with nonexistent profits from those products. My assignment has been to monitor General Micronet's activities. I can't give you any details except to say that Mr. Goggin here has been manipulated and financially damaged by that very same company, and we think we have a very good case. The SEC will be turning evidence over to the Justice department in a matter of hours."

"Why are you running then, Miss Telfair?" Hamilton asked politely. "Why don't you just call in some help? The FBI or the ATF. Hell, I'm sure even the local sheriff would be more than glad to help." He glanced in Abram's direction.

Jenna looked worried for a split second. "Ah, we're severely undermanned at the SEC and I'm having to protect Mr. Goggin by myself. We happen to be outnumbered twenty to one by our pursuers. Now, unless you want to get caught in the middle of a gun battle, you gentlemen will have to excuse us."

"An interesting story, Miss Telfair," said Hamilton. "Except there are no agents for the SEC."

"None that you may know of," Jenna replied airily. "The general public has no knowledge of us."

"Ah," Abram leaned forward. "I'm pretty well in the loop in that area, and the SEC ain't got nobody that does undercover work. Just a bunch of paper pushers."

Mark turned to look at him, puzzled.

"I'm the sheriff in Hermitage," Abram said as he tossed twigs and leaves on the weak flames. "I have to know these things."

Both Mark and Jenna registered considerable shock at his words. If he really was the sheriff, he might just arrest Mark as a suspect in the Archibald Scott murder. Right then and there. And if he was being paid off by corporations, Mark was in a much worse predicament.

Abram looked as if he understood their situation exactly, although it was impossible to tell his intentions. Word Hamilton, on the other hand, seemed oblivious to anything but his story.

"Okay, now. Let's get down to it." Hamilton rubbed his hands together excitedly, staring at Mark like a wolf at lunchtime. "Did you kill him?"

"Of course not!" shouted Jenna. "This man wouldn't harm a fly."

Hamilton glanced at her, then back at Mark. "Then why are General Micronet's goons after you?"

Mark shook his head in continued surprise at the journalist's knowledge of their situation. "How did you—"

Jenna was much more intent on his defense. "Mark built something that they—"

"Thank you, but I know all about his invention," replied Hamilton. "Do you mind if *he* talks once in a while?" He looked again at Mark. "Why, Mr. Goggin? No police are involved, no Bureau agents, not even anybody with the SEC." He smirked at Jenna before looking back at Mark. "You haven't done anything at least inappropriate if not exactly illegal, have you Mr. Goggin? Not doing any corporate espionage on the side? Maybe steal some schematics or secret plans for someone?"

"That is an outrageous accusation," Jenna blurted out. "Mark has only been in the GMN building once, and I was with him the whole time."

Hamilton continued to look at Mark.

"I've built every one of my inventions myself," Mark said quietly.

Abram suddenly appeared next to Hamilton. "Mr. Goggin, could you tell me why someone would offer me a hundred thousand dollars to arrest you and cause you to have an accident of the mortal kind?"

Mark was speechless. Stunned. There it was. They had gotten to the local police.

Jenna gasped, then asked much more quietly, "Who made the offer?"

"They didn't say. It's a generous offer, I must say. And by the looks of you, an easy job." Abram's eyes sparkled, although there still was no smile.

"Never mind that," Hamilton interrupted. "I want to know how you killed this Scott fella. I'm figuring some kind of planted booby trap. Electrocution or poison quills, something like that."

"Poison quills?" Abram guffawed. "Word, this ain't no television murder mystery. Maybe you ought to sit down and compose yourself before you pursue this line of questioning any further."

Hamilton didn't sit, but he did stop talking.

"Close enough," Abram said. "Now, Mr. Goggin, I'm not at all sure what's going on here. Of course, I suspect that most people reading about it in the papers don't understand what's going on either. But I'll tell you. In all my time as sheriff, I have never been asked to kill anyone before, and while

I'm sure it is an intriguing line of work, I'm much more comfortable making dovetails in maple stock. All this intrigue don't sit well, and I want to know a whole hell of a lot more of what's going on before I start to killing."

"Sheriff," Mark said, "I know you don't know me any more than you know the people who want me killed, but I can assure you that I haven't killed anyone, nor have I stolen anything from anyone. I build things. That's it."

"Really," Jenna added, trying to be helpful. "And he's not that great at that."

Everyone looked at her, and she decided to stop talking as well.

Abram regarded Mark for a moment. "I wonder if you'd let me put you under my protective custody. Until I can sort all this out. I won't kill you. I promise," he grinned for the first time. "Now if it was a million dollars? A whole different kettle of fish."

Mark shook his head. "I don't think so, sheriff. With all due respect, unless you've got fifty deputies hiding behind the trees, you're hopelessly outgunned."

Abram nodded thoughtfully. "I don't doubt that."

The group became silent for a time. The trees rustled anxiously, and the wind swept through the clearing in several directions. Leaves levitated up off the ground and swirled in the air as if in a friendly display of how simple it really is to float in the air.

"Okay, okay, I gotta see it," Hamilton spoke up suddenly, making everyone jump.

"See what?" Abram asked.

Mark eyed them both warily. But perhaps, he thought, it was time for some trust. For some reason, he felt like trusting these two. He opened the knapsack that had been slung over his head and shoulder for the last two days. Everyone drew near as he withdrew his hand from the bag, revealing four crystals, each about the size and shape of a coaster. They gleamed a silvery color like mercury, the surface seeming to slide around in constant motion.

"Damn," Hamilton breathed and Abram muttered an equally profane "Son of a bitch."

To Jenna they were like magical discs out of some kind of high-art movie. She had not been sure what to expect of the source of the Barbie dream house's gravitational revolt. But this was not exactly it.

"Why don't they float?" she asked.

"They're upside down," said Mark. "And they could probably use being charged up again."

Brad had been quiet for some time, presumably because of an unpleasant past history with either Hamilton or Abram, or both. But the glimmering objects nevertheless inspired new anecdotes in him. "Our discs at NASA needed a special vacuum electromagnetic charge. It lasted several years that way."

At long last Mark had a reply that seemed satisfactory to the task of defending his intellect. "These don't need electromagnetic or vacuum charges." A typical charge didn't last even close to a year, but he wasn't going to admit to that.

"Oh we didn't need electromagnetics or vacuums either," said Brad. "It just allowed the discs to last a long time and gave them enough power to lift heavier things. You know, cars, trucks, buses, construction cranes."

"Knock it off, Bradley," said Abram.

Mark scowled. He hoped it wouldn't come down to who was the superior liar. He thought he could give as well as he got, but he'd been told by more than one person that his eyes gave him away when he lied. An expression of obvious guilt, apparently.

"On the road to a thousand wars," Hamilton mumbled to himself. He caressed the flat shiny surface of a disc and moved his head so the reflected light off the discs shifted and changed colors. He pondered Mark's pleased expression. "Can you make a floating vehicle with these?"

"The multi-billion dollar civilization-breaking question," Mark said. "Honestly, I don't know. For the longest time I've thought the answer was no. But the magnitude of all that has happened to me in the last few weeks has made me think more about the whole thing, and now I must admit that it does seem possible. Certainly a significant number of corporations think so."

"Maybe I'm too much of a skeptic," said Abram, retreating to his fire, "but they just look like CDs with pixie dust sprinkled all over them. A pretty good piece of work, pretty convincing, but not much better than that alien cadaver they cut open on TV a while back. Now *that* was convincing."

The rest of them watched the discs sparkle prettily for a few moments longer before Mark put them away.

Hamilton watched the knapsack flap close. "I believe him," he said with finality.

"You do not," Abram said, snickering.

"Yes, I do. Don't get me wrong. It's not the discs; they look awfully fake to me. No, it's the people chasing them. If these were just four CDs dressed up in a juvenile hoax, then why are there people from major, *major,* major companies after them?"

"Greed blinds," Abram said as he stirred up the still feeble fire.

"Not when millions—perhaps even billions as you say, Mr Goggin—are at stake. All it takes is one company to decide to commit itself, and the rest will follow like jackals. Something must have convinced them, and whether it's stupid or not, it's a good story." He squatted down in front of Abram.

"Meaning what?" Abram asked, suddenly uncomfortable.

"We have to help them."

Abram sneered. "Not a chance. I'm crossing the line already by not arresting him. If I help him, the businesses will back my opponent come next election and spend me right out of a job. You remember the mayor getting backing from the big mattress company on the west side of town last year, don't you?"

"Fine, don't help then. Just turn the other way and let them borrow your boat."

"My boat? No! That's a new boat, Word. Took me forever to get the money for that." Abram turned away to sweep up a pile of sticks and dead leaves in his hands.

"All right, forget it then." Hamilton said, motioning Mark and Jenna toward a hill behind him while Abram was turned. He mouthed words silently that neither of them could understand, then said to Abram: "They'll just be killed, that's all. People who've been denied their right as a US citizen for a fair trial." Abram was still absorbed in his fire, pouring sticks and leaves on it, and Hamilton waved his arm wildly toward the hill.

Abram looked up then and saw Hamilton. "What do you think you're—"

"What was that?" Brad said loudly and in a distressed voice.

Everyone became silent. The sound was unmistakably that of helicopters approaching, at least two, judging by the stereo-like reverberation. One was still some distance away, coming from the northwest. The other felt as if it was practically there, zeroing in on them from the east.

"That was a fast hour or two," Mark said to Hamilton.

"Should we freeze or run for cover?" asked Jenna, staring at the treetops to the east. The trees were still a decent cover, but the mere fact that the helicopters had come directly at them as if they knew they were there suggested to Mark that a satellite or a high-altitude reconnaissance aircraft had located them. The trees weren't going to be much good if Mr. York already knew their location.

"Freeze!" Brad shouted, stared momentarily at everyone in abject terror, then broke into an all-out sprint due west. The others watched him go uncertainly.

Unaccountably, as Brad ran, leaves flew up in the air in places where he had not even passed through. A loud thud emitted from a small branch and the branch separated from its tree with an explosive crack and flew into the air. Then two even louder thuds blew holes in two tree trunks, sending bark flying and splitting the trunks into pieces. A third thud was muffled when it sank into Brad's lower right thigh. He went down in a rolling sprawl that became a cloud of leaves. He didn't move after that, although he wasn't so far away that they couldn't see a mound of leaves breathing heavily.

The remaining members of the party turned back to look at one another and then in every direction at once. Terror was in their faces and an open acknowledgement of their collective complete lack of combat experience.

More thuds sounded off, smashing into more and closer trees and scattering huge piles of leaves.

"Get to the boat!" Abram screamed suddenly. He ran between and past Mark and Jenna, and vaulted swiftly up the hill Hamilton had been motioning them toward. Mark and Jenna joined Hamilton in following after him.

At the top of the hill, another loud thud went off and Abram's left shoulder threw him over the crest. The three stragglers behind him found sudden wings and flew through the air, over the top of the hill, and down the other side, with varying degrees of success. Hamilton found himself sliding down the hill on top of Abram, while Mark and Jenna tumbled and slid along with a million crackling leaves.

They came to a stop at the bottom and quickly leaped to their feet. Hamilton and Abram were barely past the summit when they stopped. "Keep going!" Abram shouted at them.

"What? No wait!" Hamilton shouted at Abram, Mark, and Jenna.

It was at that moment that the helicopter from the east flew overhead. The excitement of escaping had deafened them to its approach until then, but the high-pitched, though strangely muffled, whine of its engine and the hovering aircraft's rotors pounding the air, coupled with the unignorably looming shadow above the trees, made everyone look up.

Mark stood still, cowed both by the impressive power of the machine and by the apparent hopelessness of their plight.

But Jenna was much more focused on the boat, and she grabbed his arm and pulled him nearly off his feet in that direction.

The helicopter had been going too fast to come to a complete stop and had to bank around. Its pilot mistakenly chose to come north, and that put it right in the path of the other helicopter approaching from the northwest.

The time it took them to safely untangle themselves from each other provided Mark and Jenna with enough opportunity to get to the boat.

The boat they approached did not look fast enough to outrace a quick ten-year-old, but it was decidedly more impressive than the canoe they'd run aground in. From stem to stern it couldn't have been more than twelve feet, and the sides weren't high enough to keep out the water lapping into it, even resting as it was now. Mark had seen boats like it on fishing shows on television, and the tall seat at the front proved that conjecture. The boat was moored to a tree, nestled in a small inlet away from the stronger main current of the river like a parking space.

Jenna reached it first and leaped over the two-foot gap between the bank and the boat itself. Her weight and momentum as she landed pushed the boat out farther so that Mark had to adjust his leap for the longer distance.

It was a doomed effort from the start, and Mark was convinced of that before he left the ground. His hands and feet flailed in the air, and he landed in the water with a loud smack, spraying considerable water—with some justice—at Jenna.

Her adrenaline peaked, Jenna ignored the spray and started the engine before she tried to help Mark aboard. He reached the boat and easily pulled himself over the low sides. The fact that the water was only three feet deep also helped.

Jenna peered just over the side of the boat at the hill where Abram and Hamilton remained, as Mark staggered sopping wet over to the controls. There were half a dozen more men surrounding Abram and Hamilton now, brandishing sleek powerful-looking weapons. She wondered if the two men would be killed and if she would be killed before she ever found out. Despite the continually mounting evidence, she could still not believe that the company she had worked for so diligently, whose proud code of professional ethics she had believed in for all these years, was behind all this.

Mark slammed the throttle into reverse, and the motor whirred like an overtaxed blender. But the boat did move. They eased out into the heavier current and slid into place.

In the wrong direction.

The sound of more thudding bullets hitting the boat's hull kept their heads ducked. Sections of wood splintered or separated from the rest of the boat with instantaneous swiftness as bullets flew around them.

It quickly became apparent that the current was too strong for the engine to force the boat around the right way. But Mark remembered that a lot of these fishing boats had smaller trolling motors that might at least speed them up and put them in the general correct direction.

The water was rough but not dangerously so, and the boat made decent speed downriver.

"Is this the main river?" Jenna shouted above the sound of the water and the whine of the motor.

"I don't think so," Mark shouted back. Frankly, he didn't care where they went, so long as it was moving away with some speed. They had been seen and shot at, so the helicopters would be returning.

The river didn't meander to any great degree, and it felt as if they were moving along well. Mark and Jenna both began to think optimistically of escape when they heard the noise of powerful motors nearing. They looked up for the helicopters, but there was nothing there.

Jenna turned to look behind them. "Oh, no!"

Mark turned to look as well. He took in a sharp breath and twisted the throttle harder, though it was already as far as it could go.

Two much larger, and most importantly, much faster boats were chasing them, catching up with them at shocking speed.

Airboats.

Chapter 24

"There they are!" screamed Drake Endicott through Mr. York's head-phones.

Mr. York looked downriver at least three hundred yards and could just make out a boat. But it was impossible to identify the occupants from that distance. And after all the misfortune they'd had in the last half a day, he was not inclined to assume they were Goggin and Telfair.

From their slow searching crawl, Endicott accelerated his single-seat airboat to a deafening roar, pulling away from Mr. York. Despite his misgivings, Mr. York accelerated as well. It would not do to leave events to play out under Endicott's influence.

That had happened often enough of late.

The morning had started well. A satellite that was normally pro-grammed to sit over Cuba and the Caribbean had mysteriously veered off course so that it was directly over the central states of the US of A. Mr. York knew better of course. In a week, an obscure science journal would publish a brief press release from a cable company no one had ever heard of saying that one of hundreds of satellites in orbit had malfunctioned and gone off course. No one would notice. That's the way it worked.

In any case, that satellite had already pinpointed six possible targets not far from Goggin's house. Two to the north they eliminated with quick fly-overs from helicopters. One just a mile or so west of the house turned out to be a horse that power lines and trees above it had blocked from view enough that it looked from space like two people. Two other sightings to the south were a pair of actual people, and they had been frightened completely out of their wits by the army of motorcycles, Hummers, and military helicopters that descended on them. That fiasco was Endicott's first effort of the day, and one of the innocent targets nearly got shot, saved only by Endicott's poor aim.

The sixth and final target was just a bit farther south and in a river. Mr. York and Endicott had begun reconnaissance on their two airboats at that point and had come so fast upon the two wading hunters who were their target—much the same way as they were even now, with Endicott accelerating wildly toward their objective—that they were shot at. Mr. York looked down at the bent metal rod under his seat where a bullet had ricocheted.

Left with no targets, the various teams had fanned out in all directions to search for the fugitives. That was what they were now, according to the news media: fugitives. Such a designation would both help and harm their efforts. Obviously it would help because people might recognize Goggin and notify the media, making the search much easier. But it was also a setback because it limited how hard they could go after Goggin. After all, it wouldn't look good on television having employees of a dozen companies, none of them members of law enforcement, gunning down someone, even if it was a fugitive.

As they searched, reports came in from the staff monitoring the satellite, detailing half a dozen more possible targets. More flybys had eliminated the majority of the sightings. Endicott was attacked again, this time by an irate fly fisherman.

The one thing that the satellite was unreliable in finding was boats, and canoes in particular. Despite the symmetry that all boats have, which should have made them easier to spot, they were next to impossible to pick out along a flowing body of water. With all the trees obscuring the view and objects presumably floating in the water, too many possible sightings that might have been boats turned out to be fallen trees. Who knew how many other targets the satellite technicians had ignored, figuring they were just more fallen trees?

But they kept at it, and Endicott kept terrorizing innocent people, until they came to where they were now. Any reasonable person would have stopped charging at targets a long time ago, opting for a more surreptitious approach. But Endicott maintained his single-minded focus regardless of the consequences.

Mr. York had considered having one of his men take Endicott out. But professional courtesy made him hesitate, and besides, his best sniper had missed hitting the three men who had been with Goggin and Telfair, going through a dozen rounds until he got two of the three. Mr. York figured the man would end up shooting him instead of Endicott and he did not intend to be killed so close to the resolution of this particularly vexing project.

They were a mere two hundred yards from the fishing boat now. Resolution was literally in sight. Endicott's boat continued to pull ahead, and Mr. York could now add the feeling of being soaked to the sensations of cold, itching, and the putrid smells that infested his body. He was no longer indecisive about eliminating Goggin and Telfair. He rarely did so, but when it was absolutely necessary to the fulfillment of the project's requirements, he did what he had to do. He had held out hope that he could just coerce the answers they needed from Goggin, but his patience was at an end.

He could tolerate Drake Endicott no longer.

What infuriated Mr. York more than anything else about Endicott was his complete lack of professionalism. He was more a Jekyll and Hyde sort who charmed the office and then committed murder as a leisurely pursuit.

As they came within a hundred yards of the fishing boat, Mr. York could positively identify the occupants. It was indeed Goggin and Telfair. Mr. York unclipped his gun so it could be drawn quickly, and prepared himself for the distasteful task he must soon perform.

At fifty yards the river became shallow and choppy enough that both craft began to bounce, many times, painfully so.

Then, at less than twenty yards, with water spraying everywhere and the boats careening violently over rocks, stones, and whitewater, Endicott was hit by a tree branch. He should have seen it coming. A six-year-old boy would have seen it coming. It was the same stupid prank that any six-year-old boy did on hiking trips. The boy grabs a branch, pulls it with him, and lets go so that it smacks into the person behind him. In this case, Goggin must have grabbed a low hanging branch of considerable size, overtaxed his boat's engine in order to pull it taut, then let go as Endicott closed in.

Endicott was quick enough to pointlessly fire his pistol at the branch before it knocked him and the pistol off the airboat's high chair and against the safety cage where the fan was housed. Without someone to control it, the boat slowed, then turned sharply left—into the path of Mr. York's own craft.

Rather than try to whip drastically to the left to get out of the way, or, better still, turn his boat neatly to the right and avoid the collision altogether, Mr. York rammed his craft straight at Endicott's boat. An outsider looking on might have thought he was hoping to vault over the top of it, or that he was hoping the other craft would be out of the way by the time he got there. It would have been difficult to tell. But a simple glimpse into the searing furnace of Mr. York's retinae could have told that outsider the truth: he rammed it, hoping something terribly painful would happen to Endicott himself. It was unseemly to so openly dispose of a fellow member of the corporate espionage family, and Mr. York would never have admitted to such a thing. To be honest, he didn't want Endicott dead, just out of the way. For a very long time. Years, if at all possible. Other members of the family would have thanked him.

As it was, Endicott's airboat crumbled under the weight of the craft above it—the seat, engine, cage, and fan collapsing and mixing together in an ugly mess. The engine stubbornly continued to spin the fan, creating an element of considerable danger. Endicott was fortunate to have immediately been squirted out from between the mess to where water was gushing over and through smooth river stones. It was so shallow there that he was in no danger of drowning as he lay there in a foggy daze.

Mr. York was more fortunate. He was not thrown from his airboat at all. Whether he had intended to or not, his craft slid through the spinning, dangerous pile of boat parts without capsizing or disintegrating into a similar mess. But the cage and propeller were torn from the back of the boat by the out-of-control remains of Endicott's boat, just as Mr. York re-entered the water. The cage dinged and screeched against the whirring propeller until one caught on the other. Together they shot backward, dropping into the water with a harmless sploosh. Mr. York and his airboat smoothly slid into the water and slowly decelerated until they were both bobbing up and down like a warning buoy.

Just as he turned to survey the damage, the airboat, unbalanced by the lack of weight in back, began to roll over. Mr. York abandoned ship rather abruptly. The craft continued to roll until only its underbelly floated above the river's surface.

Looking downstream, Mr. York was not at all surprised to see that Goggin and Telfair had made good their escape. He was surprised to see a line of motorcycles, three or four at least, lined along the western shore, just sitting there. He was even more surprised to see both of his helicopters hovering uselessly upriver.

He ran toward the parked bikers, screaming "What the hell are you standing around for?" but stopped himself when he realized he was no longer attached to his headphones and they wouldn't be able to hear him without them. Instead he threw rocks at the motorcycles and pointed in the direction of their departing quarry. The men understood and flew off through the trees downriver. The helicopters also joined the chase, relieving him of having to weigh the risks that came with throwing rocks at helicopters.

The silence after they left was eerie and aggravating. It was like listening to the electric devices that pump water endlessly over small stones and rest on so many executives' credenzas. With an impulsiveness that was unlike him, Mr. York took out his revolver and shot the river until the gun clicked on empty.

"He he he!" giggled Endicott, now standing next to him and rubbing a sore shoulder.

Mr. York turned in his direction and advanced with death in his eyes.

"That was funny," said Endicott, not immediately understanding. When he did, he frowned and reached into his drenched coat.

With a fury completely alien to the professional demeanor he had honed to cool perfection over the years, Mr. York deftly gripped the pistol that emerged from the coat the instant it appeared, tore it savagely from Endicott's grasp, and threw it into the river behind him.

The two men stood facing one another.

"You have been a torment to me from the moment we met," said Mr. York, struggling to maintain his composure. "I despise arrogant people, and I despise them more so when they have no reason to be arrogant. I despise people who kiss ass because they have no backbone. I despise people who talk too much. I despise people who have no ethics or standards, even in an occupation like this. And most of all I despise sissy pretty boys who think they're tough."

Mr. York reached out and jabbed Endicott sharply in the chest. "You are all of that, Mr. Drake Endicott. Suave and fabulous. And not an ounce of a redeeming trait within three feet of your body. Is there, Mr. Drake Endicott?" He poked Endicott again, hard enough that Endicott took two steps back to keep from falling over. Endicott jutted his chin out defiantly and bunched his hands into fists, poised to let fly a rain of crushing blows.

But there was murder in Mr. York's eyes. It was a look that Endicott had never seen in anyone. Not in himself, not even in the men he had treated so shabbily throughout this ordeal. He himself had murdered before, but he had done it in a dispassionate way, a devil-may-care extinguishing of someone's life from a distance. And it had just been business.

The malice in Mr. York's eyes said this was personal.

Endicott began backing away. "Now wait a minute there, Yorkster. We're on the same team, aren't we? I mean, I know I may have botched a few things. But I said from the beginning you were the expert, didn't I? I was learning from you. Hey, so I'm not a great listener. What can you do?"

"I haven't decided yet," Mr. York said, stepping toward Endicott.

"Yorko, Yorko, let's not lose control here. Let's be professional. That's your creed, right?"

"There's no one here to know."

"Ah, but you'll know, there Yorksly. It'll weigh on your conscience."

"I'll suppress it. I've done it before. Everyone has. Even you, I imagine."

Endicott was, for once, at a loss for words.

Mr. York came within arm's reach and set himself for a fight. Endicott was small, but he knew better than to make anything of that. Some of the best combatants he'd met were closer to five feet tall than six.

Endicott appeared to have set himself too, but not in a way that Mr. York would have judged the ideal stance for exchanging punches. There was tension and worry in Endicott's eyes. It was difficult to tell what he might be thinking.

"Aaaaaaaaaaa!" Endicott suddenly began screaming. At the same time, he spun around and took off in the direction opposite of Mr. York. "Somebody help meeee!" he screamed.

Five steps off the riverbank was a steep, almost unscalable hill. Endicott could have taken ten steps to the right and had a much less steep climb to look forward to. Or he could have taken another ten steps to the left, around a pair of trees jutting out over the river, and not have had to climb any hill at all. But in his panic, he did neither.

Mr. York watched in dismay as he scrambled up the sharply inclining hill. Endicott had always displayed such conceit and bravado that Mr. York had hoped the ass would stand his ground and put up a good fight. But this was just embarrassing. "Get back down here. Take it like a man, for God's sake."

Endicott stopped halfway up. "You'd like that, I bet, Mr. Yuck. Perhaps another day. Ta ta!" He turned and hopped confidently up. "You know, you are the least fun person I have ever worked with," he said, breathing hard as he climbed. "And you think you're so t—"

A fist-sized stone caught him between the shoulder blades, and he fell against the hill, then slid, rolled, and tumbled back down to the bottom of the hill, coming to a stop at Mr. York's feet.

"Nice throw, huh?" said Mr. York.

Endicott grimaced from pain in every part of his body. It hurt to move, and after some preliminary exploration, he decided not to.

"Get up!" bellowed Mr. York. He grabbed Endicott by his expensive leather jacket and hauled him to his feet.

"Wait a minute," Endicott wheezed. "Wait a minute! You can't do anything to me. I have a contract. With your employer. Libson Goosy...Gibson Lucy!"

Mr. York paused to consider the ramifications, then shrugged. "I can always get another job."

"Not in our business!" Endicott screeched. "Your reputation will be destroyed. You won't be able to work the DOW again."

Working the DOW meant working for the biggest and most powerful corporations, ones that were members of the DOW Industrial Average. Mr. York knew what he meant. Pretty obvious really. "I'll contract out."

"You're not the type."

"Shut the hell up." Mr. York grabbed Endicott by the lapels and shook him distractedly while he tried to decide what to do with him. He'd already punched him once. It had felt good, but he was searching now for something to make Endicott cry and foul his pants. At the same time, if he did it right.

Endicott had put his hands up in supplication and had closed his eyes in anticipation of having one or both eyes hit with something. He whimpered like a bullied child.

Mr. York looked at the man in his grip shaking and whining, and he considered not doing anything to him at all. But that would set a bad precedent. Endicott would think he'd gotten away with something, and he'd have to endure the whole nightmare all over again.

Maybe he'd just punch him once for each eye. They would hurt for a while, and maybe Endicott would give him some space from then on.

He doubled his fist, cocked his right arm, and rocked back when a motorcycle jumped off the far bank and landed in the water, drenching them both. Mr. York released Endicott, who slumped limply to the ground.

The motorcycle slid to a stop, and the rider quickly removed his helmet.

"Mr. York! We've got them!"

Chapter 25

The bear didn't look happy.

Matthias End had never actually seen a happy bear, so it was possible that none of them ever looked happy. But he had seen some that didn't look quite as angry as this one did.

End and Nathan Hamper had been running hard since they heard the many roaring engines coursing through the forest. It seemed probable that Mr. York was finally there and had caught Mark's scent, or maybe even Mark himself.

They had run until pain introduced itself to Nathan's weak lungs and to End's bruised everything else. As they slowed, they could see the flash of headlights and revving motorcycle engines swerve through the trees. It was within the realm of possibility that Mark was on one of the motorcycles, but since the bikes weren't chasing each other, it wasn't End's first choice for a place to look.

Helicopters circled overhead just as End and Nathan gave up running completely, too exhausted to do more than plod along. They were coming to a pretty good-sized cave with a spring disappearing into it. The running water was twenty feet across and bluer than a tropical vacation brochure.

That's where the bear made its appearance. And that's where they were now, roughly twenty years later. Or so it seemed.

End stood at the center of the entrance to the cave, at the edge of the spring. Nathan stood at one side of the entrance, ten feet from End. The bear was twenty feet away, growling and pacing back and forth as if it couldn't decide whether to eat them both now or save one of them for later.

What would be the odds of encountering a bear in addition to all the other calamities they had suffered so far?

"Hey!" said Nathan, pointing at the bear, "there's a bear!"

End squinted at him, dumbfounded. Where had he been?

"Do you think it'd let me pet it?" asked Nathan.

"What? Well, yes I think it would. But then I think it would smack you around a bit. I know I would."

Nathan shook his head. "Don't be an idiot. Bears are friendly. I used to watch Smokey the Bear all the time when I was a kid." He stared at the bear, lost in the marijuana-intensified recollections of childhood. "No...no, that was Yogi the Bear."

End watched with a morbid blend of fascination and horror, like watching real-life disaster programs on television, as Nathan stepped toward the bear. A growing dread filled him with each step Nathan took.

"Nathan."

Nathan continued to step slowly forward, hand outreached as if to pet the monster that was surely forty feet tall.

The feeling of dread became all-consuming to End. Strangely it felt worse coming from a direction other than the bear.

"Nathan."

"What?" Nathan finally answered, turning at the halfway point to his new pet.

End didn't move. "There's a bear behind me."

Nathan peered into the darker gloom of the cave. "No, there's two," he replied happily. "You know, I think this might be a family. Papa Bear, Mama Bear, and Baby Bear." He pointed to each one of them as they were introduced.

Outside the immediate danger of bears, the din of scrambling motorcycles had been joined by something tremendously loud, a single engine making a horrific racket. The bear outside the cave, Papa Bear, increased his back and forth pace and whipped his head up and down, emitting a worried growl each time he changed direction.

"Oh, poor Mr. Bear," cooed Nathan. "Is bad old machines being too noisy?" He resumed his approach, holding his hand out again to pet the beast. His other hand offered a brownie.

"Don't feed the bear those things," End hissed, appalled. "If there's anything we don't need right now it's a bear that's angry *and* hallucinating." The cave made his voice louder and Papa Bear stopped to look.

For the first time, End heard the shuffling back and forth that Mama and Baby were doing behind him. An adrenaline-induced sense of purpose filled him. He had no idea how one was supposed to escape bears, but he was definitely not going to stand still in the center of a crowd of them. Slowly, sliding one foot in the dirt and then the other, he reached the side of the cave. At that point, he turned to see the two behind him.

There was no baby bear. It was just two more monumentally huge bears. And nothing was cute or babyish about either of them.

Teenagers are ignorant little shits, he thought, eyeing Nathan venomously and trying to slow his heartbeat. Nathan moved closer to his own demise with each step.

Fine, let him get himself killed, End thought. "Nathan," he said.

Nathan was within the deathblow of a paw.

There, he's about to be killed. What an idiot. "Nathan, step back toward me."

Nathan held out the hand with the brownie first, which was smart, relatively speaking. Better to feed the bear something besides an arm. He also wisely set it on the ground rather than expecting that the bear would take it from his hand without taking the hand with it.

End drew himself up to his full height and said in a strong, calm voice. "Nathan."

Nathan turned to him as if suddenly awake. "Yes?"

"Come here."

In a fog, Nathan stumbled toward End. The last five feet, End grabbed him and pulled him toward the steep grassy hill that sloped up, around, and over the cave.

The bear sniffed at the moist cake and lapped it up along with several leaves. A series of pondering crunches drowned out the motorcycles and some of the awful noise coming from the single engine automaton. They didn't drown out the helicopters, though.

"My God that's a big bear!" shouted Nathan, suddenly petrified at seeing a real live bear. He frowned. "Where'd he get that brownie?" Nathan almost headed out to rescue his brownie when he thought better of it. "I think he swallowed it already."

The bears in the cave yowled at the growing clamor of the approaching helicopters, then roared a warning to their drugged brethren, and disappeared inside the cave. The outside bear, Papa, reared up on its hind legs and roared a mighty challenge to the flying machines, which might actually have been impressed if Papa had been facing in their direction.

End was tempted to turn tail and run, straight up the side of the sheer hill if necessary. But he'd heard that bears chased people who ran from them. And he couldn't leave Mark to his own devices. Mark had no devices. At least not the mental ones he'd need to escape this army alive.

At that instant though, a helicopter flew directly over the bear's head. The bear's boldness left it instantly, and it bolted due west for parts unknown. Another helicopter flew in front of it and the first one flew back to the north of it. The bear swerved away from the awful things, straight toward End and Nathan.

End saw it coming and knew they'd never get away. In any direction. He threw Nathan to the ground behind him, said a quick prayer, and set himself to face the bear, bunching up fists that would only make a self-respecting bear chortle.

"Mighty is the Hand of the Lord!" End bellowed defiantly. He wondered if he'd be killed instantly by the lethal swipe of a clawed paw or by the mauling bite of its terrible fangs.

The bear's bravado however was long gone by the time it reached End, and anyway, it was quicker and just as convenient for it to change direction again, lumber into the safety of the cave, and avoid any more noisy things.

"Son of a bitch! Did you see that?" screamed Nathan, his voice filled with both terror and excitement. He regarded End, standing above him. "That was pretty stupid, you know that?"

End's own adrenaline detonated like an explosion. "Yes! I know it was stupid! Do you think I would do anything that stupid for no good reason? I was saving your ass! Stupid!"

There ensued a brief but demonstrative tirade, with Nathan as the audience, whereby End absolved himself of his fear and tension with such gusto and volume that he became concerned he might hyperventilate. It began barely coherent and pretty much finished that way.

"Feel better?" asked Nathan, dealing with his tension less physically with a lit joint.

End sank to the ground, out of breath, his back against the side of the cave mouth. "I...I can't...believe...you'd feed a bear...your...damnable drugs! Stupid, dumbass...teenager."

Nathan just giggled and inhaled.

The scene that had been unfolding farther out in the forest was becoming louder. The motorcycles had circled and moved over to somewhere just out of sight, in the direction where the spring disappeared into the trees. The helicopters alternated between circling harmlessly, soaring swiftly this way and that, and hovering. None of it seemed worth the effort because it was plain to them that they weren't chasing anyone or were even aware of anything happening on the ground.

The noise emanating from the spring off in the distance became louder still, especially with the bear gone, and End and Nathan stood up to get a better look.

The view was not the best, what with tree trunks and branches and the odd clump of leaves getting in the way, but there was definitely a boat, or boats, approaching. It was going to be impossible to tell who the occupants were until it was too late, so End prepared for the worst.

There followed the calamitous sound of a crash, still out of sight. End and Nathan could just make out a tidal wave of water splashing everywhere, perhaps movement of a wild and drastic kind, and not much else. The terrible engine noise dwindled to silence shortly afterward and a single boat could be clearly heard.

The spring meandered somewhat and it was another moment before the boat rounded the final turn toward the cave. The forest came alive with roaring and revving machines. Motorcycles appeared among the trees in all directions, and the helicopters took up positions directly over the cave. Unseen rumbles shook the ground off to the east, and End guessed the Hummers were not far off.

The boat appeared then, driven inexpertly and with reckless speed, even with potential captors on all sides.

It was Mark and Jenna. "God be praised," End whispered to himself.

Nathan glanced at him as they moved toward the spring that Mark and Jenna were closing in on as well. "You sure do sound like you're still a God-fearing man, padre. I'm not completely convinced you really are a devil-worshipper."

"That's comforting to hear," said End, nearing the water's edge. "Now stay by me."

The boat was in fact a fishing boat with a low hull and high chairs, its weak motor screaming under a strain it wasn't built to endure.

Mark and Jenna recognized them immediately because Jenna pointed right at them and waved, and Mark smiled with a noticeable relief. "Hey! I know you!" shouted Mark as the boat went by them before it came to a stop. He grinned and waved them aboard.

Not far away, the motorcycles mowed down tree, brush, and woodland creature with equal disdain as they dashed toward the cave.

End looked hastily at the pursuit, then at Mark, the boat, and the cave. "What are we doing?" he shouted.

"That-a-way," Mark shouted and pointed into the cave.

"No, no, no, no!" End and Nathan shouted together. "Bears!" they shouted, pointing into the cave. They spread their arms as wide as they could go to indicate the terrible size of the brutes.

"No other options!" Mark shouted back, pointing at the swiftly closing motorcycles.

"I'll negotiate something!" End shouted.

The helicopters had dropped to the point where the group could see the pilot and a passenger. The passenger aimed a rifle at them.

End looked at the helicopters, the motorcycles, Mark and the boat, all the while shaking his head in total dread of any of the available options.

The whiz and smack of dozens of bullets ricocheting off rock nearby made his decision for him. He pushed Nathan a little roughly into the fishing boat and climbed in himself.

The fishing boat resumed its course, the motor laboring even more so with the newly added weight. The cave mouth swallowed them up, and the sound of pursuit faded into the background of the motor's violent whine filling the first main chamber.

As they covered their ears and looked behind them, more than one of them wondered if anyone had thought to bring a flashlight.

Chapter 26

"Sure is dark in here."

"Didn't anyone think to bring a flashlight? Or to ask if anyone else had a flashlight?"

"Oh, like *you* maybe?"

The cave was dark. Empty. A void. The light that had existed at the cave's entrance quickly dwindled to a speck. The boat's tiny trolling motor sped along the underground spring surprisingly smoothly at half the speed it entered with, which could only mean they were still in a very large space; Mark's driving just couldn't be that good.

And it wasn't, truth be told. The minute the speck of light disappeared, the boat began glancing off invisible objects with nerve-shattering jolts that made everyone afraid —even those that were barely touching unseen things made hearts skip a beat.

"Shouldn't we be slowing down?"

"Yeah, we're gonna crash into something, and we won't even know it."

"I think we'd know."

"We're not going that fast."

Be that as it may, Mark agreed with the invisible majority and dropped the speed to where they were all able to better relax.

"Don't some caves have bottomless pits?"

"Shut up, huh?"

Mark cut the throttle back even further. The motor still moved them along, but it was much quieter now.

"Where are we, Nathan?"

"How should I know?"

"I thought you've been all over the caves around here."

"Yeah, but not in the dark."

Someone fumbled with an object and dropped it.

"There's got to be a flashlight here somewhere."

"If you'll give me a flashlight, I'll go look for one."

"Oh, that is funny."

"Fishing boats have to have lights, don't they? There's always idiots wanting to go out in the dark to fish."

"Find the tall seat. There's probably a button on the armrest or maybe on the floor where you can step on it."

Bodies moved and shifted and predictably collided, but no one was badly injured or thrown overboard. By a piece of good fortune, Nathan located a toggle switch that brought a light to life sitting high on a pole in the front of the boat.

"God almighty," said End, standing in wonder at the long chamber they were in. Stalactites and dozens of stone straws hung down from over their heads and the water was so blue as to be almost unhealthy in appearance.

The most amazing wonder of it was that the chamber went on for hundreds of yards and might be even larger. They were all looking behind them because Mark continued to steer the boat backward even after the immediate danger had passed. So the front of the boat was to the back, and its light shone on waters they had already traversed.

Their collective fascination with their surroundings was such that at first no one suggested turning the boat around where the larger engine could be made use of. The light illuminated colors in the ancient stone that rivaled the blue of the spring water, mixed with some reds but mostly orange, in every hue. It was like the inside of a house decorated with Christmas lights during Halloween.

The other benefit of the light pointing behind them, though not yet consciously recognized by anyone, was to make plain that their pursuers had not joined them in the cave. At least not close enough to be a worry to them.

Still, someone did suggest turning the boat around. With the light and a bigger motor, they could proceed at a faster pace and still be able to slow, or at least turn, before they reached anything life-threatening.

They stood and shuffled around carefully so that they were facing the correct direction when a noise behind them, or rather ahead, reached their ears. No one could identify it, although Jenna wondered aloud if it was another boat cruising around. It would have been quickest and simplest for them to swivel the pole around on which the lamp hung. But the group was tired and mind-weary, and Mark's first thought was to turn the boat around and see what was what.

He killed the little trolling motor and there was a moment where the noise of quite a lot of water came to their ears. But then Mark fired up the bigger motor and its deafening roar instantly consumed the chamber's air-space and assaulted their senses.

Slowly the boat turned. The chamber was lowering in height as they continued along, but there was still plenty of room for such a maneuver. The breadth of the waterway made the current reasonable to deal with as well. Mark congratulated himself for a clean effort as the boat shifted into the correct position for them to see the water disappearing right in front of them.

Two or three people screamed, and someone shouted "Bottomless pit!" as they reached the edge of what was most definitely an underground water-fall. The light very briefly lit the chamber beyond, which appeared to also be considerable in size, before the boat went over.

As they fell, the lamp flipped this way and that, passengers' bodies doing likewise. The boat leaned heavily down and to the left, there being three of the four passengers on that side of the boat.

It seemed an eternity of flight—Nathan and Jenna both screamed all the way down—before they crashed into the frigid spray and water at the bottom of the falls. Again, bodies were flung every which way on impact and, miraculously again, no one was thrown overboard. End dinged his knee badly enough that it felt numb for a time. Mark was thrown into the steering wheel and came out of the landing with sore ribs. Otherwise, only shaken nerves were suffered by one and all.

"That must have been a fifty-foot fall," Nathan gasped excitedly, sounding as if he wanted to do it again.

The lamp had swiveled of its own volition, to say nothing of the force of the landing, and shined off to their left. Realizing that the light could be moved, Jenna turned it so that it lit up the falls.

The spring water fell prettily over rocks and down to where water misted upwards. It was only a ten-foot drop. Nevertheless they noticed their luck in escaping unscathed. Rocks protruded out of the falls most of the way down. Large, jagged rocks.

"It's a miracle," said End, gazing at the rocks with his hands clasped together as if in prayer, "and there's no denying it."

"The pope must be on our side, eh?" grinned Mark, patting End on the back. "Shine the lamp over there, Jen." He pointed, and she shined it on the water. "Farther out," he said.

The lamp made the water shimmer across an underground lake. Even assuming they were against a wall behind them, the other side was a good hundred yards away. And they knew from the brief glimpse they'd had before the falls arrived that they were nowhere near a wall.

The radiant glow illuminated the lake all the way to a shoreline at the end of the hundred yards.

"What's that way?" asked Nathan. It took a moment to aim it where he pointed, and the foursome gasped together.

The lake extended on and on and on. It was difficult to tell how big the entire chamber really was. The light weakened at a certain distance, and the cave walls gleamed with enough moisture to reflect the light and make it difficult to be sure how far away anything was.

"Ew," said Jenna in disgust. "I got dripped on."

"Bats," Nathan said and giggled.

"Ew!" she said louder.

"No, no, no," said Mark. "It's just moisture coming down from the hill above us. It takes thousands of years for it to get this far. What dripped on you may have been rain from a hundred thousand years ago."

"Or like some neanderthal geezer's spit," said Nathan and giggled again.

"That's disgusting," Jenna said.

The cave ceiling brightened as the lamp was aimed its way.

"You suppose there are bats?" Nathan asked.

"It's a cave, boy," End said, smiling, "there's sure not going to be any chickens."

Jenna shined the light around the ceiling. There were millions more of the stone straws and stalactites. In more than one place, the ceiling was just a hole, the light unable to penetrate far enough up to see any detail. For good measure, she circled all the way around the cave so they could get a better idea of how big it was and, more importantly, where they could go from there.

"We should keep on going," End said. "Follow the water and it'll take us out of here."

"Yeah, to the center of the earth," Nathan replied sarcastically. "I think I remember this place. We should head over there," he pointed at the dry land, "and find a way out. I remember going down a tunnel to a giant underground lake just like this one. Can't be very many of them. We find that passage, and we can just walk up until we're out."

"If it doesn't cave in," Mark pointed out.

"And there's no bears," End said, staring with foreboding at the far shore.

"I can't say I like the idea of falling to the center of the earth myself," Jenna said.

There ensued a rather heated and sarcastic debate that began with a discussion on the ridiculously impossible odds of finding a hole that dropped to the center of the earth, veering suddenly to the idiocy of allowing an underground river to dictate when and where they eventually reached daylight, if ever. Then there were a few snide comments about the likelihood of bears swimming all this way and waiting in caves so they could pounce on just four of the many millions of stupid people who wound up in this particular place. And that was hotly countered by suggestions that no person with any sense would voluntarily step into a tight space where any number of violent and/ or poisonous creatures could be lurking and where walls could close in at any moment.

The debate winner was still undecided when a great roar erupted from the direction of the falls. All four turned to look in that direction.

"Do you suppose a bear just fell over the falls?" asked End.

"Get over the bears, man!" said Nathan.

"Shut up!" someone hissed.

There was no need to be silent for long. The high-pitched whine of a choir of motors sang down from over the falls to where they sat.

"That doesn't sound good," mumbled Jenna.

"Start the engine! Start the engine!" End exploded.

Mark pushed the button to start the main motor, but nothing happened. He pushed it again, and again, and then in a panicky staccato fashion that served only to make his thumb sore. "It doesn't work. It must have gotten damaged when we fell." He waved wildly at the back of the boat. "How about the little motor?"

Jenna aimed the lamp on the back of the boat, and they very quickly discerned that the little motor was no more. "It must have fallen off when we fell."

They looked up at the top of the falls as the powerful though as yet unseen motors drew nearer. The ill-advised silence lengthened until someone shouted "Paddle!" Another few seconds passed while they searched for oars or anything to paddle with, then End gave up and began paddling furiously with his huge hands. The others joined in and the boat was off, drifting none too swiftly in the direction of a wall.

"What are you doing?" Mark shouted at End. "We've got to get to the shore."

"No, no, we've got to get back to the current," End shouted back. "That'll get us out."

"They'll catch us and shoot us before that happens."

"No, I'm sure the outside is just a little further on."

"End!" Jenna screamed suddenly. "Paddle for the shore! Now!"

End knew that was the only realistic option they had. But the memory of those bears— so big they towered above even him—back at the cave entrance gave him the shakes. It was rare for him to encounter anything bigger than he was.

The boat shifted as they paddled harder and the shore drew closer.

Mark suddenly sat up and felt his shoe. "Why is my shoe under water?"

"Pull it back in the boat, dumbass," shouted Nathan. He was sitting in front and leaning over so he could paddle with both hands at the same time.

"It is in the boat." Mark felt all around him and water was everywhere. "We're sinking! It must have happened when we went over the falls too."

"Damn, you just have all the facts, don't you," Nathan shouted from up front. There was a growing panic about the boy, despite the increasing sarcasm. "Come on!"

They were still twenty yards from the shore when Jenna looked back at the falls. "Headlights! Here they come!"

The foursome continued to paddle as hard as they could, all the while looking behind them as the light grew to consume more and more of the monstrous hall.

They reached the shore when the first boat leaped off the top of the falls. It was a good-sized boat and unleashed a fantastic launch, shooting far from the falls.

But when it impacted on the water and sunk with the force of its descent, something stopped it short. It stopped in the water as if it were anchored there. The driver moved, but not quickly. Two jet-skis leaped after the boat, to a higher altitude than even it had mustered. One landed in the same unfortunate way as the boat and crunched against the spring bottom. The driver slumped over and clutched at his abdomen. The other jet-ski sailed farther out and landed without breaking apart. But it did so without its driver, who shot over the handlebars and skidded off to the end of the chamber and almost out of sight.

A second boat appeared, more slowly, and it fell over the falls much like the fishing boat must have. It landed with a huge splash and an unpleasant shaking of the earth, but the boat remained buoyant afterward. Another jet-ski and its driver flailed through the air to meet an ugly end, but a fourth one landed cleanly.

It was time to get going.

As the others scrambled out of the boat, Mark leaned down and flipped up the covering next to the pole where the lamp was attached. With a deftness born of habit, he yanked at a big battery powering the lamp until it tore loose from its housing. He unclipped the lamp from the pole and they had portable light.

"Wait a minute," End pleaded. "They're wiping themselves out. Let's just take them out here, and we won't have to be running away from them anymore."

More boats and jet-skis shot over the falls and a larger percentage were landing without damaging themselves.

"There's too many of them," shouted Jenna above the growing noise.

"Maybe we should look for a bigger passage," said Mark, peeking into the only passage within eyesight. It was five feet tall and two feet across at its widest point.

"There is nothing else," Nathan screamed in terror and pointed back out at the lake. "Look out!" He ran for the passage entrance and disappeared inside without the benefit of any light.

The remaining three turned to the lake and saw the original surviving jet-ski driver running toward them, brandishing another of those very big rifles.

"Son of a bitch!" seethed End. "That water can't be more than two feet deep. We could've jumped out and ran out of here."

Mark laughed and shook his head as he climbed out of the boat.

End looked at him. "It's not funny! It's not funny at all!" He glanced back at the approaching man, pulled his revolver from his coat and dropped the man where he stood, in one quick motion, with one shot.

End glanced at Mark and Jenna, nodded with a satisfaction only he understood, and followed Nathan into the tunnel, grunting as his bulk wedged momentarily between jutting rocks before he too was gone, into the darkness.

Mark frowned at the man sitting in the water holding a bleeding shoulder, then shrugged at Jenna. "I thought it was funny."

Bullets exploded in the water and to the side, ten feet away, and Mark and Jenna also disappeared through the hole in the rock.

Chapter 27

The command post stood at the very top of a mountain, under which crawled the prey. Somewhere in the caves below, Mark Goggin hid. Unquestionably, it would be a pleasant surprise to hear from the team chasing them, now that Goggin had been caught. But Mr. York didn't expect it to happen.

If there was one thing he'd learned from this ordeal, it was never to underestimate the unpredictability, resourcefulness, and just plain luck of absolute amateurs. In his long career, Mr. York had encountered accomplished professionals for the most part in pursuits such as these. He'd tracked down corporate spies from Los Angeles to Berlin and had eliminated manufacturing saboteurs holed up in New York, Tokyo, and Thailand, of all places. They had all been calculating to the last, until their desperation made them all too predictable, and Mr. York had closed the deal.

"Yorkster, what's the plan, my man?" said Drake Endicott, reclining in a lawn chair.

Of course, Mr. York hadn't been burdened with as many imbeciles to work with as he did now. He glanced Endicott's way, gritted his teeth, and went back to staring at charts of the cave's complex layout.

The mountain they were atop—a towering hill really—was one of a range that spread across central and southern Missouri, known the world around for its thousands of caves. They would need to find Goggin quickly or risk losing him in the innumerable cave passageways below. The chart he had been looking at showed only the mountain they were standing on, not any of the others. It would be impossible to find him if he got through this hill and moved into the next one.

Unfortunately, the chart was not all that useful. There was no military or scientific or even business benefit to having professionals chart the passages and chambers. So the chart they were trying to decipher had been drawn up by three middle-school kids who claimed to have been in every part of the cave complex.

"Yorkenheimer, I have a suggestion."

Since the prior incident—specifically, when airboats crashed into other airboats—Mr. York had imposed an impenetrable calm about himself. He simply could no longer afford to have Mr. Endicott distracting and aggravating him into making any more mistakes or doing anything rash. That meant, sadly, that he had to listen to the man talk. Oddly, he seemed to have completely forgotten about Mr. York trying to beat him senseless. Again.

Endicott sat up in his seat with considerable excitement. "I have a friend of a friend, see, who can see that we get a couple of thermobaric missiles. Nothing better for flushing people out of holes in the ground. Those monsters'll bore fifty feet into solid rock before they explode. They'll take out this whole hill, no problem."

"They certainly will, Mr. Endicott, but our orders are to bring Goggin back alive, if at all possible, and dead only if there are no alternatives. I think we still have some alternatives and dropping missiles that will almost definitely kill him is not one of them."

"Just trying to think out of the box there, Yorko."

Mr. York felt the disgust welling up again and suppressed it instantly. "How nice," he said and went back to studying the chart.

Endicott began to whistle after a while, and Mr. York's disgust returned. He fought it off again. The charts were a major disappointment. They had positioned men at nearly all of the openings the chart identified, and they had already found that the drawing was not only not proportional to the actual sizes and distances, but in some cases there was nothing but rock where the drawings said there were rooms and passageways. In particular, they'd found that any room that was named on the chart, like Blackbeard's

Den or Monty's Hall, didn't exist. The children were apparently thinking of future expansion when they drew it all up.

He shook his head. "This won't work," he said out loud without realizing it. He instantly clamped his mouth shut. The last thing he wanted was to be perceived to be encouraging conversation with the rodent Endicott.

"Oh, I quite agree," said Endicott. "There's really only one way to find out where they are."

"I'm not prepared to sacrifice men just so you can have the pleasure of assaulting every single chamber beneath us, Endicott."

"Whoa, whoa, there, Yorkman. You've got me all wrong. I'm not blood-thirsty. I'm just enthusiastic." He waved his arms. "I'm not going to propose anything violent. I happen to have in one of the Hummers a seismic tectonic disturbance…thing. I don't remember what it's called, but it's a device that will actually see through the rock and pick out where the hallways and rooms and things are. It's not altogether reliable for finding people—we've got infrared goggles for that—but it'll tell you where they could have gone based on where they went inside."

"And it won't kill anyone?"

"If you dropped it on someone's head, it would. But it's a bit too expensive and hush-hush for us to even get at it, so that shouldn't be a big worry."

"We can't get at it? You just said it was in one of the Hummers."

"Well, I meant the radio. I'll call a friend, and they'll call a friend, and they'll call a friend, and we'll get an up-to-the-minute chart probably by the end of the day. Tomorrow at the worst."

Mr. York was plainly irritated. "They'll be in Mexico by then."

"Ah…well, that might make it unnecessary to chart the mountain if they're going to, you know, be someplace else."

"I think that's a fair statement, Mr. Endicott."

The silence reigned for almost five seconds.

"We could at least drop the thermobarics onto the hills on either side of this one. That would keep him from going anywhere else but out of the cave on this hill."

"No."

"Not even just one?"

Mr. York gnashed his teeth and refused to respond to any more of the man's lunacy. Two of his men stood looking at topographic charts to see if they could learn anything from them. He listened to them speculate pointlessly, and he eventually told them it was pointless. The topographic readings were not as reliable as the kids' pictures.

Inside a tent pitched nearby—Mr. York was partial to the idea of having a pitched tent, as if he were Napoleon or Ulysses Grant about to wage war—sat the two men they had caught just before they'd come upon Goggin and Jenna Telfair. Perhaps a conversation with them might prove enlightening, he thought.

As he approached them, Word Hamilton stood up. "Sir, I demand to know why we're being kept here."

"For your protection. Mister?..."

"My name is none of your gaw-damn business. And I have grave doubts that you're interested in our protection when you've shot two people. You have no right to hold us like this."

"Oh, I can do whatever I like. I've got all the guns."

"So, do you intend to kill us or are you just—"

"Please, sir, we won't harm either of you, except as much as you've been harmed so far. I do apologize for your catching that errant bullet. Allow me to explain. I am here to bring in a man believed to have committed a murder. He's fleeing from the authorities and is potentially very dangerous."

"You're a policeman?"

"No, I—"

"FBI?"

"No."

"Do you have any legal authority whatsoever?"

"No. I am probably the equivalent of a bounty hunter."

"Just a lot better paid," said Hamilton.

Mr. York lowered his eyebrows. "And how would you know that?"

Hamilton glanced uncertainly at Mike Abram, who was still sitting in reasonable comfort. The bullet in his shoulder had been removed, and he'd been given a light sedative. "Pretty obvious," he said. "How many bounty hunters bring an army with them?"

"Good point," said Mr. York, nodding. "I am better financed than your typical bounty hunter. How's that for an answer?"

"A good dodge," said Hamilton. "If this guy is *believed* to have committed a murder, why aren't real law enforcement officials after him?"

"I couldn't say."

"Who do you work for?" Hamilton asked.

Mr. York frowned. "What say I ask some questions for a while?"

Hamilton glared irritably at him, but he sat down and folded his arms.

"Thank you. First of all, do you know the man and woman we're chasing?"

"No idea," said Hamilton, looking away as if he were already bored.

"Yeah, I know them," Abram said.

Hamilton gaped at him.

"I don't see any reason to lie, Word," Abram said to him. "Mr. York, my name is Michael Abram. I am the sheriff of Hickory County."

Mr. York raised his eyebrows in surprise. "How do you know my name? Ah! Wait. You must be the sheriff we contacted about apprehending Mark Goggin."

"I was contacted by someone from General Micronet, Mr. York. And I was offered a bribe to capture Mr. Goggin, with your aid, and see that he has an accident."

"Oh, I'm sure it wasn't a bribe, Sheriff. They were more than likely offering a fee or possibly a campaign contribution. This particular criminal has been exceptionally detrimental to General Micronet's conducting of business, as is their right by law. They simply want to see justice done. And I'm sure they meant to say that they hoped he *didn't* have an accident."

"You know what I think?" Hamilton piped in. "I think you intend to kill Mr. Goggin."

Mr. York regarded Hamilton with a growing suspicion. "You do know the criminal then."

Hamilton drew himself up. "I can read newspapers and recognize a face. I can also recognize bloodthirsty mercenaries when I see them. The man is unarmed, and you're coming after him with enough ammo to take out the National Guard."

"I certainly hope so." Mr. York smiled. "In my business, you play it safe. I'm told the man may be a murderer. I'm not going to show up with cap guns."

"I bet the police would be very interested in knowing what you're up to, Mr. York. Not even bounty hunters can go around blowing up houses and terrorizing the countryside."

"You know about the house as well, hmm?"

"I told you, I read newspapers."

"And do you also *write* the news?"

That threw Hamilton. He glanced nervously again at Abram.

"Word is just a bit nosy. But he's also a concerned citizen," Abram said. "As is his right."

"Yes. I'm sure he is." Mr. York considered both men. "Did Mr. Goggin speak with either of you?"

"Nope," Hamilton replied before Abram could.

Mr. York sighed. "Very uncooperative of you, sir. As you have said, this case is making headlines everywhere. I certainly hope the court of popular opinion doesn't penalize you for obstructing justice."

"What justice? You're a gaw-damn lynch mob on a salary."

Mr. York glared at him, his patience at an end. "Sir, I can have you dragged up and down this mountain for a month and then shot up with so much sodium pentathol you'd tell us anything." He straightened his coat and raised his chin. "But I don't see you being worth my time."

He turned to his right. "Report" he hollered over to a table with two men monitoring radio communications.

"Front lines say target has gone into a mole hole. Lost him in the tunnels."

"Damn," murmured Mr. York. Narrow, cramped tunnels eliminated a lot of the advantage in transport equipment as well as sheer numbers in men. "Do we have men going into the hole?"

"Yes, sir."

This was going to be tricky. They didn't know where Goggin was going to come out, so they'd have to find as many exits from the cave as they could and put a couple of men on each one. Mr. York had hoped to confront Goggin himself. It had always been his policy to let his victims see him. Kind of like letting the accused see the accuser in court. But it didn't seem possible in this case.

Drake Endicott crept up and stood behind Mr. York. "What if I can get you the charts in half an hour?"

Chapter 28

The way was narrow, dank, and mostly in darkness. At the back of the quartet, Mark held the lamp, but its' light was blocked enough by Jenna and End that Nathan didn't derive much benefit from it up front. That might have been a serious detriment for the person leading the group, except that Nathan had his lighter out and turned up so that the flame was five inches high. It wasn't anywhere near blinding, but it kept him from running face first into stone walls or falling into holes.

This one passage had been the only way to go for the past fifteen minutes. No branching corridors or multiple cave entrances slowed them down to force a decision to be made. They still weren't exactly moving quickly, but with the guns coming behind them they certainly weren't dawdling. A couple of times Mark thought he heard something and flashed the lamp behind them. But nothing moved and no further noise was heard. Jenna screamed once or twice, convinced she was being groped by bats or walking mummies, but the lamp showed nothing but water dripping from the rock above her.

The usually light-hearted End remained as silent as he had been since they first left the sunlight for the darkness of the caverns. Bears were undoubtedly still on his mind, although it was not possible that a bear would willingly have tried to scrunch its way through the tiny space they were travelling through now.

"Which way do we go?" Nathan called out from up front. His voice was a tremor of nerves.

The three trailing behind him came up to a tee in the corridor.

"You don't know?" said Jenna. "You're supposed to know where we are and where we're going next." Her voice was also noticeably apprehensive. "You don't know?"

"Chill, okay? Just chill. The situation is perfectly under control. All right," Nathan pointed to the left and stared hard in that direction, "we go to the right." He turned right, and the trailing three hurried behind him.

"End," Mark said. "Hold this."

End glared at him and then at the lamp. "You hold it, you lazy son of a bitch."

"No, I need to work on something."

End grudgingly yanked at the lamp and its battery, and shifted so that he was last in the group. "I bet bears go after the last one in the group. Don't they."

"Probably," said Jenna.

"Why don't you come back and carry this, then?"

"I'm just a poor weak little girl. Much too frail to carry anything so heavy," Jenna said in an exaggeratedly timid voice that changed to her regular one. "Plus I don't want to get eaten by bears."

End sneered back and growled an expletive. Then he turned the lamp around to light up the passageway behind them. No bears.

From his backpack, Mark pulled out the large pizza tray, the altimeter, and the wires and duct tape he'd specifically packed what seemed like so long ago. From the pouch at his side he brought out the magical crystal discs that everyone wanted so much.

Jenna heard the clink of crystal and glanced back. "What are you doing?"

"Planning for the worst possible scenario."

"What's that, cave-ins?"

"No—"

"Grizzlies," End interrupted. He saw the discs too, but watched Mark more than he did them.

"No," Mark said irritably. "I want to connect them all up in case I need to hide them again or use them for something."

They maneuvered through a series of very tight rock formations before resuming their pace. Jenna glanced back again. "They're very pretty. Make very nice jewelry."

The corridor passed through a ten- by ten-foot room, more narrow spaces, and then a minefield of stalagmites and pools of water. Mark covered the tray and moved quickly as water dripped down on them like light rain.

They veered to the left this time when the corridor split in two. It continued on into yet another chamber filled with cave formations serving now more as obstacles than attractions.

Jenna stopped short. "What was that!" she whispered loudly. "There's somebody over there." Her hushed voice echoed through the chamber and would have easily been heard by anyone actually hiding. End showed the light on the corner she pointed at. The shadows of half a dozen five- and six-foot-tall stalagmites slunk this way and that with every change in direction the lamp made.

"Oh," she said and lowered her shoulders in an effort to relax.

Mark put his hand on her shoulder. She patted his hand and held the fingertips briefly before she went back to watching for more marauding shadows.

As the threesome skirted cautiously around the various obstacles, Nathan suddenly appeared from the other end of the room. "We've got a problem," he said loudly as he approached them.

"Shhh!" all three hissed in alarm. But the tense spell had been broken, and it was as if they were suddenly awake from a nightmare, standing in the millennia-old room like sightseers.

"Follow me," Nathan said, and he again disappeared from view before anyone could say "Slow the hell down, junior."

Another corridor followed the room and it inclined sharply then leveled off for fifty yards. Jenna began to run to catch up with Nathan, and Mark and End sped up behind her.

They came out into a chamber so huge that the lamp wasn't strong enough to reveal all of it. The ceiling wasn't particularly high, but they couldn't see the other end of the long room. What made the room seem even more monstrously big was the fact that the light was also not strong enough to find the floor. The passage they had taken opened to a short porch, of sorts, and then there was nothing. An impossibly deep hole in the ground that to all appearances meant they were at the end of their journey. Twenty feet away was a ledge with its own porch and an entrance to another passage. But it might as well have been twenty miles away.

"Now *that's* a bottomless pit," said Jenna, leaning out over the edge.

End turned around to the passageway they had emerged from. "Not a problem," he said. "I was getting tired of running anyway. We'll just stand our ground right here. We can pick them off as they come toward us, and all four of us can gang up on any that get this far."

"You're the only one with a gun," Mark pointed out.

"Again, not a problem. I happen to be an excellent shot."

"I saw at least a dozen people landing in that lake back there. How many bullets do you have?"

End pulled the gun clip out of the grip. He slid out the bullets one at a time. "Three," he said.

Mark nodded thoughtfully. "It's a shame it's not a more powerful gun. Then you might be able to fire each bullet through four people. That would take care of them."

End glared and replaced the bullets and then the clip. "I still think we can hold out."

"Do you really?"

End took a second to think it through. "No."

"All right then. We've got to get across. Jenna, where's the rope?"

The rope that was in Jenna's backpack was in actuality a clothesline—an old weatherworn clothesline she'd packed along with what had seemed at the time like random selections made while in extreme panic. No one felt much confidence in depending on it, but there was hardly another option.

Mark was unfazed. "Now we just need to lasso a rock over there. Anybody know how to lasso?"

"Doesn't matter," Nathan said, pointing. "There's nothing to lasso."

The opposite side was as clean as a hospital floor. The only thing that could possibly have worked was a reasonably solid stalactite, but it reached the ceiling as one solid column and presented no place to be lassoed.

"Rocks!" End began searching along the floor. "We'll throw rocks at them."

"Don't be an idiot. Rocks against bullets? Why don't you just fly us out, Superman?"

"Hey, what was that?!" It was Jenna again, an ear cocked and staring in every direction.

Everyone grew still. Shouting voices could definitely be heard, but it was impossible to tell from where.

"Maybe we're just really close to the top of the hill, and there are people standing on top of it," said Jenna, whispering again.

The voices quieted shortly, and the quartet was left staring at each other.

"I have an idea," Mark said at last.

He set the tray with the crystals on the ground and set out the altimeter, the wires, and the duct tape on the ground next to the tray. End continued to stare down the corridor while Jenna and Nathan watched Mark. In less than two minutes he'd attached the altimeter to the tray and connected the wires from the device to all four crystals.

He looked up at the light End was still holding. "I'll need a power source."

"Not this power source," End said emphatically.

Jenna impatiently shoved him back—more an admonishment of his attitude than anything else—and grabbed the lamp and battery from him.

Now the sound of running motors and engines could be heard over their heads. Or was it coming from the corridor?

Mark worked quickly, affixing the battery to the tray with more duct tape and winding wires from the device to it. Without another thought he detached the battery from the lamp and the four were enveloped in complete darkness.

"Well done," said End.

"There's a flaw in your plan, man," Nathan said. "Here." A light 'snickt' sound was followed by the five-inch flame of his lighter. "You might want to be able to see where the bottomless pit is before you start moving around, you know?"

Mark made a few adjustments and even pulled out a measuring device from his coat pocket and began prodding each wire connection. He turned the tray around to look at it from different angles, then held it out for the other three to see.

"You've all been bugging me about trying to make a car out of my invention or a rocket or something that would go." He looked down at the tray with the crystals affixed to it with duct tape, the lamp's battery and the square shape of the other device, all of them difficult to see by the lighter's poor flicker. "I didn't have the time or money or inclination to make something that fancy, but I figure I can still make it into something like a scooter."

Mark turned the tray over so that the side with the crystals faced down. He flicked a switch on the altimeter and released the tray. The other three gasped from the suddenness with which he let go of his greatest invention.

And then they held their collective breath.

The tray stayed right where he had left it. It bounced a trifle, but otherwise it hovered in the air, three feet above the ground, as if strung up by wires.

"Sweet Jesus," said End in a low whisper.

"Amen to that," said Nathan.

They all circled the tray, Mark included, marveling at it, and squatting down to peer at the underside, at the various parts of the hovering scooter.

Mark stopped and smiled as the other three stared awestruck. "It uses an altimeter."

The three glanced at him without really hearing what he said.

"It tells the crystals how many gravitons to absorb in order to maintain its altitude," Mark continued.

"Gravitons," said End.

"Sub-atomic particles emitted by all physical objects. Like protons and electrons and so forth."

End nodded as if it was obvious and really something he already knew.

"What now?" Jenna asked.

"I'll take the rope over to the other side and wrap it around that big stalactite."

"You're not serious," she said.

"Oh, believe me, I wouldn't suggest it if there were another alternative," he replied, tying the rope around his waist. "I hate heights."

Mark gripped both sides of the hovering tray—now an undeniably genuine flying platform—bent his knees and hopped up so that he sat on it. He raised his hands matter-of-factly as if it was a flawless plan and should have been obvious to them, but his hands didn't say it with much conviction.

End, Nathan, and Jenna looked over at the far side of the abyss, turned and gave the hovering invention another look, squinted into Mark's eyes one last time, and began to talk all at once.

"…of all the stupid, idiotic…"

"…might as well try to jump across…"

"…got to be some good, solid rocks to throw around here somewhere…"

"…be more likely to work if we threw *you* across…"

Mark seemed oblivious to the unsupportive opinions and stared fixedly at the long gap from the near ledge to the far one. He folded his legs up to an Indian-style position and appeared to be practicing for a sledding run down a short, more easily-managed hill.

Jenna watched him prepare with an anxious expression that grew with worry. Nathan shook his head and patted his pants pockets in agitation for something to smoke. End squinted at the floor, picking up any fist-sized stone he could find, which was nothing of consequence. He eventually gave up.

Mark sat on the platform trying to relax, though his hands clenched white-knuckled to the sides. He looked at Jenna with a cheerful expression that could not hide the lack of confidence he had in his invention. She found that doubly distressing. She hoped that wouldn't be what she remembered about him if he were to plunge into the bottomless pit.

End was the obvious choice to fling Mark to the other side, and he moved the platform around to get a feel for how it reacted to his pushing and pulling at it, while Mark remained sitting on it, waiting impatiently. "Amazing," End whispered to himself, "just the most amazing thing I've ever seen." More loudly he said to Mark, "Do you think I should practice pushing it? We don't really know how much effort it will take to get you across. And you don't want to stop halfway."

Mark's new expression was one of dismay and then total agreement. "Yes! Yes of course. Why didn't I think of that?" he said more to himself. "I could have been stuck out there forever."

"Or until the battery ran out," Nathan pointed out.

Mark shook his head enthusiastically, his forgetting to test how much to push having also been forgotten. "The device recharges the batteries with some of the energy from the gravitons it absorbs. In theory it should last months. Years. Forever."

"In theory," Jenna repeated. "Ohhh, I just don't think this is a good idea."

The men ignored her. They moved back down the passage they'd just come from. End and Nathan stood about as far apart as they thought the distance was across the chasm. End moved the platform around, with Mark still sitting on it. "It feels so strange," said End. "Like it's being held up by invisible cables." He pushed down. "You can't push it down," he said in wonder.

Mark beamed with satisfaction.

End pulled the platform back, then shoved it toward Nathan with a grunt. Mark skimmed over nothing and slowed to a stop. Halfway to Nathan. "This won't do," he said, looking down with considerable trepidation.

End tried again, rearing back and pushing quite a bit harder, his grunt part of a strong exhale of air as he flung Mark and the platform across the passageway.

The force of the push pulled Mark backward, and he almost fell off. But he managed to hold on and arrived three quarters of the way to Nathan. He looked down again.

"It's my weight, I think. The device is absorbing a lot of gravitons, but it can't negate both the platform's weight and mine without a lot of drag."

Nathan stared hard at the platform. "I should go. I'm lighter."

Jenna heard him from the far end of the corridor. "If its lighter you want, then I should go."

"Neither of you are going," Mark said without looking up.

"Good," Nathan said, breathing easier.

"And neither should you," Jenna said loudly, her voice shaking. She disappeared from sight.

Mark gazed unhappily for a second at the cave wall where she had been standing, then returned his attention to the platform. "Can you push any harder?" he said to End.

"I most certainly can."

End pulled the platform ten feet farther down the passage. He turned around, gripped the platform firmly in both hands, and broke into a sprint. At more or less the point he imagined the chasm would begin, he released Mark and the platform. It went considerably faster, but also veered toward a cave wall. The platform bumped the wall and slowed to a stop two feet or so from Nathan.

Mark seemed satisfied and hopped off the platform. "That should do the trick. There won't be any walls to slow me down. If you push just a little harder I'll make it with inches to spare."

They moved back out to the chasm. It looked darker somehow, deeper somehow, and so far down, a person's heart would stop long before they hit the bottom.

Mark took a big breath, exhaling slowly. He smiled to them and gave a thumbs up like a test pilot, or the guy in the barrel about to go over Niagara Falls. With a small hop, he sat on the platform, crossing his legs Indian-style again. He nodded to End.

End nodded back and took a last look at the dark abyss below them. He looked at the platform and frowned. "If this thing is supposed to deflect gravity—"

"Absorb," Mark corrected.

"—won't it still fall into the hole? The bottom is way, way down there."

Mark nodded in agreement and stared at the platform, the pitch-black maw he had to cross, and End. He displayed an expression of consternation that End found more than a little frightening, but suddenly brightened and spoke. "No, no, not a problem. The altimeter is on it, remember? It measures air density and adjusts the amount of gravitons the crystals absorb."

"But the ground is way, way down there," End repeated.

"Sure…sure. But the device is designed to absorb gravitons from all around. So it should take what it needs to maintain its altitude."

"'Designed?' 'Should?' I don't like the sound of that," said Jenna.

"Well, I haven't tried it on big holes. There weren't any bottomless pits at home for me to test it with."

No one felt better for End having his question answered. Still, no one expressed any further opinion on the matter either.

The scrape of boots and the echo of voices grew ever nearer. It was only a matter of time.

End dragged the platform twice as far back as he had in the tunnel. He leaned back and forth like a bobsledder about to take off.

Jenna had her eyes closed, and Nathan looked in the opposite direction.

End began to run. His stride increased as his speed did. He and Mark left the cave hall at full tilt and End flung the platform and Mark as absolutely hard as he could. He fell headlong to the ground and slid several feet before stopping, finding himself staring over the edge to the darkness below. He looked up to watch the platform's path.

Mark had leaned forward to prevent himself from being thrown off the platform when End flung him. He had expected End to throw as hard as he could, and he certainly had.

The platform sped quickly across the gigantic crevice and Mark saw that he had plenty of speed to make it. But as he reached the edge of the opposite side, the platform dipped suddenly.

Jenna screamed.

"Grab for the edge!" End roared, his voice echoing everywhere.

The platform teetered precariously backward and Mark clutched at the front edge. Being closer to vertical than horizontal, the rigged altimeter apparently couldn't decide what to do, and the platform turned over.

Mark's legs slid out from under him and over the side along with the rest of him. He was left hanging in the air, his hands gripping both sides of the platform. He desperately tried to pull himself up but was nowhere near fit enough.

He hung there, breathing hard, his eyes staring up at the cave formations that swished around eerily from the meager, and now distant, light of Nathan's lighter.

"Mark?" Jenna called out.

"What?!" Mark shouted with panic-fueled anger. The last thing he had time for right now was answering a lot of questions.

"Lower your legs."

"What the hell for? Can't you see I'm busy?" He groaned as his fingertips clung to the edge of the platform. He could feel them slipping.

"Mark, just lower your legs."

Mark frowned at the flickering stalactites. He hadn't realized it but he had pulled his legs up to his rear end while trying to climb back atop the platform and hadn't noticed that they were still locked tight against him.

He lowered one leg, then the other. First one foot, then the other, found solid ground. He put some weight on his feet, but didn't immediately let go of the platform. Finally he looked down at his feet and the ground all around him. The ledge was a foot away.

Mark smiled over at the trio waiting expectantly and stood up straight. Jenna had her hands on her hips, terror abating, but anger still apparent in her stance.

He shrugged. "All right, it didn't work exactly to plan." He switched off the device and clutched it to his chest, patting it like a favorite toy. "But it's got a lot to do. It's absorbing bazillions of gravitons coming from every direction, including me. It's got to adjust for altitude. It's got to adjust for the sudden drop in graviton energy over there and then the sudden influx over here. There's bound to be flaws."

No one gave a response on the other side.

"I got here, didn't I?" he said insistently.

"Get on with it!" End shouted from the other side.

"Oh." Mark ran over to the stalactite column with the clothesline and tied it around. The other end ran over to a similarly tall and stout stalagmite rising up from the ground on the side he'd just left. "All right," he called out.

"Okay," said End, "You go ahead, Jenna."

"What? Not a chance, buster. I can't go across that. I mean...well, I can go across it. I just won't. It's crazy! It's ridiculous."

"What did you think you were going to do when everyone else was over there?"

Jenna put her hands on her hips, aggravated at Mark all over again. "Honestly, I couldn't believe he was actually going across. It's crazy. Who in their right mind would do such a thing?"

The sound of men approaching was quite loud now, and it was coming this time from the tunnel. Nathan heard it and wasted no time. Before anyone could say a word, he bounded up to the rope, grabbed it with both hands, swung his feet up to criss-cross over it, and went hand-over-hand with such speed that he was on the other side of the chasm with Mark in less than half a minute.

"Wow," Mark said, grinning. "How come you get D's in gym all the time?"

"Because I like D's!" snapped Nathan. "Come on!" he shouted to the other side.

"Your turn, Jen," said End. "Now or never."

End could hear the shouts and echoes of the men hunting them growing nearer with every second they wasted standing around. He expected to see them charging up the passage any moment.

"It's too dark," she complained. "I can't see." The lighter had passed across the crevice with its owner. They could dimly see Nathan on the other side, lighting up another joint. Must have been hidden in an ear or his underpants, End thought absently.

"Jenna, it's time. Right now. Either climb up there or I'm carrying you across. We—"

"Okay."

"Okay? Okay what?"

"You carry me across. Just don't drop me."

"Oh, well, all right. If you really don't want me to."

The voices were joined in the passageway by plodding, scuffling feet and End knew the hunters were practically there. He scooped up Jenna, dumped her over his shoulder and grasped the rope. But as soon as both their weight was applied, the rope slunk down so that they were both hanging down into the chasm.

Jenna screamed. "What are you doing? Across, not down! Across!"

End scrambled frantically with the rope, trying to pull himself across while Jenna's arms and legs flailed everywhere as she tried to rescue herself from being rescued by him. "Hold still," he tried to shout, but his words were muffled by an elbow. The rope seemed to gain elasticity somehow because they began to sink farther into the chasm.

"This is helping me across?" Jenna shrieked. "We're not supposed to be going down!" She began clubbing End with her fists.

"Ow! Stop that!" End bellowed. He began climbing the rope, but it also continued to stretch more. It was also terribly dark and the sides of the chasm were slippery, just as everything is in a cave.

The two fought one another, panic building with every passing second and every inch of altitude that they lost.

Then a light began to fill the monstrous hole and End began to pull harder, sighting footholds on a chasm wall that had been smooth as glass in the dark. Jenna looked up for the source of the light.

It was Mark, sitting once again on the pizza tray, like a slacker genie on a metal flying carpet. Nathan's lighter was in one hand while he held out the other to grasp Jenna's hand. It was mostly a supportive gesture because the platform wasn't likely to hold her weight as well as his.

But the light was all End needed to find his footing, and emitting a powerful grunt with each step, he slowly climbed up to the ledge. Jenna slid off his shoulders onto the ground, and End crawled up the last few feet to safety.

They turned around to see no Mark. "Mark?" said Jenna.

"Down here." Mark was pulling himself up with the rope. "I'm okay," he said. "Power's running down, I think. Too much weight. Or maybe the altimeter's out of whack."

It took only another minute for Mark to reach the top, and he too crawled up and onto the ledge. His eyes were wide with fear and relief when he saw Jenna, who gave him a terrified hug.

End motioned them toward the new passage that Nathan had already disappeared into, though he wasn't likely to go far without his lighter. Jenna ran after him, and Mark followed, working to unhook the battery and reattach it to the lamp as he ran.

End trotted into the tunnel after them and then stopped to look back. It was several seconds before he saw the first man emerge from the tunnel on the opposite side of the great crevice. The man was running, and he had to slide hard to avoid plummeting to his death. Two more men were on his heels, and they also had to scramble and slide to a stop.

Roaring with triumphant laughter, End severed the rope attached to the stalactite column next to him, waved to the shaken threesome, and disappeared into the passageway.

Ah, it felt good to finally get the upper hand, he thought with some pleasure as he trotted along. Now they were in the driver's seat. It would take some doing for those thugs to get across that big hole. By then, they could be far away, riding again on the river, traipsing through more tunnels and underground caverns, or even—dare he hope it—relaxing in a car on the open road.

He ran through several more rooms and passageways until he could see a dim light up ahead which he surmised was Nathan's lighter. He noticed that it didn't move or disappear, as it would if Nathan were moving from room to room as he should be doing. As End drew closer to the flame, the boat lamp came on, and the room he was in was illuminated almost as if by the sun itself.

End reached the other three in a matter of seconds. They stood silently staring all around them, but mostly down. It was another incredibly vast cavern, like the one they'd just left with the huge hole in the center. This one was different in that there were no hidden spaces, no dark places. Just one big room with no shortage of rock formations. The ceiling was high in this room, and the space seemed to stretch out in every direction.

And best of all, the immensely huge hole blocking them from continuing on *now* was nowhere near being a bottomless pit like the last big hole. They could see the bottom just fine, thirty to forty feet down.

Chapter 29

Mark Goggin laughed. He looked at the expressions of dismay and disappointment in his comrades' faces, and he laughed. He looked at the boat lamp flickering, struggling against its battery's moribund lifespan, and he laughed. He looked down at yet another massive hole in the ground blocking them from safety, and he laughed.

He looked at the pizza tray in his hands, with the magical crystals that might well end up being the cause of his death as well as his three friends. That didn't seem quite so funny.

Matthias End was strangely quiet, staring intently at Mark and only at Mark. Nathan had no trouble speaking his mind.

"There's nothing goddamn funny about this! What cocksucker keeps putting these fucking holes in our way all the time?" he shrieked. "Are we supposed to die? Is that it? We're just supposed to solve one problem after another and just get more problems to solve until we fall in a hole and die?" He looked around for an adult to reassure him that the world was not this way, but then he remembered the adults who were available.

"This is your goddamn fault!" he spit at Mark. "All you had to do was build a bunch of worthless gadgets, make us a little money, and we live happily ever after. I can go to college and never see your fucking face again!"

Mark stared back at Nathan, shock and devastation in his face. He had not thought Nathan had such awful feelings about him. "I'm sorry, Nathan. I didn't expect all this to—"

"Yeah, well it did. And if I get killed, my Mom is gonna come after you with her Tempo. She's run over two boyfriends and a mad coyote, and you aren't nearly fast enough to get out of the way."

Jenna put an arm around Nathan. "Nathan, you don't really mean any of that, and you know it. This is no more Mark's fault than it is mine."

"Yeah, and maybe it *is* your fault. You're the one that told them all about that stupid thing," he shot an accusing arm at the pizza tray and its attachments. "Why couldn't you have just left us alone? We never did anything to anyone. All we do is sit on stools and fiddle. That's it. All day long, just messing with things." Tears rolled down Nathan's cheeks, and he blinked rapidly. "Why couldn't we have just been left alone?" He slouched to the ground, and Jenna leaned against a rock above him and stroked his hair.

Mark watched Nathan sob and whimper. He watched Jenna comfort him and then look questioningly up at Mark. Then he looked at the new hole. He stepped toward the hole until he couldn't take another step, and he looked down.

It was even farther to the other side than the last chasm. And they had left their rope behind. It didn't seem likely that the battery or the crystal discs would have enough left to power the device that distance.

Was all this his fault?

The pizza tray hung in his hands over the precipice. Drop it, he said to himself. Drop it right now. If you drop it right now, then all the killers will leave. Once he told them what he hadn't been able to tell anyone, they'd leave, and the four of them could go home.

Of course, that assumed they'd believe what he told them. And even if they did, they weren't likely to be in much of a mood afterward to help him and the others out of the cave. The four of them would still be stuck in the cave with no way out.

"I sure wish I had a joint," Nathan wailed. "Just one tiny little joint. Right now I'd smoke anything." Jenna sat down next to him, and Nathan put his head on her shoulder and whimpered.

Mark had turned when Nathan spoke, and he glanced at End. End said nothing, and indicated nothing. He merely returned Mark's gaze with his own.

With a long slow breath, Mark scanned the new chamber they were in. It seemed very much like the last one with a big hole in it. A bit more breathing room, maybe. The ground sloped away a bit more gradually along the path they had taken and, though there was a huge risk to life and limb, someone might survive the slide down and find a way out in another part of the cavernous space.

"What would you think if I slid down this way?" he asked End, pointing at the nearly sheer cliff.

End shrugged noncommittally.

Mark stared hard at him. "You're sure awfully useless all of a sudden. You're not about to go to pieces too, are you?"

"You're the boss, Mark," was all End said.

"No, I think I'm the boss," said a voice at the other end of the chasm. "Now, in any case."

They turned and it was Mr. York, standing at the edge, his arms folded and a satisfied expression on his face.

"Bit of a wide hole you've found here, isn't it," said Mr. York. He smiled with genuine fondness. "You've given us a terrible time, Mr. Goggin. But I'm afraid you're up against the finest technical equipment available in the western world. We knew where you were going down here before *you* did."

"You're totally welcome, el Yorko," said Drake Endicott, stepping up to Mr. York's side. "The United States government has been very good to us over the years."

"I don't recall thanking you." Mr. York glanced at his colleague with undisguised hatred. But his expression turned pleasant as his gaze returned to Mark. "I'm willing to offer you that job again, Mr. Goggin. It seems a tad surreal to be doing it underground when most job offers are made in the crisp, clean atmosphere of a corporate office. But it is still on the table. What do you say?"

"You don't want me. You want the device."

Mr. York nodded. "Well, yes, we do at least want the device. But it would save us so much time if you were to tell us how it works."

"I can't."

"Ha! You mean you won't, don't you? That's all right. We can help you remember, if it comes to—"

"No." Mark glared at Mr. York and Endicott, then looked away. "I mean I can't. I don't remember how I did it."

"What?" said Jenna. "You can't be serious. You must have some kind of notes. Any good scientist worth being called a scientist has a log book."

"I have a log book. I use it all the time. I write formulae and results and introduce speculation and the wildest most inane ideas I can imagine. But the creation of the crystals was the result of months of frustration. I hadn't been able to get the fusion coil to work. I had been threatened with foreclosure on my home. My great-great-great-grandparent's home. And then I had all these idiotic ideas for defying the laws of nature. But nothing worked, and I felt incompetent and useless, and I took all my ideas and all the ideas people had concocted over the years, I shoved them together, and I shot enough electromagnetic pulses through it all to polarize the moon.

"And it worked," he said, waving his hands at the insanity of the cosmos. "It worked and I couldn't believe it. I didn't know what to do. I didn't want to be another crackpot out to make headlines with a goofy invention that couldn't be reproduced." He looked into Jenna's eyes. "I didn't want to lose people's...I didn't want to lose *your*...respect." He glanced over at Nathan. "Or yours, believe it or not."

Mark looked back up at Mr. York. "So it might as well all be a lie. I never made this thing. It never happened." It was a relief for the truth to finally be out, but the anguish of having misled people who had risked their lives for him was a guilt difficult for Mark to bear.

Mr. York was no longer smiling. "That is unfortunate, Mr. Goggin, as it makes you rather unnecessary." He nodded toward his men and they came forward brandishing rifles and pistols. "I'll ask you to step back and set the device on the ground."

"I'd rather you didn't do that," Mark said. He stood over the precipice once again. This time the pizza tray and its invaluable contents hung over the chasm, on the brink of ruin. Mark dropped his hands, letting go of the tray. The wire connecting to the battery reached across the space between him and his invention and rested in his grip.

The tray hung in the space between the two groups. Most of the gasps came from the opposite side of the chasm, but Mark especially noted one behind him, where End stood.

Mr. York sneered contemptuously. "Don't challenge me, Goggin. I can finally see the conclusion to this hellish project on the horizon, and I'll be damned if I'm going to go back to square one. Do as I ask, or my men will gun you down where you stand."

Mark considered his words and raised his hand as if about to yank and disconnect the wire.

"And your friends as well," Mr. York added.

That made Mark pause. He regarded Mr. York for another moment, and then he smiled. "You'll have to kill us all anyway. How else could you explain why your company has my device without my permission?"

"Mark," said End, standing at his side. "Consider what you are doing."

Mark could feel the barrel of End's revolver pointing at his left temple. He froze.

"If you destroy this device, we will all be dead," said End intently. "But if you work a deal with General Micronet, you could be the acknowledged creator of the twenty-first century's version of the automobile. The *replacement* for the automobile, Mark. You'll have fame, wealth, power—anything you could possibly desire."

Mark turned to face End, the gun retreating but still pointed at his chest. "And what if they don't use it for automobiles, End? What if they build weapons with it? What if people lose their jobs or even their lives because of it? And all because I made a choice based on greed." He stepped back toward the ledge. "No, if anything is going to be made out of this, I'm the one who's going to decide what that thing is. Not a bunch of conscienceless business-men looking for the next great money-maker."

Mark watched End and his gun as he pulled ever so slightly at the wire. The far end came away from the battery and swung softly down to Mark's side.

The pizza tray hung in the air for half a second, wobbled badly, and dropped like a meteor.

"No!" Mr. York shouted as the tray fell to the bottom of the huge pit. From both sides of the hole, they could hear the tinkle of breaking crystal and shattering machinery, and the hollow gong of the aluminum pizza tray striking against rocks.

There was a moment of silence as if someone important had died.

Mr. Endicott became visibly agitated by Mark's actions. He pulled a pis-tol from his coat and leveled it on Mark. "That was a bad move, Marko. I think we need to kill you for that." He lowered the pistol onto his other arm to steady it and he pointed the barrel in Mark's direction.

"Like you killed Archibald Scott?" Jenna blurted out.

Endicott snickered and let the pistol hang at his side. "Scotty was a busi-ness decision, Jenna sweetheart. Orders from above, you might say."

"Shut up," said Mr. York.

"If I hadn't eliminated him, where would the leverage come from to pressure your boyfriend into coming over to our side?"

"Shut up!" Mr. York hissed between his teeth.

"But since he's obviously not right in the head either," Endicott raised the pistol again, "a quick death is about all he deserves."

"You don't make the decisions around here!" bellowed Mr. York. He was standing just behind Endicott, and as he roared his hatred, he emphasized the words with a brutal blow to the back of the head with the butt of his own weapon.

Endicott slumped unconscious to the ground yet again.

"Free at last," Mr. York mumbled to himself as he stood over an inert Drake Endicott. "I would have shot you in the head if it were allowed."

He returned his attention to Mark. "Goggin, I'm frankly more than a little underwhelmed by your attitude. Your own man there was trying to talk sense to you. Still, I understand you inventive types are stubborn and proud and evidently pretty damn brainless with the way of the world. So this is your last chance to accept my job offer."

Mark responded by folding his arms together and looking away. End had lowered his pistol and was beaming the broadest grin Mark had yet seen from him. He stared at End with a bewildered expression, heightened by the anger and confusion he felt in regard to the pistol still in End's grip.

Mr. York shook his head. "It would have been easier if you'd just turned it over. But our scientists are quite capable of reconstructing and reproducing the original. All we've got to do is make a few changes. You know, adjust a little. If you'll just wait right there, my men'll climb down and retrieve the pieces."

Two ropes were lowered that failed to reach the bottom. Mr. York was briefly angry at the seemingly constant level of incompetence his men were suddenly beset with, until he was told that Mr. Endicott had provided the rope. Mr. York nodded as if that explained everything. The two men who went down dropped the last five feet to the bottom.

That left Mr. York and one other man on the other side of the crevice.

Mark shook his head. "You're wasting your time. The crystals are the true source of power, and they're unstable. There was a fifth crystal I experimented on where I tried to strengthen the antigravitational effect by bombarding it with twice as many electromagnetic ions. But it reverse-polarized too quickly and shattered into dust. There won't be anything down there but broken equipment and a pizza tray." His eyebrows raised and lowered, and he looked back at Jenna and Nathan and the eyebrows rose quizzically again. "Doesn't a huge thick pizza sound really good right now?"

Sure enough, the two men looked up at Mr. York and held their hands helplessly in the air.

"God *damn* it! I have never had things go like this." Mr. York began to pace back and forth across the length of the ledge. "Nothing's gone right. Oh sure, I've had some badly planned projects before and badly executed ones at that. But nothing like this." He looked down at the prone figure of Drake Endicott. "This is your fault, damn you!"

He kicked Endicott viciously in the side, kicked him twice more, and then he tried to push him off the ledge. The remaining man on the ledge with him leaned frantically down to try to pull Mr. York back, all the while murmuring words to him that were presumably meant to dissuade him from anything so unprofessional.

But Mr. York would not be deterred. He shoved the man backward so that he fell into the tunnel entrance and out of sight, and then he pushed and kicked Endicott with a berserk rage until Endicott hung, just for a moment, on the edge. Then he fell.

Mr. York looked eagerly down to watch. Endicott fell halfway down the chasm and landed on the solid but relatively soft bodies of the two men who had been below, now climbing back up the ropes. They had had to climb the wall of the chasm just to get up to the too-short rope, had struggled up in partial darkness and now they were lying in a heap with Endicott on top of them at the chasm floor.

Nodding and slowly beginning to cackle with laughter, Mr. York also waved his arms and mumbled to himself, interrupting that with more laughter and a few shouts at no one in particular.

"York!"

It was End. He stood with his gun pointed now at Mr. York, who was nodding, laughing, and pointing at the gun as if that was just what he was expecting to happen next.

"Move on," said End. "You're done here. Call it an opportunity for improvement or some other garbage. But move on."

Mr. York wiped tears from his eyes, merriment still present in his expression. He nodded in agreement. "I'm sure we will meet again. Goggin, I know the innovator's mind, and you won't be able to rest until you have recreated your work and documented it. And when you do, I'll be in touch. General Micronet always gets what it wants. One way or the other.

Good day to you." He was gone with only a parting laugh that echoed out from the tunnel.

The cavern became quiet then, except for weak groans occasionally floating up from the bottom of the chasm. Nathan's lighter flickered, almost going out, and the foursome seemed to come out of their reverie.

"You should have told him to toss us the rope," Mark told End quietly. He turned to study the tall man, who put his revolver back inside his coat. "What——?" he started to say but shook his head as if he couldn't think of any words.

End grinned broadly and with more boyish exuberance than Mark had ever seen from him. "Mark! Mark, Mark, Mark!" End shouted, gripping Mark by the shoulders. "I am so sorry. So very sorry. I have been so very unworthy of you. But I had to know. I had to find out. And now I do."

"Find out what?"

End's grin faltered. "I've had a crisis in faith, Mark. Had one for years. I don't remember the last time I went to church. Or prayed. There didn't seem a reason to. What good did it do? I've prayed and prayed and prayed until my back ached and my knees were numb, and nothing ever came of it."

He looked over at Jenna. And then at Nathan. "I quit because I couldn't believe any more. The more I worked at maintaining my faith, the worse everything around me seemed to be. Society is so selfish now. And greedy. People don't know what a family is any more. No one seems to care to strive for a higher life. Oh, maybe not a spiritual one, but at the very least a more civilized one. If you're on this Earth, aren't you supposed to be doing something worthwhile? What does having a lot of green paper, or even having a lot of other junk, mean in the greater scheme of things?

"I didn't understand it. So I quit. And I got a job. A job just like everyone else. I tried to live just like everyone else. Work, eat, watch television, sleep, work, eat, television, sleep. I even had sex like everybody else."

He grinned suddenly. "I'll never be able to return to the clergy now."

End paused and Mark could see the past rolling through End's vision.

"I thought I'd learn something from it. Something deep inside that no one could properly describe to a priest. What it means to be the average man, maybe. What kinds of goals the ordinary man strives for." He stared hard at Mark. "And you know what I found? I found that most people have no goals. Oh, they may be trying to save for retirement or the next mortgage payment, or they may be trying to cut back on their drinking or swearing or violence or cheating. But that's it. No one aspired to becoming a statesman to lead the nation to unheard-of prosperity. No one resolved to end hunger or war forever. No one wanted to cure cancer or greed. No one so much as cared to read a damn book!"

Jenna spoke up. "You know there are people trying to do all those good things, Matthias."

End moved quickly over to her. "Yes! Yes, I thought so too. Once. I've said before: you learn a lot about people during confession. I had hoped that wasn't what real people were like, but I think at some point I realized it probably was."

He leaned against the rock behind them. "I had a man speak to me several times during confession about running a pharmaceutical company. He had been CEO for over twenty years. The company had been through hard times over and over again, and each time he'd pulled them out of it. But he hadn't, really. He'd coerced their manufacturing arm to weaken the strength of their most profitable medicines so they could make more money off of less medicine. He'd laid off tens of thousands of workers when they made a profit but didn't meet a number someone had made up. And he had worked with his accountants to alter the company books so things looked better than they really were.

"He wanted forgiveness. I told him he should confess what he had done to his co-workers and ask their forgiveness." End laughed. "He said I was being a bit naïve and couldn't he just get a few Hail Mary's and call it square."

End shrugged. "So I gave him what he asked for. One person after another told me things like that. Supposedly rock-solid statesmen who took money from corporations to change their votes. Farmers who were paid not to sell their harvest, while children starved. Thousands upon thousands of wealthy people who wouldn't give a dime to the poor because 'they didn't work for it like I did.'"

"After years of that and years of living the pointless existence of the common American, I was desperate. I lost interest in working and in talking to people. I didn't care about anything. When I got fired, it didn't really seem to matter, other than a vague resentment I felt about it. At the time, I just thought I'd find a way to get even with General Micronet and then go find another job."

He turned to Mark. "Then I met you, Mark. You were brash, eager, determined, idealistic. You really seemed like the kind of person I had been looking for, someone aspiring to a higher life. Yeah, a cold fusion device is a hopeless idea, but your intentions were admirable. In the back of my mind was the expectation that you were hopelessly flawed like everyone else. Greedy, selfish, out only for yourself. Certainly you have some of those traits, but not to such a degree that you'd harm someone else.

"At some point, I came to the conclusion that you must just be naïve too, like I was, and needed only to experience the world to make you as jaded and pointless as the rest of humanity. But I wouldn't know for sure until I had seen you experience the world, faced its challenges, and responded. So you became my experiment, so to speak. I tried to scare you with dead chickens, I gave you contradictory information. I left you to fend for yourself when bullets were flying. And then I threatened you with death if you didn't succumb to the American dream of wealth and power."

End grinned again. "And you did it, Mark. You stayed true to your ideals in the face of an opportunity of acquiring more wealth and power than anyone on the planet. I don't think you truly comprehend the scope of influence your device and its progeny would have had on the world."

He looked down. "I am truly sorry to have made things so hard for you. But I can't thank you enough for returning my faith to me."

Mark stared in bewilderment at End, uncertain how to respond. By all rights he should slug End for even pretending to threaten to kill him, to say nothing of deliberately putting him in harm's way so many times. But somehow it seemed unnecessary now. So he stood there awkwardly, feeling instead the sheepish embarrassment brought on by what he perceived as obviously undue praise.

"Didn't Willy Wonka do something like all that?" asked Nathan.

End thought a second and grinned. "No, he didn't have a gun. And I don't have anything so fabulous as a chocolate factory to give away."

The foursome became quiet. The only noises in the cavern were the constant tinkle of dripping water, and the moans of fallen thieves.

The lighter's flame flickered weakly. It would not last much longer. But no one seemed to care.

"You folks done in here or would you like some more time?" said a voice at the bottom of the steep hill that ran along the path leading to the chasm.

Mark squinted into the darkness then smiled in surprise. "Why hello again, Mr. Hamilton," he said. "Yes, I think we're done. Lucky you happened along."

"No luck to it at all," replied Hamilton. "I've been eavesdropping. Heard the whole thing. Saw it work too. Unbelievable! What a story it'll make!"

The four made their way down the hill, which turned out to be less steep than they had initially thought and easier still to go down if you took the stairs that had been hidden behind a pile of rocks.

"I'm not sure anyone would publish it, Mr. Hamilton," said Jenna. "It's a bit too, as you said, unbelievable."

"You leave that to me. Now. Have you folks ever signed a waiver form? It's a standard document for this type of occasion and absolves my paper of…"

Epilogue

The following is an excerpt from a column from the *Hermitage Index*, with permission reprinted by the *Kansas City Star*, the *Washington Post*, the *New York Times*, the *Los Angeles Times*, *Le Monde* in Paris, the *Times* in London, and the *Nezavisimaya Gazeta* in Moscow, among many others:

The Armies of Capitalism Come to Hermitage

By Word Hamilton

Mark Goggin is, I am sure, well known to all Missourians. A resident of Brookbury up in Benton County, he has been in the papers and on television and the center of attention on the Internet for the last week. He is, or was, the accused murderer of Archibald Scott, an inventor, like Mr. Goggin, with a deep interest in the study of antigravity.

Now I know most people think us country Missourians are too busy churning out moonshine and proposing to second cousins to keep up with modern scientific thought, but even us brainless Ozarkian ticks know the implications of the discovery—or should it be 'invention'?—of antigravity.

The secret to antigravity, I'm told, is in supercharged crystals. Charge a crystal in a certain way, and before you know it, it's floating away like a balloon. A simplistic explanation, certainly, but that's the gist of it. Can you fathom the historic boon to civilization if it really works? Frankly, I think there must be billions of crystals lying around the planet just waiting to be zapped with enough electricity to light a baseball stadium. If it really does work as advertised, and I'm not saying it does, we'll all be flying around like Peter Pan without having to pay so much as a dime for the pleasure. Assuming, of course, that you can figure out how to attach the crystals to the underside of your shoes.

(The editors at the *Index* would like to take this time to warn all you folks with fine crystalware not to be throwing sparks around willy-nilly.)

Now, if you are willing to wait for the professionals to build your dream antigravitational gizmo for you, the stars are the limit. Imagine cruising to work in a flying car or traipsing off to the shopping mall in levitating boots. No need to get off your rear end to get a beer from the fridge when you can have the fridge float right on over to you.

And why stop there? Entire cities could be located up in the clouds, if for no other reason than to give property tax collectors and air traffic controllers fits and nightmares.

It's not just a fantasy, folks. I've seen Mr. Goggin's own invention in action. It was spherical in shape, like a manhole cover, with wires and doodads sticking out all over it (that is as technical as I get). Goggin switched it on and let go, and the crazy thing sat there in midair like a football frozen on instant replay. It really did exist. I'll swear to that. At least until it got dropped, a big no-no when dealing with crystals.

But now, let's stop to think a second about the implications of such a thing. Sure, such an invention might cause all sorts of new industries to spring up, create new work and generate excitement the like of which hasn't been seen in a century. Heck, it might even save that ozone layer up there somewhere that no one has ever actually seen.

But what about the poor global conglomerates that do things the old ways? The giant car manufacturers. The big oil producers. They'll have to reorganize every last corner of their business just to keep making those billions in profits. And what about the immensely huge repair and overhaul businesses that will have to at the very least, retool to using, say, a mason's hammer and a battery charger for honing out and empowering those prime cuts of energized crystal? Think what it would do to the aerospace and military industries. What would NASA have to waste money on if it only needed a couple dozen charged crystals instead of five million tons of liquid hydrogen to get rockets off the ground? What good are heavy tanks for rolling over obstacles if you can get ones that float over everything? Surely you won't need those noisy helicopters flying about any more.

And if the global conglomerates are chewing their nails, what must the emotional state be of the conglomerates' poor CEOs whose multi-million dollar bonuses are riding on making all their big financial numbers? Who's going to save them?

No one is, my friends. The poor, lonely CEOs are left to fend for themselves, to save their vast wealth and multinational homes before the company stock drops a buck or two, and they have to settle for just the palatial mansion in the Hamptons and the other one in the south of France.

And that just won't do.

The CEOs of the mighty corporations of America will tell you they had to do something about this Goggin fellow and his cocka-mamie contraption. No one takes a CEO seriously if he only has two palatial mansions.

So a week ago, they all got together and decided to buy Mr. Goggin's device or buy the device *and* Mr. Goggin, or, failing that, get rid of both of them. Clearly the buying part didn't pan out, because there arrived in papers all over the country the anonymous accusation that it was Mark Goggin who killed Mr. Scott. If you're looking to hire someone, you don't usually try to get them arrested beforehand. And sending an army to blow up Mr. Goggin's ancestral home wasn't exactly an offer of employment, either.

The initial assault on the Goggin home, the old family château up in Brookbury, left it severely damaged, though not quite destroyed. Still, if you've ever seen it, you know what a tragedy that really is. The unbelievable and shocking thing of it is—no police came to investigate. Goggin and his colleagues were chased through forestland and down rivers and streams by military-equipped Hummers and helicopters. No military officials seemed to notice. A national park and a protected scenic waterway and cave system were heavily damaged by gunfire and explosions and vehicles. (And if Benton County and Hickory County had not had all their park rangers laid off, they also somehow wouldn't have noticed, I'll wager.) Were they all paid off? Threatened? Who knows? And who knows what all else was illegally done in order to track down Goggin and his friends and eliminate them?

I must add here that our own good sheriff and the finest cab-inetmaker in central Missouri, Mike Abram, was shot while doing his duty, protecting the lives of Goggin and his friends. (By the by, Mike is doing fine and is learning to saw with his left arm until the right one mends.)

In the end, it was only by the unfortunate destruction of his wondrous invention that Mr. Goggin and his colleagues escaped with their lives.

So I ask you: what's next? Should conglomerates be able to do whatever they want if they just give out enough money to the right people? Can't a hamburger franchise poison rivers to cripple a com-peting fish franchise? If people are dumb enough to buy trucks that roll over and kill them, shouldn't the manufacturers who produce those trucks be excused from having to fix them? It's just Natural Selection at work, isn't it?

How about company-sponsored justifiable genocide? Can't we allow wealthy capitalists to begin eliminating masses of people in various demographic groups that studies show to be disinterested in their products? Well, why not? What better reason is there for wiping out teenagers than the fact that they think Lincoln Conti-nentals look like big shiny plastic coffins? Should low-wage-earning families who don't fall in the group that can afford $150,000 houses be allowed to live? Perhaps we should just bomb the schools so our children can't learn how to make incredible new things that will someday improve civilization, thus preventing any future Mark Goggins from happening.

Mark Goggin was not the murderer of Archibald Scott. I myself, your faithful and intrepid reporter, have a taped confession of the real murderer that I have given to the investigators in the case. (Incidentally, the suspect was listed as an employee of an affiliate of General Micronet, whose representatives say has not been employed there for months. The affiliate doesn't exist anymore either. What a surprise.)

I also have eyewitness accounts from current and former employees of General Micronet about its involvement in the events described above, and I even have a document with General Micronet letterhead sent to Sheriff Abram offering him a huge fee for the capture of Mr. Goggin alive. The fee increased if he were somehow to be captured not alive.

I can promise you that it's all very solid evidence. Why else would there be such a big to-do about one backwoods inventor? The FBI is out here, the CIA, Homeland Security, even the state police came out to take a peek and get their pictures taken. There are, even as I write this, more reporters and cameramen from the world's media giants rooting around for answers and snapping spiffy pictures than the entire population of Hickory County, twice over.

All this is not just profoundly disturbing. It's not just loathsome, unconscionable behavior. It's terrifying. A corporation, as most everyone knows, is not a person. It can't be thrown in jail or executed for killing people. So if the corporation has the power to manipulate governments, the military, law enforcement, television, and newspapers (except for that bastion of liberty, the *Index*), who's to stop them from doing whatever they want?

After all, it's just business.